In the Time of

WORDS

Kenelm Winslow Harris

To Paul,
Enjoy!

Princess Tides
PUBLISHING

Library of Congress Control Number: 2006936062

ISBN: 0-9755884-1-9

Printed in the United States of America

First Edition

For Quill

ACKNOWLEDGEMENTS

$\mathscr{O}$ would like to thank family, friends, and colleagues who provided help and encouragement throughout.

Debra Day Glabeau, Morgan Day Harris, Deacon Winslow Harris,
Kenelmn Harris, Sr., Mildred Harris, Howard Glabau; Steve Harris, Paige Harris,
Judy Anderholm, Jacquelyn Harris, Dorette Weston, Carol Heston,
Andrew Menard, Ketan Patel, Dianne Saia, Michelle Caterina,
Jacqueline Franklin, Peter Franklin, Sandy Barry, David Valcovic, Patricia Cornell,
Richard C. Williams, David Goss, Duane Orlemann, Scott Sanborn,
Marc Holmes, Richard C. Miller, Ada Sullivan, Terry Beech, Patty Bond,
Kevin Stirnweis, Kerry Bertrand, Donald Valcovic, David Roper, Brad Treadwell,
Diane Treadwell, Fausto Braganti, Ginni Spencer, Dale Moore, Blair Pingeton,
Fred Bauer, The Marblehead Glover's Regiment, Bonnie Strong,
Judy Anderson, Webster Bull, Shawna Mullen, Robert W. Hugo, Richard Sloane,
David R. Andelman.

"When asked to compose the perfect metaphor for Fate,
I considered the task, then proceeded to describe a gigantic whirlpool
carving itself into the vast loneliness of a dark sea.
At the far edge, voyagers approach from every direction,
full of innocence.
As they are drawn inexorably together, the pace quickens
until they find themselves plunging helplessly into the night thunder
of the abyss."

— Akhir al-Nahr, "The Cauldron"

FOREWORD

*L*et me begin by saying that I am not a writer. The details of my life and my profession are not relevant, so I won't waste your time talking about them here. If asked to write a book of any description, I simply wouldn't know where to begin. My role is that of conduit.

This volume introduces the work of a man that I have never met. It is a story within a story. The thin, outer crust is mine and the inner layer—the magma churning beneath the surface—belongs to a man named Maxwell Blessing. As I said, I have never met the man and, until I came into possession of his writings, I never knew that he existed. Although I have made a significant effort, I have been unable to discover more than a few facts about his life.

Maxwell Blessing was born in Rhode Island during the 1950s. He was an only child and his upbringing appears to have been unremarkable. Upon graduating from high school in 1972, he went off to college on the West Coast and earned a master's degree in psychology. He came back east in 1978 and set up a private practice in Boston. It was from his own writings that I learned he made a final move to Marblehead, Massachusetts, the town in which I live.

My wife and I bought our house on Franklin Street in the mid 1980s. It is an old house, built before the American Revolution. We have spent considerable time over the years making it our own in the ways most families do: raising kids, passing the important days of our lives, and putting what time and energy we could spare into fixing it up. It was during a minor flurry of home repairs that I made a most remarkable discovery. The third floor is a finished attic space that had been an apartment and an office at various times in the past. I was trying to locate the lair of the several wasps that had been making my life miserable over the past few days. The intruders had clearly found a way in through the roof or wall, which meant they probably had a nest somewhere about.

I don't like wasps much. In fact, I had meant to call a qualified wasp professional earlier that day, but had forgotten to do so. As a consequence, there I was at 11:30 at night, tapping on plaster and shining a flashlight into the myriad crawl spaces, nooks, and crannies that any eccentric old house seems to have in abundance. It was during my survey that I found the dusty manila envelope stuffed against the chimney bricks in the back of a forgotten closet.

We had been living in the house for a number of years, but I didn't have a recollection of that particular cranny, so I had no idea whether the envelope was ours or had been left by a previous occupant. I was soon to be enlightened.

The envelope contained a manuscript of sorts, a hodge-podge of chapters, notes, and scribbles. After three solid days of decoding the most astonishing tale that I could ever imagine, I was determined to organize it and have it published.

Mostly, it is a narrative told in the first person by Max Blessing himself. Occasionally, I think, he closes some minor gaps using his professional gift for back-filling details. Other times, he seems to draw on information provided by several of the principal characters, details that provide a more revealing glimpse into their lives.

These, then, were the disparate pieces of writing that I have attempted to assemble into a coherent whole. For those of you who choose to take the journey, there will come a moment when your sense of credulity will be strained beyond reasonable limits. You will be tempted— as I was—to judge whether the words represent fact or fiction. My

In the Time of Worms

publisher, obsessed with publisher's issues, clearly found it too difficult to take that leap of faith and, as a condition of publication, demanded that the work be classified as "fiction." So be it. I remind myself that Jules Verne's *From the Earth to the Moon* was considered fiction when it was first published in 1865.

In that spirit, I give you Maxwell Blessing's story.

—*Kenelm Winslow Harris*

CHAPTER 1

*O*t is said that in the minutes just before a tidal wave hits, a harbor may actually empty itself of water. This mysterious warning is rarely understood by those who end up bobbing face down amidst the wreckage. The simple events that foreshadow great misfortune can often seem so thoroughly innocent when compared to the aftermath. Such was the phone call I received one October morning several years ago.

The day had begun as one of those aimless, drifty Sundays when time shambles along and you realize that you still haven't dressed and the newspaper lies strewn about the sofa. A day intended to be unfinished and unremembered. And so, when the phone rang, I almost didn't answer.

It was Burrage—so annoyingly reliable. He reminded me that I had promised to drive him up to Marblehead to buy a model boat for his father's birthday. Lunch was to be my reward. Looking back on all that has happened, I now realize that this day was never mine to begin with.

For years everyone told me I simply must visit Marblehead, so, of course, I'd carefully avoided the place. Truth be told, even those who decide to go there generally can't find it until the third or fourth try, then, once they do, can't figure out how to get back out again. It's more like a lobster pot than a town.

Marblehead sits crammed onto a small peninsula just below Salem on the old North Shore, a grand old attic of a place, its history drifting about like specs of dust in a shaft of autumn light. Salem, you see, is the tourist mecca in these parts, a town with more palm readers than streetlights. What with Cotton Mather, Nathaniel Hawthorne, and the famous witches of 1692, there is no doubt that Salem is *the* show. In contrast— much to the relief of those who live here—Marblehead has managed to avoid Salem's annual horde of visitors for the most part. Oh, there are the occasional tour-gawkers busing through the narrow streets and stopping long enough at Abbot Hall to see the original "Spirit of '76" hanging on the wall of the selectmen's meeting room. But most visitors don't really know what to look for after that. The town's past sits tucked away in corners and behind closed doors of ancient houses that stand shoulder to shoulder along old, twisting paths that barely count for roads these days.

Most never stay long enough to learn that the old town of Marblehead has more 17th and 18th century dwellings than any place in America. Georgian, Federal, and First Period homes sink and sag against one another like so many quaint, crooked teeth perched on jawbones of granite and brick. Tiny back yards hidden from the road are given away by the great trees that loom above moss-covered roofs and nuzzle up to crooked chimneys. Among rambling clapboard walls, pitching gables, and wind-worn sills there is not a straight line or square angle to be found anymore. Some of the earlier homes have ceilings barely six feet high, doorways even lower, and stairwells so narrow and winding that most second floor furniture must be hoisted up through a window. Other buildings are rabbit warrens straight out of an Escher print, chamber after chamber leading one into another, upstairs and down, until even the owners are unsure of how many rooms they actually have. And every detail turns back the clock—gunstock posts and boxed beams, fireplaces in each room, pumpkin-pine floors and dark cellar stairs leading down into every manner of earthen crawl space and granite passage.

Marblehead is *old*, old in a way that goes beyond the normal peeling of paint and settling of foundations. There are places on earth where lives have been so vividly lived that the residue has become embedded in the very fabric of the walls and ten thousand moments still hang in the air like just-whispered words. Places where time itself becomes a living thing that hovers among the shadows of an old closet or rests a bony hand on the back of your shoulder. In Marblehead, the living are seen as caretakers of the past and even the dust on an old book is considered a dimension of its antiquity.

Burrage and I pulled into town around noon and just as we arrived, the weather turned magical in a way that only happens on rare autumn days in New England. There was a gusty breeze blowing up from the southwest bringing an incongruous warmth to an otherwise crisp fall day. The sun, now riding lower in the October sky, shot deep golden rays through gaps in the thick purple clouds that rolled out to sea. As we slowly drove into the old village, the wind picked up and sent swarms of fallen leaves swirling through the air around us. Cavorting in the amber light, they ticked against the car windows leaving that delicious, musty scent expanding in our nostrils. Every now and then a burst of sun would explode upon the red painted wall of an old building and set it glowing brilliantly against the dark sky.

I was so entranced that I had barely noticed the increasingly eccentric quality of the streets along which we were traveling. House after house, each more aged than the next, created a continuous, rambling wall on either side of the narrowing road. It was as if we were journeying down a long, clapboard gullet, each turn in the road drawing us further from the outside world. We looked at one another and even the methodical Burrage was transfixed.

Burrage was one of those "left brain" individuals. A born engineer, he had decided instead that his calling was to write slogans for those little billboards on the tops of taxicabs in Boston. He viewed taxi tops as a powerful tool—under-utilized till now—which could be exploited to spread peace and goodwill among the general public. Matchbook covers, fortune cookie slips, and the undersides of soda bottle caps were other venues which he saw making up a potentially vast communications empire for someone with the right vision—his.

Burrage preached that 90% of what we believe comes into our brains without our knowledge. He was convinced that all this subliminal information had even greater sway over our actions precisely because we didn't know it was there. Burrage had this epiphany one evening at a pub while he was drinking a bottle of warm beer and eating taco chips and salsa. As he watched a long-haired waitress bend over to pick up some fallen change from the floor, he distractedly took the bottle cap from the table in front of him, dipped it in salsa and put it in his mouth. The ensuing ten minutes were a horrific blur of gagging, rolling on the floor, and being hoisted upside-down by the bartender and two customers who pounded him on the back. By the time the insidious cap was plucked from his throat by an Asian woman with long, slender fingers, he had convinced himself that somehow, without any conscious decision whatsoever, he had resolved to kill himself.

From that moment forward, Burrage had committed himself to saving the world from a similar fate. He reasoned that since human beings can only edit information about which they are consciously aware, we are forever vulnerable to the endless bombardment of negative messages, which slip into our brains unannounced. He never tired of explaining his theory.

"Just think about it," he once volunteered to me in his kitchen. "You're a kid standing at the blackboard trying to draw an isosceles triangle and the chalk keeps breaking and half the class is snickering because your fly is open and you aren't even aware of it! You think that doesn't affect you in ways we can't even begin to measure?"

"Jeez, Burr, that happened to you?"

Burrage was incensed.

"Maybe... how would I know! That's the *point!* This stuff happens, I tell you!"

"Look," I told him. "You could be onto something here, but even if you are, what does it mean? What can you do about it? This is life after all."

Without even looking, Burrage reached behind him and pulled up a wooden chair. With the self-assurance of a mathematician writing the final lines of a complex equation, he unveiled his secret plan.

"We can design *positive* messages that people will take into their brains without realizing it! Give them experiences just within the periphery of their senses yet beyond the awareness of their conscious minds. For example, have you ever consciously read the message on a taxi top?"

I sighed.

"You mean those little signs on the roofs of cabs?"

"*Exactly*. Can you remember any product that was ever advertised on one of them?"

Burrage was so sure of himself at this point.

"No, I can't," I said, doing my best to show how little I cared that I couldn't.

"Well, guess what," he said, tapping my forehead with his index finger. "Even though you may not know it, that information is right in here bouncing around just waiting for a way to control your life. Now maybe it gets you to eat at some Portuguese restaurant you never heard of, or— who knows? The point is it's making you feel *something*. Why not have it be something that makes you feel good about yourself?"

"I feel pretty good about myself already."

"You say that now. So did *I* until I found myself trying to jam a bottle cap down my throat. No! No! No! It wasn't any accident. I picked that cap up and I dipped it in that salsa and I *ate* it. I'm just lucky that long-fingered lady was in the room. Now, I have an opportunity here do something good and I intend to make the most of it."

The next day, Burrage had quit his job as the software guru at a high tech firm in Lexington and had taken an entry-level position with the Taxi-Talk Marketing Company. His responsibilities included taking copy supplied by the client and fitting it into the allotted space on the taxi-top. Occasionally, the client was too small to have an ad agency create the copy and would ask the folks at Taxi-Talk to write it for them. These requests were handed to Burrage. These were the moments he now lived for. He saw it as his mission to find a way to imbed messages that brought positive energy to all who were exposed to them, no matter how unconsciously.

As an example, for a company that sold chain link fences he wrote, *"Good fences make good neighbors. And good neighbors bring each other soup when they're sick."*

At first, the fence company wasn't quite sure why they were spending all this money talking about soup when what they sold was chain link. Burrage explained that a lot of people feel guilty about putting up a fence, that by equating fences with care giving, it took the hostility out of it and enabled folks to make the purchase without fear of being misunderstood. When it was put like that, the owner of the fence company allowed there might be some truth to it and agreed to give it a try. Of course, Burrage could care less about selling fences. Burrage wanted people to think about how they could be more nurturing to one another, which is why when the sign was printed, he made the "soup" line about three times bigger than the "fence" line.

But back to Marblehead. Burrage rotated his head like an owl as he tried to take in each building as we passed.

"I had no idea it looked like this," he said, as we almost lurched straight into the living room of the Faithful Bartlett house.

Many of the town's houses had a little wooden sign nailed to the front that said who built it, his occupation, and when it was built. Faithful Bartlett, clearly a risk-taker by nature, had placed his little house at the bottom of a steep one-lane road that took a sharp turn to the left immediately in front of his door. Apparently anticipating the damage that a runaway carriage might cause to his front parlor some icy, colonial night, Mr. Bartlett had cleverly placed a large granite post upright betwixt his wall and the edge of the road. My front bumper barely missed it as I spun the wheel hard to the left.

"I have no clue where we are," I exclaimed as I nudged my way along yet another tiny lane.

The downtown must have been built on the premise that most visitors would be as disoriented as I was, for the streets were nearly all one way, feeding one into another with few choices to be made. As we navigated yet another twist in the road, an old woman with a leash came shuffling toward us leading what looked to be a small, bouncing hairpiece. I lowered my window and tried to make eye contact as a prelude to asking directions. It's amazing how preoccupied an old woman can make herself look when she doesn't want to be bothered. Not willing to be ignored, I leaned my head out and greeted her just as the hairpiece went into a traditional squat.

"Excuse me, ma'am, but we're looking for the store that sells those model sail boats. We're not sure of the name. Any idea where we should be going?"

It was made clear that she would rather stare at newly minted dog dirt than carry on a conversation with the likes of me.

"Straight," she coughed in a voice that sounded as if it had been stored in a dusty mason jar for several decades. A stubby finger gave a barely discernable twitch in the direction we were traveling. As I stared at her, the wind picked up again and her straggling hair whipped across her ruddy cheek. She turned and studied me through narrowed eyes as though she was deciding what curse she should put on me. The dry, gutter leaves rose up in small tornados and pummeled dying plants in the flower boxes along the road and, for a moment, I felt as though long-slumbering spirits had begun to stir and move about in the shadows behind window shades or drift overhead deep within the boughs of the trees. A tremendous shudder made my shoulders jolt and I quickly rolled up the car window and lurched down the road.

We never did locate the store or the model boats that mystical day, yet, due to some compulsion I can never explain, I had made the decision that I would move to Marblehead.

As for Burrage, the stress of trying to find our way out of the old village stimulated loss-of-control feelings similar to those of the unfortunate bottle cap incident. He couldn't so much as swallow his own saliva until we hit Boston, so eating lunch was out of the question.

I began to pack up my apartment that night.

Within a month I was comfortably settled in the third floor garret of a large house on Franklin Street in the Old Town. It was all I had hoped for—four small rooms tucked under the eaves of a gambrel roof. The house had been built around 1750, although many of the large posts and beams were from a much earlier house built on the same site in the 1600s. The current version was the creation of a man named Orne, a colonial merchant who decided he wanted a home that properly reflected his success in business. Designed in the Georgian style so popular at the time, the home was built around two imposing chimney stacks, each containing multiple flues, which led to the many fireplaces below. The chimneys ran straight up through the house, each about a third of the way along the roofline as viewed from the street below. They were so massive that the rest of the house literally "hung" off of them.

The attic apartment that I occupied was like no other I had ever seen. Huge, old timbers were exposed in the ceiling and I was delighted to discover that they were not ordinary rafters. They were instead the round masts of long-forgotten ships, which had pounded through the brine in the Atlantic of the 17th century. The deep, smooth scars of chaffing ropes told stories of the countless gales that had finally scuttled the ships from which these beams were salvaged. On warm afternoons you could actually smell the odor of salt and tar still alive in the wood. I was amazed one day to find a small cluster of centuries-old barnacles still cemented to the underside of a beam in a dark corner of the bedroom.

The rooms themselves were finished almost haphazardly—a mix of crude plaster and weathered boards from an old barn that had long ago occupied a corner of the back lot. Yet, there were touches that almost reached the level of theatrical set design. A row of old, wooden blocks and tackle hung along the ridge beam at the highest point in the ceiling of the living room. In each room were several large, tarnished bronze cleats such as those used to tie-off lines on sailing ships. These were stoutly bolted to timbers as if awaiting ropes to lash down the roof in the event of a great storm. I used them for clothes hooks. At either end of the apartment there was a hole in the floor through which creaking wooden stairs corkscrewed down two levels to the ground. Each opening was surrounded by a section of ship's rail, complete with thick, turned balustrades still flecked with worn paint in deep tones of red, green, or black. On several of the wide plank floorboards, you could even see where a colonial carpenter had carved placement numbers into the surface with a knife.

From south-facing windows, there were glimpses of the little harbor. On many a Sunday afternoon, I would sit in the alcove of a dormer pretending to read but end up gazing off through the rooftops at the sea and imagine myself gliding silently out over the waves that slid across the rocks by the old fort.

When I moved here, I jettisoned every stick of furniture I owned and for weeks lived on an oversized feather pillow while waiting to be inspired as to the perfect decorating strategy. The more I did without, the less I wanted to replace what I'd had. There was something about the simplicity and the raw warmth of the rooms themselves that made me not want to detract from them with modern furnishings. I resolved that I would slowly collect only authentic period pieces that would reflect the old character of my surroundings.

And so I did. First, a small maple table—no more than a pitcher stand really—then several ladderback chairs, an enormous old carpenter's chest, which I used for a coffee table, a rocker, and a rope bed on which I threw my feather ticking. Eventually I collected a highboy chest in the Queen Anne style, a number of punched tin lanterns and a faded, olive-colored sideboard on which I displayed a growing collection of unleaded pewter plates, mugs and other small wear. Within several months, my abode was livable and even fit for a guest or two. My first guests were to be the family who lived below, the owners of the house. And, of course, Burrage.

I thought it would be apropos to serve a meal in the historical spirit of my new home, so I planned it around the dishes of the period. What I lacked in culinary ability, I made up for with resourcefulness by calling upon local purveyors of fine victuals. From a nearby café—a curried pumpkin soup. From a gourmet shop—English cheeses so finely aged that they smelled like the ripe end of an old goat. From the bakery—whole, round loaves of something called "gunner's bread." And from a waterfront eatery, an 18th century seafood dish called "Tench With A Pudding In Her Belly" (don't ask me what was in it, I hadn't a clue). Added to that, there were several bottles of wine personally selected for me by a postal worker who happened to be delivering mail to the liquor store when I was there. And finally, I created a frothy, non-alcoholic punch for the two children, who were, no doubt, being dragged to the affair by their parents.

At the appointed hour, there was a knock from below and I clattered down the spiral stairwell to the side door. Burrage stood there with a victorious look on his gaunt face.

"Found the place."

I nodded approvingly. "So you did. Come on up. Stay to the right... the wide part of the steps."

"Sheesh, it's like climbing a ladder going up these stairs! You ever fall?"

"You get used to it," I replied, not recounting the several times I had dumped bags of groceries navigating the climb.

"Cool place!" he exclaimed as his head poked up through the attic floor. "This is so..."

"Old?" I offered.

"Yeah, old, but really—I don't know—different. The peripheral sight lines are quite nice though. Lots of calming influences."

In the last few months, Burrage had developed his concept of unconscious messaging into a full blown science, complete with jargon, standards of measurement, and an endless array of factoids obvious, of course, only to him. Where most people might take a relaxed stroll around a room glancing at the various objects they found, Burrage would suddenly jerk his head to the left or right as if trying to sneak up on a peripheral view. Whenever he became aware that his odd behavior was being observed, he would immediately bring several fingers to the side of his chin and nod thoughtfully as though having just made a small but profound discovery.

"So, Burr, how are the taxi tops going?" I asked, handing him a glass of postman's choice.

"Oh, well, some really good stuff going on there, if I do say so. Just finished a nice piece for a tattoo parlor in Hampton Beach. I used a quote from Beatrix Potter about the importance of innocence. The owner thought I was crazy and threatened to cut off my ear, but his phone's been ringing off the hook. He loves me now. Of course, the demand for tattoos of skulls with snakes crawling out of the eyes is down a bit. Some biker actually wanted a tattoo of six little Renaissance cherubs just below the hairline on his forehead. They're kind of playfully pulling at his eyebrows or something. The parlor owner had to go to the Museum of Fine Arts to research it. Real progress there, I think."

I nodded. At that moment, I could hear my other guests begin their journey up the stairs from the floors below. Myles and Enid Castler were my landlords as well as my downstairs neighbors. They were from England and had purchased the house on Franklin Street when Myles was transferred to the U.S. by Barrows & Wight, a company that dealt in rare maps, antique books, and personal papers. An eleven-year old daughter named Elizabeth and an eight-year old son, William, rounded out the family. Their cat, an obese, nasty creature named Lady Jane, thankfully remained at home. Although I had been here for nearly two months, I hadn't really had the chance to get to know them.

"Here now, here we are!" sang out Enid as her face rose like a huge, white mushroom growing up out of the floor after a spell of damp weather. "Why, isn't it lovely of you to have us!"

She was soon fully aboard and stepped quickly to the side while the rest of the brood clomped noisily up the steps. Her head, which was quite enormous to begin with, was made to look even larger by the way she wore her hair, a kind of carrot-colored dollop, which meringued around her ears and over her crown. For all the fanfare above her neck, what lay below was considerably less memorable. She was quite short and wore a limp, maroon dress, which sagged unevenly above a pair of stubby, black shoes. Her heavy arms hung motionless at her sides but her fingers worked continuously like the legs of a lobster trying to gain traction in the air over a pot of boiling water. Her smile was sad and sincere, the smile of someone who felt she couldn't really express everything she wished.

Elizabeth, the daughter, was next. As her toe caught briefly on the lip of the final step, her face reddened and she quickly retreated to a spot behind her mother's shoulder. Unlike her mother, she was lanky and raw-boned. Pale blond hair clung thinly to her cheeks as violet eyes peeked out from her down-turned face. Her commitment to chewing a thumbnail superceded any obligation to speak for the moment. I could respect that, I thought. I was eleven once. William stepped up manfully and extended a firm hand to me. I bowed slightly and shook it.

"Welcome. Glad you could come," I said, watching the pride of completion flash briefly in his blue eyes. He, too, went to a place near his mother and stood with his arms folded carefully across his chest. His eyes darted from face to face looking for clues as to what else might be expected of him and, finding none, he settled in to watch his father finish the climb. William was of medium height and build with copper-colored hair and the look of a lad who knew far more of life than anyone could ever coax out of him. He wore a collarless, long-sleeved shirt and faded green shorts. The knot on his left sneaker was poised to come undone, displaying the contempt all shoes feel for the efforts of small boys.

Finally, with a low grunt, Myles Castler pulled his tall, thin frame up into the room and gazed about.

"Ah," he whispered. "Nicely done."

In my few dealings with the man, I had never known him to raise his voice above a murmur. Large, gray eyes bracketed a long, slender Anglo-Saxon nose. An amazing set of eyebrows twitched and danced with every thought that came into his head. He had that cool, British calm about him, a manner which suggested that life was written neatly in a book and whenever we found ourselves surprised in any way, all we need do is stand erect and wait quietly for the page to turn for an explanation. He was in his mid-fifties, I would say, with thinning gray hair and a habit of running the palm of his hand up over the top of his head and down the back where he would then draw it round his neck to the front again. I was curious how I would feel about him by the end of the evening.

"Well! Welcome, all of you. Let me introduce you to my friend, Peter Burrage."

I proceeded to complete introductions all around and herded the group to a seating area under the eaves. Within a few minutes Myles and Enid had their wine, William, a glass of punch, and Elizabeth, nothing that appealed to her. The conversation meandered here and there in a way typical of such gatherings. I gave William an interlocking loop puzzle to solve and he moved off by himself immersed in the challenge. Elizabeth sat on the floor at her mother's knee, uninspired by any of the distractions I had offered her. When the time felt right, I brought everyone to the table and served the feast I had assembled. It was well received for the most part, I thought.

"Would anyone like anymore tench?" I inquired. The platter made the rounds.

"Just *delicious*, Maxwell!" Enid bubbled to me. "How *ever* did you manage it?"

I came clean with regard to preparations and no one seemed to think the worse of me for it. The wine had everyone in a very accepting frame of mind.

"I just wanted to try something different," I explained. "Something that had the feel of the house and all the history here in Marblehead."

"Ah, well then," Myles asked, "Do you know about this house?"

"Not much really," I replied.

"Quite a history, I have discovered," Myles went on. "Among other things, it seems that the Orne lads—the sons of old Joshua, that is—were very active in the years leading up to your Revolution. Members of the Committees of Correspondence, I understand. Probably met with Paul Revere and Samuel Adams and all the rest of those rebel brigands right down there in the front parlor!"

Myles said this with the good-natured humor of an Englishman who now found himself in the curious position of owning a house in which bits and pieces of the war against England had been plotted.

"You don't say!" Burrage chuckled. "And here you are, come back to reclaim the lost colonies house by house! Very clever!"

"Oh, no, no," Enid protested, a look of concern on her face. "We'd never dream of anything like that. We *love* what you've done with it—the country, I mean—although it could do with some tidying up here and about. I'm not sure about the skateboards and such or what you've done with golf, but for the most part, you've made a fine job of it. It was simply brilliant how you Americans managed the moon-landing business and came up with that jazz music. I simply *adore* all those saxophones!"

Burrage took the compliment in the spirit it was intended and assured Enid that he did not really suspect the Castlers of being the first wave of a royal invasion force. If anything like that were in the works, he pointed out, the tabloids would have exposed it long before now.

As the conversation changed direction, I drifted away for a moment and conjured a vision of Sam Adams, Azor Orne, and the Sons of Liberty sitting in a room below, lighting pipes and tilting back on their chairs as they debated the course of American independence. In my mind, I heard the voices and tankards raised in support of the preposterous idea that Marblehead fishermen could strike a blow at the most powerful nation on earth. The primordial odor of wood smoke from my fireplace curled into my nostrils as if to remind me that the veil between past and present was even less opaque than I might think. It was true. The old Marblehead buildings seemed to resonate with deep, low notes struck long ago. These reverberations were now traveling through the centuries the way the secret song of a great whale travels along the bottom of the ocean until heard by a receptive mate a thousand miles away. As I was swept along with the current, the sound of Myles' voice pulled me back up to the surface.

"You're both welcome to tour the house and I will be happy to tell you what I know. Would you like to see it now?"

Before Burrage could even react, I blurted out an unequivocal, "Yes!"

Elizabeth took the change of venue as an opportunity to head off to parts unknown. But William made it clear that he would stick with us as we began our descent on the old wooden stairs. Within moments we were standing in the very parlor that Myles had described. The room was in the front right corner of the house. Around the ceiling was colonial "dental work" molding. Ornate floral carvings wound their way up the side panels of the fireplace. In the corner, a small closet stood tucked away to the left of the fireplace, its door cut to follow the sharp angle of the sagging ceiling.

The house had come furnished, we were told. An estate sale. It looked as if the furniture had been there forever, each piece just the right size and design for the space it filled. I could see there were many valuable antiques that matched the period of the building. My previous vision of secret meetings became even more real as I took in the room.

"This musket is quite old, I believe," Myles said as he took a long, brown flintlock down from the wall. "A birding piece they tell me. Used to hunt fowl with small shot. That's why the barrel's so thin."

He handed me the musket. Its size and weight surprised me. I held it up to my shoulder but my arm shook from the strain. It was hard to imagine anyone holding it still while aiming. Weren't folks supposed to be smaller back then?

As Myles returned the gun to the wall, Enid motioned us toward the dining room on the other side of the entry hall. As I stepped through the doorway, something heavy came hurtling against my shin. I looked down to see a great, brindle mass skittering across the floor and down the hall. It was Lady Jane, the Castlers' cat, although it looked more like a knot of debris from a clogged storm drain. I regained my composure and brushed the clumps of cat fur from my trouser leg.

"Oh, don't mind *her!*" Enid exclaimed. "She's just trying to impress you."

In fact, I was impressed with how a creature that fat could run down the hall without falling down dead.

"Quite a load there," I observed politely.

"Well, yes, we try to keep her snacking under control, but I fear she eats whenever she's nervous and it seems most everything makes her so."

Snacking? What could she snack on, I wondered. *Potato chips? Mouse heads?*

"The poor dear! We found her in the cellar when we moved in," Enid explained. "No idea how long she had been down there or who she belonged to, so we kept her on. She won't go outdoors and yet she'll disappear for days at a time. Most curious."

Indeed. Enid led us into the dining room. A brass chandelier hung from the ceiling over a long dining table. The chairs were arranged away from the table around the perimeter of the room and on every wall there were numerous mirrors trimmed with ornate gold leaf frames. They made the room sparkle with reflected light and gave the feeling it was much larger. A burnt red China trade paper covered the walls above the chair rail. A beautiful room.

"Next time we'll have to have you come here to dinner," Enid offered, her fingers dancing at the thought. "It has been a wonderful place to entertain. Why, the last time we had guests—who were they, Myles?"

"The Welkies."

"Yes, the Welkies! *Lovely* people, although I wasn't keen on the way Boden Welkie arranged his peas in a circle around his baked potato and then ate them counter-clockwise. It felt a bit Druidish to me, although I haven't the faintest idea how the Druids felt about vegetables. But you would like the Welkies—an old Marblehead family. They know the history of the town like no one else. Why they were the ones who told us about the secret stairway running up along our chimney stack!"

My head turned with a slight snap.

"You have a secret stairway?" I asked, feeling the same giddiness a young boy feels about underground forts or leafy caves beneath forsythia bushes. Myles immediately downplayed the revelation.

"No staircase that we could find certainly," he said. "We gave the place a pretty good going over, measuring rooms, tapping on walls and so forth. In a house like this there are always odd bits of space and nooks and crannies galore, but we found nothing that suggests a hidden stair. If there ever was such a thing, I'm certain a previous owner dismantled it long ago. Pardon me for a moment, won't you? The telephone is ringing."

Myles took his leave and slipped up the center staircase.

"Hannah Welkie told us it had been used to hide slaves on the Underground Railroad," Enid added, her fingers in a fury. "But her husband, Boden, said it had been there since the house was built and had been used for smuggling! Can you *imagine*? But come here—to the back sitting room. You might enjoy this!"

Burrage looked at me as if to say we should think twice about taking this too much further, but by this time, I was fairly flying down the hall behind Enid. She walked through a door that featured a delicate Palladian window over the frame. The glass was rippled with age and the light coming through it cast shadows that looked like waves washing over the plaster wall. Once beyond the door we found ourselves in the kitchen, but took a quick right into the back sitting room.

The room was dominated by yet another fireplace, this one large and clearly used for more than heat originally. There were large iron arms, which swung out over the hearth on which kettles or pots could be hung. There were also several iron hooks imbedded in the brick. To the right of the fireplace there was an amazing, primitive wooden door. No more than five and a half feet high, it was of dark wood and scarred by time like the face of one of the old lobstermen who stacked their pots around the corner near Little Harbor. It was held closed by a small wooden block that rotated on a nail. Enid walked up to the door and twisted the block.

"Now come closer, you two and look in here."

I stepped forward and leaned into the darkness. After several seconds, my eyes became used to the light and I saw what was a small pantry-like space, barely large enough for two people to enter. Books and boxes sat on shelves and in wooden cabinets built into the small alcoves of the space. It was interesting, I supposed, but nothing extraordinary.

"No, no," Enid said. "You must step *in*—further. *There* toward the back corner."

I turned to Burrage and shrugged my shoulders. We both crammed our way further back in the shadows.

"Sorry. The light's burned out," Enid explained. "Now—stand very still and listen!"

Burrage was breathing heavily through his nose, as always, and because there was spontaneity involved, he was feeling more stress than usual, which made the air snoring through his nostrils sound like a windy day.

"Burr! *SHHHH!*" I whispered hoarsely.

"I'm not saying a word!" he countered. "And besides that, my bladder is about to rupture!"

He was clearly not in the right frame of mind for standing in the dark in someone's closet. His breathing grew louder.

"Look, Burr, just stop for a second! Hold your breath."

He shot a resentful look at me but stopped his breathing. For a few seconds, I could only hear the sound of us shifting our weight and the distant ticking of the century clock on the tall armoire in the sitting room.

"Do you hear it?" Enid whispered breathlessly.

"What are we listening for?" I asked.

"Just wait," she replied.

Burrage took another deep breath and we stood stock-still. The seconds crept along and drops of perspiration began to run down the small of my back. I was beginning to wonder why I was putting myself through it when—for a moment—I thought I heard the faintest of sounds from somewhere down near the floor at the back wall. I tugged on Burrage's sleeve and held my finger to my lips and pointed to the corner. Burrage took another breath and leaned closer.

"*There*," I said, not totally sure that I wasn't imagining things. "Did you hear that?"

"I don't think so," Burrage whispered. "What did it sound like?"

"Wait!" I said quickly. "Listen there! It's like, I don't know, *waves* or something. Do you hear it?"

I now could distinctly hear a faint rushing sound, like water surging over small pebbles. As I leaned down further and cocked my head, the sound grew slightly more distinct.

"Do you hear it?" I asked, accidentally poking my elbow into Burrage's bladder area.

Burrage let out a low moan. "Jeez, that does it! I almost peed my pants!"

He noisily shuffled out of the pantry and I could hear Enid give him hurried directions to the bathroom. I leaned back in toward the corner and held my breath again. It was still very faint but I could distinctly hear the sounds of waves softly lapping on a beach. For an instant, I even thought I heard the far, sharp cry of a gull. Then, it was gone. I waited a few moments more then turned and felt my way out. As I emerged, Enid and William were staring at me with a look of anticipation.

"Well?" asked Enid. "Did you hear it?"

"I'm not sure. Do you mean that surf sound?" I asked.

"Yes! Yes! That's it exactly!" Enid burbled. "It's not there every time you know. In fact, I have not heard it more than a dozen times in the year we've owned the place. Myles claims never to have heard it of course, but he is such a doubter! Oh, I'm so *excited* for you! William and I call it the 'Ocean Room.' William here discovered it one evening whilst looking for a box of games we had never unpacked. Isn't it uncanny?"

I had to admit I was captivated by the experience of hearing ocean surf in the corner of a closet deep in the bowels of a large house.

"Do you know what causes it?" I asked. "Is it maybe a trick of the senses, like hearing the ocean in a seashell? Or maybe it's some acoustical thing, you know, like sounds bouncing off surfaces and echoing in weird ways."

"I have no idea, I'm sure," Enid replied. "I only know it can be louder when the door is shut and that it can fade away entirely in a few seconds. Did you hear the gulls?"

I nodded. "I think so."

"That's why I can't imagine it's the same as hearing the ocean in a shell. I've never heard a gull in a seashell nor has anyone else," Enid suggested. "And we're quite some distance from the ocean, behind many buildings, and, what with the automobiles and such, I've never even heard the sound of the surf from our yard or from anywhere else in the house. We simply cannot imagine from where the sound is coming. If you have any theories, please feel free to share them."

"Not at the moment," I replied, shaking my head just as Burrage was returning from the bathroom.

"Burr, did you hear it or not?"

"Hear what?"

"The sound of the ocean in the closet there."

I could tell that Burrage simply didn't want to get involved with any foolishness such as this and shook his head. But there was something about the way he did it that caught my eye. It was too quick, too certain.

"Well, it's better than having a ghost in there, I suppose!" I joked. "Nobody dragging chains around the cellar or making the walls bulge out when you walk up the steps."

Myles entered the room and calmly turned to me and said, "No, of course not. None of that around here. Enid, I hope you didn't subject our guests to this closet nonsense!"

Enid straightened her back and did her best to assume a dignified air.

"It is *not* nonsense, as you well know, Myles!" she said, then turned to Burrage and me. "My husband is a precise man but could stand to be a bit more open-minded, in my opinion!"

It seemed the right time to call it an evening. Enid led us back to the stairway and we all said our good-byes. As we were leaving, I saw Myles cast a frown toward William. I shut the door and Burrage and I headed up the steps to the third floor.

When we got to my apartment, I turned to him and demanded, "Okay, wise guy. Spill. You heard it, too, didn't you!"

Burrage was getting his coat from the chair.

"Look, don't even ask. I'm not getting involved in their goofy little parlor tricks. Those people are weird, Max, trust me. They're just playing mind games with you. And that Myles, where did *he* disappear to? Funny how he leaves and then all of a sudden there are 'strange' noises in the closet! They even had the kid doing it. At least I get to go home, thank God."

"Wait a minute. What do you mean they had the kid doing it? He never said a word."

"Maybe not to you. When we were heading to the dining room, he started giving me a bunch of bull about a guy coming out of his closet at night. Look, I know he's only eight but it sounds like it's in their genes. They need to get out and do something productive like help the homeless or something. See, that's the problem in this town—no taxi tops. No way to spread the word to these people."

Burrage had his coat on and started for the steps.

"Good dinner, Max. Never had tench before. That was a great wine though."

"Yeah, thanks. William said *that*? About a guy in the closet? The closet we were in?"

"No, the closet in his bedroom," Burrage said as he started down the stairs. "I'll call you, Max."

"Yup. Give my best to Cambridge. Catch you next week."

I watched his head bob down the twisting stairs and disappear. Typical Burrage. Always looking to avoid anything too offbeat. The irony struck me. How much more offbeat do you get than Burrage?

I started to scrape the dishes and put them in the sink. Within a half an hour, I had the place back to normal so I sat back in the rocker and poured the last of the wine into a pewter mug. As I rocked slowly back and forth, I shut my eyes and listened to the creaking of the chair on the old, pine floorboards. I thought about the Castlers and the house and everything we had talked about that evening, then started to doze.

Just as I was about to nod off, the distinct odor of warm, salt air struck my nostrils and my dreams filled with images of waves frothing over a black sand beach in the moonlight.

CHAPTER 2

*O*ver the next few years, Marblehead became more and more a part of me. It was as if I had been here my whole life, and perhaps several lifetimes before that. It felt as timeless as the old stone walls that run through the Maine woods marking where a farmer's field had long ago reverted to forest or the clop-clopping of a horse-drawn wagon swaying along a dirt road in Lancaster County, Pennsylvania. There are just certain places that feel like genuine doorways to a time long gone. Marblehead is one of those places.

Eventually, Burrage had left taxi-tops behind and gotten a job with a software company—the memory of his little brush with death having faded along with his need to explain it. He was now building computer models of insects. The models showed how particularly stubborn pests might evolve to resist the effects of pesticides. His current study revealed a futuristic cockroach that not only would breed within hours of birth but also would have sex organs four times the size of its head. Burrage showed me a picture of it. Since I didn't know what the naughty bits of a cockroach were supposed to look like, I could study the picture without embarrassment. It reminded me somewhat of a big-time country western singer, very dazzling and bloated with all sorts of iridescent fringe hanging from this part or that. It looked like it could survive a nuclear attack, never mind a cheatin' wife.

As a result of his work, Burrage had become very concerned about the need to eliminate vermin. The way he saw it, certain ecologically aggressive creatures not only weren't essential to the health of the planet, but actually threatened to squeeze out all the useful species to boot. Rats, mosquitoes, and black flies were high on his hit list. At one time he had included dung beetles just because of their name but learned that they were actually very helpful in recycling your basic filth. I had asked him if he thought, based on his definition, that human beings qualified as vermin. He said humans were not born vermin but that some chose vermin-esque lifestyles. He listed telemarketers, tobacco executives, and radio talk show hosts as prime examples. He believed that, while it would not be morally acceptable to actually exterminate them, it should be legal to publicly assault them, say with a cream pie in the kisser or a burning bag of dog mess on the front stoop. Of course, I found his comments childish and trite, but I agreed with all of them.

The Castlers still owned the house on Franklin Street and I still lived in the apartment on the third floor. Elizabeth, the daughter, was finishing middle school and had her whole life planned out. The plan was to go to a good prep school, get accepted to Harvard, and live in Cambridge. She would then go on to business school, become obscenely wealthy, and never have to do anything she didn't want to do again. Oh, yes, she had also decided her bedroom was the wrong shape and moved to the back of the house into what had been a guest room.

William was now in fifth grade and played baseball. He dreamed of pitching for the Red Sox some day. In the three short years since he had arrived in this country, he had become totally Americanized and decided that baseball was his best chance at fame and fortune. He had learned how to pitch from the stretch, scratch himself in public, and hate the Yankees, so it appeared he was well on his way. The moment Elizabeth had moved out of her bedroom, William had moved in claiming his closet was too small. Since the move, it had struck me he seemed much happier and less distracted.

Enid Castler was now a volunteer at the local historical society. Most of her duties involved genealogical research for folks who had traced their roots back to Marblehead and wanted more information on a long forgotten ancestor. Enid would scour the databases, graveyards and dusty, old town registers to track down what she could. I imagined the hours of page-turning were the perfect workout for those hyperactive fingers of hers. She had to have a minor operation the previous year. It seems she had pinched a nerve in her back bending down in the pantry of the back parlor. She told the doctors that she had been dusting the shelves in the corner. I suspected she had been straining to catch the sounds that I had heard so faintly that night several years ago.

Myles was still with Barrows & Wight hunting down rare documents, maps, and books for collectors and museums. Marblehead and the surrounding towns had proved to be a real mother lode for Myles. Two whole rooms of the house were filled with dusty parchments, lambskin scrolls and fragile leather-bound books. They had wonderful titles like *An Account of My Journies Among the Red Indians of the Ohio Territorie* by a Calvinist minister named Temperance Mooney or *The Restorative Effects of Work*, a short but passionate volume written by a member of the Hancock Shaker Community in the mid-19th Century.

Myles was constantly behind with researching, documenting, and preparing his acquisitions for delivery to their future owners. Especially the maps. There were hundreds and hundreds of them—property surveys from the 1600s, street maps, maps of colonial water systems, coastal navigation charts—even one map showing the locations of gun powder stored in readiness for the coming war with England. I found them fascinating. Many had elaborate artwork and tiny, delicate handwriting done in a beautiful sepia script. Some were faded almost to oblivion and others were mere fragments of a much larger original. All of them were the last surviving portraits of a world that had long since vanished.

Lady Jane, now in the September of her fat, self-absorbed life, would often be found sprawled on a stack of old papers like a piece of road kill. That was fine with me, since it meant fewer encounters with her in the dark, narrow stairwell. Too many times I had placed my foot on a shadowy step only to be bitten on the ankle or have a trouser leg raked by the startled Lady Jane. On the plus side, however, there were several periods over the years where she would simply be gone. One day she would be lying on the door sill tonguing away at her tangle of fur; the next day she would have vanished without a trace only to reappear weeks or even months later acting as if she had never been gone. With each reappearance, my spirits would sag. What kind of world is it that allows Golden Retrievers or innocent chipmunks to get hit by cars yet allows a foul, useless sack of doorknobs like Lady Jane to go on and on?

As for me, I was quite satisfied with the life into which I had settled. As a psychologist with my own practice, I could pretty much define my days as I saw fit. Since William had abandoned his bedroom, I arranged with the Castlers to sublet it so that I no longer had to see clients in my living room. It was quite convenient actually. William's room had two doors—one that opened onto the landing in my stairwell and another that led into the central hallway in the Castlers' home. This second door remained locked and so the room came fully under my jurisdiction. I had fixed it up nicely, I thought. Comfortable wingback chairs were clustered around the fireplace. Framed prints of early maritime art adorned the walls. I also displayed a nice little collection of whaling artifacts, some of which had come from the Charles W. Morgan, the last surviving 19th century whaler, anchored today in Mystic, Connecticut. Clients seemed to find the atmosphere quite cozy and calming.

Not that I had that many clients. The fact is I've always had a low tolerance for this line of work so I kept my client base small, seeing no more than twelve people a week. More than twelve and I knew I would start to feel like Alice free-falling down the rabbit hole. Take Godfrey Nearing, a manager in the meat department of a small supermarket. Mr. Nearing could not shake the feeling that the minute he fell asleep, his wife, Tina, would roll over and stare at him all night long. Consequently, he would lie awake staring at *her*, trying to catch her in the act. Tina would say she found this incredibly unnerving. He would say, *"Exactly!"* and accuse her of being a hypocrite. She would say he was a horse's ass. The only thing they agreed on was that I stared at both of them way too much in our sessions. We wound up placing our chairs back to back and looking out at the walls. I met with them until their insurance ran out.

One afternoon, I got a call from Boden Welkie, the Castlers' friend. It seemed he was having some problems with anxiety at night and his doctor had suggested that it might be caused by stress. I scheduled an appointment for him.

"Well, aren't *these* something!" Mr. Welkie exclaimed as he came in the door and walked straight over to the artifacts I had mounted on the wall. "What a fine pair of eel spears you have there! No doubt most people go for the harpoons, but eel spears were far more important to the early settlers, you see, 'specially when the game was scarce. Oh, I beg your pardon—Boden Welkie. Pleased to make your acquaintance."

He strode over to me and shook my hand heartily. He was full of energy, that was plain—a smallish man, round in build with a large birthmark on his left temple. He was dressed in khakis, boat shoes and a maroon cardigan sweater buttoned up the front. On his head he wore a black fisherman's cap. I guessed he was in his mid-seventies although his vigor belied his age. He gave me a sheepish look and apologized for being a few minutes late. I introduced myself and gestured for him to have a seat in one of the wingback chairs.

"So," I said. "You seem to know a lot about history."

"Well, I do enjoy it certainly, although I've come to believe that no one knows much about it when all is said and done. Too much history out there and not enough left behind to give us a clear picture, I'm afraid. Throw in modern attitudes; a changing society and it's hard to put what information we *do* have in the proper context. Most of the history you read is just someone's guess at what happened, although the historians rarely admit to it. Seems there's more status to being a teacher of history than being a student. Me, I'm just a student."

I like this guy, I thought. "I hadn't looked at it that way, but I see your point. I'd have to agree, but why don't you tell me why you came to see me today."

I crossed my leg and leaned back with that "in-control" body language that I had perfected. Boden Welkie leaned his elbows on the arms of the chair and loosely clasped his fingers in front of him. For a brief moment, a small shadow seemed to pass over his face.

"Ah, yes. Why am I here? I could make a joke about forgetting why I came," he teased softly. "But better just to get to it, I s'pose."

He took a breath and glanced up toward the ceiling.

"I've had trouble sleeping lately, no doubt about that. I just feel... uneasy somehow—something looming. I don't quite know how to describe it."

"Is anything going on in your life that might make you feel worried?" I asked.

He struggled with the thought for a moment.

"I really don't think so," he replied. "Everything's fine with me, my wife, Hannah. Our health is good and we're fine with our finances surely. It's more "looming" like I said. I feel like I'm waiting for something to happen though I haven't a notion what it might be."

"Something bad?" I asked. "Frightening?"

"I'm just not sure. It's more the unknown, I think. Something I don't understand."

It seemed the right moment to try a theory, but I had to be delicate.

"Do you think... I mean we're all getting older. Do you think you might be feeling anxiety about—"

"Death?" he said. "Is that what you're asking?"

I nodded.

"You know I've asked myself that a hundred times," he answered. "No, I don't think I fear death for myself or even for Hannah, my wife. In fact, it's almost the *opposite* I'm feeling."

"I don't follow you," I said, shifting in my chair and crossing my other leg.

"I don't know. I feel I truly understand death. I respect it. I know its place in the scheme of things, so to speak. For me death is as acceptable as birth, all part of the same thing. But this—this feeling—what happens when death isn't *there* somehow? Do you see?"

"I'm not sure I do," I replied.

"Oh, I know, it's so hard to put into words. Think... think of a note played on a piano. The hammer strikes the harp and the note is born. A wave of sound pulses outward, reverberating like a ripple in a pond. Each ripple reaches the ear, loudly at first, then softening until the ripples fade to nothing and the note is gone. Passed on, you might say. There is a beauty to that—a clarity. It was here, it fulfilled its destiny, and then it was gone and what was left was our appreciation for having heard it. Are you following me?"

"I think so," I replied, although I hadn't a clue where he was going with it.

"Very good. Now what would happen if the hammer struck the harp and the ripples kept coming?"

"Kept coming?"

"Exactly. Just kept flowing out into the room, reaching your ear again and again, never fading, never... dying. No clarity. No definition. A present where there should only be a past. How would you feel about the note then?"

I hadn't anticipated this kind of conversation, I have to admit. We weren't talking about being afraid of spiders or choking on a bottle cap here. I wasn't sure how to answer.

"How would I feel about it? I suppose it would start to get on my nerves. I guess I'd probably leave the room before it drove me crazy."

I looked across at Mr. Welkie. The small shadow had grown and his face was dark with a subtle terror unlike anything I had ever seen in a patient of mine. I looked into his gray eyes and it was as if I was looking into twin crystal globes in which a great storm was growing, clouds thick and heavy racing across the sky. His fingers gripped the arms of the chair and wisps of white hair stood on end as if the air was charged with electricity. His mouth was frozen and dry. I began to rise from my chair to help him and in that instant his eyes closed and his head fell slightly forward. His hands relaxed and he looked up at me with a faint smile of exhaustion. Both eyes were now at peace and I slowly sank back in my chair.

"Are...are you all right?" I asked gently.

"I don't know," he answered deliberately. It wasn't expressed as if he was confused. It was expressed as if he meant exactly what he said. I tried to reassure him.

"You *are* all right," I told him. "You're sitting in a chair in my office. No pianos. No sounds that don't end. You're not going crazy. Something has you upset, I think. I'm going to try to help you to figure out what that is. Are you hearing what I'm saying?"

He nodded.

"Good. Now let's think about what you just told me."

He looked at me for a moment, then nodded again, gathering his strength.

"Okay," I continued. "Now, what I heard you say was that something isn't behaving the way it should in your view. Is that a fair statement? Something you didn't expect is happening and you want it to stop. Does that sound right?"

"I think that's probably right," he said. "But I have no idea what it is. And I'm not sure anything's happened yet. It's all so confusing."

"I can see that. You know, you are very articulate, Mr. Welkie. You have a gift for expressing abstract thoughts very well. Can you give me another example of how this feeling operates?"

Boden Welkie leaned back in the chair and rested his head against the cushion. His eyes closed and for a minute or so, he fell into a deep stillness. When his eyes finally opened again, he began to speak quietly but very clearly, as if every word was exactly right.

"How much do you know about Marblehead, Mr. Blessing?" he asked me. "Not as it appears today. I mean historically."

I thought for a moment.

"Oh, I know about the fort. I know that *Old Ironsides* once came into the harbor to escape British warships or something. And I know about Glover's Regiment. They rowed Washington's men across the Delaware. They were from here. There are guys in town today who dress up like them and march around Marblehead sometimes... up at Burial Hill. A few other things I suppose."

"Have you ever heard of Old Dimond?" he asked studying my face.

"Old Dimond? No. Haven't heard of him I don't think."

Boden Welkie closed his eyes and began to talk. I sat back and listened to every word.

"Old Dimond, his first name was Edward, I believe. I'd have to look up the dates, I can't recall them exactly. He lived here in Marblehead long ago, the late 1600s, early 1700s down in the Barnegat district near Little Harbor in what was later called the 'Old Brig.' Those years were filled with happenings we can't even dream of today. In 1692, Salem was in the midst of the witch trials, of course, and a black shadow covered the small villages on the North Shore. It even reached into Marblehead. Did you know that Wilmot Redd, the old crone who was accused and hung, lived near the pond behind Burial Hill? And that one of the witnesses who spoke against her at the trial lived in that house right over there?"

Mr. Welkie pointed out the window. Just across Franklin Street stood the Ambrose Gale house, built in 1663, one of the very oldest in Marblehead. Dark brown-black clapboards and moss-encrusted wooden shingles still covered the walls and roof. It looked as if it hadn't changed in more than 300 years. He continued.

"That's right. Ambrose Gale. And there were other things as well. These waters were alive with pirates back then. Many came from

Marblehead itself. John Quelch, Ned Low—others. You must have heard of 'Screaming Woman Beach' right down here at Lovis Cove. That's where pirates brought a captive ashore one night and brutally murdered her. Cut off her fingers for her rings. The townsfolk heard her screaming through the night but not a one went out to help. You see, all the men were out on the Grand Banks fishing and only women, kids, and a few old men were left here in town. They found her ravaged body stripped of clothes and half buried in the sand. They say her screams were heard for years after.

"And of course, there were the storms. Back then, the town made its livelihood fishing the Grand Banks, far out there to the northeast. The lives of the men were hanging by a thread. Fleets of wooden ships would put out of the harbor and be gone for weeks at a time, families never knowing who would come home and who would not. Death was so much a part of life back then that fear and dread were as natural to feel as hunger and thirst. If a man fell overboard, the ship never turned back. Everyone knew that by the time they came about, the icy water would have done its job and the body would be far below the waves. And the storms; the storms meant death for dozens, sometimes hundreds at a time. Howling nor'easters and sudden gales could take down entire fleets! Three times in Marblehead's history that's exactly what happened. The last time they never recovered from the loss. Too many dead. Those left took to making shoes to earn a wage. The great fleets were gone forever."

Boden Welkie paused and rubbed the birthmark on his temple.

"Old Dimond had another name, you know. He was also called the Wizard of Orne Hill. Old Dimond was believed to be a magician, a conjurer. A bizarre and reclusive man, he was held in awe by the townspeople who believed he had incredible powers. Apparently, he used his powers on behalf of the townsfolk and so, while feared, he was held in high esteem. His most notorious acts took place at the top of Burial Hill. When the fleets were out on the Banks, Old Dimond would be seen at night climbing up among the stones, cocking his head into the wind as it blew in from the sea. It was said he could hear the storms approaching the fleets and would yell his warnings out into the darkness or dispatch his phantoms, Redcap and Bluecap, to carry his instructions. There, so many miles out in the ocean, the sailors would receive his warnings and sail out of harm's way.

"You can look it up in the old logs. The men swore they heard the sound of him in the wind and recorded it just as I've told you. And there are many descriptions of him standing atop the hill, bent into the storm, his cape blowing in the snow or rain, arms stretched out into the fog, calling in his high, thin voice."

It was a truly fascinating tale, no question. And in fact, I now remembered that I had read bits and pieces of the story in books of local legend, although never told in so riveting a manner.

"And what does Old Dimond have to do with you?" I asked, as a chill shot down my back.

"A voice in the wind, I s'pose," he replied, his eyes far away. "Have you ever been sitting in a room late at night and think you heard someone speak to you only to look up and see no one there? That's how it feels— something calling just out of reach. That's all I meant."

Boden Welkie seemed to have shrunk even smaller as he sat there in the wingback chair. If not for his white hair and translucent skin, one almost could have mistaken him for a young boy lost in the vastness of some great melancholy. Where was the path back to that wonderful vigor that had filled the room the moment he had arrived just a short time ago?

For the first time in my career, I was genuinely frightened. It was as if his fears had become mine and we were now simply two helpless souls adrift on a dark sea. I struggled to shake the predatory dread that threatened to overwhelm me. As I closed my eyes and arched my back, I felt waves of naked terror flow outward from my fingertips, back to their dark source like wraiths fleeing the first light of dawn. Soon, my sense of self began to reemerge and I filled my lungs with the pure air of reality. I turned toward my patient.

Boden Welkie had also begun to reverse his descent. He leaned forward with his elbows on his knees and stroked his face with both hands. Muscles frozen with strain began to soften and the color again rose in his cheeks. Tired but whole again, he lifted his head and beckoned me to sit back in my chair.

"So now you know, Mr. Blessing. I haven't dared to express any of this to anyone before. Certainly not to Hannah. I have felt from the beginning that to do so would unleash something I could neither understand nor control. Each time, it feels more powerful, like a great wave finally come to crash down on me. And yet, I have no sense that I will die. It is more a feeling that I will be dragged down below into a world from which I can never return. And my worse fears may yet be realized," he said, staring at me with genuine concern.

"And what are those?" I asked, feeling my muscles begin to tighten again.

"That I shall take others with me, Mr. Blessing," he replied, as he rose and walked out of the room.

I found it impossible to shake off the effects of my strange encounter with Mr. Welkie. Never before in my career had the boundaries between a patient and myself been so utterly blurred. It was as if every word he said was meant for me. Every fear he expressed seemed to become one of my own. After he left the room, I had collapsed in my chair unable to stir for the better part of the afternoon. When I finally did rise, I felt like someone ravaged by illness. For the next week, my nights were fitful. I was continuously thirsty. I recoiled at the thought of food. And even the most minor frustrations sent me into episodes of anxiety and self-doubt.

Seeing patients had become a struggle and I felt barely present in my sessions with them. The rest of the time I stayed up in my garret, sitting in an alcove and staring out the window toward the harbor. I was a mess. I realized that I had to snap out of it somehow. I called Burrage.

＊ ＊ ＊

"Max, you look like you've been dragged through a knothole," Burrage observed with his usual tact when I arrived at his door. "What *happened* to you? You sounded really weird on the phone—on the edge."

In fact, I felt like a stray cat stuck on a roof with no idea how to get down. We got into my car and headed down Massachusetts Avenue toward Boston.

"I've just been working too hard, I think."

"*You?* Yeah, right, Mr. 12-hour work week! All right, you do look totally washed out, so what's up?"

Even the thought of recounting what I had gone through with Boden Welkie sent a wave of nausea running through my stomach.

"Hey, Burr, I really just want to talk about something else right now. What's up with you? What's with the arm?"

Burrage's left arm was wrapped in an elastic bandage and held by a sling.

"Sprained my elbow. I was sleeping and I had a dream I guess. I started flailing away and fell out of bed. I've been putting a lot of time in on head lice lately. The computer models are enough to make your blood run cold. Tough to get stuff like that out of your mind."

I knew the feeling, although I had to smile at the image of Burrage duking it out with mutant head lice in his sleep. Me? I just wished I could sleep these days, at least what I used to think of as sleep. The last few nights my mind had been filled with disjointed thoughts that made no sense. I would toss and turn, then drift into a kind of anxious stupor until my alarm went off. It certainly didn't feel like sleep. As we crossed the bridge into Boston, I realized I had to talk to someone about what I was going through.

"Listen, you remember that night a few years back when you came out to dinner with the Castlers?"

Burrage nodded. "Yeah, I remember. That lady—the wife—Lyddie, or something."

"Enid," I prompted.

"Right, Enid. She was the one who stuck us in that closet, wasn't she? Bet they had a good laugh over that!"

"Hey, c'mon, she was serious about that. And listen, I heard it," I said. "And you know what? I think *you* did, too."

"Heard what? The ocean? Do you know how many things in the world sound like the ocean? Millions. It's like when you eat snake or wildebeest, everything tastes like chicken, right? Hey, my sinus cavities make a sound like the ocean every time the pollen count goes up. What's the big deal!"

"Uh-uh. This was different. You could hear the waves crashing, the surf running up the beach over the rocks... and the birds! You heard the gulls, too, *didn't* you?"

Burrage was in his scoffing mode.

"Who knows what we heard! And even if it was the ocean, it could have come from anywhere. God, Max, you're only a block from the harbor. Why shouldn't you hear the ocean?"

"I'll tell you why. Because I've never heard the ocean from that house. Not inside or outside, windows open, windows shut. Never. But I heard it clear as a bell in that pantry. But let's not argue about it. That's not why I brought it up."

"Fine," Burrage answered. "Why did you?"

"That night you told me about something William said. Something about a guy in his room. What was that all about?"

"Right, the little kid. It was his closet. He told me some guy had come out of his closet one night."

"And?"

"And nothing. That was it. Cripes, the kid was like seven years old or something. What *doesn't* come out of a kid's closet?"

"Maybe so, " I replied. "But why did he tell you out of the clear blue sky? What was the point?"

"How should I know? Heck, we were taking the spook tour at the time, if you recall—hidden stairs, talking closets. I'm sure he just thought he'd join the party. Although his father didn't look too pleased."

"What do you mean?"

"His dad. He looked at the kid like he had spilled a double helping of beans. Shushed him right up. Nipped in the bud."

I thought about the look Myles gave William when we were saying good night. Probably just didn't want his son getting carried away by his imagination. That's understandable. Anyway, I'd looked in that closet a hundred times hanging up my coat. Solid plaster walls all around, nothing ever amiss. I took a left turn onto Boylston Street.

"Let's go have a beer somewhere. I'll buy," I said. "Tell me where we should go. I never get into town anymore."

Burrage pursed his lips and thought. "How about that place we used to go to on Broad Street? Great Irish musicians jamming there tonight. I could definitely use a Guinness. Head lice love beer. Did you know that?"

I headed toward the Custom House Tower.

"Anyway," I continued, "I had a real interesting session last week. A patient of mine told me all this stuff about a bunch of Marblehead legends, myths really. One of them was about an old man, a wizard who supposedly lived 300 years ago near Little Harbor. 'Old Dimond' they called him. I'll tell you the story later if you want. But when I heard it, it's like a door started to open and now I feel like I can't shut it again."

Burrage pointed to a parking place and I slipped the car in.

"What are you talking about? What door?" he asked.

"I don't know. It's like a feeling I just can't shake. It's got me spooked, I guess."

"Well, I have the cure right in here, my friend. Great music, great suds, and authentic colleens from the auld sod to bring 'em to the table!"

Burrage held open the door to the pub and we found ourselves at a small table in the far corner. Sure enough, there were about a dozen musicians with fiddles, tin whistles, accordions, and goatskin drums all warming up near the bar. Within a minute the black-haired waitress had two pints in front of us and we were wiping the foam from our upper lips. The music began in earnest as feet commenced to thump the floor and heads began to nod up and down in time. Burrage turned to me and took another long drink.

"Now *that's* great music! You know, Max, I never understood why you just up and moved there in the first place. Marblehead I mean. It's quaint and all that, but the whole town just seems full of cranks, eccentrics, and flakes. Look at that family who owns your place. It's like they couldn't be happier than to think their closets are haunted. And let me tell you, Marblehead has a very nasty powder-post beetle problem. Those little suckers will have your rafters falling down on you some night and you won't know it till it's too late."

"What the heck are powder-post beetles?" I asked, not needing anything more to worry about.

"Eat right through your timbers. Worse than carpenter ants. You can see carpenter ants. All you see of these little scum are the piles of sawdust they leave on the floor. I'd think twice before I leaned too hard on anything made of wood."

I was about to reply when a picture hanging on the wall over our table caught my eye. At the same moment Burrage became distracted by a fetching young fiddle player who was tossing her hair as the bow slid wildly across the strings. As I squinted my eyes, I realized that the artwork inside the frame was not a painting, but an old map—a map of the coast north of Boston. There was no date that I could see, but it was certainly an antique judging by the crudeness and lack of accuracy. My gaze wandered up the coastline north from what is now Boston Harbor and I was able to pick out the peninsula where Marblehead sits today.

The town was indeed shown on the map, as were parts of Salem. The paper was quite brown and stained with age and the artwork was very faded. As I stood up for a closer look, I noticed nine small, black crosses clustered throughout what is now known as the Old Town. I thought it odd that these markings were the only specific details on the map other than a few small roads and a number of boxes that seemed to represent buildings. There was no writing or labeling of any kind other than the words "Marble Hedd" and an ornate "north" arrow coming out of a nautical compass.

How strange, I thought. It surely was not a map that could be used for navigation or much of anything else that I could see. I supposed that the black crosses had something to do with deaths, although, spread out as they were, I doubted that they signified graves. A large water stain crept down from the upper left side and pushed rust-colored ripples out over the drawings. As I took another sip of my ale, I spied a small character of some sort in the lower left corner almost hidden by the dust that had built up on the glass. I drew my eyes to within a few inches and made out the letter "Q" written in a flowing hand with ink so pale and faded that it looked to have been drawn with weak tea.

This new discovery caused me to look more closely at other areas of the map in hopes of finding some other detail that would shed some light on its purpose. As I systematically scanned each quadrant, the pub continued to fill with people and the old Gaelic music increased in both volume and pace, swirling through the cigarette smoke and dim light. Across the room, several patrons began to shove chairs aside and throw themselves into a classic jig the likes of which had probably been danced in cottages and pubs since the Middle Ages.

In this light it was hard for me to distinguish between stains, dust and artwork. At one point, I thought I could make out a small arrow pointing into Salem Harbor but it turned out to be a cobweb that fell away when I brushed my fingers across the glass. The rest of the parchment seemed devoid of meaningful details, however. I was about to sit down and turn my attention back to the lively throng across the room when I caught the barest glimpse of a pale shape hovering over the ocean just to the east of Brown's Island. I strained my eyes and honed in on the rendering. The shape was as transparent as the small "Q" below yet, as I studied it, I could clearly make out the lines of a figure carefully drawn in thin, brown ink. The drawing was that of a woman in a long, pleated gown. My eyes took in every detail as they rose up her torso.

"Hey, Burr, look at this," I said as the music in the pub began to rise in a frenzy of fiddles, whistles and drums.

"What? Look at what? I can hardly hear you!" Burrage said, turning his head.

"Here, by the island on this map," I shouted, barely audible above the din. "Tell me what you see."

Burrage pulled himself reluctantly out of his chair and came around the table. He leaned forward and tried to make out the little drawing next to my finger. His head swung back and forth, trying to lose the reflections in the dusty glass. He finally stood still, squinting for several long seconds.

"Oh, yeah, well... it looks like a woman of some kind. Yup. *Holy jeez,* is that what I *think* it is?"

We both stared at the map and at the delicate drawing of the young woman drifting out across the water. Her left arm extended straight out from her body and in her hand she held what looked to be a large hourglass. Below the hourglass was the number "1863" written in a tiny, spidery hand. This was followed by several rows of small, round dots faintly drawn in red ink. In her other arm, barely discernable in the dim light, she clutched her own severed head.

C H A P T E R   3

By the next day, my mood had changed entirely. I felt totally energized. Burrage was convinced that the drawing on the map was a fake, probably done as a fraternity prank by those MIT guys, he said. The map did seem a bit too melodramatic to have been authentic and yet, I found I couldn't get it out of my mind. It's not that my rediscovered sense of well-being could be traced to it, but the map had an uncanny way of shouldering aside other thoughts and positioning itself squarely in my mind's eye. After several days of trying to ignore it, I admitted defeat. I told myself that the map would fit so very well on the wall beside my whaling artifacts. The next afternoon, I drove into Boston and went back to the pub with the intention of making an offer to the owner.

It was around 3:30 when I walked in the door. The place was empty save for a bartender and a pair of elderly gents seated on stools at the far end of the room. The old men were engaged in an animated discussion about the upcoming city council elections and who was going to represent Southie (or South Boston for the uninitiated). It was far from an argument. In fact, they were falling all over each other agreeing with everything that was said. It was clear that the conversation was not a debate but rather an exercise in male bonding. At such moments, the key ingredients of the bonding process are, in no particular order, ale; an "us vs. them" topic, like politics; a common enemy, in this case, pointy-headed intellectuals; and finally, two people looking for a little instant validation. I predicted that within five minutes the mood would change and one would say something that would have the other trying to choke him. That's the way two male bonders get over the feeling that maybe they just got a little *too* bonded.

I walked over and asked the bartender if the owner was around. He immediately pointed me toward the old men at the end of the bar. I sighed and made my way toward them. I was careful to wait for the right moment because I knew that males in the act of bonding generally don't like spectators. Finally, one of them got up to go to the bathroom and I made my move.

"Pardon me, but the bartender there told me that you were the owner," I said, addressing the remaining fellow in the most respectful tone I could muster.

He looked me up and down and I could see he was trying to decide exactly which level of disdain to inflict on me. The man was short and wiry with a shock of snow-white hair shooting out of the top of his head like a troll doll. His face was florid and his nose looked like a purple potato that had been hastily wired to the space between his intensely pale blue eyes. A checkered cotton shirt was falling out of his pants and gapped open halfway down the front, barely containing the explosion of hair that enveloped his chest and threatened his throat. His mouth revealed a row of yellow teeth as he grabbed a cigarette with his lips and pulled it from the pack.

"You some kinda salesman?" he sneered.

"No, not at all," I hurried to assure him. "I'm—"

"Not happy with the service then?" he shot out before I could finish.

"No, the service is fine. I only—"

"Who we got here, Eddie!" his companion growled as he came out of the men's room zipping his fly as he walked. "Looks like some kinda inspector ta me!"

"Oh, *yeah?*" Eddie snapped. "You an inspector, then? I ain't payin' nobody off for nothin', pal, if that's your game! I own this place 45 years and I ain't never paid nobody nothin', my friend, so don't even *think* about it! Now what you lookin' for?"

I'm off to a good start, I thought. *Just get things sorted out for the man as quickly as possible. Just a little over-reaction on his part*, I told myself.

"No, no, really," I said, giving it my most earnest tone. " I'm just here to ask about a map I saw last week, that's all."

"A map? What map? Somebody give you bad directions or somethin'? You should get yourself a good atlas, my friend! I don't get into that. Too many damn tourists don't know what the hell they're doing, so they think I got nothin' better to do than stand around givin' directions! Go ask a cop or some other damn thing. I'm busy here. Got things to do. Ask Joey," he said, pointing to the bartender. "Joey, *hey!* This guy needs—"

"Whoa, whoa, *whoa!*" I said, starting to wonder if I could ever get control of the conversation. "I don't need directions, all right? I just wanted to know about that map on your wall back there," I said, turning and pointing across the room to the table Burrage and I had occupied so recently.

The old men craned their necks and squinted across the dimly lit tavern.

"What, a map on the wall?" the owner asked. "What you talking about?"

"Here," I said walking over to the spot and touching the map with my finger. For an instant, I felt a pulse of energy move up my hand and cause the hair to stand up on my arm.

The two old men climbed down from their stools and strolled slowly over to the place where I was standing. They studied the wall for a few moments. The friend was the first to speak.

"Watch out, Eddie, prob'ly some treasure hunter thinks you got a treasure map," he grunted, setting his jaw to let me know they were not men to be taken lightly.

Eddie looked at me suspiciously.

"What you care about this map?" he asked. "You got some idea or somethin'?"

This was really getting out of hand. It was to the point where whatever I said would only feed their imaginations and kill any chance I had of coming to a reasonable accommodation. I lowered my eyes and tried to decide if I shouldn't just forget the whole thing and go back to Marblehead. That would certainly be the reasonable choice. But something wouldn't let me walk away. Something inside me had become too attached to let go. I was struck by the compulsion I was feeling.

"Look. I'm not a treasure hunter. I'm a psychologist. I just thought it would look nice in my office because it's a map of Marblehead and my office is in Marblehead, that's all. It's no big deal," I said.

The old men looked at one another for a sign of how to proceed. Eddie, the owner, decided to play it close to the vest.

"How I know that? How I know you're not that guy who found that sunk ship off Cape Cod a while back? What *then?* Maybe you think I should just give you this treasure map so you go get rich all over again! Then what I got, heh? *Nothin'!"*

My mind raced. It was like being in a bizarre situation comedy. The conversation was out of control. Yet the worse it got, the more I wanted to prevail. I hated the way I was reacting. It was a formula for disaster.

"You can look it up in the phone book. My name is Maxwell Blessing. I'm a psychologist in Marblehead. I saw the map and I liked it. I thought I might offer you something for it, but if you think it's a treasure map, fine. Go buy a shovel."

I turned away feigning disgust. I started for the door, then shot a glance to see how they were reacting. Eddie had put on his glasses and was examining the map in detail. His friend loomed over his shoulder. I paused and waited to see what they might conclude. After a minute, Eddie turned away.

"*Jeez Christ,* can't hardly see anything at *all* on 'er! Looks like some cemetery or somethin'!"

His friend put in his two cents.

"I dunno, Eddie, I read about stuff like this. Some old lady cleans out her attic and some sharpster buys somepin' at her yard sale for 50 cents and winds up with a million bucks! I *seen* it!" he scoffed, looking at me accusingly.

"Right—fine," I replied, edging closer to the door. "The hell with it. I was going to offer you a hundred dollars for it because I thought it would look nice on my wall, that's all. I don't know anything about any treasure, but if you want to talk yourselves into that, go right ahead. Just forget the whole thing!"

I played my hand and walked purposefully toward the door. Much to my chagrin, they let me leave without saying a word. *JEEZ!* I thought! *What now?*

As I drove back up Route 1A toward home, the dark cloud which had enveloped me for the past week began to creep back into my soul. I reacted with anger. What WAS this all about, anyway? Was I having some sort of nervous breakdown? Had I experienced an emotional transference as a result of my session with Boden Welkie? I had no answers. I felt as though I was slipping over a cliff and that my rational mind was not going to save me. I began to feel strongly that I had to rely on my gut to find the way out. And my gut kept leading back to that ridiculous map! Desperate thoughts began to present themselves for my consideration. Should I go back and offer $500? $1000? $10,000? What was it worth to me, after all? My peace of mind?

Or, should I just skip the formalities and return tonight and simply swipe it off the wall when the music gets going and no one is paying attention? That idea appealed to the part of me that wanted to see Eddie have a stroke once he realized he no longer had the map or the hundred bucks. The jerk!

It took all of 10 seconds for me to realize that Eddie knew my name, occupation and the town in which I lived. As satisfying as swiping it out from under his nose would be, I was still rational enough to know it was out of the question. So, what then? After a few minutes of angst, I remembered the one person who might have a shot at it. Myles Castler. My god, the man made a career of separating owners from their antiquities. I would ask Myles.

When I got home, I immediately walked over to the Castlers' front door and rapped several times with the big brass knocker. Within seconds, a bustling Enid opened the door.

"Oh, Maxwell!" she burbled. "What a surprise! Is something wrong upstairs? The throne is functioning properly, I hope?"

Enid leaned forward with a look of deep concern as she inquired about the state of my plumbing fixtures, both biological and otherwise. I had come to realize that the orderly functioning of the bowels was of great concern to her. She was forever slipping newspaper clippings about roughage under my door. At least once a week, she handed me a brown paper sack of bran muffins. And if there were any sign of commodish distress, a plumber would be summoned within minutes to resolve the problem. What had inspired her to become such a student of the alimentary system, I had no idea. I just knew I had other problems to solve at the moment.

"No, no difficulty with anything like that, Mrs. Castler. Is Myles at home by any chance?"

"Oh, I'm certain he is, Maxwell. Why, he's in the study, I think. Won't you come in?"

Relieved to have gotten beyond the subject of porcelain and other personal concerns, I followed her stocky frame as it gamboled down the darkened hallway. As I stepped into the study, Myles was seated at his desk, examining some old letters with his magnifying glass. He glanced up and greeted me with a faint smile.

"Maxwell, how are you? Just trying to catch up on a few things here, but that can wait. No problems with the apartment I hope?"

"No," I replied. "Nothing like that. The apartment's fine. I actually came for another reason altogether."

"Well, sit down and tell me what's on your mind then," he offered, pointing to a small wooden chair in front of his desk.

I obliged.

"It's about an old map, " I began. "A map I found in a tavern in Boston recently."

"A map is it?" he answered, warming up to the subject. "What sort of map? Is it very old do you think?"

"I don't really know," I said. "It looks old enough but I have no idea if it's authentic. The thing is, I want to buy it but the owner is a little difficult to deal with."

"Ahh, I see. Do they not want to sell, then? Or are they looking to pinch every penny from your pocket!"

I proceeded to describe the entire encounter. Myles nodded his head knowingly and smiled that small smile of his.

"Well, as I'm sure you know, in most cases it's simply a matter of money. That treasure business was unfortunate, however. Makes the old fellow imagine all his hopes and dreams could be wrapped up in it, I'm afraid. That could poison the well, so to speak," Myles reasoned, knitting his brow. "If that's the case, he may never let it go. At the very least, I recommend that you not contact him again for a few weeks, even longer if you can bear it. If you go back to him too soon, he'll become convinced you think it has great value. Much of the acquisition process is simply waiting them out. That's your only hope, I'm afraid."

When I got up to my apartment, I was thoroughly depressed, not only because the task at hand seemed hopeless, but that I had become so obsessed with the map in the first place. What was going on with me that I felt so invested in owning a piece of paper that had no documented age, origin or value? I called Burrage to ask his advice. That, of course, only made me feel worse. Burrage thought I was behaving pathetically and I couldn't argue with him.

✳ ✳ ✳

The next day I moped around the house until about mid-morning when I finally decided to go down and pick up the paper at the side door. As I felt my way down the dimly lit stairwell, I heard the throaty hiss of Lady Jane as she slunk rat-like from the landing ahead of me. I had come to hate my encounters with her, here on the shadowy stairs. It was the psychological equivalent of wondering whether a scorpion had crawled inside your shoe during the night. Only in this case the danger was stepping on a tail and having a pint of adrenaline shoot into your heart as she screamed or bit or clawed at your feet.

By the time I reached the lower landing, she had disappeared, God knows where. I opened the door and bent down to get the paper only to find Burrage standing on the step poised to ring my bell.

"*Cripes!*" I exclaimed, still on edge from my encounter with Lady Jane. "Where did *you* come from?"

Burrage had a smug look on his narrow face that immediately told me something was up. With a smooth motion he swung his hand from around his back and revealed the map, still in its old wooden frame. I let out a whoop.

"How did you get it?" I asked, as a horrible thought crossed my mind. "You didn't steal it, did you? They know where I live."

Burrage's calm, triumphant expression never left his face.

"Certainly not. At least not in the way you think," he answered.

"What do you mean? Tell me how in the world you got it!" I demanded, stammering with both incredulity and relief.

"Why don't we go upstairs and I'll tell you everything."

Within seconds, the map was propped up on my sideboard and I was pouring Burrage a glass of cold orange juice. I was nearly hyperventilating. Burrage was enjoying my suspense. I felt the sudden urge to shake him violently if he didn't start talking. He sat in a chair by one of the dormers and began to hold court.

"It was quite a surprise the way things happened," he said. "Especially after everything you told me."

"So?" I prodded.

"Well, I had wanted to go back there anyway, you know—to the pub to see if that fiddle player might come in again. You remember her?"

I nodded.

"So, I walked in about nine and headed over to the table where we sat last week. So there I am and I figured I'd take another look at the map. Well, there it was and damned if there wasn't a sticker in the corner with a *price* on it!"

"You're kidding me!" I gasped.

"Nope. Five hundred bucks, he was asking. I thought, this might lead to something, so I asked to talk to him. He was in the back, so I had a Guinness while I waited. In the meantime, the music had started and damned if that cute little fiddler wasn't sitting right in the middle of it again! So, I'm tappin' my foot and drinkin' my pint and this old codger pokes me in the back and asks me what I want. He sits down and I ask him what he'll take for the map. He points to the price and I kinda scoff at him. Well, he's about to get up and leave when this Godzilla-sized roach crawls right across his hand. The old guy looks like he's about to jump out of his skin and shakes it off, right into my Guinness! Can you believe it?"

Burrage didn't wait for my answer.

"So, anyway, I jump up and start yelling at the guy about the Board of Health and pain and suffering and lawsuits. I'm ranting and raving, putting on a great show. Max, the place went dead quiet. I'm yelling about roaches and he's trying to shush me up. It was great. Finally, he says to me, 'I'll give it to you for a hundred bucks.' The map! He's pointing to the *map*. I couldn't believe it. I pull out my wallet and he hands me the map. Is that sweet or what! That was it. The whole thing took maybe fifteen minutes from the time I got there. A stinkin' cockroach! You know what they say—can't live with 'em, can't live without 'em."

Burrage slumped back in his chair and took a breath. It was truly amazing. I looked over at my prize.

"I owe you big-time," I said walking over to the map and bringing it into the light by one of the windows. "Now I just have to figure out what the heck it all means."

That afternoon, I called Myles on the phone to see if he would make time to see me. Within ten minutes he had the map out of its frame and sitting on his desk. Training two strong lights on the strange document, he stood up and thoughtfully considered what was before him. Every once in a while he would swing an illuminated magnifying glass over the document to examine a detail. Every time he found something that interested him, his magnificent eyebrows would dance and twitch above widening eyes. The process was punctuated with a variety of purring sounds that revealed the level of deep contentment he was experiencing. Solving time puzzles, I had decided, was what Myles Castler seemed to love above all else.

I coughed slightly to remind him of my presence.

"Ah, yes, I know you're curious, aren't you?" Myles said in a distracted voice as he immersed himself in scanning every inch of the parchment.

"I am... a bit," I replied, biting my tongue to conceal my agitation.

"Well. This map is..."

Again he became lost in a long silence as his mind reacted to some stimulus far more intriguing than anything I had to offer. I knew that my presence was not conducive to the level of concentration he sought to achieve; yet I simply could not pull myself away. I was crawling out of my skin. I sought resolution. I needed to know that the roller coaster that had taken over my emotions in the last two weeks was coming to a stop. I wanted my life back the way it was. I craved the mundane. There was something about coming to an expert like Myles that caused me to hope that clarity was only an eyebrow twitch away. I wanted him to roll back the storm clouds and calm the wind that whistled through the widening cracks in my sense of reality. How that was going to result from examining a scrap of pub flotsam, I had no idea.

Myles motioned me to join him behind his desk so that we could both view the map from the same vantage point. The yellowed surface drew us down toward it.

"Most unique in many ways," he said.

"How so?"

"Contradictions," he replied. "See here."

He pointed to the compass rose that dominated the upper left quadrant.

"Look at the detail in this artwork here. It's quite beautiful really. Even though it is fairly primitive when compared to the meticulous symbols of trained cartographers, it shows a level of complexity beyond that of the map itself. Why would the maker put the bulk of his efforts into what was basically a decorative element?"

I had to agree. The coastline was crude, although the area around Marblehead was somewhat more detailed. But the compass had to have taken far more time to create than any other aspect.

"Maybe he was just showing off," I offered. "You know, like the scrimshaw drawings the whalers did in their spare time."

"Ordinarily I might agree with you," Myles countered. "But why would someone who was seeking attention position the north arrow as he has done?"

I looked again. Incredibly, as carefully drawn as the compass was, the north arrow pointed to what was obviously due east.

"Holy cow!" I remarked. "What's *that* all about?"

"I haven't a clue at the moment. I can only imagine that the compass was not intended to show true north at all but had some other purpose. Now another thing. Look here," he said, pointing to the map artwork itself. "See how rough the drawing is? I believe that this map was most likely created to do a very specific job and was drawn with just enough skill to accomplish the task at hand. It was not done by a cartographer or a surveyor for use as a general reference. It is not a navigation chart or a street map. It shows no boundaries or name references other than that of the town itself, our own 'Marble Hedd'. I see it as more of a sketch than anything else, meant to communicate some limited message and then be discarded. Drawn on a napkin, so to speak. Therefore, the fact that such a map still exists after all these years is quite remarkable."

"What do the little crosses mean, then?" I asked. "Any idea?"

"Well, then, the crosses. On a map such as this, a cross symbol could mean most anything—a place where something is located, a path someone had taken, a series of events and so forth. What did you imagine they might represent?"

"Deaths? Graves maybe? That's what came to my mind," I replied.

"Possible, I suppose. For the most part, they do not correspond to the locations of the graveyards in Marblehead, although this first one is in the vicinity of Old Burial Hill. Who knows? But keep in mind, crosses have always been one of the most common symbols used on maps and generally have nothing to do with death per se. The fact that they appear to be concentrated in the Old Town is interesting, however, and might provide a clue if we only had some other information."

"What about the 'Q'?" I asked, pointing to the single letter near the bottom of the page.

"It's purely a guess, but I think it may be the mark of whomever created the map, an initial or something. You see? It appears at the bottom like a signature. If that's what it is, it strengthens my belief that this was an informal note between people known to one another."

That, of course, left only one other element to interpret.

"Ah, yes, the headless maiden. A bit chilling, isn't she?" Myles remarked in a tone that betrayed his fascination with such a delicious mystery. "Clearly allegorical, hovering over the sea. Note the hourglass held in her extended hand, bringing the element of time into the equation. My first thought was that it might be a death warning, as in 'the hour of death is at hand.' But I really don't know if that's it at all. Usually

such a warning would incorporate a death's head— a skull—or perhaps a
hanged man or weapon. I've never seen such a message conveyed using a
decapitated woman, unless, in this case, the threat was aimed at a woman.
It is a powerful image, however, meant to evoke strong emotion. Not the
usual fare for a map."

"And the small red dots?"

"Some sort of shorthand I would think, although at first glance the
meaning is not obvious. Latitude and longitude perhaps, indicating a
location? A crude inventory of a ship's cargo? Again, more information is
needed to put it all in context. And see here, the tiny number below the
hourglass, '1863.' I would assume that was a date, but, given the style of
the maiden's dress and the general condition of the paper, 1863 seems too
recent. This document is exceedingly barren of the sorts of details which
would give it clear meaning to an outsider."

I was afraid of that.

"Is there any way to get more information?" I asked.

"Well, the most obvious next step would be to determine the age as
closely as possible, then try to figure out the composition of the
parchment and inks used. If we could get a clear fix on the year, we could
see what else was happening around that time. All these things are clues
that can bring us closer to the maker and the meaning. I can send it to a
colleague in London who specializes in that sort of thing."

I needed to think about that. On one hand, I wanted to understand
every possible detail about the map. On the other, I felt a strange
reluctance to let it out of my sight. What if it should be lost? A nervous
chill shot down my spine.

"Do you have any theories?" I asked tentatively.

"About the paper? I am quite certain that we would find that it was
imported from Europe. It is very well made, which is one of the reasons it
has held up so long in spite of the obvious distress it has suffered along the
way. The inks were probably made locally from plant material and berries.
They are badly faded which may indicate the chemistry was not as

archival as the better imports would have been. As to the age, without more detailed tests I cannot say for certain, but my best guess is that it was drawn sometime in the late sixteen, early seventeen hundreds. It is quite authentic, I believe, and one of the most intriguing pieces of work I have seen in quite some time, worth considerably more than the $100 you paid for it. Do you want me to send it off to London?"

"I'm not sure right now," I answered, trying to let Myles know I appreciated his interest. "I'm sure it's the right thing to do, but I think I just want to live with it for a little while first."

"Most understandable," he answered. "After all, you just acquired it and you should take some time to enjoy it, Maxwell."

Enjoy it, I thought. *Not likely.*

That evening, I hung the map on a wall in my office on the second floor. As I stood back to make sure it was placed correctly, I was interrupted by the sound of the telephone.

"Mr. Blessing?"

"Yes?" I answered.

"Boden Welkie."

The muscles in my neck stiffened.

"I'm afraid I cannot make my appointment tomorrow as scheduled," he said in a voice that sounded pale and far away.

"I'm sorry to hear that," I replied, feeling both disappointment and relief. As unnerving as our first meeting had been, I instinctively felt that I had to see things through with Boden Welkie, both for his sake and for mine. At the same time, though, I was not sorry for the cancellation. "Nothing wrong, I hope."

There was a short pause and I heard a soft, empty chuckle.

"Oh, no," he answered. "Storm's comin' is all. Things to do."

"I see. Well, would you like to reschedule now?" I asked.

"Reschedule? No, not now," he replied. "I have to go. I'm sorry.

Someone's at the door. Have to go."

"Of course. I'll speak to you soon, then," I said, as I heard the click on the other end of the line.

That's funny, I thought. There were no storms in the forecast that I knew of. Must be one of those folks who feels it in his bones.

The next day was bright and sunny until about 11:00 AM, when the barometric pressure suddenly dropped steeply. Some thick, dark clouds formed to the north, but blew out to sea before lunchtime. By noon the sun was riding high in a cloudless sky and my spirits with it.

CHAPTER 4

As the days wore on, I felt my sense of equilibrium return to me. Lady Jane had disappeared for the second time in a month which made life in the stairwell considerably more serene. Burrage had finally mustered the courage to ask out the comely Irish fiddle player from the pub and was pleasantly surprised when she accepted. He took her out to dinner at one of the finer all-you-can-eat buffets on Route 1 only to discover she was leaving the country the next morning. As she explained in her melodic Irish lilt, she was on her way to the Amazon rain forest to photograph a variety of small, warm-blooded vertebrates for an Irish nature magazine. Her prime subject was to be a species of hairless mole that carried its young in its mouth. The idea so repulsed Burrage that he couldn't finish his marinated mushroom caps and he had her home by 9 P.M.

As for me, I threw myself into my work as never before, seeing upwards of fourteen, even fifteen clients a week. Dealing with your standard, run-of-the-mill wackiness was like a balm to me after the penetrating angst of Boden Welkie. Folks who couldn't bring themselves to go to the dentist, pee in the woods, or touch the veins on their wrists without throwing up; they were my kind of clients. People who ate lint, bring 'em on, I said. My confidence soared.

Boden Welkie hadn't called back and I kept putting off trying to reach him. I had observed him walking up Orne Street one windy night but he had not noticed me and disappeared around the corner up near Gas House Beach.

And I had seen on the late news where Eddie McCool, the owner of the pub on Broad Street, had been raided for selling liquor for seven months after his license had been revoked. What made it newsworthy was the fact that when police arrived to close his place down, he had retreated into the small kitchen in the back and locked himself in the walk-in freezer. By the time the Jaws of Life could be fetched to open the door, he had been found sitting, stiff as a board, on a carton of frozen shepherd's pies. It was a sad story. But not that sad.

Then, one evening, as I was finishing up some insurance forms for several of my clients, the doorbell rang below. I opened the door and there on the step was Hannah Welkie, Boden Welkie's wife of 52 years. She was dressed in a gray skirt and dark green sweater, which she clutched at her throat against a chilling easterly wind. She looked frozen and I immediately insisted that she come in out of the cold. She huddled on the landing and in a voice fraught with urgency, asked that we go up to my office.

As she quickly picked her way up the narrow stairs, I noticed how thoroughly under-dressed she was for the blustery winds swirling outside. The thin sweater had not even been buttoned and she was wearing a pair of light pink house slippers. Strands of her snow-white hair drifted haphazardly out of a hastily gathered bun on the back of her head. I was certain this was not the way Hannah Welkie would present herself under normal circumstances. Clearly, her haste reflected a great deal of distress.

As we reached the second floor landing, I pushed open the door and invited her to enter. She quickly found a chair by the fireplace and leaned forward imploringly, her gray-green eyes alive with need. She was a tiny woman, in scale with the cozy antique home she and her husband shared on Hooper Street. With her gaunt cheeks and haunted expression, I could envision her walking the unpaved streets of the old town two or three hundred years ago as the wife of some long lost fisherman. At the moment, she seemed a living link to that vanished time, filled with the painful experiences of a world we can no longer imagine.

Her skin was almost translucent, the color of milk as it's poured from pitcher to glass. Delicate veins formed pale alluvial fans at her temples and disappeared in the worried furrows of her brow. Her thin lips were almost colorless and trembled slightly as she began to speak.

"Mr. Blessing, I'm so grateful you were here! I simply had no idea where to turn. Boden had mentioned how thoughtful and reassuring you were when he came back from his meeting with you."

"Is he all right, Mrs. Welkie? Is there a problem?"

"Oh, yes, I'm afraid there is an awful problem. Mr. Blessing, Boden is—I don't know how to explain it. His spirit has seemed so troubled lately, obsessed and filled with desperation. And yet, I have no idea what has happened. At times he looks right through me. Doesn't hear a word I say. It's as if I don't exist for him. I'm terrified, Mr. Blessing. Absolutely panicked!"

Her small face quivered with emotion and she sat charged on the edge of her chair, as an iron filing might be held upright in the field of a magnet. I felt myself instinctively pull back so as not to be drawn again into the vortex of Boden Welkie's world. And yet, I realized that Hannah could not long sustain her role as her husband's only bookmark to reality. Clearly, each day that passed, the story grew steadily darker. I now knew that I had to overcome my own sense of vulnerability and actively attempt to intervene.

"Where is Boden now, Mrs. Welkie?" I asked.

"He's gone out on the island again, Mr. Blessing, and with the weather coming in, he'll catch his death!"

"Which island? How did he get out there?"

"Gerry Island. The tide was out, but it's getting so dark. I'm afraid he'll be stranded!"

Gerry Island was a shallow knob of land that rose up from Little Harbor. It was a small island, only a couple of acres covered with wild grasses, brambles and several haggard trees standing watch. Amazingly, one could actually walk out to it on a spit of pebbles that materialized when the tide went out. But twice a day, like the Red Sea, the waters came swirling back when the tide turned. And with the full moon only a day away, the tides were running high and the autumn Atlantic was once again as cold as dungeon stone. Anyone who missed the turning of the tide would be trapped for hours on the exposed island, a most unpleasant prospect with the night that loomed ahead. Hannah looked at me plaintively.

"I thought to call the harbor master, but it's so hard. Boden's moods. Then I thought you might know what to do!"

I immediately rose from my chair and went to the closet where I snatched a heavy, yellow slicker and my woolen watch cap. I also grabbed the large flashlight from the shelf and flicked the switch to make sure the batteries were in good order. I turned to Hannah Welkie, telling her to go back home and wait to hear from me. I wanted to get a quick read on the situation first and then decide if the harbor master was going to be needed. I would then call Hannah with a report, hopefully that her husband was already safely landside and on his way home.

I stumbled down the stairwell and raced outside into the thickening darkness. The gusty wind sent a branch stinging across my cheek as I ran down toward the back gate and the harbor. Small, hard drops of rain began to knife into my face from the northeast. I glanced above to see enormous thunderheads boiling up thousands of feet into a night sky so black that even the lights of the town below could not illuminate it. Within the dense mountain of clouds, I could see the throbbing glow of distant lightning bolts dwarfed by the storm that spawned them. I had never in my life seen a night like this one.

I ran through the back streets and in a minute found myself scrambling across the wet sand of Gas House Beach. As I looked out into

the harbor, I saw the shadowy hulk of the island barely outlined against
the heaving darkness of the sky. Harsh gusts of wind assaulted the grass
and shook the trees creating a scene of building violence across the water.
I looked to the pebbled causeway that curved tenuously out from the
beach until it made landfall at the jumble of old foundation stones spilling
down the slope of the island's lee shore. Even now the black water
growled up and over the path, raking the small stones as the tides began
to flood back into the harbor.

I knew that it would not be long before all trace of the causeway
would disappear beneath the tidal surge, making foot travel to and from
the island impossible. I flicked on the flashlight and directed it out toward
the rocks, only to see the beam evaporate in the sheeting rain. I had just
reached for the phone, when, high in the wind, I thought I heard a faint
wail rise above the din of the pounding surf. I narrowed my eyes against
the gale and tried to scan the island shore but could see nothing in the
shadows and spray. I hesitated for a moment, then took off at a run down
the beach and plunged out along the path into the harbor.

With each flying step, the frigid waters swirled around my ankles then
briefly receded until the next wind-driven wave frothed over the track. I
clenched my jaws against the shock as I crashed across half-submerged
rocks and shell fragments. My legs buckled time and again, knees and
ankles twisting in my headlong race against the rising tide. A sense of
unreality soon enveloped me and the roar of the storm became a whisper
far away at the end of a long tunnel, though the blood pounding through
my ears sounded like a torrent. Puffs of moist heat warmed the skin of my
neck as it escaped from my clothing below.

As I reached the halfway point, a succession of white-topped waves
swarmed across the causeway bringing the numbing waters up to my
thighs. My run became a staggering slog as I tried to bring my knees ever
higher above the tides that threatened to engulf me. I could no longer feel
my feet as the cold stole all sensation and I struggled to keep my focus on
the now-hidden path to shore. The narrow ridge of pebbles fell off to

either side and the deeper water with its ripping currents would prove disastrous should I stray. As I fought my way toward the rocks, a rising anxiety kept my legs moving ever forward.

Then, when I was only a few yards from the island shore, I felt a heavy thump and a searing pain shot through my left knee. In the inky waters I saw a jagged, black shape glistening just at the surface. It was a large timber carried on the surge, splintered and spiked like the end of a broken bottle. One shard had grazed my leg and I saw that my pants were torn. I reached down and felt the watery warm sensation of blood that washed away clean with each successive wave. I knew I had to get to shore.

As the seconds became eons, my motions toward shore became almost unconscious. Finally, with a jolt, I found myself on the wet rocks of the shore. I shook off my disorientation and peered up over the crumbling stone foundations of a building long gone. Within moments, I had ascended the banks and stood braced against the driving wind that howled across the small plateau. My leg had begun to throb with pain and I could see the dark stain growing around the tear in my trousers, but only one thought held sway—finding Boden Welkie.

I set off around the north perimeter, paying close attention to the rocks below and then sweeping my gaze over the whipping grasslands above. I again tried the flashlight, but to no avail. The beam would disappear within a few yards. I even tried to call out, but my words were knocked out of the air by the wind and blown tumbling back over my shoulders. Step by step I made my way along the narrow, dirt walking path that skirted this side of Gerry Island. Even bathed in the golden light of the softest summer day, the tiny island had always had a haunted feeling to me. Perhaps it was the stone ruins of the several small houses that had once brought life to the barren ground or perhaps it was the arrowheads that locals mined from the primeval soil, remnants of the long-vanished Naumkeag tribe. I only knew that I never felt quite alone walking its empty shores.

My left leg had begun to stiffen in the cold and the pain was spreading further from my knee. My brine-soaked feet felt as though a thousand pins and needles were working their way under my skin. Even with the increasing discomfort, I guessed that I could circle the island within the next twenty minutes, but I began to wonder what I would find once I had made my way back to the tide flats. If the storm worsened, the currents would be too treacherous for the return trip to the mainland. I also was becoming increasingly convinced that my entire search was in vain. I was nearly to the seaward point and there was no sign of life to be found. I was now certain that Boden Welkie was long gone and yet, here I was, once again drawn into his nightmare. I increased my speed, spending less and less time exploring every crevice and boulder. As I rounded the point, the wind, with no land to interrupt its relentless drive to shore, escalated to near hurricane force. I quickly turned my back to it and began my return trip along the southern edge of the island.

As I lowered my eyes to more carefully navigate the twisting path, I was suddenly paralyzed by a ferocious howl that seemed to penetrate directly into the back of my skull. Instinctively, I dove to the ground and covered my head with my hands. For a fleeting moment, I pictured school children in the 1950s ducking for cover in that laughable attempt to escape the cosmic finality of a nuclear blast. Frozen with fear, I clung to the earth not daring to breathe as cold rivulets of rain trickled down my burning neck and began to pool in the mud beneath my chin. The unearthly sound was not repeated but was replaced with a low, undulating groan, which did nothing to lessen my sense of dread. After several moments, my fear of *not* knowing what lay behind me superseded my fear of knowing and I slowly rolled over on my left shoulder and lifted my face back toward the headland. I was not prepared for what I saw

Standing with his back to me was the barely discernable figure of a man. Dressed in dark clothing, which tattered and blew in the ripping gale, he towered wraith-like on the stone wall high above the multitude of rocks which paid homage before him in the storm. His arms stretched outward from his shoulders to the left and right, giving him the aspect of a great, black gull hanging suspended in the wind. He was hatless and the hair danced and flamed about his head like pale, white fire whipped to a frenzy. He never moved and yet the waves, the winds, and the very sky churned around him, an extension of his will.

At first, I thought the ghostly sounds were simply the voice of the storm, which even now seemed to explode upon the town from the sea. But as I fixed my eyes on the specter, there was no doubting the source. As his voice rose, the skies began to fill with a thundering display of lightning bolts hurled from the belly of the storm. The blasts grew so numerous that within a few seconds the clouds were dancing with the jagged after-images of a hundred mammoth strikes, a colossal fireworks crescendo. As the maestro raised his arms ever higher, the air began to crackle with static energy and the acrid scent of ozone was so thick it became suffocating.

Arms thrust skyward, the figure stood at the very epicenter of the storm. And as I watched in awe, an enormous thunderhead rolled in directly over us and released a flash of light so brilliant that I was temporarily blinded and had to turn away. When darkness returned, I looked back toward the wall in time to see the man's body fall backward and disappear into the sea of blowing grass. In that instant, my fear left me and I rushed to the spot where he fell. I pulled back the tattered arm that covered his face and found myself staring into the glowing embers of Boden Welkie's eyes.

✳ ✳ ✳

To this day I have no recollection of the hour that followed. They say that we were found lying at the edge of the surf on Gas House Beach. By the time I was revived, Boden Welkie had been lifted into the ambulance and Hannah was sitting at his side. The fireman who brought me the blankets and hot tea, told me that I had first been spotted staggering out of the water with an unconscious man draped across my shoulder. The storm had ended and as I rolled my head skyward, a few stars twinkled diamond-like in gaps between the clouds scudding westward across the black velvet sky.

By eleven o'clock, I had been delivered to my door and helped up the stairs to my office. I was exhausted to the point that I could barely move and a chill had settled deep inside my bones. The heavy wool blanket was still wrapped around my shoulders as I sat huddled in my chair and I knew I should go upstairs and jump into a warm shower. A strange inertia had overtaken me, however. It was as if my mind needed time to catch up to what my body had just been through. A cold wind was howling once again and tiny hailstones began to peck at the windowpanes. I dragged myself from my chair by the fireplace and reached into the woodbin for some small logs, which I tossed on the andirons. After sliding a starter log beneath the stack, I leaned down and lit the edges of the paper. Within minutes, I had a fine blaze dancing against the sooty bricks of the hearth. As it was designed to do, the shallow fireplace sent waves of heat outward into the room, so I once again settled into my cozy wingback and allowed the glow to penetrate my damp clothes.

My eyelids grew heavier and my face began to prickle as the warm air washed over my chapped skin. My head fell backwards and I squirmed into a position that would take the pressure off of my injured knee. The scrape had been cleaned and bandaged tightly by the paramedics but it still throbbed with a dull pain whenever I moved. I would decide in the morning if it needed further attention. As my eyes closed, every muscle in my body proceeded to shut down and within minutes I was in a state of deep rest. It was almost as though I had been paralyzed.

As my mind began to replay the events of the last few hours, I took comfort in knowing that Boden Welkie would now get the level of help that he really needed. It was clear tonight that he had been in the throes of a full-blown psychotic episode and that some sort of drug intervention would be required to stabilize his situation. Intensive psychological treatment, perhaps even a period of hospitalization would be the likely outcome. I felt badly for Hannah. She was so confused by it all and I knew that, at her age, dealing with the next few months would be very difficult. I resolved to call her in the morning and offer my support.

I slowly became infused with a deep sense of peace. I knew that my recent period of good feeling had resulted more from avoidance than resolution. Now, however, I was finished. I had overcome my fears. I had, literally, looked the storm in the eye and brought my client to safe harbor. And while I would have preferred it by way of the comfortable environs of my wingback chairs as opposed to the hostile landscape of storm-swept Gerry Island, I had to admit that I was rather proud of my performance on this strange night.

A log shifted in the fireplace and a plume of glowing embers scattered up the flue.

I'm not really sure what woke me.

It might have been the clammy chill that hung in the air as the dying coals gave up on the drafty old house. Or, it could have been the white noise of the heavy rain that had begun to pepper the roof and lace the windows with drops as fat as June bugs. Shifting in the chair, I felt the wet warmth of my clothes sticking to my back and thighs under the tent I had made of my heavy blanket. The cold green light of the street lamp melted on the walls as the water ran down the panes of glass. I was cramped and sore, yet reluctant to let the last of the warm air escape from beneath the blanket, so I tried to find a new position and drift back to sleep.

The first creaking sound was woven into the dreamy sleep-world to which I was trying to return. In my mind, I was in the cabin of a bygone ship rolling in the storm. The dripping shadows on the walls were caused by the spray of white caps, the dampness in my clothing the result of fog rolling in from the Grand Banks. In my dream, a simple "creak" became the sound of timbers twisting against the swells or cleated lines straining in the wind. But before sleep could steal me away, a second creak sounded loudly enough to cause a lazy eyelid to squint open and blink in the darkness. As my mind strove to place the source of the sound, a deep, muffled thump brought both eyes to attention. I was immediately transported back to early childhood, where a branch tapping on the window or a night bird calling in the darkness might cause me to freeze with cold terror.

Ordinarily, I would have assigned the noise to the Castlers bumping about in the rooms below, but I knew the family was gone for the weekend peeping at the autumn leaves in Vermont. Of course, it could be Lady Jane back again, I imagined, from yet another of her sabbaticals to hell. But even on her best days, the porcine Lady Jane had not the heft required to produce sounds of this magnitude. In my childhood-throwback frame of mind that really left only two possibilities: a madman with an ax, or a ghost—with an ax. These prospects led to a few seconds of icy dread during which my eyes grew so large that they began to water from the dust that settled on them.

Within moments, my more adult sensibilities took control and my childhood panic gave way to simple cold fear. Who on earth could be making such noises at two o'clock in the morning? Another muffled bump—this one slightly louder. *Where was it coming from*, I wondered. The muscles in my neck stiffened to the point of pain as I raised my head ever-so-slowly from the arm of the chair. The last few flickers of light glowed eerily in the black hearth sending shadows pulsing across the floor like tiny demons. Small drops of perspiration began to bead on my forehead and upper lip as my skin flushed and my heart began to race. Another thump and a few seconds later, yet another, followed by a faint shuffling sound.

There was no question that someone or something was coming closer, but from where? The noise seemed to originate from within the room itself, not from the stairwell behind me or the hall beyond the opposite door. Another bump, louder still! My heart pounded and I sat bolt upright in my chair, the wool blanket sliding to the floor. A chill went through my entire body as the cool air hit my wet clothing. I slipped silently from the chair and instinctively backed toward the wall, never turning away from the corner that seemed closest to the source. I made no sound as my hand touched the rough old plaster behind me and I flattened myself in the shadows next to the large grandfather clock that stood ticking quietly near the stairwell door. As rain continued to hiss across the windows, I could see the tree limbs shaking violently in the wind.

My thoughts churned. Should I get out of the room and run upstairs?! What *then?* If someone were approaching, he would surely hear me! Should I run downstairs and out of the house? That made more sense, but where would I go, half-dressed in this miserably cold storm? On one hand, the police station was too far away, yet if I knocked on a neighbor's door, I would scare them half to death. And over *what?* I had no idea what I was running from. What if the Castlers had come home early? Maybe the sounds were simply echoing in some crazy way from another part of the house. Another thump. *My god!* I tried to make myself sink back into the wall itself. My breathing slowed to nothing.

The room went quiet for what seemed an eternity. I could hear the blood pounding in my ears as a drop of sweat trickled down my back and I shivered in the chilly air. With my heart in my throat, I slowly brought my head forward and peeked around the edge of the clock to survey the room. Now that the fire was down to a few smoldering embers, only the glow of the nearby street light gave any illumination. My eyes flitted from object to object hunting for any clue as to the source of the strange sounds. I was about to relax my posture when I caught a small but certain movement out of the corner of my eye. I caught my breath and shrank back quickly into the shadows but managed to maintain my view of the closet door next to the fireplace.

As I stared through the dying light of the fire, I began to think my eyes were playing tricks on me until, once again, I saw a movement. It looked as though the edge of the door was slowly moving away from the door frame and opening into the room. From my angle it was hard to see into the closet itself, but I had no doubt that the gap was widening. I gazed in disbelief as the timeworn iron hinges began to emit a low groan. Suddenly, about half way up along the edge of the door, I saw a sight that made every muscle in my body clench. Two blackened fingers curled out of the darkness and—almost tenderly—caressed the edge of the door, forcing it further away from the frame.

My senses reeled. Even if escape were possible, sheer terror had drained every ounce of strength from my trembling legs and it was all I could do just to remain on my feet. At that moment, a bright flash of lightning lit the room and I prayed that whoever—whatever—was in the closet had not seen me. Then everything changed. Where once the light had been blinding, now there was none. The storm had knocked out the power and the streetlights had gone dark. The room was now dungeon-black but for the waning glow of the embers. While thankful for the darkness, I was horrified to realize that the intruder was now virtually invisible!

A feeling of vertigo took over and the room began to spin.

My mother's voice seemed to whisper in my ear. "No one there. Only some old clothes on the closet door."

To steady myself, I tried to dig my fingertips into the chair rail at my back. As I did so, I heard the hinges groan again and the heavy tread of a shoe on the soft pine floor.

"Just the sounds of an old house."

I squinted out into the darkness and tried to get a glimpse of the invader, but to no avail. About all I could see was a hulking figure that seemed to change shape against the dim shadows of the room. At first, he simple stood there, like a wolf smelling the wind. His head turned as he scanned the room, finally stepping over to the hearth where he bent slightly to warm his hands over the coals.

"Just your imagination."

And yet there he stood, a dim silhouette with a head of long, unkempt hair and thick clothing that hung loosely over his large frame. After a moment, he grunted softly and brought himself erect, leaning back and rolling his shoulders as if to loosen stiff muscles in his back. I heard the muffled clink of metal as he slowly turned away from the fire and peered about the room. I hugged the wall and closed my eyes, praying I would not be seen.

I heard him take several heavy steps toward the opposite wall, then watched as he ran a shadowy hand along the whaling tools that were hanging there. He was breathing heavily through his mouth, and I could hear him laboring above the sound of the wind and rain. I tried desperately to make out some detail of his clothing but the darkness was too thick to penetrate. I could tell that his coat hung down quite low, almost to his knees, and the sleeves were cut full with sizable cuffs. His trousers looked quite ragged and very loose fitting. Perhaps a homeless man rummaging about for something of value, or so I hoped believing that if such were the case, he would likely prove harmless.

As he continued his methodical journey around the perimeter of the room, I realized that it was just a matter of time before our paths would cross. Homeless or not, he was enormous and clearly had led a rough existence. When he saw me, would he panic and run? Or would he become enraged and attack me? In any case, I did not wish to make myself known until the last possible moment.

Sidestepping a chair, he started slowly toward the clock and I could not imagine the shadows would hide me much longer. I swallowed hard and pressed my head hard into the plaster, feeling a sense of panic begin to take over. But then, when he was about halfway across the room, he stopped in his tracks and turned toward the windows. Two paces brought him to the wall and I realized he was standing in front of the map I had recently hung between the sashes. He reached up carefully and pulled it down from the wall, turning slightly in my direction as he tried to angle the frame for a better view.

The lightning flashed again and at last I caught a glimpse of him. He was terrifying. As thunder rumbled ominously, I saw a dark, cruel face— sunburned I thought—covered with filth and a scraggly, unshaven beard.

His jet-black hair was knotted and uneven and grew raggedly down from beneath a dirty purple cloth, which he had tied around his forehead. His mouth curled open to reveal a set of horribly rotting teeth which ground together as he tried to view the map in the flickering illumination of the lightning. Filthy fingers clutched the sides of the frame as he brought it closer to his face and it was then that I noticed the most hideous aspect of all. His right eye was completely gone from his head and all that remained was a cavernous hole, black as pitch in the shadows that fell across his cheek. I nearly shrieked out loud, but, thank God, was able to contain my shock as the room fell black once more.

Nearly beside myself with fear, I felt the strength leave my legs altogether and my body began to sink toward the floor. As my weight pressed against the side of the grandfather clock, it began to rock slightly causing the floorboards to emit a soft squeak. I held my breath and glanced up expecting to see the monster looming over me. Instead, he had turned and was making his way back toward the closet door, the noise of the boards apparently lost amongst the sounds of the storm. With a quick look over his shoulder, he stepped back inside the closet and I watched as the door swung slowly closed behind him.

In my exhausted state, I must have lost consciousness for I slept for the rest of the night and the better part of the following day. When I finally awoke, I lay shivering on the floor with nothing to greet me but the tick-ticking of the grandfather clock that towered above. My hands were as cold as ice and my bandaged knee throbbed as I struggled into a sitting position and collapsed back against the wall. I let out a long, slow breath and tried to sort out what had happened. I realized that I had had a dream, probably brought on by my exhaustion and perhaps a bit of fever. My cheeks felt flushed. I was a fool not to have gone up to my apartment and taken a long, hot shower. I could have spent the night curled up in a nice, warm bed instead of sprawled out in damp clothes on the bare floor.

No wonder I had been hallucinating.

It was now late afternoon and the sun was sinking rapidly through the tree limbs outside my window. My eyes went to the hearth where thin, gray feathers of ash nodded gently in the updraft of the flue like ghostly anemones on the floor of the sea. The only thing out of place seemed to be me. I let out a soft yelp as I staggered to my feet, sore muscles and aching head punishing me for my imprudence. I leaned my left hand against the wall and waited a few moments for my circulation to catch up with me. As I casually gazed across the room, my attention instantly became riveted on the empty patch of wall. The map, of course, was gone.

CHAPTER 5

I stepped out of the shower and grabbed the towel. I knew exactly what I *should* do. I should call the police. The police would send over an officer who would ask me questions. The officer would then go to the closet and open the door. After poking around for a few minutes, he would conclude that there was no secret passage, no intruder, and that I was either drinking or exhibiting symptoms of acute psychosis. I knew this because only an hour ago, I had spent a significant amount of time poking around that very closet and had found absolutely nothing that would corroborate my story.

Plan B, of course, was Burrage. I dressed as quickly as I could and called him on the phone.

His silence spoke volumes. After hearing me describe the events of the last 36 hours, Burrage made it clear this was not something he cared to deal with on any level whatsoever.

"Burr," I prodded. "C'mon, Burr, you've got to help me figure this out!"

A deep sigh on the other end of the line.

"Call the police."

"Look, Burr, I already explained why that would be totally useless. Now are you gonna come up here or what?"

"What about the closet freaks—your landlords. This sounds right up their alley," he said, his voice growing more agitated.

Let's face it. This was not left brain stuff. This was the part of life that Burrage had worked so hard to avoid. For him, it was right up there with folks who think they see the Virgin Mary in a sticky-bun or people who believe that their cat actually cares about them. I had no time for his cynicism. I needed help.

"Burr, I need you to come up here _now_," I said, using my most uncompromising voice. "The Castlers are in Vermont till tomorrow night. Besides, they would think I was crazy. I know you think I'm crazy too, but listen—and this _is_ a threat—if I can't get to the bottom of this, then I'm coming down there and bunk with you, got that? I'm not spending another hour here the way things are. So what's it gonna be?"

"Jeez, Max, it's 9 o'clock at night!" Burrage moaned.

My threat hung in the air. Forty-five minutes later I heard him at the side door.

"So I'm here. Let's get this over with," he snorted.

I took him up to my office where I had left everything as it had been the night before. The still-damp blanket lay on the floor. The cold ashes of the fire were scattered on the hearth. The closet door stood open, just as I had left it after mustering the courage to look inside. Yes, I'd had an iron poker in my hand at the time. I had checked every inch of the plaster walls and ceiling. Solid as a rock. There was no trap door in the floor. All the closet contained was some summer clothes that I was storing and a couple of boxes of old college books that I had shoved up on the shelf over the clothes pole.

As I stepped to one side and invited him to examine the closet for himself, Burrage put on his very best "weary" expression and sighed as he stepped to the door. Within a few short minutes, he emerged from the alcove and turned to me with the most insufferable "I-told-you-so" look on his face. I knew it was the price I would have to pay for having dragged him up here, so I ignored it.

"Okay," he challenged. "Now what?"

I pointed to the wall where the map had hung.

"Gone!" I exclaimed. "How?"

Burrage walked over to the wall, looked at the empty picture hook and made a quick turn back to face me.

"*You* took it."

I choked for a moment and stared incredulously at my accuser.

"*I* took it?" I repeated.

"Exactly. You were exhausted. You said you felt feverish. You got up and acted out some dream/sleepwalk thing and hid the map somewhere. Case closed, Watson. I'm sure you'll find it stuffed behind the hamper or something. Now go to bed and let me go home."

"Oh, no you don't!" I shot back. "I know I've had some weird stuff going on lately, but I know what I... look here!" I barked, striding quickly back to the closet. "He came out of *here*, he took the map and he went back in! Look, you sit in that chair where I was. I'll show you!"

I grabbed Burrage by the arm and hustled him over to the wingback, not giving him the least opportunity to protest. Then I quickly slid in amongst the hangers and pulled the door closed behind me.

"You watching?" I yelled through the door.

"Wouldn't miss it," he yawned.

I reached down to the old iron latch and was about to lift up on it when I thought I heard the faintest of sounds coming from the floor to my right. I cocked an ear and listened until—there it was—the faraway cry of a gull! As my pulse quickened, I tried to lean down in the narrow space and sent the wire hangers tinkling against one another.

"Enough with the dramatics. I'm feeling stupid enough as it is," I heard Burrage snap from the other side of the door.

"*SSSHHH!*" I countered. "Come over here!"

I unlatched the door and let it swing open. Burrage leaned forward on the chair.

"Is this how it happened?" he asked.

"*No!* Come over here. Listen!" I commanded, tugging his sweater to bring him down towards the floor.

"Oh, Christ, not *this* again! Listen, I gotta get up in the morning. I'll call—"

"Will you *shush* for a second!" I scolded, cupping my hands over my ears. "*THERE!* Listen there!"

I pointed to where the left wall met the floor. Burrage reluctantly squatted down and turned his ear to the wall. For several seconds we heard nothing and then, clear as a bell, three sharp cries like those of a sea gull echoed faintly near the floor. We glanced at each other and I could tell Burrage had suddenly gotten very serious. I dove on my hands and knees, crying out as my injured leg thumped against the floor.

"What'd you do to your leg?" Burrage asked.

"I told you, it happened on the island, but that's old news. This is amazing! It's just like what we heard downstairs that time, only much clearer. Help me here," I ordered, as I started to run my fingers along the crack where wall met floor. "There's gotta be something here."

I tore at the floorboards, but they wouldn't budge. The left-hand wall was actually the side of the chimneystack so it was all solid brick. I grabbed the poker that Burrage had retrieved from the fireplace and began to tap it against various bricks. They were all solidly joined with mortar.

"Max, look at that!" Burrage exclaimed, pointing to the mortar layer between a row of bricks about two and a half feet above the floor.

It was difficult to see details inside the shadowy closet, but as I looked more closely, I could tell that this particular layer of mortar had pulled away slightly from the row of bricks above. I stuck my fingernail into the seam. It ran the length of the wall, about three feet from front to back.

"Burr, put your finger here!" I said. "What do you feel?"

Burrage placed his hand near the seam and felt the draft of cool air. He followed the crevice to the back wall.

"Hey, Max, you know this crack? It seems to continue. Wait; look down here, just above the first row of bricks along the floor. See that? It keeps going. Feel the air all along here? This is weird."

Burrage traced his finger along the entire length of the seam. When he was finished, he had scribed a rectangular slab of bricks about three feet wide and two feet high that had become detached from the surrounding bricks. I pushed at the slab with the poker and felt it give slightly. I continued to exert pressure at different points along the edge until, about half way down the backside, the slab moved about half an inch into the wall.

"Burr, look at this. It *moves!*"

I pushed harder and heard a soft grinding sound as the back of the slab swung slowly into the chimneystack, while the edge near the doorway swung out from the wall.

"Look. It's on some kind of pivot," I exclaimed, as I arched my back to get enough leverage in the cramped closet. "Help me."

Burrage braced his knees against the door frame and got into position to lean in on the poker. As we grunted and strained, the slab swung further and further into the wall until it was perpendicular to the opening. True enough; it must have been on some kind of vertical bar that ran into the bricks above and below. Burrage and I stared into the blackness as a steady draft of dank, musty air blew past our faces.

"So, now we know," I said softly, an involuntary shiver running down my spine.

Burrage sat back on his heels and took a deep breath.

"This is no flue," he noted. "Look at this."

He pointed to the small area of inside surface that was now visible. It was sheathed with thick oak boards from which a fine rain of wood dust sifted down to the closet floor. Burrage leaned down and examined the wood.

"See these little channels here in the wood? Powder-post beetles. No way they could survive in the heat of a chimney flue. And anyway, who lines a chimney with wood in the first place?"

We looked at each other, as the larger question became inescapable.

The practical Burrage took charge.

"Okay. Do you have a light or something so we can see what in the hell this is?" he asked.

I immediately went to my slicker and dug the flashlight out of the pocket and put it in his outstretched hand. Burrage crawled deeper into the closet and flicked on the light, while I leaned in over his back and watched as he directed the dim beam into the gaping black void. The light was almost instantly swallowed up in the darkness as we strained to identify some detail that might explain the nature of our discovery. After a few moments, our eyes grew more accustomed to the dark and we gradually began to make out a narrow, vertical shaft as it revealed itself in the shadows. Everywhere, dust and cobwebs formed a thick fur on the surface of the brick, creating an eerie, gray world deep in the bowels of the chimney. It reminded me of those scenes on TV where they film some shipwreck on the ocean floor miles below the surface—colorless, covered with soft gray algae, everything looking quiet and dead.

Burrage moved the beam along the back wall and I heard him gasp as the light fell on a row of heavy wooden rungs climbing up the shaft from the blackness below. I could see what looked like a splatter of pale candle wax clinging to the edge of the uppermost rung. At that moment, I felt as if my sense of boundaries had been altered forever. Here I had been living in a world of order and normalcy, seeing clients in this room, when, barely six feet away, the world I knew abruptly ended and another clearly began. My reality was melting like a snowball tossed into the sea, all my naive beliefs disintegrating with the last pieces drifting down into the gray, dead fathoms below.

At that moment, Burrage suddenly turned toward me and I fell sharply backwards. Staring directly into mine were the glowing eyes I saw on Gerry Island—the eyes and the face of Boden Welkie. I was so unnerved that I immediately turned away and covered my face with my hands. Then, within an instant, I heard Burrage calling to me from very far away.

"Max—Max! Are you alright?"

I looked up to see my friend bent over me with a look of near panic on his face.

"What's wrong?" he asked. "Are you sick? I turned around and it looked like someone cold-cocked you with a two-by-four, for god's sake!"

"Jesus, Burr. I thought it was *him!* Boden Welkie—your face! It was him, staring at me. I swear to god!"

"All right, all right. Just try to relax. Are you okay now?" Burrage asked cautiously.

"Yeah, yeah, I'm okay," I answered, still shaken by the shock of it all. What was *wrong* with me? I felt like my mind had been poisoned, cursed with terrible visions that I could neither predict nor control. I couldn't live like this and I knew I had to find a way to get to the other side of it. I shook off the shiver in my spine and sat up leaning against the door frame.

As I was about to suggest we call it a night, the distinct sound of waves running over a beach echoed up from the depths. There was no mistaking it this time. Burrage and I leaned in toward the shaft and the sound of sea birds rose and fell with the tide.

"That's it," I cursed. "I'm done. No more mysteries, Burr. I'm getting to the bottom of this right now. It'll either cure me or kill me, but it's not going to drive me crazy any more."

"What are you talking about? Are you telling me you're going *in* that god-awful hole?"

"Yep," I said, as I stepped out into the room and grabbed my jacket. I snatched up the poker and took the flashlight from Burrage. "I can't live like this, Burr. I can't. I don't know what's real and what's not anymore. For years I've been telling my patients to do the hard things—to look their fears in the eye. Sometimes the only way out is to go in. I hate the idea of it more than I can tell you, but I feel it in my gut. It'll never leave me alone."

"You're crazy. You have no idea where that shaft goes, what's down there, *who's* down there. If that guy you saw last night exists, then *he's* probably down there! What then? This is nuts. My god, get the police over here. Let them figure it out."

"You know, Burr, if I listen to you anymore, I'll start to think about what you're saying and if I do that, then I won't go. And I *have* to go, so stop using common sense on me. There's nothing about this that makes sense, all right? Now, if you want to be useful, you could wait up here in case I need help. If I run into any trouble at all, I'll yell. Then you can get the police over here."

I could tell Burrage was having none of this and planned on calling the police as soon as I was out of sight. I stepped up to him and looked him in the eyes.

"Burr, I'm *asking* you. This is one of those big favors a friend asks once or twice in a lifetime. I need to do this my way. All of this isn't happening down there in that tunnel. It's happening up *here*," I said, tapping my forehead with my finger. "It goes way beyond a hole in the wall or even some shadow in the night. By going down there, I start to get my life back. I feel that, Burr. You have to let me do this."

Burrage hated moments like this. He was so used to solving problems with common sense. There were rules to govern the decisions you made. To let amorphous "feelings" lead the way was a totally alien concept. I was asking him to give up control. It was like asking him to drive his car blindfolded. But he knew I meant it and that, as a friend, he had to go along. But god, did he hate it.

"JESUS!" he shouted and paced back and forth across the room. "God almighty! Okay! I'll wait up here for 15 minutes! That's *it!* If you're not back in this room by then, I don't care what you say, the police are being called! Agreed?"

I nodded. In fact, I was glad. This whole thing was scaring me to death. I *needed* to be back in 15 minutes. Burrage took a deep breath and put a hand on the back of my neck and gave me a small squeeze.

"You turn back if you see so much as a spider, Max, you understand?"

"Thanks, Burr. I mean it," I said, as I stepped through the closet door and knelt on the floor. I handed Burrage the poker and light.

"Hold this till I get on the ladder."

Burrage aimed the light on the rungs once more and I got on my hands and knees backing myself up to the opening. I paused for a brief instant, then reached my right foot back into the shaft and out into space. I felt the temperature drop suddenly as the cold, damp air hit my leg. I stretched a little further and, finally, felt the opposite wall with my toe. By this time, I was almost prone on my stomach and I searched with my foot until I felt it come to rest on the edge of the second rung. I gave a quick jolt as a large, frigid drop of water hit the back of my leg just above my sock.

I looked up at Burrage and nodded that I was okay. I finally worked my other leg through the opening and soon had both feet solidly on the rung so that I could push up with my hands and guide my body slowly back and down into the shaft.

I was shocked by the nature of the cold that immediately began to envelop me. It was nothing like the cold of a winter's day or a plunge in the harbor. It didn't feel like it affected my body so much as it did my will. The light from the room above suddenly radiated the warmth of everything good and safe in the world, whereas here in the shaft there was nothing but the coming darkness. I felt myself being drawn back toward the light and it took every ounce of resolve to slide a foot down to the next rung.

"You okay, Max?"

"Hand me the light."

As my hand extended out of the opening, it was as though I began to thaw. Burrage gave me the light and then the poker. As I drew them inside, the chill returned and I felt a wave of nausea in the pit of my stomach.

"Max?"

"I'm okay," I lied.

I shoved the poker into my belt and twisted around so I was facing the ladder. Taking the flashlight, I immediately shined it downward and let my eyes adjust to the light. The shaft swirled with dislodged particles of dust descending into the void below—like snow caught in the headlights on a dark winter night or a cloud of plankton streaming through the ocean depths. The old wooden rungs led steadily downward until they disappeared in the blackness below my feet.

"All right, then," I said and lowered my left foot about two and a half feet to the next rung and then brought down my right. The wood creaked painfully with my weight and I looked at the nails that secured the rungs to the rails in the shaft. They were old, iron nails—spikes really—hand-forged and cut with squared heads. Around each nail head, the wood was stained red with oxidized iron from the years of moisture. The wood itself had turned soft and damp in spots, clearly in a progressive state of rot. I prayed they would hold just a brief while longer.

The sound of the surf played steadily in my ears and actually began to sooth me as I forced myself to begin my descent. I looked up and could see Burrage's head silhouetted inside the opening as he watched me make my way downward.

"Everything okay?" he asked.

"So far," I coughed. "It's just so musty down here, it's hard to breathe. I think I see the bottom, though."

As I peered through the gloom, I could barely make out a small, flat landing about twenty feet below. I reckoned that would be a good dozen feet below the level of the cellar floor. As I was about to resume, my eye caught a glimpse of several small, pale objects that had been placed in a tiny niche between the bricks to the left of the ladder. I leaned over to get a closer look, and saw that they were the stubs of about half a dozen candles nestled in the cobwebs, the largest being about three inches in length. The sight of them instantly reminded me that I was not alone and I shut my eyes to fight off a wave of anxiety. After a moment or two, I reached out and carefully plucked each one from its perch and dropped it into my jacket pocket.

Within a few minutes, I had completed my descent and was standing at the bottom of the shaft. Here, the space widened into a tiny room about six feet square. Small piles of brick dust gathered in the corners and a large, red centipede rippled out of the rotting coils of an old hemp rope that lay near the base of the ladder. The walls were fairly covered with the delicate silken egg cases of spiders from the previous season. All long gone, I hoped. As I turned to explore the area behind me, my hand passed through a thick veil of spider webs and I instinctively recoiled, dropping the flashlight on the hard floor. As it clattered across the stone, it suddenly blinked and went dark.

"Oh, JEEZ!"

"What is it?" Burrage echoed down from above. "I can't see your light at all!"

I squatted down and soon found the flashlight, but after several shakes, slaps, and a long stream of curses, I realized I had lost my light for good.

"Burr! The flashlight's gone," I heard myself saying as the darkness closed in around me. The dust-filled air felt too thick to breathe. My head began to swim as a sense of vertigo enveloped me and I felt myself begin to black out. I went down on one knee. "Burr—"

✳ ✳ ✳

When I awoke a few minutes later, Burrage was kneeling next to me holding the candle from my mantlepiece.

"Max, we're getting out of here now. Can you walk?"

I propped myself up on an elbow and coughed up some of the dust that had been collecting in the back of my throat. Burrage hauled me to my feet and I steadied myself on his arm. Without even looking up, I said, "I'm not leaving."

Burrage angrily shook his head.

"Look, Max, I should have called the cops before I came down here, but I didn't want to take the time until I made sure that you were okay. If you don't come up with me now, that's just what I'm going to do."

I shot a look at him.

"Ten minutes. That's all I want. Did you see *this?*" I asked, pointing to a low tunnel about three feet high that disappeared in the rock to the left of the ladder. Burrage looked at me with total disdain and turned away.

"Listen, Burr. I'm as weirded out by this place as you are—*more* even—but at least now there's two of us. You can stay here or come with me, but I'm going to see where this goes."

With that, I pulled the longest candle stub from my pocket and lit it from the one in Burrage's hand. My candle was still damp from the condensation in the shaft and it sputtered and hissed until the moisture burned off the wax. I bent down and peered into the low tunnel and could see that it took a sharp bend to the left. Just at that moment, as I turned to ask Burrage what he was going to do, a large, dark shape came hurtling toward me from the blackness in the passage. Before I could react, the phantom crashed into my right shoulder and with a horrific scream, clamored up the first few rungs of the ladder and disappeared into a crevice behind the rails.

"*Jesus Christ Almighty!*" Burrage yelled as he flattened himself against the wall, still clutching his precious candle. "What in the hell was that?"

As the adrenaline shot through my arms and legs, I caught my breath and gathered myself together.

"Lady Jane," I muttered.

"Lady *who?*" Burrage shot back as he circled around toward me, careful to keep the crevice in full view.

"The cat. The Castlers' damn cat!" I replied. "So *this* is where she goes."

"Well, where'd she go just now?" Burrage asked, his eyes still wide with disbelief. "She went up the ladder and just vanished!"

"There's got to be a hole in the bricks up there. She must get out into the cellar somehow. Anyway, she won't come back as long as we're here.

That's not her style. Once she gets your eyeballs to pop out of your head her job is done. She's probably off somewhere licking whatever it is she licks."

Every cloud has a silver lining and in this case it was that Burrage decided that he would rather strike out through the mysterious tunnel than risk having Lady Jane attach herself to his face if he tried to climb back up the ladder. That resolved, we turned our attention back to the passageway.

Progress was difficult. The tunnel's rough-hewn ceiling was just low enough that, even hunched over, you couldn't quite stay on your feet. This meant we had to crawl across the uneven stone on our hands and knees, one hand anyway, while we held our candles in the other.

The tunnel had been carved out of the solid rock ledge that lay under so much of the Old Town. This was a feat in itself. The coarse, dark walls were stained with decades of seeping water and, in some spots, eerie deposits of mineral salts formed glistening white fingers that reached downward and brushed our hair as we passed. As we slowly made our way along, the mood grew more somber and forbidding. It was a journey of compulsion more than choice. Every movement forward brought a deeper feeling of separation from things familiar. Our sense of security extended only so far as the flickering light of our candles could penetrate the pitch-black world around us.

We spoke little and my attention was drawn once again to the sound of the ocean as it filtered toward us out of the darkness—rising, falling— sometimes disappearing altogether. If this were an old smuggler's tunnel, as the legends suggested, it made sense that it would open out on the edge of the harbor somewhere. But I couldn't imagine how such a thing could have gone undetected through the centuries. Marblehead Harbor was far from remote. It was surrounded on both sides by waterfront homes. Nearby Fort Beach was always busy in the summer with families swimming and picnicking. Armies of kids chasing green crabs had explored every crevice in the rocks a hundred times over. And the small harbor itself was absolutely teeming with pleasure boats. It was inconceivable that even the smallest opening would escape discovery.

"Max, I got to stop for a minute."

I could tell Burrage's allergies were kicking up from all the must and mold. He was breathing heavily through his mouth and had begun to wheeze. We came to a halt in a section of the tunnel where the path widened slightly and sat back against the cold rock wall. I blew out my shorter candle to conserve our light and let out a long sigh of exhaustion. A pebble or stick was digging into my buttocks and I wriggled over a few inches to retrieve the offending clutter.

"How far you think we've come?" I asked Burrage, as he peeled a long strand of melted paraffin from his thumbnail.

"Far enough," came the terse reply.

I tossed the bit of stone at his shoulder, playfully trying to break the mood. He grunted and picked it up looking to return the favor, but as he drew back his hand he stopped and brought the object nearer to the light of the candle.

"What?" I asked.

"Some kind of bone," he replied.

I slid closer and looked at the small, gray morsel as he turned it in his fingers.

"Let me see that."

I took it from his hand and held it close to the flame. I then took the candle from him and turned back to the spot where I had been sitting. There in the dust were two more small bits, which I collected and brought back to examine.

"These *are* bones," I confirmed as I laid them end-to-end. "More than that—they're three bones of a finger."

Burrage recoiled.

"Like—a *human* finger? Are you kidding me?"

"No question. Before I dropped out of med school, I saw a lot of stuff that I'd just as soon forget, but *that's* someone's finger."

"Jesus *Christ!*" Burrage cried, leaping to his feet and rubbing his hand on his trouser leg.

We both looked at each other in surprise as we realized that he was standing erect in a tunnel that up until now had been no more than three feet high. Burrage held his candle aloft and we could see that we were seated in a small, stone chamber and that there was a second ladder that led up into another narrow shaft.

I stood up stiffly. "Whoa. I wonder where *that* goes?"

"Or *that!*" said Burrage, pointing to another tunnel that forked off to the left from the main passageway.

I re-lit my candle and began to examine the makeshift ladder. This one was quite different than the one we had descended. Where our ladder had been stoutly attached to the wall of the shaft and constructed with iron spikes, this apparatus was far more spontaneous. It was made of irregular scraps of wood that had been lashed together with bits of hemp and could not have been more than a dozen feet long. At the top, it came to rest against what appeared to be a small platform wedged in the shaft above. The light from my candle was too weak to view much beyond that.

As I turned to join Burrage, I saw that he was studying an area of the wall near the second tunnel and as I leaned over his shoulder, he brushed the cobwebs from the surface of the stone.

"Look at this," he whispered.

There, carved in the rock surface, were three crude circles stacked in a small pyramid formation. I tugged on his sleeve, then led him over to the ladder and held my candle near an area on the stone just below the shaft. As the flame flickered in the draft, we could just make out the Roman numeral "IX" scratched in the surface of the rock.

"Did you see one of these in the shaft where we came down?" Burrage asked.

"Uh-uh," I replied. "What do you think? Should we head down one of the tunnels or see what's up there?" I asked, pointing into the darkness at the top of the ladder.

Burrage looked furtively toward the tunnels.

"I think we should go up the ladder. It could be another way out of here, and that would suit me just fine. If it is, then we can decide what to do from there."

Fair enough, I thought, and I gestured for Burrage to take the lead if he preferred. He was only too eager.

Within a minute, Burrage was standing on the platform above and holding his light so that I could follow. I blew my candle out, dropped the warm stub back into my pocket and began to ascend the rungs. The ladder swayed and shifted under my weight but felt sound enough and I quickly made my way toward the base of the platform.

"What do you see up there?" I asked Burrage. "Is there a door of some kind?"

"Sure is," he whispered. "Look at this."

I leaned back from the ladder and looked over the edge of the platform where I could clearly see a small, wooden door about two feet square. On the right was a length of old chain that was attached to a large iron ring imbedded in the stone next to the door. The chain was joined to the door by an old, rusting padlock. I could tell Burrage was just aching to somehow smash open the lock and climb back into the real world.

"Should I—"

His request was suddenly interrupted by the sound of something moving heavily through one of the tunnels below. Burrage quickly extinguished the candle and we froze in the darkness of the shaft, suspended precariously above the floor.

"*Max*," Burrage whispered urgently from above.

"*HUSH!*" I countered, as loudly as I dared.

I strained my ears, as the sound grew ever closer. It was a ragged, scraping noise—almost rhythmic in cadence, neither fast nor slow, approaching with a deliberation that sent a chill down my spine. I could feel the ladder begin to sway under my nervous weight. *Oh, God, don't let it climb up this ladder*, I prayed silently, squeezing my eyes closed with the horror of the thought.

On it came, taking forever seemingly, dragging its way toward the chamber below. The scraping sound was now joined by an occasional clank of metal against stone. Perspiration began to bead on my forehead finding its way through the grime into the corners of my eyes. I ground my burning eyes into the back of my sleeve. The scraping sounds were now so distinct that I knew the source was almost upon us. I forced myself to look over my shoulder and steal a glance toward the floor below. A dim, bluish glow began to illuminate the stone chamber and faint shadows crept slowly up the walls. My heart began to pound and the dust on the ladder rungs turned slippery beneath my damp, clammy hands. *What in the world made me come down here?*

As the approaching light grew brighter, I could see the rays reaching up the ladder rung by rung. As I looked downward, I realized with horror that my shoes would be visible from below, for I could see the light creeping across the front of my toes! I thought I should make my way up one more rung so that I might be fully hidden in the shadows, but as I shifted my weight, the ladder began to sway and I realized the movement would be easily noticed from below. I immediately stopped my climb and held my breath until the ladder was still once more.

At that moment, a lantern was thrust forward and the room seemed to fill with an undefined black form that emerged from the tunnel with the three circles. I watched as it swept beneath my ladder obscuring the lantern light and casting huge, dark shadows across the floor and walls. It stopped for a brief moment and then, with a soft growl, swung out of the chamber and disappeared down the main tunnel toward the sound of the tides. Within seconds, all grew dark once more with only the occasional flicker of light from the rapidly receding lantern. A sudden rush of air in the shaft hit my wet skin and sent me into a spasm of shivering. I clung to the ladder until the episode passed.

I could hear Burrage's labored breathing as he fought to subdue his panic. A broken whisper squeezed out from the bottom of his throat.

"Was that *him?*"

I closed my eyes and relived the scene from the night before—the ominous figure, black and shadowy, my own terror of being discovered.

"I have no idea."

"Max, listen. We're in way over our heads with this! You *know* that! We have no idea what we're dealing with. We have got to get out of here—get the cops involved."

He was absolutely right. Here I was with a fireplace poker and a three-inch candle stub, chasing phantoms through the darkness. It was right out of a horror movie and I hated horror movies. Facing your fears was one thing; meeting them in a pitch black, subterranean dungeon was another. What was I thinking?

"Okay, Burr, no argument. Follow—"

My words caught in my throat as every muscle in my neck constricted. A second light now approached and the unmistakable sound of movement through the tunnel once more had us paralyzed with dread.

"Oh, shit," Burrage whispered and once again we held our breath and waited shivering in the darkness.

The approach was much more rapid this time and my adrenaline level rose accordingly. The lantern light bobbed and flickered into view and once more a black shape burst into the room below! This time, however, it did not hesitate but immediately rushed across the floor and disappeared like a ghost train booming past the platform leaving a wake of swirling dust and shadows melting back into the darkness.

Burrage's response was immediate.

"Down, Max! Do it *now*. That thing could come back any minute and we're not gonna be here if it does!"

I quickly felt my way down the ladder and within seconds I was standing on the chamber floor. As Burrage followed in the darkness, I was struck by something that had just happened, but I couldn't quite get a handle on what it was. I felt Burrage nudge me as he hit the ground and re-lit his candle.

"Let's get moving," he commanded and started toward the tunnel from which we had come.

"*Wait!*" I exclaimed, grabbing his shoulder. "He came from there!"

I pointed to the tunnel we were about to enter.

"He didn't come back from the tunnel we just saw him go down. That *wasn't* the same guy. It didn't even sound the same, the way he moved. They both went down that way," I said, pointing into the darkness. "Down *there*, toward the sound of the waves!"

Burrage hesitated for just a moment.

"Whatever! All the more reason for us to go *this* way," and he turned toward the opposite entrance.

I knew he was right but I couldn't help but feel a certain thrill at the mystery that was unfolding, although I had no idea what any of it meant. I turned to follow but when I got down on one knee to avoid the low ceiling, yet another light appeared heading down the tunnel toward us.

Burrage immediately backed out and flattened himself against the wall.

"*Damn!* I can't <u>believe</u> this. Another one! What the hell do we do *now?*"

"This way," I urged, and pulled him into the tunnel with the three circles. "Nowhere else to go!"

In we dove, stumbling along and shielding the candlelight as best we could, for it would have been impossible to navigate in the darkness. Fortunately, this tunnel was a good two feet higher than the first, allowing us to remain on our feet as we hunched our way through the dim glow. The floor rose and fell haphazardly and took numerous turns and as we hurried along, I noticed odd bits of clutter on the floor—rusting chain, a pile of barrel staves, even an old shoe. I kept glancing over my shoulder to see if we were being pursued, but with the twists in the tunnel, I simply couldn't tell.

At one point the tunnel took a sharp upward slope—so steep, in fact, that we had to crawl on all fours to reach the top. When it leveled off again, I saw that the sides and roof were no longer ledge, but earthen and held up by stout timbers and planks of hardwood. Hundreds of roots, large and small, penetrated the passage, almost clogging it in several places. I wondered if the tunnel would disappear altogether, leaving us trapped like moles in the dark, damp earth. Burrage began to show the strain as the walls closed in on us.

"This is bad. It's too *small!* I gotta go back!"

"Burr, hang on. We *can't* go back yet. We don't know—"

Burrage shouldered me aside and started to fight back through the tangle of roots that seemed to thicken with every step.

"Burr! Don't do this! We'll be okay," I pleaded, but it was too late.

Burrage was flailing now, attacking the roots with his right hand while trying to shield the candle in his left. The situation was deteriorating and I desperately tried to think of what I could say or do to calm things again. A steady rain of loose dirt began to shower down from the ceiling. As I tried to keep up with Burrage, my face and arms were lashed by stiff roots snapping back in his wake. Finally, I made a lunge for his sleeve, but as I did so, a large clod of soil fell from between the timbers overhead and knocked the candle from his hand. And as a choking rain of dirt continued to sift down on us, we were once again plunged into blackness.

"*DAMMIT!*" Burrage coughed. "Where'd the damn <u>candle</u> go?!"

"Quiet, Burr!" I hissed. "Calm down and take one of mine. You have the matches."

I reached into my pocket and fumbled for one of the stubs, but as I was about to hand it over to him, I saw the glow dancing toward us on the wall.

"Burr, look *there*. Get down!"

We both immediately hit the floor of the tunnel and watched as the light grew in intensity. We were hidden for the moment by a sharp jog in the tunnel but I knew it would only be a matter of moments before our pursuer rounded the bend and would be upon us.

"Burr," I whispered urgently. "Our only chance is to grab him the second he rounds the turn—surprise him. Then maybe we'll have a chance. Try to hit his legs and I'll see if I can knock him over. Then we'll take off in the dark."

Burrage grunted a tenuous agreement and we lay on the bone-chilling earth awaiting the moment of truth. It was not long coming. The lantern swung around the corner and Burrage dove forward into the leg that followed. The figure fell hard against the wall of the tunnel, yet managed to hold tightly to the lantern. I sprang up and lurched toward him looking to bowl him over while Burrage, hopefully, kept hold of his leg. As I lowered my shoulder for the impact I glanced up and, with a feeling of total shock, twisted off to the right just before smashing into his chest.

"William!" I cried.

CHAPTER 6

Burrage and I sank down to the floor of the tunnel and tried to gather our wits. Poor William was speechless and stood wide-eyed against the wall, still clutching the small brass lantern in his hand. He wore a dark blue Red Sox sweatshirt under his down vest and had a red wool stocking cap pulled low over his face. The bottom of his jeans were splattered with mud and the laces of both sneakers trailed loosely in the dirt. His eyes darted nervously back and forth as he searched our faces.

"William," I said, as calmly as I could, "what in the world are you doing here?"

He shifted his weight from side to side and looked at his feet. For a brief moment I suspected he was going to say something, but a small cloud passed over his face and he seemed to swallow his thought. I decided it would be best to shift the attention for a moment or two and let him get his bearings.

"You okay, Burr?" I asked.

Burrage was still trying to recover from the strain of the entire ordeal. His breathing was rapid and shallow as he cupped his hands around his nose in an attempt to filter out the dust that still hung in the air around us. I noticed a bright scarlet blotch on the back of his hand—blood oozing from a cut that mingled with the sweat and grime.

I leaned my head back against the wall, shut my eyes, and tried to make sense of all that had just happened.

"I need to go home now."

It was William's voice bringing me back to the moment.

"William," I asked again, "what *happened?* Why aren't you in Vermont?"

He glanced behind him and then at me.

"We just got back," he answered. "My dad... We came home early."

"But how did you get down here of all places? Did you know about the tunnel?"

"No. I was in the cellar."

He paused and his skin flushed slightly.

"Then what?"

He suddenly shut down and just stared at me. I could see in his eyes a fierce need not to tell me what it was that could possibly entice a young boy to climb down into such a place. I know I would never have had the guts at his age. I figured he must have caught a glimpse of Lady Jane making her getaway and found his way down. Probably afraid of getting in trouble.

"Where'd you find the lantern?" Burrage interjected.

"The study," he answered carefully.

"So then what? You just decided to explore all these tunnels?"

Again, his eyes hardened and I knew we would get nothing more from him at this point.

"Are you lost, too?" William asked, his voice sinking.

What to say now. While I knew William must be very glad to have found help, he was clearly agitated and as desperate to get the hell out of here as we were. His voice was dry and his chin trembled as he spoke. His eyes were everywhere as if he expected something to come flying at him any second. Little wonder after what we had just subjected him to.

"William, listen, I'm sorry about, you know, us grabbing you like that. We thought it—"

I hesitated. Was William even aware of the dark figures in the tunnels? Somehow I didn't think so and I didn't want to make him even more frightened than he already was.

"We didn't know who you were, that's all. Are you okay?"

He gave a small nod.

"All right then. Time to get back up and get home," I said, trying to sound like the task involved no more effort than going to the store for some milk.

Burrage gave me a sarcastic glance, but I knew he also sensed the need to keep things upbeat for the boy's sake. I proposed a strategy.

"I say we head back and leave the way we came. We have the lantern now and that helps. But I think maybe we should cover it a little bit and keep as quiet as we can, because, you know, there could be small animals or something down here and we wouldn't want to scare them, right?"

William seemed to get extremely nervous at the thought of small, unknown animals that might be lurking in the shadows, so the idea of traveling in stealth mode had great appeal. Burrage took his scarf and draped it over the lantern in a way that only a small slit was left to illuminate our way. I reached down and pulled the iron poker from my belt and explained to William that if any small creatures were foolish enough to come near us, I would have no trouble discouraging them. As he took stock of my martial stance, I could see his confidence falter, but he dutifully fell in behind Burrage and we set off down the passageway.

With the lantern shrouded as it was, there was precious little light available to help us pick our way through the clutter of the rambling tunnel. The going was slow, made more so by frequent stops. Any noise, any thought that the light flickering on the walls ahead might not be from our lantern was cause for an immediate halt to make sure we were not in danger of discovery. Several times we stood pressed against the cold stone, listening breathlessly to the sounds of droplets echoing in a distant puddle or some small creature scurrying through the darkness. I wondered how our extreme caution was affecting William. Did he suspect that there might be more than the errant wharf rat afoot?

As we made our way, I couldn't help but wonder how someone as young as William could ever end up in a place like this. It seemed inconceivable. It was all I could do to keep from screaming off down the tunnel. And I at least had a companion. Would I have ever gone this far alone?

I realized that I hadn't paid much attention to William since moving up to Marblehead. No reason I should have. I'd give a little wave when we passed on the sidewalk or as I headed down the yard to take a stroll near the harbor. He had always been polite, respectful, quiet. But I had been struck by his determination to look me in the eye, not easy for a shy boy of ten or eleven. It occurred to me that on the few occasions I saw him with a friend, it was always someone new. No one came around regularly. Yet, he didn't seem like a sad child, just preoccupied.

For me, here in this cold, dark place, the sunlit memories of childhood felt as distant as the warm, green earth must feel to an astronaut circling the dark side of the moon. The only real worries of my youth—the big kid down the block or the surly German Shepherd that got loose every so often—evaporated the moment I entered our cozy little house and plopped myself down to listen to baseball on the radio. On those glorious summer evenings, the buttery smell of my mom's grilled cheese would fill the room and I would lie back on the big sofa, the epicenter of a universe that existed solely for my gratification. Any needs that weren't met by a loving family and the general prosperity of the era, I met through my considerable powers of imagination.

Young boys, happy ones anyway, live their lives with no more sense of purpose than a well-fed house cat. Once lunch has been stuffed inside his belly, the average small boy is a blank slate. The only practical use to which his brain can be put is to decide whether the stick in his hand would make a better pirate cutlass or Ninja sword. I wondered if William felt the same.

My thoughts jarred to a sudden halt. Burrage stood motionless at the front of the procession and craned his head slowly around a sharp curve in the tunnel. He then turned cautiously back to William and me.

"We're back to where the tunnels split."

I squeezed past William and joined Burrage. A few feet ahead was the ladder that we had explored earlier—a dead end because of the padlock on the door above. Across the room we could see the low tunnel that led back to the chimney and, hopefully, our way home. And just to the left was the larger passageway down which the two mysterious figures had disappeared.

"*There's* our way back," Burrage said, pointing across the stone floor. "Do you hear anything moving out there?"

I listened for a moment, but I only heard the sound of the mysterious waves down the large tunnel. Burrage covered the lantern completely to see if there was any sign of a light heading our way. Nothing.

"Coast seems clear," he whispered. "Let's cross over with the lantern dark, just in case."

We felt our way to the mouth of the low tunnel and ducked down and began to crawl up the path on our hands and knees once more.

"How you doin' there, Will?" I whispered back over my shoulder.

Silence.

"William, how's it going?"

I grabbed onto Burrage's foot and tugged.

"Burr, light the lantern. *Damn!*"

Burrage rekindled the lantern and we looked back behind us. William had vanished without a trace.

"*Christ!*" Burrage exclaimed, "Where's the kid?"

"We've got to go back," I barked and took the lantern while reversing myself in the tight passageway.

"Where could he have gone?" Burrage asked, incredulously. "He was right behind us!"

I had no idea. Had he taken a wrong turn when we came out into the chamber? Did he freeze up when the lantern went out and stay where he was? Or was it something more unthinkable?

We quickly made our way back to the small chamber and I immediately ducked into the tunnel from which we had come.

"*William!*" I whispered as loudly as I dared. "William, where *are* you?"

Nothing. I turned back to Burrage.

"Go look up there!" I said, pointing to the ladder. Burrage made a quick assent and returned empty-handed.

"Where the hell *is* he?"

I was starting to feel panicked.

"He's got to be down *there* then," Burrage said, gesturing toward the large tunnel.

"Oh, Christ! Burr, we've got to go after him!"

Burrage winced, then nodded and we both plunged down the unexplored passageway. Neither of us wanted to discuss what we feared most, that he had been taken from under our noses in the dark. That seemed inconceivable—no noise, no cry for help, no light of any kind. The trouble was that everything that had happened was inconceivable. Why should we be surprised at a phantom kidnapping.

"Slow down," Burrage pleaded. "We don't know what we might be running into!"

I stopped for a moment and listened for any noise from up ahead. It was very still. Even the sound of the waves had ceased. *How could he have gotten so far in the dark*, I wondered. We crept forward more cautiously, twice passing the entrances of tunnels that branched off in other directions.

"Wait a second," Burrage whispered. "Turn out the lantern."

Thinking he had seen or heard someone approaching, I quickly doused the light and looked about nervously for any sign.

"See that!" Burrage exclaimed.

As my eyes began to focus, I realized that we were no longer standing in the pitch-dark as before. The walls of the tunnel were streaked with a pale, iridescent glow. This remarkable phenomenon—some sort of algae,

I guessed—created enough light for us to make our way forward without
the use of the lantern.

"That helps," I replied. "At least we don't look like a subway car
coming down the tunnel anymore."

A low mumble was the reply.

"Come again?" I asked.

"What?" Burrage answered.

"I didn't hear you, that's all."

"That's because I didn't say anything."

"Oh, jeez."

We stood stock-still. We could hear the voices echoing softly all
around us, a grunting sound, then a low, hollow laugh followed by a sharp
rebuke. The words were unintelligible, but they reverberated ominously
through the passageway, bestial rumblings from deep within the bowels of
the earth. Instinctively, we dropped to a low crouch as our pulses
quickened yet again. Burrage whispered hotly near my ear.

"What the hell is that!? Is it coming closer?"

"I don't think so," I said in a hushed tone, straining my ears. "Hard to
tell how far away it is in these tunnels."

"So what now? We can't just keep walking till we stumble into them!"

My mind began to swim. We absolutely should fly the hell out of here
to get help. But what if William had been taken by some degenerate low-
life? It could be too late if we went back. Besides, I reasoned, we could run
into trouble no matter which way we headed.

"We've got to keep going. Let's just take it slow and be totally quiet!"

Burrage nodded. He knew the stakes, but, my God, the choices were
unforgiving.

We pressed on, stooping low and sliding along near the passage wall.
My hand brushed against the rock and several small globs of algae began
to glow eerily along my knuckles. I flicked them off with my fingers and
they fell to the tunnel floor like tiny, green drops of liquid metal. The
tunnel took several sharp turns and as we rounded each corner, the distant

voices shifted. The phosphorescent glow on the walls seemed to wax and wane like cold moonlight in the forest, sometimes bathing us in sulphurous gray-green light. Other times we were swallowed up in shadowy grottoes of black stone.

My sense of time disappeared completely. Whether we had walked for five minutes or fifty was indiscernible. At that point, we arrived at a crossroad in the alien world of which we were now a part.

The "Hub," as Burrage named it, was a small, irregular room from which no fewer than seven separate tunnels snaked outward through the relentless layers of stone. It reminded him of a chamber in an anthill and, for a few irrational moments, he had convinced himself that perhaps we had stumbled into some sort of mutant colony of giant, rock-tunneling insects. He imagined conga lines of black, shiny ants the size of Shetland ponies, abdomens bobbing, antennae twitching as they scuttled through their subterranean lair. Some would be carrying eggs like huge grains of boiled rice; others would be bringing food to the nest—William? The whole fantasy fell apart when he had to admit that even giant ants would end up above ground on occasion and that such an event would likely have been mentioned in the police log of the local paper.

Even in the dim glow of the algae, I could see several more of the mysterious pictographs carved in the rock near the tunnel entrances—a crude boat, a well, a tombstone, and so on.

Suddenly, the distant voices grew markedly louder.

"They're headed this way!" Burrage whispered urgently.

"In here," I answered, ducking down a tunnel and around a bend.

The scene in front of us left us completely astounded.

We found ourselves in a large room—much larger than anything we had seen up till now. It was fully 30 to 40 feet long and nearly as wide although the ceiling was still very low—no more than six or so feet at the most. The walls were studded with heavy, rough-hewn timbers and on several of them, small candles flickered inside blackened tin lanterns. Massive barrels and wooden crates were stacked along the perimeter, particularly at the far end, and a number of large chests lay randomly scattered about the floor. Here and there, a small fish or chicken bone poked out of the damp sediment covering the ground, but otherwise, the area was relatively uncluttered. An enormous black cauldron sat on a hearth in the far corner below a narrow shaft that exited up through the stone ceiling. An archaic-looking cupboard stood next to the hearth and I could make out a number of tarnished cups and plates stacked along several rough plank shelves that had been wedged between the timbers.

"My God, someone's been living down here," Burrage whispered, as we slowly walked across the floor.

"Quick, Burr, they're coming!" I said, pulling him toward the crates stacked along the far wall.

We rushed to the far corner, squeezing our way behind a large pile of casks that lay on their sides in the shadows and within seconds we had succeeded in hiding ourselves from view. Just as I stretched myself out along the base of the wall, an enormous, dark shape darted from behind one of the barrels and leapt to the ground not twelve inches from my face. I barely managed to stifle the scream, which got as far as my throat and then stuck there, trapped by constricted muscles and sheer will. As my eyes bulged out of my head, a leprous looking sewer rat bit down on a fat centipede that hung writhing in its jaws, then made a quick about-face and padded silently into the darkness. I didn't want to think what other little horrors might be creeping about down here in the shadows.

Burrage apparently felt a little too exposed where he was and somehow managed to step over me and take a position exactly in the spot the rat had just vacated, a fact that I decided not to share. As we lay head to head on the dank earthen floor, a new nightmare made its presence known. A hundred tiny legs began to make their way across various parts of my body—down near my ankles, along my arm and on the back of my neck. I glanced at Burrage and I could see he was just about beside himself trying to fight off the tiny horde.

"Oh, Christ!" he rasped, digging a finger into his ear. "I'm in hell here,

Max! These damn things are crawling into—*everywhere!* I'm starting to feel like a goddam dead bird!"

He was working himself up into a full-blown rant. I was about to intervene when we both realized that something very strange was happening around us. A candle in the nearest lantern suddenly puffed out. Then, one by one, in perfect sequence, the half dozen remaining candles also expired, leaving us awash in blackness so dense that it actually felt difficult to breathe. Burrage went silent and even the body-crawlers seemed to freeze with suspense. Here, waiting in the utter darkness, a vision of the great storm clouds over Gerry Island billowed up before my eyes—so thick, so looming that I felt they would roll down and smother us like a dust storm. Was it only in my mind? Lightning blazed jaggedly across the inky darkness and I braced for the crash of thunder that was sure to follow, but there was only silence. I shot a glance toward Burrage, but could not see him, only the afterglow of the flashing bolts across my eyelids.

"Burr! Are you there?" I whispered hoarsely.

"Yeah, hush up! I'm right next to you," he hissed back at me.

From his answer it was obvious that he was unaware of anything that I was seeing. I shut my eyes and tried to shake off the hallucination. When I opened them again, I saw Burrage staring wide-eyed toward the doorway across the chamber. As I turned my head in the direction of his gaze, a dim, yellow glow began to intensify at the mouth of the tunnel and within seconds, a bobbing lantern appeared.

A dark figure entered the room followed by four others. The leader took a candle and proceeded to relight the lanterns that had gone dark just moments before. As each flame flickered to life, a startling scene was revealed. Four men stood clustered by one of the trunks in the middle of the room and were soon joined by the lantern bearer. They were nothing short of astonishing.

The lantern bearer was a robust man with a full beard and large eyes, which darted about the room as he carefully placed the light on the trunk before him. He wore a large kerchief over closely cropped hair and several aboriginal tattoos peeked through gaping tears in the sleeves of a grimy, linen shirt. A large, gold tooth flashed brightly, like sun off the water in the dark ocean of his face. His trousers were cut so full as to drape in baggy folds past his knees and they were extremely ragged and worn. About his waist was a dark sash and across his chest, a great leather strap from which hung a short, curved sword. As I looked more closely at his sash, I could also see a short-handled ax with a cruel, arcing blade and what appeared to be an antiquated pistol of some kind. He stood silently, hand on sword hilt, exhibiting the stoic demeanor of a veteran warrior for whom readiness is a way of life.

I glanced at Burrage who stared at me with a look of absolute disbelief.

The other men were outfitted in similar fashion, though the details of their dress and equipment varied widely. One fellow had the short, muscular look of a bulldog. Long blond hair was gathered club-like behind his head and contrasted with the burnt red complexion of his craggy face. He held the stub of a clay pipe in his teeth and stood with his arms folded across his chest, his head cocked to one side. Pale blue eyes hid behind the narrow slits of his eyelids like hunters in a duck blind.

Lurking behind him was a taller man, thin faced and with a slender build. A black tricorn hat perched on his head and his lank, brown hair was gathered at the rear with a black satin ribbon. His pale skin was far less weathered than that of the others and his clothes showed less wear. He had the look of someone who worked with his head more than his hands—a schoolmaster or clerk. I couldn't help but notice the subtle expression of disdain, which arched an eyebrow and added a sarcastic curl to his cold smile.

The fourth man was dressed most formally in black velvet and white shirt; however, all of his clothes showed a great deal of wear and were quite frayed. This condition extended to his gray-pallored face, which sported a week's worth of stubble. He was an older man with cavernous, reddened eyes, as if he had not slept in some time. He wore a tall, black felt hat with a broad, round brim and several goose feathers stuck randomly about the headband creating the appearance of an unkempt nest. There was a certain wisdom in his eyes, but loneliness as well, I thought. He had the aspect of one who knew what he wanted but had never managed to acquire it.

The last figure stood slightly apart. He was quite tall and had long, brown hair that fell in tangled curls over the shoulders of a dark coat. His laced shirt featured an ornate jabot cascading down the front of his chest. He wore a large brimmed hat with a dark maroon ostrich feather that quivered nervously with every movement of his leonine head. He, too, had a full beard, which framed a dark and brooding face. Fathomless eyes burned from beneath close-knit brows and his mouth was clenched so tightly as to appear sewn shut. Brown fingers extended from beneath an oversized cuff and curled around a crudely made crutch that tucked under his left armpit. I could see him listing slightly as he sought support.

There was a vigilance about him, but not the kind that scanned the horizon in search of a distant enemy; it was more the look of a man who sensed that the real danger lay no further than the eyes of those around him. I thought I also detected a certain grim contentment, an awareness that whatever his life had become, he not only had accepted it, but had discovered that he actually relished it.

Suddenly, the short fellow with the pipe took a step to the rear of the lantern bearer and, as quick and silent as a scorpion, flashed a dagger across the poor man's throat! At first, there was simply a look of shock on the victim's face. Within seconds, a thin, scarlet line appeared just below the jawbone and the first rivulet of blood made its way down through the dirt and perspiration on his neck. His fingertip dabbed gently at his throat and he raised it to his eyes. I could see the color leave his face as he realized what had happened and he immediately sank to his knees. He pressed his fingers against his throat and moaned piteously as he tried to determine if he was indeed moments from death. The tall man with the crutch stumped forward two paces and surveyed the damage.

"Ah, well, Ned Buckett," he growled in a thick French accent. "You are not dead today. Monsieur Snitch has a light touch, does he not? Think on it, *mon ami*."

The group watched coldly as the hapless Mr. Buckett tied a dirty piece of cloth around his injured throat then hesitantly rose to his feet. Taking a second lantern from the wall, he slowly made his way to the other end of the chamber and disappeared back down the tunnel. The deadly Snitch wiped the blade of his dagger on his trousers and returned it to the sash behind his back.

"We shall see if our message has been heard," the tall man intoned, as he motioned the remaining contingent to exit as well. One by one they began to slip out of the room.

At that moment, Burrage, who was practically apoplectic with distress, decided to begin breathing again. As his throat began to unconstrict, the air that had been trapped in his lungs rushed out his windpipe and made a sound something like a broken party horn. We both froze once more as the tall man stopped in his tracks and turned in our direction. He cocked his head slightly and scanned the room. After several nerve-wracking moments, he appeared satisfied that nothing was amiss and swept silently down the tunnel.

The tiny legs resumed their march across my neck.

CHAPTER 7

"He's had a terrible shock, Mrs. Welkie," said the puffy-eyed young internist as his notes skiffled across the clipboard. "At his age—the exposure, the fall he took—we'll have to see how he does over the next twelve hours or so. The fact that he has still not regained consciousness is not good, frankly. He seems to be struggling. I'll talk with Dr. Sanborn this afternoon and see what he thinks. He knows your husband's history—maybe we'll find a clue."

The doctor gave some last minute instructions to the floor nurse and left the room in a swirl of white polyester and the lingering odor of breath mints. Hannah Welkie sat stone silent next to the bed. Her husband's hand, discolored from the I.V. needles and unresponsive to her touch, rested in her own. Her sad eyes watched as the muscles of his face jumped and twitched beneath the pale, wrinkled skin. His brows tightened into deep gullies over clenched eyes and several low growls rumbled softly in his throat.

A profound sense of guilt had begun to take root in Hannah's anxious mind. Should she have been more aggressive in getting him help, she wondered? She sat and gazed listlessly at the man with whom she had spent the last fifty-seven years of her life.

It shocked her how quickly their world had fallen apart. It struck her, too, how utterly dependent she had become on her husband's reassuring presence in her life. Always strong-willed and never one to shrink from

any challenge, she had always assumed that when the time came to deal
with losing him, her natural strength would see her through. But there
was something deeply disturbing about the manner in which Boden
Welkie had come to his current condition. Had he been the victim of a
sudden illness or struck down in an accident, she believed that, for all the
pain and sorrow such an event would cause, she would have known her
role and had access to her reserves. But *this!* Nothing had prepared her for
the rapid and mysterious transformation of his personality. It was as if he
was slowly being absorbed through a membrane into a dark, invisible
world. His body was still here, living and breathing. But the rest of him
was gone.

The dry air in the room caused her unblinking eyes to burn and a thin
tear began the slow journey down the side of her nose. She did not even
know if he wanted her with him at this point, and the pain of that
thought was almost unbearable. Better to go home and sleep, she
reasoned. Clear her mind and gather her strength for the days ahead.

She gently placed her husband's hand on the white blanket that lay
across his chest and gathered herself to leave. She pulled on her sweater
and walked toward the door, then paused for a moment. Turning toward
the bed, she discerned a tremble in his lips and saw the color rush into his
face like a storm surge. In an instant, Boden Welkie's eyes blazed open and
he sat straight up in his bed. In a voice as chilling as wind off the water,
he called out, "Thy word thy mark as 'twer in blood! Each soul upon the
rail take heed! The god of storms thy deeds shall set against the vessel
'neath thy feet! For there upon the waves thy hearts make blackness
blacker still!"

With that, Boden Welkie's face drained pale and he lay back against
his pillow, the tempest sinking below the surface once again.

Burrage and I lay for long minutes before either of us dared to stir.
When we finally sensed that the visitors were not coming back, we

struggled to our feet. I made my way cautiously out into the candlelit room and stood with an ear cocked, listening for any sign of movement.

"I don't hear anything," I whispered, motioning Burrage to join me.

We were at a complete loss for words. I found a seat on one of the wooden crates and Burrage soon followed suit.

"Max," he began, then stopped when another wave of disbelief swept over him.

"I know," I replied, although I knew nothing at all.

"Max, did we just see someone get his—you know—throat cut?"

I nodded.

"Well, does that mean those guys weren't acting? They were *real?*"

"I have no idea what they were," I answered.

"Jesus, Max, they looked like... *pirates*, for God's sake!"

Burrage stared at me. It was inconceivable.

"Let's think this out," I answered.

"Think *what* out?" Burrage huffed. "Whatever we come up with won't make any sense! Are they real? Ghosts? Hallucinations? And where's that kid, anyway?"

That last question jolted me. After the scene we had just witnessed, finding William took on a sense of extreme urgency. And Burrage was right. Trying to get a grip on reality right now was a waste of time. Somehow we had to get William and then get the hell out of here. We could figure the rest out later. I stood up and motioned for Burrage to follow and we cautiously made our way over to the tunnel entrance once again.

"Look, Burr, we may only get one chance at this," I whispered. "We absolutely have to find William and we can't risk being seen by these guys, so listen! I'll go on ahead about fifteen yards or so, then you follow. That way, if I run into trouble, you'll know it and can stay hidden. Now, if I don't get caught, you take off and head back to the ladder and bring back help. I'll try some of the other passageways and see if I can find William. That way, there's less chance they'll find us both. You keep the lantern, you'll need it. I've still got some candles."

Burrage thought for a moment and realized this was probably our best shot. He nodded then looked back over his shoulder nervously and gave me a little shove to get moving. I took a deep breath and headed down the tunnel.

Within a minute my eyes had adjusted to the dim glow of the phosphorous and I moved forward as quietly as I could. When I finally emerged in the Hub, I examined each tunnel and tried to decide which one was the most likely to lead to William. The small, carved drawings were the only clues as to where the tunnels might go. Our original passageway was marked with a key symbol. The carving of the well also intrigued me. William might be thirsty and head that way. Or he might head down the tunnel with the boat symbol thinking it would come out at the harbor and offer a chance of escape. Other carvings of a gravestone and a noose were not at all inviting. My instinct told me he would choose the boat and freedom.

I ducked through the entrance and made my way along as quickly as I dared. The floor became more cluttered with debris and the odor of dead fish grew stronger as I went. Suddenly, I heard the sound of several footsteps rapidly moving in my direction from up ahead! I began a stumbling retreat, hoping that once I got back to the Hub, I could slip down another tunnel and lose them.

The pursuing footsteps grew louder and more rapid. I realized they must have heard me. Now in a complete panic, I took off at a run. Scraping against the walls and tripping over objects in the dim light, I now abandoned all pretense of secrecy. My heart racing, I burst into the Hub and made a quick right toward the tunnel with the symbol of the well. At that moment, a burst of light flashed through my head and I felt myself begin to tumble as if I was weightlessly rotating in space. The world grew intensely quiet and dark and amorphous shadows began to swirl all around me. I could no longer tell if my eyes were open or shut and a searing pain exploded down the back of my head and my mouth filled with dust. Then, utter blackness.

✳ ✳ ✳

I awoke to the taste of blood in my mouth. Bits of dirt caked my lips and ground against the front of my teeth as I searched for damage with the tip of my tongue. Spitting out a mix of grit, blood, and saliva, I tried to shake off the dull pain in my head and open my eyes. I sensed that I was in a sitting position, leaning against a rough stone wall that dug into my shoulder blades. Something in my eye caused it to tear and as I reached to wipe it, I discovered that my arm could not move. Turning my head I saw that my wrist was clamped tightly in a crude iron ring that was pinned to the wall with a great metal spike. My other wrist was similarly shackled.

The discovery left me incredulous. The idea was so absurd that my first instinct was a bitter laugh. I shut my eyes again and slowly shook my head. I felt a strange calm—a sense that my fate was no longer in my control and that I was free from the pressure of making the right decision, finding William or making an escape. I had failed and at least I could now rest.

I opened my eyes and peered through the flickering yellow light that emanated from a bit of candle on the opposite wall. The only entrance to the room was secured by a small door made of thick iron bars. This was padlocked on the outside. My attention was immediately drawn to a curious sight indeed. Two stout cords hung down from the middle of the ceiling. One held a chunk of dark bread and the other, a wineskin. The wineskin, clearly full of liquid, was dark and moist along the lower side and every now and then a drop would run down the seam and fall into the dust below. A damp spot about four inches in diameter had formed where it landed. Clearly, the presence of even this paltry offering was intended more to madden me than to sustain me. As I stared at the bread, a fat roach scuttled silently down the cord and got to work on a small section of crust.

"Max?"

As soon as I heard my name, my heart sank. I turned to my right and there, in a patch of shadows across the room, lay Burrage, his chin nodding against his chest. Both arms were drawn straight up over his head and chained to a single ring imbedded in the rock. His clothes were filthy, as if he had been dragged through the dirt and his hair was totally disheveled.

I let out a disheartened sigh.

"You look awful."

Burrage snorted wearily.

"It's a good thing you can't see yourself," he replied.

The realization that we had no chance of help began to sink in. It was clear that Burrage was already as depressed as I was becoming.

"How long have we been here?" I asked quietly.

"A couple of hours, I think. You going to be okay?"

"My head's killing me. What the *hell* happened?!"

Burrage raised his head and rotated it in an attempt to stretch out his neck muscles.

"Well, basically, you got clocked by that guy's crutch, the big guy with the limp," Burrage answered.

"You *saw* it?"

"Saw the whole thing. I had just come into the Hub when you came tearing through. That guy was just standing there waiting and clubbed you right in the back of the head. Jeez, I thought he killed you. Then these other two guys were right on your heels and they jumped me. I just went limp and they pretty much left me alone—except to throw me in here, of course. Really, Max, I thought you were gone. I couldn't see you breathing."

We both sat silently for a while.

"What now?" Burrage asked, only because there was nothing else to say.

"Christ," I sighed. "This is not good. Who *are* these guys?"

My question was interrupted by the grinding squeal of rusted metal.

The padlock on the door fell from its hasp and landed with a dull thump in the dust. The door swung inward.

I could feel the iron shackles dig into my wrists as my arm muscles involuntarily tightened. The passageway outside the now-open door was black as pitch. A sudden current of musty air penetrated the room and made the tiny flame flicker wildly on the melting wax stub. Otherwise, all was still as death. I glanced over at Burrage. I could see real fear begin to creep into his eyes and I quickly looked aside. I knew I couldn't allow myself to give in to my own raging trepidation.

I squinted into the void beyond the bars and a great chill immediately shot down my spine. The unwavering eyes of Boden Welkie burned through the darkness and bore into my own. His head seemed almost disembodied as it slowly floated toward me, then burst through the doorway into the pale candlelight. I immediately turned away and buried my face in my shoulder, feeling the same sense of dread that I had felt so many days ago when we first had met.

"So, yer nay dead after all," a strange voice growled with more than a hint of regret.

I turned my head to see a figure towering over me, silhouetted against the candlelight. Boden Welkie was gone. The shadowy details revealed a broad face, which seemed to match well the Highland brogue. A tattered shirt hung precariously from burly arms, and equally ragged trousers luffed about his legs. His only weapon appeared to be the venomous-looking dagger that protruded like a fang from beneath the thick sash about his waist. The expression on his bearded face was one of complete contempt and a total disregard for my well-being.

"I see yer wee friend hae ta'en ta 'is supper, such as it is," he sneered, plucking the hapless roach from his perch atop the bread.

With a quick squeeze, the insect was separated from both its life and its innards, which now hung in a sticky thread from the tip of a blackened thumbnail.

"Them as steal from others shall no' prosper for long!" he grunted, well pleased with his thinly veiled threat.

That said, he smeared the tiny carcass across his shirtfront and turned his attention to Burrage, who looked positively stricken.

"As sorry a pot a' slum as I ne'er hoped ta see, the pair a' ya!"

Giving Burrage a half-hearted kick, our tormentor turned toward the sound of two new visitors entering the room. The first I recognized immediately as the tall man with the limp—the one Burrage claimed to have knocked me senseless with the heavy staff he now held beneath his shoulder. He had to duck quite low to enter and I could not see his face until he raised himself up before me. His dark eyes surveyed me as one might a gutted fish hung from a yardarm with no more use than as a resting place for flies.

Behind him appeared a second man. He, too, had been among the group in the storeroom—the gray man with the goose feathers in his hat. His worn face gave no hint of his manner or intent, but he clearly carried himself as one with a certain degree of status. His deep voice resonated as he spoke.

"They come from the Key by the looks of it, Cap'n. Too many eyes would have seen 'em otherwise."

The accent was hard to place, English for sure, but very different than any I had heard. The Frenchman fixed me with a stare, then spoke.

"This has the stink of Worms on it, *n'est pas?* Have you found him yet, Monsieur Quill?"

"Not as yet, Cap'n," the gray man replied.

"And our little bird, Ned Buckett. What song does he sing?"

"Nary a peep. Becalmed 'e is. Prayin' for a one-eyed wind to blow 'im out of harm's way no doubt!"

The captain turned his attention to the hapless Burrage, prodding his midsection with the heavy crutch.

"He has the look of a squid with all the best parts pinched off, does he not? Well, this a puzzle indeed."

I could see Burrage begin to shrivel and I sensed that we were at a crisis point. There was the sickening realization that our situation, however incomprehensible, was deadly serious and that any misstep could lead to quick and dire results. And yet, I had no sense of how to deal with it. What would they respond to—a show of defiance, subservience, courage, fear? My mind madly raced through a backlog of stored images, scenes from movies where the captive stands up to his captors; childhood experiences where the victim of a playground bully desperately strives to avoid abuse. I was not good at this sort of thing but my instinct told me that Burrage would be even worse. Burrage would fluctuate between self-pity at the unfairness of it all and sheer panic, neither of which would endear him to people such as these. I knew that if we were to avoid serious harm, it would fall to me to navigate our way through the dangerous waters ahead. I decided to take the risk that if the situation deteriorated, I would respond with as much bravado as I could muster and hope that a display of boldness would elicit at least a modicum of respect. The captain continued his advance on Burrage.

"You have the look of a cull, *mon ami*. A common thief! How you found your way to us I do not know, but I have no doubt we shall discover it. Perhaps you would prefer to simply admit to the indiscretion. You could then proceed with begging my forgiveness, a gift which I have been told by some that I bestow too readily."

As I looked at the Frenchman's icy expression, it was clear that forgiveness was probably the last gift this man would ever be accused of bestowing in too much abundance. From his ever-widening eyes, I could see that Burrage was rapidly melting down.

"Come then, *monsieur*," the captain continued as softly as a serpent coiled to strike. He fingered the stock of an ornate pistol that hung from a leather strap under his coat. "Unburden yourself."

Burrage was now virtually incoherent.

"I—no—we're just—please, we want to leave!"

"No doubt!" the Frenchman roared, his companions joining him in the joke. "And so you shall. Ditty Gunn. Take this man to the crab pool and bid him good journey."

As the Scotsman moved toward him, Burrage's face drained of color. I instantly realized that this was all meant for my benefit and that it was my tongue they wished to loosen. I also sensed that a true accounting of our reasons for being here would never pass muster. I had no doubt that our captors had survived precisely because they never accepted the benign explanation for anything. They smelled smoke and if we were ever to escape our predicament, I would have to lead them to a bit of fire.

And there was something else. Even in our brief experience with these men, there were several clues that they were dealing with troublesome issues that went beyond our unexpected presence in their midst. This Ned Buckett was clearly having a very bad day, but it was uncertain how these other factors might impact our situation. Still, at the moment the Frenchman was exercising all the control and I knew we had to find a way to gain a little for ourselves.

"So, you know about all this!" I blurted out, not quite believing that I had said it.

But at least for the moment, my words had the desired affect. The Scotsman temporarily ceased his efforts at dragging poor Burrage to his feet. The captain turned in my direction. It was clear that a response from me at that moment was what he had fully expected. Burrage, who was now teetering on the brink of incontinence, sat gaping as the Frenchman took two stumping strides in my direction.

"Well, it is good some men still place a value on their mortal souls. Confession is the only true path to God, is it not, Monsieur Quill?"

With a wry smile, the gray man nodded his agreement, "Aye, Cap'n, an' it sets my heart soaring just to see it. Why, if all of us was to drop anchor in the Firm Sediments o' the Good Book, there'd be none adrift on the Shoals of Perdition, that's certain!"

"They're from the Key. Jus' listen to 'em!" Ditty Gunn observed with grave concern. "An unholy thing they're here at all! We all signed the Articles! There's the De'il at work here and that's sure. 'Tis a business for the Company ta decide, bless my soul!"

Quill looked to the captain, who had paused to consider his course.

"Aye, 'tis true, Cap'n. The Articles forbid it and was signed by all. 'Twould mean a tally by shares to go against it," Quill pointed out.

"Damn your soul, Ditty Gunn!" the captain thundered. "The Devil's at work—and he has one eye! *Belay!* I will know what I must know."

Turning back to me, the Frenchman drew his flintlock pistol and pointed it directly at my forehead.

"Now then, name the traitor who brought you here!"

His voice went through me as if the gun had fired and, for a moment, I was frozen. How could I explain what I knew nothing about? And even if I could, I was clearly on the wrong side. My mind fought to construct a story that would buy us time.

"Please!" I choked. "Something to drink. My throat... I can hardly talk!"

The captain nodded to Ditty Gunn who used his dagger to cut down the leather wineskin that hung from the ceiling. He snatched it up from the floor and tugged the wooden stopper out of the throat. Holding the bag a few inches from my lips, the Scotsman tipped it forward until a thin stream of clear liquid splashed into my mouth and ran down my chin. I took a deep swallow before I even knew what I was drinking. The warm burn washed down the back of my throat and into my belly. It was the most lethal rum I had ever tasted and it took my breath away. As the warmth spread down through my extremities, I realized that another swallow might cloud my thinking and the result could be disastrous.

Gunn held the bag forward to administer another dose. I shook my head.

"So, you have had your drink, *mon ami*. Now explain yourself!" the captain barked, his patience clearly running thin.

I glanced over at Burrage, who simply looked down like a condemned man.

"It's true," I started out. "We came here... looking for someone. We, uh, we looked around a little bit and, uh, we realized it was wrong to be here so we were trying to find our way back. That's when you found us, I guess, and you thought we were trying to steal something, it sounds like. And we were, actually... Food! We needed some food. Although, if we could just get out of here, we wouldn't need any food. We could find some up there, if you would just show us the way out."

I saw the thumb pull back on the firing mechanism. Candlelight glinted along the rough, crooked edge of the flint that was clamped tightly in the jaws of the hammer. I could imagine the spark it would make as it struck the frizzen and ignited the powder in the pan. The flash would then find its way down the hole and into the barrel where a large, lead ball was packed against 50 grains of black powder. The powder would explode and hot gasses would immediately expand sending the ball careening down the barrel, out into the candlelight, through the bone at the front of my skull and into the soft tissue of my brain.

"*Buckett!*"

The word hung in the air. It was the sound of Burrage's voice and my eyes left the barrel of the pistol and glanced over to see my friend straining forward against his chains.

"It was Buckett. *He* told us to come here. He... he told us not to talk to anybody."

The Frenchman turned to Burrage. His voice was calm, almost gentle.

"And when did Monsieur Buckett tell you to come down here. Please, I would like you to tell me that."

Burrage shot a look in my direction and shifted uncomfortably against his shackles.

"He just told us... last night."

Quill and the Scotsman looked at one another. I could tell something was very wrong. I looked over toward Burrage to see if he had picked up on it, but he was too engrossed with getting the words to come out of his mouth.

"We aren't really sure what he wanted us to *do*, though."

The captain stretched out to his full height and lowered the pistol to his side.

"That is truly a miraculous thing, *n'est pas?* Imagine, Monsieur Quill! Ned Buckett, a man who has not said a word since his lying tongue was cut out of his head on Hispaniola 20 years ago, Ned Buckett *spoke* to these two men only last night."

The air left my lungs in a rush. *My God.*

Burrage simply stared ahead, made numb by the thought of the certain death about to befall him.

The captain motioned for Quill and Ditty Gunn to join him in the corner on the opposite side of the cell. Turning their backs on us they briefly held council, then fell silent. Turning toward us once more, the captain studied me for a few moments, then quickly ducked through the doorway and left, followed closely by the Scotsman. Quill waited until they were gone, then slowly walked back to where we lay trembling against the stone.

"Have ye 'ad business wiv a one-eyed man or spoke to such?" he asked, looking first at Burrage and then at me.

Burrage and I again glanced at one another.

"I'll tell ye plain. If ye wish to live another hour, ye will say what ye know and say true. The Cap'n, I never seen 'im spare a man what hath lied to 'im so bold as ye. It's only the Articles what saved yer scales and ye can set yer wager there, by thunder.

"The Cap'n's gone off to lay 'er before ship's company and I go now to join 'em. It could go hard wiv ye, that's certain. Ye don't belong here, yet, here ye be an' it can't be undone. But if you've a chance to save yerselves, pray set yer words to the mark. That's all I can say to ye."

With that, he turned to leave.

"Who *is* the captain? What is this all about?" I asked, unable to withhold the question any longer.

Quill spoke as he retrieved the lock from the dirt and set it back to work.

"Bartholomew de L'Hiver, a Frenchman o' redeeming qualities."
He paused, as if about to say more, then melted away in the darkness.

C H A P T E R   8

*H*e was a large man, well over six feet tall with big bones and a full face. When he stood erect, however, there was a considerable hunch to his shoulders that caused his head to ride lower and closer to his chest, giving him the look of someone trying to avoid scrutiny. But there was no ignoring him because, in fact, he looked hideous. His most grotesque feature was the eye; not the pale blue eye that was in perpetual motion, darting this way and that, seemingly able to rotate a reptilian 180 degrees. It was the eye that was conspicuous by its absence. To the right of his nose was a dark crater, lined with tortured skin that had turned almost black from the years of exposure, grime, and disease.

When he was born, he had two wonderful eyes—bright, blue—ready to drink in the innocent visions to which all children are entitled. The son of a struggling poet and a startled milkmaid, his birth above a tavern on the London waterfront was, in itself, unremarkable. Four weeks before the child's entrance into the world, his father had made the mistake of publicly reciting an unflattering sonnet aimed at the local magistrate. He was promptly bundled off to a prison hulk where he died of an infected rat bite within a matter of weeks.

For two years the young child was raised with the help of the milkmaid's great aunt, an alchemist (or witch, according to those who availed themselves of her services). The aunt was Aifric Wormsley, named for the 12th century bride of Olaus the Swarthy, King of Man. Her specialties were poultices for the treatment of parasites such as common lice, toe weevils and various pests of the nether regions, although she was rumored to dabble extensively in the black arts as well. She conducted her business from an abandoned privy that she had moved from its original location behind a butcher shop to a site off of Billingsgate Wharf near Lower Thames Street. Her customers were mostly fishmongers and prostitutes who would step up to her tiny booth to purchase a penny's worth of dagger root paste or a pinch of belly bitters. It was Aifric Wormsley who gave the baby his name: Melchior.

When the boy was 29 months old, his mother, Dolora, suffered a freak accident while leading a small herd of cows back to the milk yard one spring evening. As she leapt to avoid treading on the body of a dead crow, she slipped on the muddy path and one of the huge beasts stepped on her throat, crushing her windpipe. She rose to meet her Maker the following morning. Melchior was to spend the next nine years as his aunt's apprentice.

Even for the times, his life was harsh. His days, often 20 hours long, were spent gathering wild herbs, begging in the streets, or committing petty crimes. Other hours were given to mixing Aifric Wormsley's homeopathic inventory or participating as a foil in her fortune telling. And whenever one of her potions required a few drops of virgin's blood, his arm became the source.

Shortly after his eleventh birthday, three key facets of his life converged: his knowledge of the black arts, his total absence of a moral compass, and an unwillingness to tolerate his aunt's abuses any longer. One night, as Aifric Wormsley lay in a gin-induced stupor, young Melchior mixed a caustic syrup, which included, among other ingredients, molten lead and ox urine. This elixir was then poured into her left ear and after 15 excruciating minutes, she, too, had slipped the bonds of her earthly existence and proceeded to wherever it is depraved alchemists go.

Within hours, young Melchior Wormsley was making his way to the

Port of Bristol where he signed on board the merchantman *Dalliance* as a carpenter's apprentice, then sailed off to the West Indies. He had with him: 14 shillings, a cruel dagger that he had removed from the chest of a footman he found floating in the Thames, a large piece of yellow cheese, and a silver ring fashioned in the likeness of a human skull. He had cut the ring from the hand of his late aunt. It had been designed so that one's finger passed between the upper and lower jaws of the gaping mouth. Aifric Wormsley had used the ring as a medium for communing with the dark powers and had even named it—Evil Tom.

Melchior Wormsley never arrived in the West Indies. Three days out of Bristol, *Dalliance* came under the scrutiny of a heavily armed Spanish vessel and began what would be a four-day chase across the Atlantic. Three hundred miles northwest of the Azores, the Spaniard overtook *Dalliance*, firing several nine-pound balls into her sails as a warning. When the merchantman hove to, she was immediately boarded by cutthroats under the command of Fernando Cruz, also known as "The Sea Cook," so-named for his penchant for roasting his enemies on a pig-spit. The year was 1682.

After the obligatory deprivations, several of the most troublesome of the *Dalliance* crew were simply thrown overboard while the rest were forced to sail to Spain where both cargo and ship were sold. Melchior and the fifteen remaining Englishmen were deemed fit for labor and promptly shipped on a galleon to Hispaniola where they were sold into slavery. Their new master was Eduardo Leonadis de Leone, the owner of a small sugar plantation. Within twelve years, only two of the original *Dalliance* company were still alive, Melchior Wormsley and a seaman by the name of Ned Buckett.

In the third year of servitude, a most unfortunate episode occurred. Ned Buckett, exhibiting extremely poor instincts, complained about the live maggots he had discovered in the slurry he was eating. Within an hour, his tongue had been torn from his mouth and nailed to a tree next to the huts where the plantation slaves were housed, a sign to all that they should be grateful for any unexpected protein that might wriggle its way into their diet.

It wasn't until nine years later that Buckett and Wormsley were able to take advantage of the chaos following a devastating hurricane and escape along with six other Englishmen and a Dutchman named Van Weir. Hiding in the remote countryside for several months, they eventually made their way to the north coast where, after murdering a Catholic missionary and his two Indian servants, they took possession of his small boat, an open 26-footer with a gaff-rigged sail. Under cover of darkness, the fugitives set out to the northwest, making for Isle de la Tortue, a former buccaneer stronghold that was still the occasional stopping place for a number of vessels operating independently in Caribbean waters.

Within a month of making landfall, all eight joined a crew of vrijbuters, Dutch privateers, who had visited the island to take on water and hunt for wild pigs. However, the newcomers soon became disenchanted with the indecisive Dutch captain and it was agreed that the nine would leave the vessel at the earliest opportunity. That turned out to be Port Royal, the once flourishing haven for pirates, privateers, and freebooters. Although struggling to recover from the earthquake of 1692, the Jamaican port continued to serve as a rendezvous for ships and crews plying the waters of the Spanish Main, the trade route between Spain and the New World.

While the band was awaiting the right opportunity to sign on board a ship, the Island of Jamaica was invaded by Jean-Baptiste du Casse and his buccaneers and within a short time, they had overrun the place. One of his lieutenants was Bartholomew de L'Hiver, an ambitious man who had grown weary of his status as an underling. Upon arriving in Port Royal, de L'Hiver patched together a crew of smugglers and rogues from a wide range of nationalities and backgrounds. Wormsley and his fellows were among them.

One moonless night, he led his new recruits out to one of du Casse's corsairs, which was anchored in the harbor. Once the interlopers had crept aboard and made their presence felt, the few men left guarding the ship exercised superb judgment and immediately joined the new owners. The ship, *Le Cheval d'Or*, was a trim vessel, fitted with 12 guns and a staggering arsenal of small arms and powder—the perfect craft for their purposes. Within a year, *Le Cheval d'Or* had taken over 20 prize ships, though, none was carrying the type of rich cargo that the crew was seeking.

It was during this voyage that Melchior Wormsley truly found his calling and honed the skills he would need to pursue it. On numerous occasions, the victim ships were large enough or foolish enough to believe they could hold off the assault of de L'Hiver and his band of brigands. In the ensuing battles Wormsley discovered, much to his perverse satisfaction, that he had a real gift for mayhem. Part of this success was due to his size, which he used to simply overpower many smaller opponents. His weapon of choice was a heavy cutlass with a scallop shell hilt. Wielding his steel like a machete, he slashed and ripped his way through armed encounters using his superior reach to offset his initial lack of experience. But with time, he learned the art of the cutlass, the dagger, and the pike and, most importantly, the deadly cunning that he would need when dealing with enemies and friends alike.

After a year, *Le Cheval d'Or* visited Isle de la Tortue for fresh water and found itself sharing a small cove with an English privateer captained by Edward Deevish. Deevish, in fact, turned out to be a poor leader and was demoted by his crew after only two weeks at the helm. However, at the time the two vessels converged, the idea of finally serving under an English commander appealed to Wormsley, Buckett and several of their mates. So, by mutual consent, they left de L'Hiver and joined the Englishmen aboard the *Trident*. This turned out to be only one of many bad associations over the next decade and Wormsley did little more than survive a succession of unlucky ships and ill-fated expeditions.

On one of the last of these, he had the misfortune of losing his right eye as the result of an encounter with an axe-head. As he was following a boarding party up the side of a Spanish brigantine, the fellow above him took a musket ball square to the face and fell backwards from the taffrail. On his journey to the water below, the dead man's body brushed past poor Wormsley and, as luck would have it, the spike end of his boarding axe scooped Wormsley's eye completely out of his head. He was forced to finish the day's work with the remains dangling on his cheek like a pocket watch.

He somehow survived the subsequent infection by keeping the ravaged socket packed with a poultice of pork fat and saltpeter, but the experience transformed him forever. He progressed from being merely a soulless brigand to being a mentally unstable one as well. There seemed to be no limit to his capacity for treachery, paranoia, and bizarre behavior. He would often be discovered in deep, mysterious conversations with Evil Tom, the silver ring that he had somehow managed to avoid losing all these years.

Among his fellows, he was both feared and reviled, although his prowess in a fight was still highly regarded. But most would have little to do with him, if not for his unpredictable nature, then for the sorry state of his hygiene. In an era when cleanliness was universally in short supply, Wormsley, or "Worms" as he came to be known, had taken the concept of filth to a different level entirely. With rotting teeth, running sores and skin stained with the bilge-slop of his daily existence, Worms was a portrait of human decay.

It was the decay of his buccaneering life, however, that once again brought him back to a ship captained by Bartholomew de L'Hiver. Marooned on a tiny island in the Bermudas, Worms and a small contingent of his shipmates were picked up one day by de L'Hiver, who was on a journey to the New England colonies. There, he intended to sell off two ships of molasses that his men had captured near Santo Domingo. De L'Hiver was desperate for men to crew the two prize vessels and gladly took on those he knew to be able mariners. Along with Worms, Ned

Buckett, and Van Weir was a New Englander named Jack Wiggin, who had become known to shipmates as Jack Wager thanks to his penchant for gaming; William Reddish, who was called simply Snitch; and Thelonius Daggett, a Cornishman of limited mental dexterity. This was the crew that sailed north and, in the process, was to change my life.

Burrage was a mess—completely shell-shocked. His mouth gaped open and his eyes simply stared into space. As for me, my head was throbbing thanks to the blow I had received from the Frenchman. The fact that I couldn't reach back and survey the damage made the injury seem even more onerous. I imagined a fractured skull with blood and brain oozing out from beneath my hair. After all, our recent encounters had already proven that no flight of fancy, no matter how dark, was too awful to be true.

We lay in an exhausted trance for what seemed a long time. At one point I closed my eyes and tried to sleep, hoping to fortify myself for whatever might lie ahead, but it was no use. I remained in a state of semi-consciousness, a perilous condition when your mind is wracked with fear. Every sound, every sensation, every thought became a trigger for runaway images of chaos and destruction. A Calvinist preacher couldn't have painted a more lurid picture of Hell and all its torments than I had managed to conjure up with a simple climb down a ladder. The need to flee was so strong, the fact that I was totally immobilized nearly drove me into a frenzy. I could finally understand how an animal might chew off its own leg to escape from a trap.

As tortured thoughts raced through my brain, a sixth sense caused me to glance up toward the cell door. There, sitting like a bloated hobgoblin on the other side of the bars was the ubiquitous Lady Jane. She stared at me with disdainful yellow eyes and indulged herself in the unexpected pleasure that my suffering provided. It was a windfall for her, clearly. I was struck by how seamlessly she managed to fit into this landscape of depravity—like a sociopath in Times Square or a fungus on a rotting log. I screamed at her and kicked a handful of loose dirt in her direction. My futile efforts only intensified her sense of superiority and she basked in the glow of my simmering hatred.

Suddenly, like a small disturbance on the surface of a pond, her calm demeanor was interrupted. At first, she merely rotated an ear slightly off-center. Then, her head jerked quickly to the right and she hunched down her body, staring off into the void behind her. Her tail began to writhe violently from side to side like a snake that had just been separated from its head. Finally, she crouched down low to the ground and silently slipped away in the darkness.

For several eternal seconds, all was deathly silent. Burrage sensed my anxiety and also began to scan the shadows beyond the cell door.

"What is it?" he whispered to me. "Do you see something?"

"No," I replied. "Just a feeling I got. I don't know why."

We both continued to peer into the darkness.

"Maybe they're coming back," he said.

"Maybe," I agreed.

At that moment, I caught a glimpse of an icy blue light shimmering in the inky blackness. It was just a pinpoint and it reminded me of the first pale star you see just after sunset. It seemed to move slightly and then blink on and off several times before it vanished altogether. I heard the soft clang of metal, then—nothing. The hair on my neck stood straight on end.

"Something's out there," said Burrage as his breathing became shallow and rapid. "Something's moving."

We stared until our eyes stung with the strain. I became suddenly grateful for the stout iron bars that separated us from the mysterious realm beyond. A moment later, the temperature dropped about 15 degrees and the strong odor of salt air and low tide filled the tiny chamber. A thin, gray mist curled slowly through the bars and droplets of moisture condensed on our iron chains and chilled our bare skin. The fog grew thicker until it became as dense as smoke and the tiny candle flame was reduced to a pale halo upon the wall. Even the smallest sounds from our moving became magnified and echoed from the walls like the noise of a stone dropped down a well.

I heard the cell door begin to creak and groan as if someone was trying to force it open. Peering through the thick vapors that now filled the room, I saw that the outworn padlock was still in place upon the hasp, but as I looked more carefully, I could see it shiver and wobble as the door strained against it.

"Oh, God—who's *that!*" Burrage quaked.

"Where?" I asked as the candle flame began to flicker wildly in the mist.

Looking back toward the door, I again saw the pale blue light, only this time it was no longer a mere speck blinking in the darkness but an orb burning coldly, staring at me. As I watched it float hypnotically beyond the bars, I saw a shadowy face slowly come into focus around it. First, the dark brown skin and the thick, frowning brow; then the sunburnt nose leading down to a grim, motionless mouth; and, finally, the shock of black hair that fell about the face in ragged chaos. A brief glint of gold shot through the bramble of hair, then disappeared. Across the cheekbone, I could see the dark lines of an aboriginal tattoo that laced downward only to become lost in the stubbly growth that covered the lower cheek and jaw. The right side of the face was still in shadow and invisible to me as was the body, which, I prayed, the apparition still possessed. The vision filled me with even greater sense of foreboding than that of the haunted Boden Welkie.

Still the iron door ground against itself and at times appeared to bow inward as if from some great outward pressure, although no physical object could yet been seen. The lock twisted and shook and tiny flecks of rust sifted down from the iron hinges. Finally, a black claw of a hand curled itself between the bars, grasping the iron between its fingers and gave a mighty wrench! The door shuddered, but held firm!

I looked up to see the eye blazing with cold fire. Just at that moment, voices could be heard approaching from down the tunnel and the face vanished as if a shroud of black velvet had been thrown over it. The mist evaporated and the candle flame settled into a steady, gentle flame once more.

✳ ✳ ✳

I felt the pressure of a hand on my back as I was shoved along the stone passageway. A set of iron manacles cut into the skin around my ankles. These were joined to one another by a heavy chain, which dragged in the dust as I walked. My arms stretched out before me, drawn by a second chain that was held firmly in the bear-like paw of Ditty Gunn. I could hear Burrage's labored breathing as he stumbled along somewhere in the darkness behind me. The passage wound downward for about forty yards or so and we turned into several side tunnels, finally emerging in the large storeroom where we had first laid eyes on our captors. Upon entering, we were pushed roughly to the ground and lay face down on the cool, earthen floor. I wiped the dirt from my lips and managed to pull myself into a sitting position.

"*Alors*, get them to their feet!" barked the familiar voice of the French captain, Bartholomew de L'Hiver.

Strong hands grasped my shoulders and hauled me up to a standing position next to Burrage. I raised my head and stood wide-eyed at what I saw. The room was literally filled with a cast of characters straight from the dark-hued brush of Howard Pyle. Pyle, an artist known for his gritty, hard-bitten illustrations of buccaneers from the Golden Age of Piracy, a period spanning roughly a hundred years from the early 17th to the mid-18th century. I had seen such illustrations in several books that Myles Castler had leant me because of my interest in New England maritime history. As I slowly scanned the room, those images now surrounded me, larger than life and in three dimensions, living, breathing beings from a time long past and impossibly far away. For a brief moment, pure wonder replaced sheer dread and I drank in the mystery of the journey that I had taken.

Each individual stood in stark contrast to every other, although all shared the ragged, timeworn nature of both costume and features. Virtually every piece of cloth, some quite finely made, was now tattered with holes. Scraps of fabric hung in shreds about a shoulder or knee. Once rich shades of burgundy, purple, or green were now muted by the effects of hard use, dirt, and weather and all took on a deep gray hue as though filtered through the dark glass of time. Yet, every now and then, a bit of silver thread or the sheen of fine velvet would reflect the soft candlelight and bring a flash of color or the sparkle of past glory to the tertiary palette of the room. Most feet were covered with old leather shoes, some buckled, others corded. Some feet were bare, although because of tar, dirt and calluses it was not immediately obvious.

Hair was worn long for the most part, though often gathered in a seaman's braid or left hanging loose about the shoulders, and was infused with the same grime and dishevelment as the clothing. Skin was weathered and taut, ravaged by thousands of days in tropical sun or freezing salt spray and often adorned with exotic tattoos or bits of shell or silver imbedded in an ear or hung about the neck. Such teeth as were visible resembled wood more than ivory—yellowed, broken or rotted, if there at all. Perhaps I was most struck by the evidence of extreme violence, which seemed to exist everywhere I looked, missing fingers or a whole hand, half an ear, a misshapen limb. There were the countless scars etched into faces, arms, necks and chests, some blood red, others black, and yet others pale and ghostly, as if carved by spirits with blades of vaporous steel.

The company was lightly armed. The occasional flintlock pistol hung from a shoulder strap or lay tucked into a sash worn around the waist. More common was a dagger or even a small seaman's ax. Heavier weapons—cutlasses, rapiers, pikes, or muskets—were virtually absent on the men, although several cutlasses and a dozen muskets were racked upon the far wall. The exception was a pair of stout hearties stationed near the passageway. Both were armed with several pistols and a cutlass each.

The multitude sat on barrels, kegs, or crates or stood silently in the shadows. Now, as I gazed at them in a circle around me, I became acutely aware of the expressions frozen on their mask-like faces. To say they were hardened would be an understatement. Almost to a man, they revealed a potent combination of fear and defiance. It struck me that these were men who had known much of both and that their ability to transform one into the other was what made them who they were. I, despite my shackles and exhausted condition, clearly inspired no small degree of anxiety in those around me. And as I watched, their trepidation slowly grew into a fierce determination that they would deal with me on their terms, not mine. Eyes flashed, mouths curled into sneers, and hands clenched into a fist or around the handle of a dagger. I shrank back as the palpable feelings of enmity hit me in waves.

"*Monsieur Quill*, stand to your duty," the captain continued.

All heads turned to the gray man as he came forward several paces and stood facing the Frenchman. He held a scrolled parchment in his left hand and brandished it as he spoke to the assemblage.

"Free men of the Comp'ny," he began, his baritone voice rolling smoothly from his tongue. "As was writ by us in the Articles and signed by us also, the Comp'ny hath spoke its mind regardin' the use o' the prisoners standin' now before us. As free men all, accordin' to shares, we agrees that these men shall stand duty as apprentice to the Comp'ny and shall provide such service as befits that station and shall be granted such return also. For these services and accordin' to the Articles, each shall receive one-quarter share ta be paid at the reckonin'. That's done!"

As I listened to Quill's words and tried to decipher the meaning, it dawned on me that he might be talking about us! I searched the faces of those gathered and saw nothing but the same disconcerting glares as before. A sturdy seaman, who I recognized as the knife-wielder that had dealt with poor Buckett, stepped forward and asked to speak.

"Put 'em to work, so say I—but as apprentice? Think on't! We ain't at sea where they can roam a deck with naught but brine 'twixt them an' home. How can they do their service hung in chains, but if done wi'out, what's to keep 'em from slippin' their cables? Who knows what mischief they could then bring upon us!"

Several in the mob grumbled their agreement.

"Here now, Master Snitch," replied Quill. "Seein' as ye hath the good o' the Comp'ny at the foremost, you shall serve as master and tutor for the one, and Ditty Gunn t'other! And fear not, they'll not be entirely unyoked."

With that he gave a motion and the burly Scotsman stepped forward with hammer and iron in hand.

"Ditty Gunn. Make fast the prisoners," the gray man ordered.

In a few swift strokes, Gunn had freed us from our shackles and I gratefully rubbed my tender wrists with my fingertips. But no sooner had one burden had been lifted, than another was laid down. Heavy collars of iron were placed around both our necks and quickly locked with padlocks. Each collar had a large ring attached to it.

"Here now," Quill continued. "When at their labors they shall be fitted thusly! When at rest, ye shall anchor 'em fast to the wall or some such place with a length of chain. Gunn shall 'ave the key."

Seeming none too pleased with his assignment, the man called "Snitch" nonetheless allowed that the restraints seemed adequate and he stepped back into the crowd. When the murmurs had died down again, the quartermaster addressed the room and the company quickly dispersed, ducking down tunnels like weasels down a rat hole. Soon, there were none left with Burrage and me but Gunn, Snitch, and the captain. He stumped over to where we stood and turned to face us. I knew every word he said would be critical to our survival.

"You are now apprentice to the ship's company, which means that instead of lying comfortably chained to a wall, you will have to work for your supper," he chuckled coldly. He then brought his face close to ours and spoke with all the ritual grace of a swaying cobra about to strike. "Do not run. Do not steal. Do not fail in your service, or even the Door will not stand between you and a Spaniard's death!"

With that, he turned on his heel and left the chamber.

I awoke to a painful wrench on the iron collar around my neck. It was Burrage who, in the throes of a fitful dream, had jerked into a sitting position. The chain, which had been threaded through the rings on both our necks, was securely wrapped around the base of a stout timber that stood near the cook's hearth in the storeroom. My entire body ached from the hours spent sleeping on the bare floor and my head, though not as severely injured as I had first imagined, still throbbed with pain every time I moved my neck. I sat up blinking and shook Burrage to get him fully awake.

Scattered about the storeroom, which also served as the tavern when our captors felt the urge for a noggin of spirits, were the prostrate bodies of a half dozen rogues who had drunk themselves into unconsciousness a few hours before. One of these was Snitch, who now lay draped over a large crate; his head flung back like a dead squirrel. I watched with fascination as a cloud of small insects flew about the open chasm of his mouth, flitting back and forth through his exhalations like tiny hawks soaring on a thermal above a sinkhole. Every now and then, one would disappear between his lips, some to reappear a few seconds later, others never to be seen again.

"Max..."

"Yeah, Burr?"

"Do you see what I see?" Burrage asked.

"You mean the bugs?"

"Yeah. What's wrong with these people."

"I don't know, Burr, but frankly, considering everything else that goes on down here, having a few bugs in your mouth probably doesn't register real high on their list of worries."

"Well, it's making me sick," Burrage exclaimed, then moved on to the bigger, more obvious question. "What in God's name do we do now?"

"I just keep trying to wake up," I sighed.

Burrage pulled himself over to the timber and leaned his back against it. It was the first he had spoken since his ill-fated story about Ned Buckett.

"At least it looks like they're not gonna just—you know—*kill* us," he whispered. "If we can just hang on without pissing them off, maybe we'll get a chance to slip away. What do you think this apprentice thing is all about anyway?"

"I have no idea. All I know is I have to eat something, drink some water. Where's that guy with the key? You see him?"

"Uh-uh," Burrage replied.

It felt for both of us that the first wave of panic had passed. We were still alive. It sounded like they were planning to use us somehow, which I assumed, meant they had to feed us. I could see scraps of food—bread, some kind of meat—left sitting on various surfaces about the room. They, too, were surrounded by clouds of insects but I wasn't feeling picky at that point.

Just at that moment, Ditty Gunn strode into the storeroom and paused for a moment to make sure we were still where he had left us. He then walked over to one of the sleeping men and picked up a pewter tankard that sat a few inches from his outstretched hand. With a quick gulp he drained the contents and proceeded on to several other cups and bowls, repeating the process each time. With a wipe of his sleeve across his mouth he again turned to us.

"Ha' ya slept well, then?" he asked, enjoying our misery. "I'll wager ya could do wi' a bit a food now, could ya na'?"

He snatched up some of the table scraps and tossed them down to us as you would a dog. Unwilling to give him the satisfaction, I let the food lie untouched at first.

"Suit yersel'!" he snorted.

"We need some water," I said firmly, hoping he would respect a show of confidence, no matter how contrived.

"Do ya indeed?" he answered gruffly, yet still, he went to a barrel and dipped two wooden bowls in the contents and set them on the ground near my feet.

The greasy bowls did, in fact, contain water, tasting somewhat mossy but cool and wet, a godsend for our parched throats. We divided up the bits of dry bread and several scraps of pork fat and feasted hungrily. As I chewed the grisly pork, I asked Gunn what was to be expected of us now.

"You'll earn yer bread, I can promise ya tha'. You're marked for the Works," he answered.

"What are the 'Works'?" I asked.

"You'll find out sooner than ya may wish!" he grunted. "Now, I s'pose I shall know yer names?"

"Our names?" I replied, suddenly feeling like I was avoiding a telemarketer. "Maxwell. Maxwell Blessing. And this is Peter Burrage."

The Scotsman spat wetly on the ground near my feet.

"English nae doubt," he sneered. "Nae Scotsman would present himsel' so foppish as the two a' ya."

Gunn turned and filled another water bowl. After taking a drink himself, he threw the remaining contents in the face of the sleeping Snitch, who, sputtering angrily at his rude awakening, toppled to the ground and began to swear blue fire. As Gunn looked on with amusement, Snitch clambered to his feet and took a threatening step toward his antagonist who in turn, calmly drew the dagger from his sash and leveled it at the stocky seaman's throat. Snitch, momentarily knocked off stride by this show of force, stopped in his tracks and considered his options. Then, carefully wiping the water from the stubble on his chin, he allowed as how he could go along with a little joke and that no real harm had come of it. I could see, however, that there was no humor in his tone and I got the distinct feeling that the "little joke" would not be forgotten. Snitch struck me as one with whom you did not want to trifle, for while he played the part of a deferential man, he had the cold, calculating eyes of an assassin who knew how to bide his time.

Gunn, on the other hand, left nothing to the imagination. Though not huge in stature, he carried himself like a fist poised to strike the chin of any man who offended him. And like many of his war-like race, he seemed more than willing to perceive an offense, even where none might be intended. Whenever he entered a room, his fellows were careful to give him a wide berth rather than risk being misunderstood. It was difficult to relax when he was about and that, I came to discover, was precisely why the French captain used him as his unofficial sergeant-at-arms. The fact that Gunn was also a Jacobite gave the Catholic de L'Hiver an additional sense of comfort among a crew that was otherwise top-heavy with Calvinists, agnostics, and Anglicans.

"Time ta see our new shipmates ta their posts, Master Snitch!" Gunn announced, as he unlocked our chain. "They're ta haul timbers up from the tide cave ta the auld works 'neath the kirkyard. Take the quiet one and I'll t'other."

With that he snatched me by the back of my jacket and hauled me to my feet. Snitch, grabbing a lantern, led the way, followed by Burrage, me and finally, Gunn. There was no small talk.

Once in the Hub, we took a right turn down the tunnel with the boat carving in the wall near the entrance. This was the very passageway that I had tried to explore just prior to my knock on the head. As we walked along, I realized that it was larger than most of the others—a good six and a half feet high and four feet wide in most spots. After traveling about 20 yards or so, we came to a massive wooden door made of oak timbers and enormous iron fittings. Gunn and Snitch slid a heavy wooden bar out from behind a large iron staple imbedded in the door frame and pushed the door outward. As soon as it swung open, the sound of the tide echoed through the tunnel and the air was heavy with the pungent odor of brine and tar. The sharp cry of a gull echoed loudly.

I looked triumphantly at Burrage who gave me a brief, grudging nod in return. Here, finally, was the source of those mysterious noises we had first heard in the Castlers' pantry years before. How ironic that such beguiling sounds would find us in such dire straits! Even so, I could not help feeling glad at the thought of the sea so close at hand and as we walked on, my step lightened.

After several minutes, we had reached our destination.

We were standing in a small cave, no more than 25 feet across and 10 feet high. But, unlike the other passages and chambers, this one was natural, having been created by some geological cataclysm eons ago. In fact, we could see where one side of the cave had once been joined to the other and where the fissure ran up along the ceiling in a long, craggy scar. The floor of the cave consisted primarily of jagged stones that had fallen from the ceiling and filled in the floor below.

Interspersed among the boulders was a soggy moraine of sand, crushed mussel shells and bits of black kelp, a brackish soup attended by swarms of flies. The stench of decomposing marine life was almost unbearable. And yet, penetrating the murk, a single, pristine shaft of sunlight sliced along the far wall, a warm, glowing messenger of deliverance. Clearly there was an opening and the thought that we might be so close to a patch of blue sky or a breath of fresh air was like an elixir!

Snitch allowed little opportunity for lifted spirits as he shoved us toward a pile of old ship's timbers and drift logs piled loosely to one side of the cave.

"Step lively!" he hissed.

Ditty Gunn now came forward.

"So ya see where the timbers are set," he said, walking to the far end of the cave. "Now, come wi' me ta bring in the rest."

With that, he disappeared behind the shelf and into the halo of light. Burrage and I eagerly followed and discovered that the opening did indeed lead to the sea. We emerged like moles blinking back the radiance of the midday sun and feeling the light wash across our cheeks like a warm towel.

The cave was imbedded in a wall of solid rock, which met the ocean and disappeared below the waves at our feet. The cave opening was actually at the end of a shallow ravine and partially sheltered from above by a long rock outcropping, which angled up and over us. I could see that the tide was out and that the ocean would actually enter the cave when the tide was at its peak. Gunn led us down the rocky trough to the edge of the water where several additional lengths of timber lay washed up on the boulders.

"Now then, these must come inside, as well," he ordered, pointing to the scattered logs. "An' take care nae ta be seen!"

Burrage and I moved out onto the rocks as far as we could. In reality, being seen was exactly what we were hoping for. I realized we had emerged from beneath the low cliffs that surrounded the base of old Fort Sewell, which lay at the entrance to Marblehead Harbor. The ramparts above, although not visible to us at this angle, had long been planted in grass and fitted out with blacktop walking paths. On a day like this one with blue skies and balmy temperatures, the place would be alive with joggers, dog walkers, and folks sitting on benches taking in the view. And if they couldn't see us here down below, surely a lobsterman or late-season sailor would spot us as they made their way around the point.

As we did our best to fumble around with a six-foot log that lay wedged in a small crevice, I twisted my head around to see if I could spot a passing boat, but the narrow channel between the fort and Marblehead Neck was empty. Strange, I thought, on a day like this. Gunn barked a quick order to get on with things.

Burrage tried to get his hands under the base of the log and lift from below. He yanked upward and the log suddenly came loose, teetering over the boulder and down to the water's edge. As we picked our way carefully among the rocks to retrieve it, I glanced again at the water. I had the eerie sense that something was amiss. Suddenly it struck me and I stood motionless gazing out over the water.

There were no lobster buoys bobbing in the channel or in the outer harbor. As I looked across the mouth of the harbor, I couldn't see the lighthouse in Chandler-Hovey Park at the far end of Marblehead Neck. My eyes followed the far shoreline and as the reality began to sink in, I grabbed Burrage's arm to steady myself.

"Burr!" I said, my mouth so dry I could hardly get the words out. "The houses on the Neck—they're all gone."

CHAPTER 9

*T*he boy sat shivering in a dank alcove near an old stone well. His fingers felt especially numb as they cradled the cold handle of the iron poker. William had found it lying in the dust in one of the tunnels off of the Hub and, although he had no idea how it got there, he suspected the worst. In any case, he was glad to have something with which to battle any unwanted guests, large or small.

His copper hair lay stiff and crusty against his forehead and as he tilted his head back against the rock wall, he realized how completely exhausted he really was. Although he had no watch, he guessed it had been eight hours or more since he had slipped away from his companions and continued the search for his father. The whole situation had simply gotten out of hand. Although he hadn't actually seen anyone, he had heard enough of the ghostly voices to know he was in a very bad spot indeed. Worse, he had no idea what fate might have befallen his father.

It had happened so unexpectedly upon their return from Vermont. He had just thumped his empty suitcase down the cellar steps when he observed Lady Jane disappearing into a crevice in the chimney foundation. His curiosity awakened, William had knelt down to see where the enigmatic cat might have gone, when suddenly, a dark figure had slipped past the opening on the other side of the bricks, briefly silhouetted in the glow of a faint light. The startled boy had nearly jumped out of his skin. Moments later, William distinctly heard the voice of his father echoing through the shaft and reasoned that the mysterious phantom must have been he. Within minutes, William had retrieved the small lantern and some matches from the mantlepiece and somehow managed to wriggle through the opening in the bricks. By the time his feet touched the bottom of the shaft there was no one to be seen, so he struck out through the tunnel following the distant sound of footsteps.

All that seemed so long ago. Now, he deeply regretted his impetuous leap into the throat of this dank, Gothic world. Any vestige of self-confidence was quickly eroding. And it wasn't simply the events of the last day that had deepened his feelings of vulnerability and isolation. In recent weeks there had been the voices late at night, as he lay awake in his bed, the footsteps in the hall, and the cold drafts that seemed to come from nowhere. He had wanted to leap from beneath the covers, run to his father, place each dark thought into those large, steady hands and watch them melt away in the warmth of grown-up reason and reassurance. But he never did. Each time he had tried to move the words from his brain to his tongue, a look in his father's eye would make him pause—something smoldering faintly just beyond reach. And so William's dark thoughts would sink back down into the silent regions of his mind.

So now he was here, a place where every boyish fear had somehow taken root and grown into a vast subterranean garden of gloom. His father was gone. Maxwell and that Burrage fellow, where were they? Harsh language and soulless laughter echoed through this seemingly endless catacomb, always just around a bend or with disembodied closeness. He struggled to free himself from the dark thoughts that had begun to sap mind and body of the strength he would need to go on.

He looked again at the fathomless pool of water as it lay black and still within a mossy turret of ancient stone. If he leaned out over the pool and looked up, he could see the lichen-covered rocks that lined the shaft and disappeared into the black void above. William decided that someone at the surface must have sealed it long ago. Here at passage-level, a number of stones had been carefully removed from the wall of the well, just above the water line, allowing tunnel dwellers to dip a bucket or jar into the pool. William had hoped the well might offer quick access to the world above and had been profoundly disheartened when he found it did not.

As he sat praying that some means of escape would magically present itself here in the shadows, his mind drifted back to his last day at school. Four days earlier he had been sitting in history class, heavy-lidded with his chin resting on the soft flannel sleeve of his shirt. Half-listening to Mrs. Gambino as she described the mathematical precision used to build the Great Pyramids, he became distracted by a tiny movement a few feet away on the window sill. Peering beyond the tumbling motes of dust that slowly migrated through a slice of sunlight, his eyes came to rest upon a drama in miniature. A fat, black fly lay on its back in the dander next to an old straw wrapper and a larval blob of melted crayon. The fly's tiny legs would pedal furiously for a moment or two, then suddenly stop as the last few watts of energy were spent. Each time its wings beat against the peeling paint, the ebbing carcass would rotate in tiny half-circles, its world upside down, its instinct for survival reaching beyond the limits of its life span. Within moments it became one of a dozen feather-legged cadavers strewn about the sill, each the victim of a closed window and a mindless need to be on the other side of it.

William had gazed about the classroom. To him it seemed like fly nirvana. Bits of half-eaten sandwiches in the trash can. A dripping faucet in the sink. No barn swallows swooping about looking for a quick bite. True, it was not the infinite space of the great outdoors, but still a generous, climate-controlled habitat that seemed more than adequate for the modest needs of a housefly. And yet, some primordial instinct had caused each of those little creatures to expend an inordinate chunk of their short time on earth bashing their tiny bodies against dusty panes of glass.

As he leaned against the tunnel wall, William came to the conclusion that, if he was going to get out in one piece, he couldn't panic. He had to adapt to his new surroundings and bide his time. If he focused on survival rather than escape, he actually might live long enough to come upon an open window, so to speak. Right now he had water. If he was careful, he might be able to slip back to the storeroom that he had discovered and liberate some food as well. Beyond that, he would focus on avoiding discovery. In this way, he felt he might buy the time needed to locate his father or at least find his way back to the surface.

Braced by the clarity of his new resolve, William leaned through the breach in the wall and took several long draughts of cool water from the surface of the pool. Warmed by a hearty shiver, he set his chin, firmly grasped his slender sidearm, and set off down the tunnel. At least for the moment, his spirit of adventure soared and his fears were tucked away.

As a pirate captain, Bartholomew de L'Hiver was one of a more shadowy species of seagoing predator. Unlike the notorious l'Ollonois, Rackam, and Teach, all of whom used their bloody reputations as a psychological shot across the bow, de L'Hiver preferred an ominous, disorienting silence. Where Bartholomew Roberts chose to pummel, sending vast flotillas in bold assaults against entire cities, Bartholomew de L'Hiver chose to haunt. He would stalk a merchant ship the way a vampire stalks a maiden, materializing out of the darkness like ectoplasm then leaving his victim adrift on the currents, empty and unexplained.

Unlike those captains who saw their ships as grand ornaments proclaiming their success, de L'Hiver fitted out his vessel as a messenger of fear and despair. He purposely allowed his ship to weather like the bones of a great fish bleaching in the sun. The sails he left to molder in dank holds until stained with mildew. He then hauled them up to be scrubbed with a special solution of hog bile, sulfur and resins which killed the rot and saturated the fibers with an ethereal, gray-green pigment, leaving them streaked like shrouds in a crypt. Where practical, he had them cleverly slit or gaffed in ways that made them appear shredded, yet left them undiminished in strength and performance. Above the water line, the hull was smeared with tars and oil to resemble rotting wood. The overall effect was exactly what he sought: a ghost ship dredged up from the nether world; a vision that would cause the stoutest sailor's heart to sink to the bottom of his boots.

To further the effect, de L'Hiver chose to approach his victims only from a bank of fog or the deepest shadows of night. A few lanterns might be set burning about the deck and his men would stand motionless at their posts or drape themselves as if dead amongst the rigging, their clothes in tatters and made gray with wood ash. Their faces and hair would likewise be powdered with ash and their eye sockets blackened with soot. The result was devastating—a ship of death, manned by wraiths or corpses. Those fool-hearty captains who lingered long enough to question their eyes soon found their ship overwhelmed by ghoulish boarders who swarmed down the lines like spiders on silk thread. Within minutes the hapless ship's crew had either been sent lifeless over the rail or, in rare instances, had a few likely hands added to the ranks of their captors.

Many buccaneers preferred to destroy the evidence of a raid by burning a victim ship. Not so de L'Hiver. He invariably chose to let the empty hull float off like the husk of an insect, sucked dry of its contents and cut loose from the web. He felt that when found, the mystery of its demise only deepened the fears of superstitious mariners. They, in turn, would pass the tale along in every dockside tavern from New Spain to Newfoundland. The latent horror these tales provoked only worked in his favor the next time his ship emerged from a fog bank. Even in instances when a prize ship managed to outrun him and slip away, the survivors only fed the panic with tales of the haunted vessel that had come upon them in the night. While pirates like Blackbeard, Low, and others inspired fear with the black flags they flew, de L'Hiver had managed to turn his entire ship and crew into a symbol of death and doom.

As effective as his strategy was in spreading terror among merchant vessels of the late 17th and early 18th centuries, what is more striking is how perfectly de L'Hiver's style manifested his inner nature, for he seemed born to the crypt.

Among his many backbreaking jobs as a peasant laborer, de L'Hiver's father had been a grave digger in post-Richelieu France in the village of Boult. In February of 1663, the impoverished Jean-Georges Claveau and his wife, Ninon, grieved at the sight of a new infant son. So deep was their despair that they neglected even to name him until they realized he would survive his first few weeks in the world. And so Bartholomew Claveau began his life.

Louis XIV, the Sun King, sat on the throne of France and for the great masses of poor in that suffering land, a new mouth to feed was as welcome as any other pestilence of the time. Throughout the province, vast herds of humanity migrated slowly through ravaged fields in search of half-rotted roots, carrion, or the straw with which to make "bread."

Throughout his early childhood, Bartholomew helped his father gather the corpses from roadsides and hovels. These they brought to nameless graves in the field outside the churchyard where they were stacked often five or six to a hole before a foot or two of soil was tamped upon them. Bartholomew would strip off any remaining rags and his father would then attempt to sell them for a trifle in the village. The task was theirs because few had the nerve to risk the disease that invariably claimed those that performed it and, in fact, when he was eight years old, Bartholomew saw his father bloat and die of a hideous gastric malady. His mother had herself succumbed to the pox two years after his birth and each of his four brothers and sisters was dead before he arrived. How he survived at all was a miracle beyond explanation.

With his father's death, so went Bartholomew's livelihood. His legacy however, was an intimate knowledge of the small abbey and the comings and goings of the brothers who served it. For the next several years, he lived entirely in the shadows sleeping by day in cellars and venturing out at night to steal scraps from the larder or, more often, the waste bucket the brothers used to feed the abbey's hogs and chickens. Compared to some others in the village, he ate like a king.

To pass the time, he explored the maze of subterranean passageways that led into the various crypts and tombs of well-to-do citizens who had been buried over the centuries in and about the abbey. He soon discovered that several of these graves had not yet been completely plundered of their valuables by the clergy and he eventually amassed a small collection of rings, lockets and bits of fine lace. On hot summer days he would lie about toying with spiders or newts until he fell asleep amongst the cool bones that lay scattered about the granite vaults. At night he would awaken and walk, pale and thin in the moonlight, through the churchyard and out into the woods and fields. Rarely did he see the sun and for seven long years not a soul knew he was even alive.

Finally, at the age of fifteen, he gathered together his small horde of treasures and walked by night until he reached the port of Calais. Once there, he exchanged his worldly goods for some decent clothes, several months of lodging and an unembellished Spanish rapier that had been part of the booty auctioned off by the crew of a French privateer newly returned from raids off of the coast of Portugal. His money having run out, he slipped aboard that same vessel and hid in the hold until the ship was several days out to sea. When finally discovered by the ship's cook, Bartholomew was hauled on deck where he was awarded 40 stripes and a blow to the head for his thievery. The punishment would have been far more deadly in nature but for the fact that the crew was shorthanded. Bartholomew was given a corner in the forehold and put to work learning a privateer's trade. When asked, he gave as his name as Bartholomew de L'Hiver, meaning "of the Winter," having been born in that season of ice and darkness.

Burrage and I stood silently gazing across the waves as gulls swooped down toward the deep blue water of the channel. I swallowed hard as I took in the alien landscape on the opposite shore. The fine, oceanfront homes—gone. The clusters of old maples and rich landscaping that ringed the harbor, the Corinthian and Eastern Yacht Clubs—all gone. All that was left was a long, rolling peninsula of rock and grasses with the odd clump of scrub pine or brambles nestled here and there along its spine. My eyes followed the shoreline all the way down to the low, pebble causeway that attached Marblehead Neck to the mainland. It was completely barren.

Off in the distance, I saw what appeared to be a pair of ragged-looking cows, two meandering specks that picked their way slowly up the rise toward a bank of clouds castling up over the headlands. It was like a postcard from northern Maine. Every detail that might have suggested the town of Marblehead had been scoured from the earth. Burrage was the first to speak.

"This isn't right, is it?"

"Uh-uh," I softly intoned. A harsh jerk on my iron collar brought me back to the moment. Ditty Gunn let out a cold chuckle.

"I guess yer heads is in a wee muddle, are they no'?" he observed with amusement. "Yer no' dreamin', I can tell ya tha'!"

Gunn seemed to sense that until we got our bearings, we'd be little use for the job at hand. Still, he was clearly amused by our anguished confusion.

"Yer no' deceived," he went on. "An' yer still where ya thought ya was. Same harbor. Same town. Ya just arrived a bit earlier than ya wished, is all."

It was almost impossible to believe that we somehow hadn't been transported to another, less inhabited place, the Maine coast, New Brunswick. But I sensed he was telling the truth. That this was Marblehead.

"How long ago?" I asked, barely believing I was asking the question.

"Three hundred years," Gunn answered. "Or there about, bein' as yer from The Key."

I shut my eyes.

A second later Burrage shook me out of my stupor. His eyes pleaded for help that I couldn't begin to give him. I knew he was going into one of his mind-locks, the way he did when he just couldn't cope at all. With impeccable timing, Ditty Gunn brought us back to the task at hand.

"Come now, ya simple squid!" he growled. "There's work ta be done and I ain't disposed ta do it mesel'! Fish that timber and be quick about it or there'll no' be supper fer ya this night!"

I motioned to Burrage to heft an end and we wrestled the heavy beam up over the rocks and into the cave where we added it to the pile.

"And the rest!" hissed Snitch, who sat puffing a clay pipe. "There's a dozen yet ta be brought in. I've seen dead men wiv more spark than the two o' ye!"

So, for an hour or more, we toiled until the stack of timber nearly touched the slanted ceiling of the cave. When Gunn was satisfied there were no more logs to be had, he bade us sit down on the rubble of the cave floor and passed a small goatskin of greasy water. While we drank, he studied us closely.

"Yer brain is still widdershins, I'll wager!" he mumbled. "A fine bit o' sorcery, I'd be thinkin', is it no' true?"

I glanced up and nodded. Sorcery indeed. As good an explanation as any I could muster.

"Well, I canna bring ya peace wi' the whole of it, but I must tell ya this much. If ye've a prayer ta see kith an' kin again, ya must ne'er venture outside this cave wi'out leave o' the Captain or the comp'ny o' yer mates. For yer own good, I tell ya this."

I was struck by the almost comic irony in this warning. Here we sat, shackled—enslaved—eating scraps of god-knows-what and drinking puddle water for all I knew, breaking our backs and breathing the aroma of dead crabs! And this thug—this kidnapping, brutish, nightmare of a man was telling us what was good for us. I almost laughed out loud, but one glance at the deadly serious looks on the faces of our companions caused me to swallow my bitter sarcasm. I took a different tack.

"Why is that?" I asked without expression. "Are you concerned we'll run off somewhere?"

Snitch immediately doubled over with laughter, spitting brown juice down the front of his shirt. I turned angrily toward Ditty Gunn, but before I could blurt out my indignation, he silenced me with a burning stare.

"Run off, ya say! Now tha' would be a pretty sight. An' where would ya go then, my pretty boys? The village? Why, you'd be lucky the old women dinna chop ya fer bait afore ya said yer name! You'd be penniless an' beggin.' No' an attractive prospect in this town, me wee dandies! Acourse, ya could try an' hide, filch a chicken an' such or some fish from the flakes. Don't get pinched though, laddies, for they'd haul ya up a stout tree by yer thumbs an' set the dogs about ya! Then, when ya was dressed out proper, they'd cut ya down, dip ya in a pitch-pot an' heave yer bones down the tide line. Run off, indeed!"

I was incensed at his low opinion of our ability to make our case, no matter what the year. After all, it was still a town of churches, sheriffs, magistrates and the like—a town of laws! And we had broken none, as opposed to our felonious companions. I felt certain the decent citizens of Marblehead, no matter how mean their lives, would welcome the opportunity to burn out the nest of rats living beneath their tiny village.

"Just thinking of us, I'm sure," I replied, careful to control the true level of disdain I felt for him. "I'm sure you have no concern for how the local citizens might view *your* activities here."

My mere hint of betrayal caused an even darker cloud to pass over the faces of both our captors. Ditty Gunn pulled me to my feet and breathed his words hot and slow into my face.

"Dunna make idle boasts or make lightly a threat ta any in the comp'ny, ya wee man. Ya don't begin ta know the half o' what ya speak. There's no' a soul in the village wouldn't drag yer poxy body back ta this cave and have a penny fer it! A third the comp'ny were born here or close enou'. You an' yer sorry lapdog are now apprentice ta the comp'ny, a *part*, ya see. The enemy we fear is the same one you should as well! An' it's time ya seen 'em."

With that, he dragged me roughly across the stones much as one would a sack of chickens. Pushing me out into the sunlight, he grabbed a fistful of my hair and jerked my head eastward and pointed out to sea.

"*There!*" he spat. "They ride high on the horizon!"

Still wincing from Gunn's iron grip on my hair, I strained my eyes to look out in the direction he indicated. Burrage was stumbling just behind me, his throat turning crimson from the pressure of Snitch's fingers wrapped about it. I couldn't see a thing other than the islands beyond the harbor,

"I don't know what you're pointing at! Do you mean the island?" I choked.

"Not *there! THERE!*" Gunn growled and I followed his gaze to a spot out in the water just beyond what I knew as Cat Island.

Beyond the rocky point to the right of the island I finally saw what he was so determined I should see. Three thin masts rose up behind the low granite hill. The sails were furled fast to the spars and it was clear that the ship lay at anchor. A second set of masts rose and fell several hundred yards northeast of the first and further out. That was all I could discern as the details were lost in the distance.

"Ya see now?" Gunn demanded.

"The ships you mean? I see two ships. What do they have to do with me?"

"Wi' *us*, ya cursed bloat! Wi' the whole comp'ny! The one is a man-o-war—*Catamount*—of Queen Anne's own navy. T'other, well, tha' be the knot fixed about our necks then."

Burrage managed to pull himself free of Snitch's grasp just before he passed out. Choking, he, too, looked out at the vessels riding the swells beyond Cat Island.

"What... what do you mean by *that?*" he rasped.

Gunn looked back at the nearly suffocated Burrage, still held roughly by iron collar.

"Cut loose o'im, damn ya!" Gunn barked at Snitch. "He's no use wi' his throat mashed like a pippin, now is 'e!"

Gunn released me as well and strode a couple yards forward to where the tide had started to rise ever closer to the mouth of the cave. He raised his voice to be heard above the pounding.

"T' other is our own ship, *Anne Boleyn*."

Enid Castler turned on the burner beneath the kettle and pulled a box of shortbread from the pantry shelf. They had just arrived home from Vermont minutes before and Myles had immediately repaired to his study. She knew he would welcome a late evening snack. Placing the freshly brewed tea on a wooden tray, she shuffled off down the hallway. After several sharp knocks went unanswered, she turned the handle and pushed the door open with her hip.

"Goodness, dear," she scolded. "You really must pull your head out of the clouds once in a while. See here, I've brought you some tea and shortbread."

Barely raising his head, Myles looked out over his spectacles and nodded to his wife. He set down the magnifying glass and leaned an elbow on a tall stack of old books sitting on his desk.

"I'm so sorry... didn't hear you quite," he apologized, gazing at the tray which was set before him. "Yes. Tea will do nicely. Thank you."

As he tucked a linen napkin into the front of his collar, he asked, "Are you quite tired, I suppose?"

"I'm satisfactory, considering the long drive. I must admit, I wish we could have stayed one more day as we had planned."

"Yes, well, I do apologize. You were most understanding. I simply had to get back to my work. Quite urgent, I'm afraid. Yes, indeed. And William, has he brought in the bags yet? He really should be in bed."

"He's got most of them in from the car," Enid nodded and tugged at a shank of orange hair that had broken loose and fallen down across her forehead.

"What keeps you so thoroughly fixed?" she asked, beginning to gather some of the old teacups that had collected on his desk. "You've barely caught your breath since we got back. Is it that book of charts you were going on about last week?"

Myles took a sip of steaming tea.

"No, no," he replied, watching her leave. "Just an old book on 17th century encryption."

A few minutes later, he had drained the last of the tea from the small china cup. The drive home had been exhausting and he felt another cup would keep him alert for the long hours of work ahead. He called to his wife, but when Enid failed to answer, he set off to find her.

A quick visit to the kitchen and a call down the cellar stairs were equally fruitless. He finally decided that she must be helping William bring the last bags into the house and had simply neglected to let him know. Climbing the stairs to the second floor, he noticed that the door to Maxwell Blessing's office was slightly ajar. That was odd. Myles peeked in the door.

"Everything all right, then?" he inquired as loudly as he dared.

Silence. He slowly pulled back the door and peered about the room. Almost immediately, his eyes fell upon the closet door that stood wide open revealing the low brick gateway.

"Oh my!" he gasped, kneeling down to examine the yawning, black chasm within the chimneystack. A hundred thoughts rushed through his mind and a bead of perspiration stood out upon his upper lip. "Oh my, indeed!"

Within minutes, Myles had retrieved his large flashlight and was carefully picking his way down the rickety ladder into the void below.

❊ ❊ ❊

As William approached the Hub, the haunted voices began anew— low murmurs and dark curses—all uttered in barely intelligible tones and with heavy accents. He paused, not knowing if he should reverse his course or simply push onward and hope that he would not be discovered. He realized that the path behind led nowhere but to the well—a dead end. He went on.

When at last he arrived at the Hub, it was clear that the loudest voices were emanating from the storeroom. His empty stomach growled regretfully. After several seconds, he decided to try the tunnel marked by the symbol of the small boat. At least that might prove to be a way out. Shifting the poker to his other hand, he set off.

He had not taken three steps when an enormous face materialized out of the gloom only inches from his own! Shaken to the core, he swung the poker in a great arch, hoping his desperate lunge would catch his assailant off guard. Instead, the force of the thrust caused him to spin on his heel and land hard on the floor. Immediately, he felt a rag being stuffed in his mouth and his arms being lashed behind him! With a heavy tug, he was hoisted up and tossed like a bale over a broad shoulder. His captor ducked below an archway and into the Hub. William groaned as he realized he must be on his way to the storeroom. But then, the man ducked into a smaller tunnel and sped down the passageway at a fast trot. As the Hub disappeared behind him, William was overcome with fear and despair.

After several minutes, the bone-jarring run had ended and William was thrown down upon a heap of moldering canvas and broken spars. He took in a deep breath of musty air and tried to hold back the sobs that he felt rising up from his belly. They caught in his throat and he lay coughing into the filthy rag that still filled his mouth. Not only did the rag make it hard to breathe, but it tasted of rancid cheese and grease.

William turned to get his first close look at the man who had abducted him, the mysterious Ned Buckett.

It took only a minute for William to realize that the ragged fellow could not speak, a fact that only made his anxiety grow. Who was this horrible man? What was his plan? William could only imagine his picture flashing up on the six o'clock news—the search parties, his parents weeping, pleading for his return—one that would never come. He felt truly ill and with great effort spat out the grimy rag from his mouth. He shot a glance at his captor to see if retribution was going to result. Buckett, in fact, at first made a move toward him but then merely raised a dirty finger to his lips to caution silence. William nodded.

Sensing he was in no immediate danger, William peered about the tiny alcove. Buckett had lit a candle and placed it carefully on a small ledge. In the resulting glow, William could see that he was in some sort of storage space, one filled with coils of rope, wooden kegs, and the type of hardware one might find aboard an old ship. The alcove had been carved out of the tunnel wall, although he had no idea which tunnel he was in. Across the way, he saw a narrow passage that quickly went black as pitch. The air seemed more still and dank than anywhere he had been before. He almost felt a pressure in his ears as if the atmosphere was too heavy for the space it occupied.

He nervously studied the burly sailor who now sat on the floor of the tunnel near the opening in the far wall. William had no real difficulty accepting that the man sitting a mere ten feet away from him was a pirate. He was still a child with an active imagination, someone for whom pirates were as likely as big game hunters or astronauts, other sorts of men he had never encountered, yet had no doubt existed. The question here, as in any case where pirates might be involved, was what kind of pirate was he?

His father had educated him to the fact that some pirates had been rather decent when it came to dealing with captives. Edward England, for example, had been known for his mercy and good nature. Some captains had even allowed a captured vessel to sail off with all hands or even half her cargo. William hoped that he was in the company of such a fellow now.

The man seemed quite worried, William thought, strange behavior for one so large and heavily armed in the presence of a mere boy. What could he possibly have to fear? It was then that William noticed the dark red crease across the fellow's throat. William swallowed hard and wished his hands were free of the biting cords that bound them behind his back. He wondered if he dared ask if they could be removed.

He was about to speak up when he noticed the candle flame flickering wildly as if buffeted by fast moving air, the kind created by movement in the tunnels. Ned Buckett sensed it, too.

As the seconds passed, Buckett became more agitated and William felt his own anxiety begin to well up once more. There was a sound now, a low, hollow tone somewhere between a whistle and a moan, like wind blowing through a narrow space. As the noise rose and fell, Buckett edged his way to his feet and turned his head nervously from side to side, backing slowly along the wall. Just as he reached the black opening in the wall, a filthy hand darted out of the darkness and grasped his tunic in a powerful grip, twisting the fabric and nearly lifting Buckett off the ground. With a startled gurgle, he was drawn into the shadows of the passageway, leaving William staring wide eyed and wondering what was about to befall him.

As he pulled frantically on the cord binding his hands, William heard harsh whispers coming from the shadowy tunnel. It was at that moment, in the flickering light of the candle, that he noticed the small, crude skull carved in the rock beside the entrance. It fairly matched the symbol he had seen in the Hub and the thought of it made him shiver. Several seconds later, Buckett emerged, his face an ashen gray and his jaw set hard against the gristle of his neck. He strode purposefully toward the spot where William lay and with a single motion, the barrel-chested seaman hauled him to his feet once more.

Holding William firmly at the throat with one hand, he reached behind his back and drew forth an evil-looking knife with a curved blade and a handle of yellowed bone. William's body went nearly limp as Buckett spun him round to the back. The boy shook as he waited for the thrust he knew must come and nearly collapsed at the sensation of his hands suddenly cut free from the leather cord. It took him several seconds to accept the fact that he was not dead and he immediately burst into

tears. Buckett, in a curious display of respect, allowed William a moment
to compose himself.

"Where am I? Who was talking to you?" William asked, turning his
head round and forgetting for the moment that Ned Buckett could not
answer.

The old sailor merely put a finger to his lips again and took hold of
William's arm, leading him off of the mound of old canvas and down the
main tunnel. The candle had been placed in a punched tin lantern and
little points of light danced across the craggy walls as they walked.
William realized they were moving further away from the Hub and deeper
into the tunnel of the skull. The fact that his hands were now unbound
made him feel slightly more hopeful that his fate would not be as grim as
he first had feared.

After several minutes at a brisk pace, they arrived in a curious spot
indeed. The tunnel had been rising steadily at a steep angle and it now
opened up into a low, domed room that was riddled with burrow-like
passages. These plunged crookedly off in many directions, some sloping
further upward and others dipping slightly down. It also appeared that
many of the passageways crisscrossed one another, the effect being that of
a great, neolithic termite mound. Buckett bade William sit upon a low,
oblong chest that lay half-buried in a clutter of dead leaves and dust
against a far wall. A number of lanterns burned deep within the warren of
tunnels and bathed the walls in a pale wash of light that seemed to glow,
liquid-like on the granite. Here and there, veins of dark earth broke
through the stone surface of ceilings and walls and root tendrils hung
down like the feathered legs of great insects. Mounds of loose dirt formed
small, conical piles along the floor.

William leaned his back against a wall of hard-packed soil and tried
to reassure himself. His heart had been pounding since the first encounter
with the seaman and a vast reservoir of adrenaline made it almost
impossible to resist the urge to explode down the tunnel or lose his keeper
in the maze of tunnels that surrounded him. However, the very fact that

he now sat unfettered made him suspect that any attempt to escape, no matter how likely it might appear, would somehow be thwarted in a way he could not yet surmise. How else to explain the casualness of Ned Buckett. And there was something else. His instincts told him that lurking just beyond his view was a dark presence that might prove far more dangerous than anything he had encountered up until now. Better to repress any impulsive actions for the time being.

Within seconds, his caution was validated. The sound of advancing footsteps began to echo from the direction that they had just come. William glanced quickly at Ned Buckett who, although in a state of high alert, was nonetheless composed. This suggested that the visitor was expected, a prospect that caused William's spirits to sag. He unconsciously pressed his body a little deeper into the shadows and narrowed his eyes in anticipation.

The steps grew brisk as a glowing halo of light bounced forward, heralding the stranger's approach. A nervous tremor worked its way down William's back and through his legs, which gave an involuntary jerk. The motion caused the unsecured top of the chest to slide open several inches. William glanced down, following the path of dim light that now illuminated a small area within. His eyes finally settled on a dark object, which was barely visible below the lid. At first he thought it was a knot of rags grown hoary with cobwebs and debris. As his eyes adjusted to the darkness, his mouth immediately went dry as dust.

It was a *head!* Eyes turned to leathery knobs and hair like a disheveled nest of white cornsilk in which rested a great, misshapen egg long gone to rot. Thin, leathery lips were pulled tightly back to reveal silent rows of blackened teeth sitting shoulder to shoulder as if in church, struck dumb and dead in their pews by some sudden, unforeseen cataclysm.

The sight so staggered him that William felt as though he could no longer breathe. It was as if a powerful force was pressing down on him and that he would soon be driven through the lid and into the terrible chest below! He gasped for air and pushed against the chest with all his might, suddenly breaking away and falling back into the room. Buckett, not knowing what was occurring, jumped to his feet and lunged wildly, trying to catch hold of the frantic boy's arm. William spun away in a frenzy of terror and stumbled blindly toward the main tunnel, turning his body to avoid the hulking seaman who now pursued him with desperate abandon.

Darting to the left and beneath Buckett's outstretched fingers, William rushed madly out of the chamber. And then, almost instantly, he found himself in the iron grasp of the mysterious stranger. The force of their collision had knocked the light from the stranger's hand and for a moment they were left struggling in the darkness. With a groaning twist, his assailant spun William around and pinned his arms behind him, forcing him out of the tunnel and back into the lantern light.

"Dear *God!*" the terrified boy heard a voice say. "William!"

William felt himself suddenly slide free and he spun about mirroring the incredulous expression on the face of his father, Myles Castler.

For a timeless interval, they simply stood staring at one another. It was not apparent which of them was the more thoroughly shocked. Once his body would again obey his mind, William rushed forward and buried his head in the folds of his father's heavy wool sweater. As he stood trembling with relief, the boy waited for reassuring arms to encircle him. He felt the hand upon his shoulder, but sensed a touch that was somehow tentative. As long as he had known him, William's relationship with his father had been defined almost solely by intellectual parameters. As in some British families, each member stood to some degree apart reflecting a certain determination to leave one another's emotions unencroached upon. Yet, William found his father's response cool to an extent that caught him off-guard and touched a dull pain deep within his heart.

Sensing the boy's state of mind, Myles realized that he had to take immediate action to resolve the situation.

"Mr. Buckett," he began, carefully pushing William to the side. "What is the meaning of this incomprehensible state of affairs?"

As soon as he said it, Myles remembered that the man he was addressing hadn't the remotest capacity to respond. "Where is he?" Myles then demanded, as if to himself.

William could barely keep up. His head was reeling.

"Keep the boy here. I'll find him myself!" Myles growled. With that, he retrieved his fallen light and quickly disappeared down the passage.

CHAPTER 10

After a brief respite, Burrage and I were returned to our labors. Our main task was to drag the heavy timbers, one by one, from the sea cave back to the Hub. From there, we were assured, the final leg of the journey would be even more taxing. As afternoon turned to dusk, the tide rose ever higher causing the cave to take on water. Before we knew it, we were toiling up to our knees in a cold, murky stew of floating debris. The work was exhausting and monotonous but it gave us time to reflect on the incredible revelations of the past few hours.

As hard as it was to believe, it appeared that we had, through some unimaginable contravention of physical law, been delivered to an as yet undetermined year in the early 18th century. I was infected with a sense of awe that bordered on giddiness; yet, at the same time, I was tormented by the knowledge that I was now totally out of control of my life.

The issue was no longer merely a matter of escape from bondage but escape from an entire world. Every fearful emotion that had plagued me since my first meeting with Boden Welkie was revealing itself in three dimensions before my eyes! When my fears were abstract, I could at least play at keeping perspective. But here, every dark thought, every moment of dread had a face as real as my own.

Burrage had remained remarkably intact, considering. I would have expected a far higher level of angst than he was exhibiting and, in fact, his complete immobilization would not have surprised me. Yet, here he was functioning at an almost superhuman level of acceptance—no dramatized whining, no righteous indignation, not even the asthmatic flailing that so often signaled the collapse of his emotional underpinnings. I confess, I found some measure of reassurance in his apparent ability to make peace with our new reality. Of course, the thought did cross my mind that whenever Burrage seemed most in control, it was generally because he had compensated with some borderline psychotic fantasy. The taxi-top episode was only one example.

I had deduced from bits and pieces of conversation that our final destination, "the Works," was a network of small tunnels. Apparently, the passageways in that sector had become unstable and needed to be reinforced with pilings to avoid collapse, hence, the gathering of timbers.

Once we had completed the backbreaking task of moving the posts from the sea cave to the Hub, we were permitted to fall back on the pile and catch our breath. In a grudging show of approval for our efforts, Gunn rewarded us each with a few sips from his rum skin. The liquid carved a channel down my parched throat and dripped like molten lava into my empty belly. It amazed me how a few drops of this crude elixir could have such an immediate and stimulating effect. Though thoroughly drained, I felt an immediate surge of energy to every muscle. And the results were not merely physical. An unexpected sense of euphoria proved a balm to my scorched psyche. I could see that Burrage was reacting in a similar manner.

Snitch observed our transformation with thinly disguised disdain. His look told us very clearly that rum or no rum, he thought no more of us than he would a dead roach on the bottom of his shoe.

"We shall see if ye polish up so pretty after a dozen marches to the Works, my fine yeomen!" he jabbed. "Rum 'as a way o' chargin' double for its services, ye may discover!"

Satisfied he had put us in our place, he gave Burrage a stout kick to the leg and bade us both rise and resume work. Hoisting a slippery log upon our shoulders, we looked about for direction. Ditty Gunn quickly motioned us toward the passageway directly across the room. As we ducked to enter, a small, carved skull grinned a dark warning from the wall.

We were not two steps down the passage when Ditty Gunn grabbed me by the shoulder and motioned me to an immediate halt. He and Snitch plastered themselves to the wall and strained their ears back toward the Hub. A great rushing sound began to rise toward us, like a strong wind blowing through the woods. Without thinking, Burrage and I dropped the timber to the tunnel floor and leapt to the wall as well. Staring out into the dim lantern light of the Hub, we saw the first figure emerge from one of the other tunnels as if propelled by a load of gunpowder. He staggered to the center of the room and stood like the hammer of a cocked pistol, straining against the spring. Within seconds, a dozen of his fellows burst into the room and took their places on high alert.

"Lively!" the voice of the gray man bellowed as Bartholomew de L'Hiver entered the Hub and filled the remaining space with his stormy countenance and flashing eyes. Down every side tunnel I could see many other heavily armed men cuing up like street gangs, waiting.

"Lively, ya spew-guts and hold-yer tongues, I say!"

Everything was suddenly still as death. Quill spoke again.

"All ears for the Cap'n now. All ears!"

De L'Hiver stood in the middle of the hard dirt floor staring intently at his boots. One could almost see the thoughts swirling in his brain like thunderheads before the storm. The air was so charged with portent that I half expected to see blue flames of electricity dance across his body in the dim light. Then in an instant, he came about to face the company.

"The time has come, *mes amis!*" he boomed.

Not a member of the assembly moved a muscle.

"The *Dartmoor* has now joined her sister north of the island and Sir Robert is preparing our welcome, have no fear! He means to see us dancing upon the Dock or sealed up like Tower rats! Old Beckie Broo has told our Jack that most of the folk above are gone—off to the woods for fear the town shall be burnt and them all with it! So, *mes amis*, how will you choose?"

My mind raced trying to catch up to the meaning of his words. I guessed that the *Dartmoor* was yet another British frigate and that she had joined *Catamount* out beyond the island. Apparently, this Sir Robert commanded the vessels and was planning some sort of assault on our stronghold and the wise citizens of Marblehead had decided to clear out before disaster struck. As a quick glance from Burrage confirmed, the really important question was how the company would react and what that would mean to us. Mr. Quill was the first to speak.

"We all knows the up and down of it, that's certain. An' we all has a pretty fair reckonin' on who steered us to it, as well!" he began, raising an arched eyebrow to the crowd. There were several angry grumbles of assent to his remark. "But done is done an' there ain't naught to gain wishin' it were different. But I says there ain't naught to gain settin' a course for a 32 pound ball neither! Stay below and damn the guns! If that means we be marooned, so be it! Bide our time. Who knows but, by an' by, we finds a back door what no one knew were there. Better a live rat than a dead dog, says I!"

As I listened, I was surprised at the silence that followed. Within seconds, another voice chimed in. It belonged to a thin young man in his early twenties who boldly stepped forward from one of the passageways to be heard.

"Easy words, Master Quill, for a man wiv no wife, no family! Me, I got a wife, a mother, an' her all blind besides. Do I leave 'em to starve now whilst I bury meself alive in this pit? I'll take me chances on deck wiv a pike in me hand first!"

An immediate chorus of approval reverberated through the tunnels.

"Aye! Are we ship's worms to live in the dark?" shouted another stout fellow. "I'd sooner die in the sun than shrivel like an old pippin down here!"

More cries of support. Quill raised his voice above the din.

"Belay yer boastin'! Ye're all full o' piss an' powder now, ain't ye though! Will ye feel so bold when yer boat's stove in an' yer thrashin' about in the cold, black water prayin' for a ball in yer brain?! How about yer poor, blind mother then, I ask? They're two ships o' the line an' what are we?—nine jolly-boats wi' nary a swivel gun ta answer! Think on't!"

The thin man stepped to within inches of the quartermaster's nose.

"If ye've not the stomach for't, then say so damn ye, Tobias Quill! Then let the hands decide if a change is in order!"

The challenge was plain but Quill was having none of it. As quick as lightning, he slipped a pistol from his sash and smashed it across the young man's forehead. The poor fellow fell back into the arms of his companion and lay stunned and bleeding on the cave floor. Several of his mates angrily reached for their weapons and moved toward the defiant quartermaster, but before more mayhem could ensue, the low, menacing voice of de L'Hiver brought matters quickly to hand.

"If any here wish to issue a challenge, then do so according to the Articles and be prepared to suffer fate if you fail. 'Tis your right to call for a vote, Thomas Peeler. But failing, it's two toes from the left foot as you well know. Do you wish to proceed?"

Fortunately, the stricken Peeler had recovered enough of his faculties to consider the consequences of his rash threat and painfully shook his head. Quill, satisfied that his manhood was intact, returned the pistol to his sash and looked to de L'Hiver for the next word. The Frenchman continued.

"Mark me! Only a fool does Her Majesty's work for her! Shall we kill ourselves, then? According to the Articles, each man must decide for himself according to shares! All for the caves, say 'Aye'!"

Quill came back with a firm reply, but was met with silence all about him.

"All for the boats?" de L'Hiver continued.

The answer thundered forth like a broadside. Weapons flashed in the gloom and men began to press forward. Muscles flexed beneath ragged garments and eyes simmered as the agitation spread from man to man. Like a mob about to explode in some terrible act of violence, the crew of the *Anne Boleyn* fed off the release of pent-up emotion. De L'Hiver stood calmly in the eye of the storm, a small smile revealing that he'd gotten the answer that he had wanted all along.

I glanced over at Tobias Quill. The gray man had sunk back against the wall, his pale face frozen with anger at the turn of events. I couldn't help but wonder what lay behind his fierce need to stand against his shipmates. But more to the point, I dreaded to think what might be coming next. The company was clearly preparing for some bold action that would take them out of the caves, but to what? A desperate attempt to escape, or more frightening still, a bloody confrontation with the enemy standing ready off of Cat Island? I couldn't understand why they simply didn't slip out in the darkness and head inland away from the threat lurking in the harbor. There seemed to be nothing to fear from the local inhabitants who, if anything, saw the company as brethren.

And then there was the issue of the British. I realized that I had no idea how I should view the two warships standing watch only a mile off shore. On one hand, they seemed to represent the closest thing to legal authority in these bizarre circumstances. Would they see Burrage and me as victims of brigands and, thus, entitled to their help? Or would they consider us all fish in the same barrel, one common enemy to be punished or destroyed. From what I knew of history, they might even choose to take us as unwilling recruits in the Royal Navy, as a press gang might procure crew from a dockside tavern or merchant ship. I had read that life aboard a man-of-war was tantamount to slavery, fraught with cruelty, danger, and deprivation. I could not imagine surviving such a fate.

And yet, it all ultimately seemed so completely ridiculous! Even if we were given the best treatment by Sir Robert and his crew, what of it? How could we explain ourselves? Where were we to go even if given a choice? We had no money, no destination; we didn't belong here at all! There seemed little to gain at the hands of the Royal Navy and potentially everything to lose. As incredible as it sounded, our chances could prove better with our anachronistic band of cutthroats. At least they offered some access to the path back to our world, if only we could stay alive long enough to discover it. The image of William flashed through my mind. I hoped more than ever that he had somehow found his way back to the loving arms of his parents.

The great commotion rumbling off in the distance barely registered in William's brain. As he sat shivering on the floor in the passageway, his freshly bound wrists grew numb under the cruel leather straps that now held them behind his back. A wary Ned Buckett assumed a perch upon the old pine coffin by the wall. As Buckett stared moodily in his direction, William lowered his head to avoid eye contact. The old seaman clearly felt caught off-guard by the boy's panicked response to the grim contents of the box. But Ned Buckett's feelings meant little to William at this point.

How does a twelve-year-old boy begin to recover from what he had just experienced? The profound shock of his father's betrayal had seared William to the heart and turned his thoughts sharply inward. Suddenly, where he was and what might become of him were of little import. But as he pondered the meaning of it all, he was drawn deeply into his past.

Myles Castler, you see, was not William's biological father. At the age of six, William and his nine-year-old sister, Elizabeth, had been adopted in Great Britain by Myles and his new bride, the former Enid Carp, who had met one chilly, June afternoon in a small curio shop in the Devonshire village of Okehampton. Enid had been on a motor coach tour of the southwest districts with her garden club and Myles on one of his procurement expeditions for his new employer, Barrows & Wight. All it took was tea in the grassy ruins of Okehampton Castle and a long walk through the moors for the pair to agree that they would correspond.

Within six months they were married and a year later they relocated to America with their new family. Barrows & White purchased the house on Franklin Street to provide Myles with a base of operations for his work in New England.

As with most small boys who longed to be loved, William had proved very adaptive. From the beginning, he made it his goal to seek his new father's attention and find ways to earn his approval. As his father lived a life of quiet self-sufficiency, so too, did William develop an air of unruffled detachment. While not unfriendly, he eschewed close relationships with male friends in school. Observing the formal manner with which his father responded to Enid and Elizabeth, William concluded that love must be something experienced at arm's length. Myles' passion clearly was his work. Likewise, William chose to invest his emotions in baseball even though it was painful that his father showed no interest whatsoever in sharing the game with his son.

In any case, William spent six years nurturing the hope that somehow his adopted parent loved him after all. And it was his ability to cling to this belief that anchored him. Now in an instant, William's entire sense of his place in the world had fallen to pieces. He had no reason to do anything or be anywhere other than where he was at this very moment. In comparison to what he had already suffered at the hands of his father, there was little that Ned Buckett could do to harm him. He let out a quiet sigh and leaned his head back against the stone.

The next thing William knew, he was being dragged to his feet and a blazing lantern thrust full in his face. Straining his eyes to see beyond the light of the candles, he could make out the faces of two men gazing directly back at him through the haze. He did not recognize them and assumed that they were there at the bidding of his father and had been sent to dispose of him once and for all. As he turned his head away from the light, he saw Ned Buckett cowering in the dust, a look of stark terror on his face.

"So, Neddie, lad! This is where ye been hiding since old Snitch put steel to your throat, is it?"

The voice belonged to a third man who now stepped from behind the others and addressed the stricken Buckett in a silky, refined tone.

"And what have we here, then?" he asked, nodding in the direction of poor William. "A fine pup gone astray from the litter, it seems! And ye not sharing your good fortune with the comp'ny, Ned?"

The pirate who had spoken chuckled darkly at his own wit, but the words were not out of his mouth before one of his companions stepped back nervously, eyeing William from head to foot.

"See 'ere, Jack!" the man whispered, his watery blue eyes widening as he spoke. "The lad's not from the cove—just look at 'is clothes, will ya! He's like the others, God save us. No good'll come of it!"

"Aye," said the third man. "No good! Leave 'im, says I. Leave 'im ta the rats an' let's away afore we finds ourselves chartin' a course for the Dark Door! Ye knows well what we all agreed."

The man called Jack stepped back quickly and placed a finger to his narrow chin. His   concern grew as he realized the truth of the matter. He brought his face close to William's ear and his hot breath made the hair stand up on the back of the boy's neck.

"How now then, lad? Use yer tongue! From the Key are ye?" he asked.

William, never having heard the term before, shook his head slowly and looked down at the ground. The answer did not sit well with his questioner, who stuck a long finger beneath William's chin and roughly raised his head again.

"Don't play the fool with me, my young puppy! We'll see the truth of't soon enough! Bring 'im and Buckett, also!" the man barked as he turned his attention to the poor seaman. "Ye see, Ned, yer absent from yer post, it seems. I shan't think that the Cap'n will look kindly on such poor attention ta duty!"

The man with the watery eyes responded quickly. "Take 'im?" he said, referring to William. "Not I! Tis the Devil's work an' that's certain! I'll 'ave no part!"

"Nor me neither," agreed his companion, taking Ned Buckett by the arm. "I'll bring Ned, then, but I says we acts like we never seen the lad. Leave 'im, for God's sake, an' make no mention, lest he bring a curse down upon us all."

Ignoring their pleas, Jack Wager took hold of William's collar and abruptly herded him down the tunnel.

"See to yer cargo then, damn ye," he chided, as he disappeared into the shadows. "The pup'll be on my tether where his fierce teeth can't find yer arses, my brave boys!"

No matter how the situation continued to deteriorate, Burrage seemed to be taking it all in stride. Here I was feeling more lost and desperate by the hour, yet Burrage was reacting as if he was at the movies! Every word, every movement the brigands made, Burrage's eyes glistened all the brighter with boyish fascination. I could hardly believe it. I wanted to shake him out of whatever little Hollywood fantasy he had managed to conjure and get him back to the dry-mouthed, pants-wetting anxiety any normal person would be feeling.

At that moment, several mates made their way into the Hub and in turn reported to the captain.

"Very well, then. That leaves only Jack Wager still out gathering shirkers," de L'Hiver announced to the assembly. "Each mate with a full crew make ready your boats! I will join you in due course. Away now, *mes amis!* The hour is upon us!"

A deafening roar filled the air and the tunnels exploded into a frenzy of activity. From every passageway a steady stream of armed men gushed forth. Faces that only recently had been more like death masks, frozen with misery and boredom, now became engorged with the ferocious vitality of warriors on the march. A hundred cutlasses clanked ominously against stone and steel. Braces of pistols, sometimes three or four to a man, hung from leather straps slung high across bare chests and burly fists gripped the handles of fearsome boarding axes, blunderbusses, and pikes.

The dust from the floor of the cave rose in a cloud to the tread of 300 feet and quickly enveloped the moving figures in a golden, silty glow. It soon became an awe-inspiring, animated tableau of almost hypnotic power. How often through the ages had bands of desperate men risen up—just so—and answered a heart-pounding call to battle? How many Celts or Vikings, Highlanders or Huns, Zulus or Saracens, Mongols or Sioux had marched out into the early morning mist toward a waiting enemy just as these men were now doing?

On one hand, my modern sensibilities rejected the base instinct that carried men to the battlefield at all, and yet, even I was not immune to the terrible majesty of the scene before me. As for Burrage, his primordial brain had so overwhelmed his philosophical gentility that I had to remind myself that he was still from my century. His muscles quivered and he strained forward as if being absorbed into the consciousness of the army, which now streamed through the Hub and disappeared down the passageway leading to the ocean. His face took on the look of a hungry man peering at a roast. Even Ditty Gunn could not help but notice the metamorphosis of my friend's demeanor.

"Easy, laddie," he chuckled softly. "'Twas in yer soul all along, were it no'? Perhaps ye 've a wee dram o' the thistle in yer blood after all!"

Snitch, too, was chomping at the bit and took a step toward the surging mob, but Gunn pulled him back with a sudden jerk on his waist sash.

"No' sa fast," he growled.

Within a short time the host had passed us by and as the last lanterns disappeared down the tunnel, only Quill and de L'Hiver remained in the Hub. It was then that Gunn motioned to his companion to lead us out to join them.

"Ah, yes," the Frenchman sighed at the sight of Burrage and me. "A puzzle indeed. What do you say, *Monsieur Quill?* Shall our new shipmates have a taste of life tonight?"

Quill immediately strode forward and angrily protested.

"Take them wiv us to sea?" he sputtered. "'Twould be madness itself! Ye know what the Articles says— 'Ta make no Acquaintance wiv Time Folk' it says!' 'Tis a curse they be here a'tall, by thunder! An' if one o' them should die? Why, 'twould mean our mortal souls, Lord preserve us!"

The Frenchman was quick to respond and gave no quarter.

"'Tis a curse indeed, but done is done! The Articles say that none shall die by 'our hand,' is that not so?" he roared.

The quartermaster would not relent.

"An' where's the difference, I asks, if ye cuts their throats wiv ye're own blade or just leads 'em ta the man what does it? Dead is dead, by thunder, an' there's no denyin' yer part in't! An' what o' the rest o' us? When the Door opens fer one, shall it not open fer all? Leave 'em stay!"

"And how shall I do that?" the captain chafed. "If all goes well, we shall be gone a fortnight or more. Do they die here in their chains then? Would that not bring the curse upon our heads as well? And you know we can never see them free."

Quill stalked back and forth silently pondering. It was clear he had no answer. On one hand, our fates seemed fixed. We were to remain in this nightmare of a world until nature or British steel took its course. And yet, the captain said something that gave me the smallest glimmer of hope.

"If you free us," I asked, "is it that you're afraid we will come back? With others from our time? Because if that's true, then you're saying that it's still possible for us to return to where we came from. Isn't that right?"

The captain glared at me.

"Silence!" he bellowed. "It is no matter! You sealed your fate when you entered the tunnels, did you not? We did not ask you here. You are a disease that has no cure and so you shall accept your fate. If you die, it shall not be by our hand but by your own. But mark me, you shall never, *never* return!"

"But we wouldn't come back, I promise you!" I stuttered. "Why, you'd never see us—"

With a lightning motion, de L'Hiver swung his crutch like a cudgel and caught my jawbone just below the corner of my mouth. I spun away from the blow and managed to keep my feet, but the message was clear. The conversation was over. We would not be allowed to go. And yet, I took more than a little solace in the knowledge that if we could somehow survive long enough to escape, we might find our way home.

My thoughts were quickly interrupted by the sound of several men entering the Hub from one of the other tunnels. I immediately recognized the unhappy Ned Buckett being prodded along with a cutlass in his ribs. And then, to my utter horror, I saw William in the grasp of the unsavory Jack Wager. As dismayed as I was by the sight, Quill and de L'Hiver were beside themselves.

"*Mon Dieu!*" the captain thundered. "Is there no end?"

"So what then? Does we take a boy as well?" Quill shouted.

De L'Hiver hesitated for a moment and realized there was no more time for talk. A decision had to be made.

"Bring them! Bring them all!" he ordered and started for the tunnel.

"But what about Worms?" Jack Wager asked. "I couldn't find 'im anywhere!"

"Leave the pestilence to his rathole and curse his bones!" the Frenchman replied. "I am well done with him!"

As we hurriedly entered the tunnel and began to make our way toward the sea, I heard a sound echoing from behind. Glancing back over my shoulder beyond the hunched figure of Ditty Gunn, I'm sure I saw a pale, blue orb burning in the darkness.

and caught my

CHAPTER 11

After we slogged our way through the flooded sea cave, we finally emerged once more into open air. How different the scene appeared, now bathed in the brushed-pewter light of the night sky. High, thin clouds drifted over the waning moon like smoke passing over a silvery ember. Overhead, unobscured by the glow of modern cities, the Milky Way spilled diamond flecks from horizon to horizon. And though the night might be described as dimly lit by most observers, for men just ascended from the bowels of the earth it was positively radiant. I could even see the masts of the two vessels spiking up above the shoreline of Cat Island like leafless tree trunks stark against the sky. A third ship, presumably the newly arrived *Dartmoor,* was stationed just to the north at the head of Salem Harbor.

As we picked our way along the rocky shoreline, the sea was as placid as a lake and the waves could barely be heard lapping gently against the granite boulders. We were heading away from the open ocean and toward the small village on the inner harbor. I was struck by the almost total absence of trees, so different from the Marblehead that I knew, but I guessed that the need for firewood and building materials had denuded the immediate area and created this barren, almost apocalyptic, landscape.

The town itself seemed deserted as it squatted before us, a dense clutch of ragged, clapboard dwellings, some of which seemed barely worth the trouble to construct. Had the residents been about, perhaps one would have seen a hint of wood smoke curling above a cobbly chimney. But the village was as silent as the graveyard that rose above it, huddled against the small, wooden church atop Burial Hill.

As I struggled to find my footing, a distant movement caught my eye. There, amongst the black gravestones on the hillside, I saw a dim point of red light circling out toward the ocean to the north where it was soon joined by one of pale blue. Like tiny sparks of St. Elmo's fire, they flashed faintly against the horizon, then rose up toward the heavens and were lost in the stars. A high, thin wail, like wind coursing through a jagged windowpane, briefly sounded across the still, dark water that separated Gerry Island from the mainland.

A hard shove from Snitch brought my attention back to the task at hand and as we rounded the inner shoulder of the point, the tiny cove beside Fort Beach was a cauldron of activity. Nearly a dozen stout longboats, each about 25 feet in length, were in various stages of loading men and preparing to depart. In fact, several were already underway, slipping between the jagged rocks that poked up through the smooth, inky waters of the cove. Referred to as "jolly boats" by the crew, each made station for three to four pairs of oarsmen as well as a helmsman on the rudder and carried between 10 and 15 fully armed men.

Within minutes, a flotilla of nine craft made its way out of the cove and began a long, snaking journey across the harbor toward the Neck. Burrage, William, and I were in the last boat to shove off. We, along with Snitch, Jack Wager, Buckett, and a half dozen stone-faced buccaneers, huddled in the chill night air. The contingent was joined by the gray man, Quill, who sat staring at me from across the plank on which I was seated. Surprisingly, Burrage and I were not put to work straining our backs at the oars and I assumed that this was only because we were not trusted to understand the commands and manage the synchronized stroke required to keep up with the experienced seamen. But we were soon given our own job to do.

"Skin yersels!" commanded Ditty Gunn, as he tossed a large canvas sack at our feet.

Burrage and I looked at one another, having no idea what was being asked of us.

"Yer clothes, laddies—all o'em. Send 'em o'er the side," he explained.

"Our clothes?" I asked. "It's freezing out here!"

"The boy, as well. Then put on such finery as may take yer fancy," he snickered, much to the amusement of the crew, and he emptied the contents of the sack.

It was a pile of rags not unlike the garb of our companions, but clearly the dregs of the wardrobe. I held up several limp, crusted items and I could swear they crawled in my hand. The stench—a mixture of mildew, filth, and prodigious bodily aromas—took my breath away. Noting my squeamish behavior, Gunn decided to get things rolling. He quickly stood me up, spun me around and brought the blade of his dagger up beneath my shirt. With a quick downward stroke, each of the garments on my back had been split from collar to waist and torn from my arms. I realized there was no escape and I finished the job myself with Burrage and William following suit. Within ten minutes, we were all newly outfitted in clothing that we could neither understand nor identify.

"Well, ain't ye the pretty lads now," spat Snitch from his oar, as we watched Gunn stuff our old belongings—shoes and all—into the canvas sack.

Before securing the bag, Gunn reached down in the shadows below his seat and fished up two black iron balls of solid shot about three inches in diameter. These he clanked into the canvas as well, then tossed the lot over the starboard side and into the sea. Within seconds, the remnant bubbles broke surface amidst the eddies of our dipping blades and yet another link to our world slipped away beneath the waves.

✳ ✳ ✳

Shivering on the open water, we watched the tiny armada as it reached the far shore and swung northeast toward the mouth of the harbor. The boats were still in single file and stretched out like plot points on a map. All the men were now hard at their work, backs bent and arms straining against heavy oars. They had settled into a steady rhythm, kept moving and on course by the clipped commands of Ditty Gunn, who manned the steering oar. I looked over at William who sat huddled against the gunnels. It occurred to me that he had not made the slightest effort to make contact with either Burrage or me, choosing instead to keep his eyes lowered at all times. It felt exceedingly odd. Here we were, three castaways adrift in another universe, and yet we might as well have been strangers. From what I could see of his expression, he seemed completely shut down. *No wonder,* I thought, but as of yet, there had been no chance to try and connect. I was burning to know what had befallen him from the time that we had separated.

It was here that the lead boat broke out from the shadows along the shoreline and began a determined sprint across the outer harbor toward the rocky hummocks near the southern end of Cat Island. Eight oars rose and fell in perfect cadence as the low-slung hull plowed briskly through the gentle waves. The other boats quickly followed suit. I was not good at estimating distances, but the island looked to be about a mile out from the mainland. I could not for the life of me imagine why we were heading directly toward the anchorage of the formidable *Catamount*. I had assumed that if de L'Hiver was truly planning to fight, he would have chosen some sort of ambush on the shore, thus depriving the British of their greatest advantage—their powerful ships' guns. But out here, sliding across open ocean like so many toy boats in a shooting gallery, what chance had we against battle-ready ships of the line? Quill picked up on my sense of alarm.

"A touch o' the fantods, 'ave we?" he chuckled darkly from out of the cowl of his cloak.

"What? Surely we're not headed for that ship, are we?" I flustered.

"Now which ship might that be, mate?" he inquired.

"*That* one," I replied, pointing toward the larger of the two. "The warship."

"Now, that would be a sight, by thunder!" he coughed. "Aye, an' her wiv sixty guns an' 200 muskets ready ta blow us back ta Perdition's shore! Nay, lad, even a Frenchman ain't so fuddled as ta take on the likes o' her."

"Then why are we headed straight for the island?" Burrage piped up. "I mean, it's only a couple acres, even if we landed, couldn't she blow us to bits from the sea?"

"Ah, very sound advice, I'm thinkin'," Quill responded with a slight lilt to his voice. "You 'as the makin's o' a captain, an' that's certain!"

"Well?" I demanded, tiring of his condescension. "Where *are* we going, then?"

"Steady, lad," he answered, his voice returning to a harsher tone. "But, I s'pose there's no harm in't. It's time ye knew what's expected o' ye, in any case."

Now that I had gotten his attention, I really wasn't sure I wanted the information after all.

"We'll be making course for the island, in all truth," he continued. "But not ta go ashore. Nay, we'll use the rocky hill as a mask, so ta speak. Can ye see the decks o' the ship?"

I peered through what was left of the moonlight and realized that I could only make out the masts.

"No." I replied.

"Ah," he said. "Neither can they see us then. I meself served on a man o'war, an' I can tell ye, bein' as we ain't looked on as a proper enemy, Queen Anne's navy thinks no more o' us than they might a silverfish ta be ground beneath the heel o' their boots! An' what does that mean ta us, ye may ask? Just this. It means they'll 'ave no watch in the maintop atall—no man higher than the deck-watch this time o' night."

"So, we mean to sneak up and attack the ship?" I asked, still not clear on why I shouldn't be in a blind panic.

"Nay! Nay!" he scoffed. "Not the frigate. The *Anne Boleyn*, lad. That's who we make for. They'll 'ave no mor'n a sailin' crew aboard 'er, that's certain—10, maybe 20 men in all. Why we'll 'ave throats cut an' be underway afore Sir Robert makes 'is mornin' water! That's what we're about."

Quill sat back, apparently satisfied that the logic of the plan would have a reassuring affect. Clearly, he had no clue that for Burrage and me, *any* plan took us far beyond our tolerance for danger.

"So, what do *we* do?" Burrage asked. "I mean, we don't even have any weapons."

"Why, acourse ya don't!" Quill retorted. "An' pray, what would ye do if ye *had* one? Nay, ye'll be left ta tend the jolly boats until the ship be taken. One o' ye wiv a cutlass?" Quill shook his head in disbelief at the idea. So did I.

Strangely, Burrage was not of the same mind. Showing a bit of trepidation, he managed to get the quartermaster's attention once more.

"I understand, I do," he began. "But, do you think that, well, that maybe I could *borrow* one of those cutlasses? Just a small one, in case, you know, someone jumped in our boat or something?"

I don't know who was more dumfounded, the grizzled old buccaneer or me. Even William took time out from his self-absorption to glance up at the remarkable Peter Burrage.

"Well, ain't ye the plucky codfish now!" Quill responded with a gnarled grin but not a small touch of newfound respect. "So, ye wants ta go a-rovin', does ye!"

I glared over at Burrage and gave him a sharp nudge with my knee. He gave me a fierce look of indignation.

"Well!" he argued. "It wouldn't *hurt*, would it? We need something to defend ourselves!"

I couldn't believe my ears. Peter Burrage, a man for whom an anonymous sneeze on the subway evoked fears of epidemic. A man who would rather have his bladder explode than use a gas station men's room. What was happening? Was this nightmare rising to still higher levels of absurdity? I immediately felt the need to bring him and everyone else back to reality.

"What the *hell* are you talking about?" I barked, no longer caring who heard me. "We're not defending anyone! We're staying as far away from cutlasses and cannons and everything else as we can! Understand?"

I looked at Quill, surprised at the power of my rage to push my fears aside.

"You can keep us in this boat, I know that. You can even knock us around. I know *that*, too! But you can't do *one* thing, can you? You can't *kill* us! There's some curse that means you got to keep us alive and safe."

I paused to gauge the effect I was having on my captors. Quill sat motionless. Even Snitch gave no reply. I sped on. "In fact, you need to make sure that I'm happy enough not to do something unhelpful, like raise my voice when we pass that ship in the dark. Am I right?"

When I woke up again, I was lying face down in the puddling slew on the floor of the jolly boat, cold murk slopping about my cheek as the hull rolled in the swells. As I moved to get up, I felt a heavy weight bearing down on my neck. It was the thick heel of the quartermaster's boot. I also realized that my hands were secured behind my back and a foul rag had been stuffed in my mouth. My head was throbbing with pain once more. It appeared that I had yet again failed to properly assess the boundaries of my situation.

"*Whisht!*" came the harsh command from the gray man as he emphasized his point with a kick to the ribs. He did, however, allow me to roll onto my back and get my bearings.

I looked up just in time to see the stars slip behind a huge, black shape now looming overhead. We were soon swallowed up in the shadows below and I realized that it must be the hull of the *Anne Boleyn*. As we held close to her stern, her mizzenmast towered high above her bulwark, spars and lines crisscrossing in the dark sky like the web of a great spider spun to trap seabirds as they rode the night air. I could just make out others of our small fleet circling silently toward her bow and disappearing round her wale.

It was another of those instances when the sheer romance of my bizarre journey held me spellbound and caused me to lose myself in the dark grandeur of the moment. I was witness to a thing that had, until now, lain invisible and untouched deep within the vaults of an age long forgotten. Like a grassy barrow, no more than a peculiar hump bedecked with wild flowers and butterflies, yet down below, antideluvian bones and dust-covered days lay unrevealed to modern eyes. But here the bones were fitted out with flesh and sinew, alive once more in the service of mysterious and desperate men.

The quartermaster again dug his boot into my side and held a crooked finger to his lips. I could see Burrage and William sitting just above me, both as entranced as I. Our boat moved a little farther forward then hove to amidships. From here, the main and fore masts added even more magnificence to the fantastic vessel riding the waves just a few yards to larboard. It was as Quill had said. The only sign of life aboard her was the pale glow of a lantern swinging over her stern far below the crossjack yard.

I lay spellbound as three of our companion boats gently, silently nuzzled up to the hull. Large bundles of rags had been lashed along the rails of each boat to muffle the sound of any bumping that might occur once the boarding commenced. After several tries, a loop of line was skillfully tossed over a mooring bollard, which could barely be seen peeking over the topgallant rail just below the foremast. Once it was made fast, a wiry seaman, stripped of all weaponry save a dagger clenched hard in his teeth, quickly made his way up the side and disappeared over the rail. Within seconds several lines were dropped from above and secured by eager hands in the boats. I wondered what signal might begin the assault. I soon got my answer.

Staring with rapt anticipation, I caught sight of a dark shape about five feet in length being lowered just over the starboard rail near the aft cabin. As it slid beneath the surface of the sea, it made no more noise than a small stone might make. Yet, I knew it must be the remains of some hapless sailor who had, but a moment before, sat puffing on a clay pipe or gazing up at the stars. As the blood drained from my face, the magic and romance went with it.

In an instant, the sides of the ship were aswarm with dark figures hoisting themselves up the lines and springing over the rail! My heart began to race and I strained to get a glimpse of what might be occurring up on deck, but it soon became clear that this fight was never intended to take place in the open. Muffled cries could be heard as panic spread below decks—the distant clash of steel and a single pistol shot reverberated deep within the belly of the ship. In a matter of minutes it was over and the soft, presumably lifeless bundles, each properly weighted with a load of chain shot, began to appear in the gun ports and slipped gently into the sea.

Jesus, I thought.

Even Burrage seemed set back from his brief flirtation with manhood.

"Mr. Gunn!" the quartermaster exclaimed. "Make way for larboard side an' prepare ta board!"

Ditty Gunn stood at his oar and gave the commands that started us round the bow of the *Anne Boleyn*. The sky had gone blacker with the setting of the moon but there was still the starlight to paint the edges of objects in pale relief. The sea had grown more restless and our boat began to trough the swells that now drove in steadily from the northeast. As we made our pass beneath the bowsprit, the hull rolled heavily down toward us and I felt Burrage's hand seize my arm. At first I thought he was alarmed at our nearness to the rolling ship, but then I saw it etched in the starlight—a severed head rising and falling with the sea!

A jolt passed through me and I struggled to my knees. The face was ghastly, eyes wide with shock and mouth agape, telling the tale of a cruel and violent death. The head was held tightly in the weathered right arm. The torso, clad in peeling paint, lurched forward with frozen urgency, the left arm extending toward the horizon.

"God almighty, Max! It's *her!*" Burrage gasped.

Indeed it was. Anne Boleyn herself, captured in the throes of her final agony; ghostly eyes steering the course of the ship she now graced with her oaken corpse.

"So then, 'tis yer first meetin' wiv our Lady," Quill grunted. "Mind ye, don't look 'er in the eye lest ye be the next ta join 'er!"

As he spoke, Quill directed one of the seamen to cut me loose. With my hands free and my mouth clear once more, I sat myself down next to Burrage. Realizing he was about to speak, I nudged him firmly with my elbow. But then, it was William who made the unfortunate comment.

"It's like the lady on the map," he offered, to no one in particular.

I immediately cleared my throat and tried to change the subject, but it was too late. Quill was on his feet and at the boy's side in an instant.

"What's that ye spake, lad?" he asked in a quiet voice that could not hide the urgency in his tone. "A map?"

William shifted uncomfortably and glanced at me for guidance. With Quill's full attention upon us, it was impossible to give my young friend any hint of direction. In reality, I had no idea which way to go to begin with. I was flabbergasted by the similarities between the carved figurehead of the *Anne Boleyn* and the faint drawing on the map that had been taken from the wall in my office. And yet, given the circumstances of the map's disappearance, it seemed more than likely that the figures were one and the same. Now, coupled with Quill's intense interest in the document, I felt the need to learn as much as I could while saying as little as possible. I waded in.

"Yes, a map," I interrupted. "A small thing, actually, a proven hoax drawn up by some college students in the 1970's. I thought it was an interesting bit of artwork, so, I managed to purchase it as a decoration for my office."

I realized Quill was having difficulty keeping up with my modern references, but he had a way of getting to the heart of the matter.

"An' the boy, here," he continued in a hoarse whisper, glancing at William and making sure he was not heard by the rest of the crew. "What do ye make o' *his* words, then? This map—how does she configger? An' mind, not too loud!"

I struggled to stay focused on the task—how to answer his questions, yet say nothing.

"Oh, there was a picture of a lady in a long dress, is all. I suppose that's the connection," I offered.

I could see Quill suspected that I was being elusive and I began to sense that the situation was taking a truly dangerous turn. But just as I began to prepare for the worst, he took another tack. He turned to William.

"An' her head, lad?" he asked. "Were it set proper on 'er shoulders, or were it in 'er arms, like the Lady 'ere?"

We all gazed over at the rolling bow. William nodded, affirming the latter. Quill pressed harder.

"An' were it a map o' this 'ere town? One wiv' a brace o' black crosses on 'er?" he persisted.

"I... I'm not sure. I never noticed much about it. I hardly looked at it," William stammered, the stress beginning to take over. "That's all I know."

The quartermaster's eyes bored into the boy for several long seconds. Then, seeing no additional treasure to be dug, Quill turned again fixing me with a stare that pinned me like a beetle to a board.

"Take care, now," he snarled. "Play the fool an' there ain't a Article writ what'll save yer lyin' carcass from the gibbet! The crosses, then?"

I had no doubt that he would see through any attempt to evade the question.

"I guess there might have been marks of some kind... maybe crosses," I teetered. "Maps have all kinds of things on them. Anyway, the map is gone. I don't even have it, so I can't really help you much more."

For the first time Quill looked thrown off.

"Where?" he demanded.

"I have no idea. Stolen, I assume. It was just gone one morning," I continued.

"So, *that's* what brung ye here, eh!!" he whispered in a voice barely audible above the sea. "Come lookin' for Old Buckett's Bible!"

As Burrage, William, and I sat in the stern of the long boat trying to absorb all that had just been said, Quill immediately cautioned, "On this matter speak no word ta any man save me! Swear it on yer mortal soul an' that o' yer very mother, by thunder!"

At that moment, we reached mid-ships on the larboard side and the flurry of activity exceeded that on the starboard. Men had sprung into the rigging and were hard at the task of making the *Anne Boleyn* ready to get underway. Other hands had set about scuttling the long boats and one by one the small vessels swamped and disappeared beneath the dark waves. Our boat was the last to off-load and we labored to get ourselves safely over the rail before it, too, was sunk below us.

As soon as we reached the deck, Quill immediately set off to find Bartholomew de L'Hiver. I couldn't help but wonder how much he would choose to share with his captain. But I now had no doubt that Tobias Quill was familiar with the map and, perhaps as the large "Q" suggested, even the creator of it. Knowing that much gave me an unexpected feeling of calm even though many other questions remained unanswered. I sensed that perhaps my knowledge of the map and its possible whereabouts might provide some valuable leverage.

For now though, we were hard pressed to know exactly what we were to do next. Ditty Gunn filled the void.

"Lively there, ya squid!" he barked. "Find a place at the capstan an' prepare ta weigh anchor!"

Gunn was now in his glory, back on the deck of his ship as first mate and taking over the business of getting underway. Burrage, William, and I joined five other hands on the capstan bars and awaited orders. As a predawn wind began to rise from the northwest, the timeless excitement of a ship preparing to sail infused everyone around us. Even in the hard-bitten faces I could sense the unmistakable pleasure each man felt standing once more on a rolling deck, liberated at last from exile in the tunnels.

Orders were passed quietly. It was clear that no one wanted to alert the watch on the deck of *Catamount*, which stood off the island about a quarter mile astern. High above our deck, the trees and footropes were now crowded with mariners hard at the business of unfurling canvas and setting the lines. Royals, topgallants, tops, and jibs—one by one the sheets burst forth from the buntlines and began to waffle in the stiffening breeze. I was shocked by the decrepit look of the sails, each one more ragged and stained than the last. I wondered if they would hold any wind at all.

"Weigh anchor, laddies!" came Ditty Gunn's command. "Backs to it, now!"

Bending forward into the capstan bars, we extended our arms and fought to make headway against the immense weight of the chain cable. At first our feet slipped on the damp deck and we struggled to find purchase and push as one. Then, ever so slowly, the great wheel began to turn. From below decks, I could feel the steady *thunk* of the pawl as it caught the rim and the windlass began to groan. The men around us took up a dark, chanting melody which brought pace to the task and we soon felt the *Anne Boleyn* pulling steadily along her tether. Once free of the bottom, we continued at a dead lift until the great hook broke surface and was made fast to the cathead. At last, the sheets filled and our extraordinary vessel immediately bent to her course and made way toward a horizon that had just begun to brighten with the pale glow of dawn.

Within minutes of our departure, the peace was suddenly shattered by the crash of a thundering explosion. Burrage and I rushed to the larboard rail in time to see a thick donut of gray smoke rolling out from the hull of *Catamount*.

"Twenty-four pounder," came the casual comment of a smallish buccaneer who shared the rail several feet away.

"Is she firing at us?" I asked, wondering if we should be heading for cover.

"At us? Nay!" came the reply with an amused Irish lilt. "We've crossed 'er 'T.' She can't bring 'er guns ta bear, praise be. Nay, that'll be a call ta 'er sister, *Dartmoor*. They seen us sure an' ol' Sir Robert must be in his treacle now he knows we're off!"

I could see that we were looking directly at *Catamount's* bow-sprit and realized that her impressive array of large guns was indeed aimed parallel to our course. With her still at anchor and sails furled, she had no means to come about and show us her broadside. I could make out the tiny figures as they began to swarm her deck, shocked out of their sleep by our brazen escape, but it would be many long minutes before either of the Queen Anne's frigates could get under way and take up the chase.

"Won't they catch us? There's two of them, after all," I went on.

"Not likely," our companion chuckled. "We're no match in a fight, what wi' only sixteen twelve-pounders, but our sweet *Annie* can outrun any man-o'-war ever built, light air or gale, ye can lay wager ta that. Nay, they know they're done an' it's all fer show now. The only ones ta suffer will be the watch, poor lads."

Sure enough, by the time their masts were dressed with sail, *Catamount* and *Dartmoor* were several miles astern and growing smaller by the minute. I felt a confusing sense of relief. Even Burrage turned to me and grinned. Nothing made sense.

"So, we really kicked some *butt!*" Burrage chortled, bringing a sharp glance from me. "Very professional, eh, Max? Like a SWAT team! Took the entire ship without losing a man!"

The Irishman continued to monitor the progress of our pursuers, then turned to us.

"Nary a man lost, 'tis true, but for poor Ned."

"Ned?" I demanded. "You mean Ned Buckett?"

"Aye, the very same. Found below, Ned was, wi' a ball in 'is brain."

CHAPTER 12

*T*obias Quill was an enigma, even to himself. While he had adapted as much as necessary to his life as a rover, there were aspects about him that went beyond one's image of a buccaneer. For one thing, he was actually quite educated for his time, having spent two and a half years studying for the ministry at Harvard College and when in the company of a gentleman or lady, he could demonstrate a most charming facility with the language. Once he had become absorbed in his new life at sea, however, he discovered that speaking with refinement among his fellows did little to endear himself to them, for piracy was as much a reaction against the calumnies of the upper classes as it was a path to wealth. In fact, it could be credibly argued that pirate society, despite all its hedonistic instincts, was western civilization's first experiment with many of the principles of modern democracy and socialism.

In the so-called "Golden Age of Piracy" that spanned the 17th and early 18th centuries, a number of unique factors converged. The first was the official encouragement and even financial support given to the maritime industry known as "privateering." Privateers were essentially boatloads of thieves sponsored by certain governments to raid the merchant shipping or colonies of countries with which they were at war. The captain of a privateer vessel often carried one or more "Letters of Marque," documents granting him permission to inflict his depredations upon selected enemies. The plunder accumulated as the result of these practices was generally divided among the crew, the boat owner, and the sanctioning body. In short, privateering became a most cost-effective means to both harass and weaken an enemy nation while enriching one's own coffers. It also became a training school for generations of pirates.

The second factor was the emergence of trade routes that were both staggeringly treasure-laden and difficult to protect. The Mediterranean, the coasts of Africa, and the Indian Ocean all offered opportunities for sea-going raiders to abscond with grand cargoes of spices, jewels, silks, and slaves, with comparatively little risk to themselves. But the mother lode of all treasure routes was that known as the Spanish Main, the long and perilous journey made by Spanish ships from South America, Central America, and Mexico. Beginning in the 16th century, great fleets of treasure galleons were loaded with billions in gold, silver, and jewels pillaged from New World civilizations such as the Incas, Aztecs and Arawaks. But to reach the coffers of Seville, the fleets had to run the gauntlet of the West Indies, the Greater and Lesser Antilles, and the Bahamas.

The thousands of large and small islands that made up the West Indies were under the control of no one power. Spain, England, France, Holland, and other European nations all claimed ports and strongholds throughout the Caribbean Sea, but even then, hundreds of islands lay beyond the reach of European authority. In short, privateers and pirates throughout the Caribbean enjoyed the ideal environment from which to operate, access to food, water, stores, manpower, and tens of thousands of square miles of ocean and uncharted islands in which to hide from the meager forces sent to stop them.

A third factor was the enormous chasm that separated rich from poor in the harsh social landscape of 17th century Europe and the colonies in the Americas. It was a world in which the very few held virtually all the power and wealth, while a large underclass held none. For the poor life was likely to consist of backbreaking toil, disease, malnutrition, and an early grave. The legal system, such as it was, existed only to benefit the noble and merchant classes.

For many, indentured servitude or outright slavery began in childhood and ended only in death. Even the so-called "free man" lived a life that by today's standards would be considered grossly inhumane. And most unfair was the fact that a member of this underclass had virtually no legitimate vehicle with which to improve his station in life, either socially or economically. This, more than any other single factor swelled the ranks of pirates and privateers. As dangerous a calling as it might have been, piracy was no more brutal than life in the Royal Navy or on a sugar plantation, and those occupations offered no hope of reward.

The profession spawned a number of socially radical ideas as well. For example, pirate crews often sailed under a contract created to protect the interests of each individual member. Sometimes referred to as "articles," these agreements might include the mechanism by which the captain and officers were selected and their power limited. The articles also recorded the number of "shares" each man was to receive when spoils were divided. The captain and officers often received little more than the average seaman, creating a distribution of wealth far more equitable than that in European society. Some crews even instituted a rudimentary health insurance system, providing compensation for injuries sustained in the line of duty.

While some pirate captains, such as Blackbeard, used fear and intimidation to solidify their power on board ship, many captains served strictly at the pleasure of the crews they commanded and could be voted out of office by a simple majority if they did not produce. In addition, there were often strict rules with regard to fighting, gambling, drinking, and petty theft that were imposed to minimize friction among the crew. And though life was still brutal in many respects, even a lowly seaman enjoyed a sense of power over his own destiny that was unprecedented in mainstream society. And strangely, it was this chance to explore the nature of a more egalitarian society, far more than treasure, which had first attracted Tobias Quill to life as a buccaneer.

Quill had been raised in the small New England town of Ipswich in the Massachusetts Bay colony. His father, James, had been a farmer of some stature in the community, which accounted for Tobias' opportunity to study at the fledgling Harvard College. His first years there saw him immersed in religious studies that both fulfilled and inspired him. In fact, he had every intention of completing his education and living his life as an ordained minister. However, during Tobias' third year, his father suddenly found himself accused of a lengthy list of crimes. These included heresy, adultery, and consorting with members of a Quaker sect. This shocking turn of events led Tobias to leave the college to help his father defend himself against charges both knew to be false.

As it turned out, the plaintiff was a wealthy Salem landowner who had long coveted the Quill family holdings. In less than a week's time, the elder Quill had been dragged from his home, tried, and convicted. The trial judge, it seems, was also senior deacon of a Calvinist congregation gathered beneath the pulpit of the Reverend Constant Prowst, a truly Machiavellian sort who had a goiter below his left ear. Prowst just happened to be the brother of James Quill's accuser. By the vernal equinox, every acre of the Quill lands had been sold at auction and was in the possession of Edward Prowst of Salem. And, in one final breathtaking act of greed, Prowst accused the Quills' hired woman of complicity, resulting in a sentence of indentured servitude to his brother, the good Reverend!

Tobias was outraged. The fact that a man of God could be an accomplice to such blatant injustice made him all the more bitter. He took what money he had left and booked passage to England where he strove for over a year to put his case before a sympathetic ear. When his last farthing had been spent, he was no closer to justice than the meanest beggar in Newgate. Distraught, he found himself wandering the docks of lower Thames Street and within a day, he had been knocked unconscious by a press gang and taken aboard His Majesty's Frigate, *Honor*.

Four seven long years, Tobias Quill served as seaman, gunner's mate, foretopman and cook aboard a progression of vessels in the Royal Navy. He was at sea almost constantly, giving him no opportunity for escape. In his time, he saw shipmates savagely beaten for minor offenses, keelhauled, crippled, starved, and hanged. He watched boys, some as young as eight years old, taken into service and brutalized to the point of suicide. Finally, he himself had reached a state of despair that nearly had him leap from the moonsail yard one night off the coast of Hispaniola. The next morning, however, changed his life forever.

As the sun broke the horizon that day in June of the year 1684, the watch called out a ship standing six miles off the larboard bow on the lee side of Ile-á-Vache. Suspecting she might be a pirate, the captain set out to chase her down. As it turned out, haste was unnecessary, for the mysterious vessel had run aground on a narrow reef and was helplessly awaiting the tide to set her free again. The officers of Quill's ship, *Revenge*, saw no urgent need to fire upon the small, yet unidentified barkentine and it was decided that she should be boarded instead. Carefully, the gunboat maneuvered to within 20 yards of the helpless craft and hooks were tossed across her rail. The few crew visible on her decks looked peaceful enough.

Quill was chosen to be one of the boarding party and he joined the others sliding across the grappling lines. One of the last to reach deck, he landed just as a wave of heavily armed men poured forth from the hatches below! Quill immediately dropped his weapons and was shoved aside as the crew loosed the hooks and threw them into the sea. Just at that moment, a swell rolled in from the north and lifted the small vessel from her perch and within seconds the pirate crew was on the shrouds dressing canvas and rounding up the small contingent of British seamen who had managed to reach her deck. The captain of *Revenge* was clearly caught off guard by the sudden turn of events and stood at the rail commanding his gunners to prepare to give fire. But the order never came.

As the crew of the barkentine looked on in amazement, the great guns of the frigate stood ready, yet silent. Soon the newly freed ship had turned herself 60 points to larboard and began a mad dash for the far side of the island. It was clear that *Revenge* could not breech the reef, but it was still a mystery as to why she would not fire. Finally, Quill stepped forward and pointed to a young ensign among the boarding crew.

"This is why," he said calmly, as attention turned to the small clutch of captives. "He is the captain's son."

So, in the blink of an eye, Tobias Quill found himself on a new ship and with a new life.

Like many in his trade, Tobias Quill went where the wind and fortune took him. One vessel on which he served, *Gwenhwyfar*, even spent a year plying the waters off of Madagascar. And while the life of a buccaneer made any man leathery and harsh, Quill never completely lost his humanity. His passion for justice had even led him to a central role in the mutiny aboard the bark, *Scythe,* a notorious ship under the command of Giles Crowe. Crowe was perhaps the most ruthless individual Quill had ever experienced in his 20 years at sea; after his service in the Royal Navy, that was no small claim.

On a clear summer day in July of 1697, *Scythe* overtook a Dutch flute after chasing her for several days off of the Araya Peninsula. The undermanned vessel had finally surrendered without a shot and served up her cargo of slaves resignedly. Crowe however, was not in the market for slaves that day and had counted on a prize that would require less maintenance. Angry at the time he had wasted obtaining a cargo he did not want, Crowe ordered the Dutch crew below with the slaves and, after locking them down, set the ship afire. The young wood took five hours to burn down to the waterline and the screams of the victims could be heard until the blazing mainmast crashed through the deck and brought the rigging down after it.

To complete the nightmare, three of Crowe's own men dared to grumble at the pointless cruelty, so the Captain had *them* set ablaze, as well, and thrown into the sea. Horrified at the day's events, 23 members of the *Scythe's* crew met secretly in the cable hold at the bottom of the ship to plot a coup. In the end, Tobias Quill, at the time a master gunner, led a rush on the main cabin and took control of the ship. Not a man aboard, save the captain, protested. Crowe was deposed and left to fend for himself on a barren island southwest of the Lesser Antilles where it is said he was eventually devoured by a voracious species of carcass beetles as he lay immobilized with hunger.

Quill's eloquence in shaping the revolt and his administration of a fitting punishment earned him a serious measure of respect from his fellows. And while he himself deferred consideration to take over command, he was elected quartermaster and came to be considered the conscience of the crew. In fact, he was held in such high esteem that a dozen or so of the current crew of the *Anne Boleyn* had followed him to that ship when he signed on with Bartholomew de L'Hiver. It was well known that they would never have submitted to the command of a Frenchman otherwise. Quill, however, had recognized the need for a leader of de L'Hiver's abilities and had served with the captain ever since.

And so, for the twenty-five years since his ill-fated journey to London, Tobias Quill had wandered the globe, his life a deepening mystery. With each year that passed, his need to know what had become of his father grew ever more subordinate to his fear of finding out. This ambivalence left him becalmed, so to speak, and the driving force of his early years, the reclamation of his birthright, had no more strength to propel him forward than a sail luffing in a thin breeze. Sapped of his indignation, he had grown careless with the gifts of his life. A formal education was given no more expression than the keeping of ledgers and a melancholy diary. His passion for a just and moral life was twisted to fit the often self-serving definitions of the roguish world in which he lived. And his agile mind was often viewed as a complication by those around him.

✳ ✳ ✳

The black figure was barely visible against the night shadows that fell across the rocks outside the sea cave. With the one-eyed rapture of a raven watching June bugs trundle across a garden path, he followed the tiny line of long boats as they broke beyond the Neck and began their run across the outer harbor toward Cat Island. The distant craft rose and fell in silhouette against the flinty glow of moonlight as it played across the dimpled chop.

He was at first taken by surprise; he was not expecting so bold a maneuver by the French Captain. It was unlike de L'Hiver to put his enterprise at risk when two British frigates hovered so close at hand. The figure rubbed a gnarled finger in the empty socket above his right cheekbone and sat himself upon a smooth granite boulder to consider the meaning of this unforeseen development.

"Tell me, Tom," he purred in a thick, grainy voice, engaging the silver skull ring that grinned back at him from its filthy perch upon his left hand. "Where they off to? Old Worms needs ta know the whole of't, 'e does, every word!"

The ragged man sat back and brought Evil Tom's gaping mouth close to his ear and waited for a reply. As always, Tom didn't speak out loud. Instead, his messages gathered spontaneously like a swarm of flies in a dark corner of the fetid swamp that was Melchior Wormsley's brain.

"So, they thinks ta sail off, they does—back ta Maracaibo like as not! An' Old Worms left 'ere ta rot, they thinks. Not likely! Nay. Back they shall come, shan't they, sweet Tom? Lookin' for Buckett's Bible and the *rest!*" he croaked with glee, taking the faded, old map from his coat and holding it up against the night sky. "Aye, a golden guinea for every star, Tom! That seems fair, don't it now?"

With that he rolled the parchment in his hand and returned it to his pocket. With a satisfied chuckle, he hunched his way back into the black hole below the ledges.

✳ ✳ ✳

Exhaustion had crept across the deck of the *Anne Boleyn* like a great, dull cloud. Any man still not held to his task had long since curled up wherever he could find a patch of deck and a coil of hemp to rest his head. Some even slept high aloft, a shoulder or leg looped precariously through a bit of rigging in hopes of avoiding a fatal plunge below.

The night had been long. The extreme physical and mental exertion had drained most everyone of wit and will. The few still at work were so only at the pleasure of Ditty Gunn's sharp tongue and menacing eye. When I awoke, I found myself still draped across the capstan bars, my left arm pinned awkwardly beneath me. Carefully unfolding myself, I sat down heavily and rested my back against the whelps so that I might gaze out into the bright, new day.

About ten degrees above horizon, the morning sun hung like a great, glowing peach against the broad swath of vermilion to the east. As my eyes scribed an upward arc, the sky went from pink to pale orange to pale blue, becoming a deep azure high above the towering masts. A surprisingly warm wind began to gust and soon the ship was booming through the rolling swells with a leviathan grandeur that belied her grizzled appearance. The diving bow threatened to drive her needle deep into the belly of the sea, only to come pounding up in a frothy torrent of white spray that soared high above our heads. I felt like Ahab lashed to the great white whale as it careened through the boiling foam on its way to Perdition! The feeling was indescribable!

The tossing sea soon had all hands awake again and clinging for dear life to the nearest line or yard. I glanced above me and saw William's upturned chin as he faced into the following wind, his hair in a halo of copper flames that danced madly round his head. A feeling of heavenly bliss softly radiated out from behind his closed eyes and I thought I had never seen him so fully at peace.

Burrage, too, was up on his feet, his head swiveling on his neck as he tried to take in every detail of the astonishing moment in which he found himself. I could tell he was aching for a more substantial role in his own dream, some task he could perform that would make it more real than he would otherwise dare to believe. I was struck, uncomfortably so, by the strange transformation that I was seeing in Burrage's manner. Where only hours before there was trepidation and a need to escape, now there was an incongruous sense of exhilaration and a need to participate. It was becoming clear that he, and probably William as well, were being thoroughly seduced by a perverse sense of romance and adventure that grew with every new experience.

"Sail! Sail two points off the larboard bow!" came the faraway cry from the main top.

All eyes turned to the southeast and fought the heavy roll of the ship. As the bow rose up on each swell, I caught a glimpse of tiny, dark sails silhouetted against the shining sea far on the horizon. Just to starboard, I could make out the long low profile of Cape Cod as it swung away to the west. It was clear the distant vessel was headed around toward Buzzard's Bay.

"Shall I make for 'er, Cap'n?" shouted Gunn above the rush of the wind.

"Nay!" came the reply. "Hold steady east by southeast whilst we have this charming bit of wind to blow us on our way. Sir Robert may be slow, but he is the bulldog, *mes amis*. I'll not have him find us aground on some sand bar because we chased a cargo of bobbins. Hold steady."

The Frenchman's words were an abrupt reminder that we were, in all likelihood, still being hunted by two British men-of-war. I glanced back into the wind and could see no sails astern. For this I was grateful. I had come to accept that capture by the English held no good outcome for me or my two companions. And yet, I knew that every hour spent racing to the southeast took us further from home.

The deck was now alive with the ragged minions of *Anne Boleyn's* crew as they slithered down the lines or poked up through deck hatches like so many feral cats. Seeing them for the first time in full sunlight was truly startling. When bathed in the glow of candle-lit tunnels, the men had seemed ruddy and robust—like chiseled bronze figures striding purposefully through N.C. Wyeth's paintings. But here in the bright glare of day, they seemed altogether more *fragile* somehow, faded and drained of hue. Yet, it was more than mere coloration. There appeared to be a subtle translucence to their forms, as if their tenure underground flitting through time had robbed them of some degree of their temporal substance. And yet, we still shared the same dimension. A sudden chill shot through me and I turned away.

"Up, ye lazy she-goats!" came Snitch's harsh command. "Seems ye're given some favor this day, tho' taint my wishes, that's certain!"

With that, he had us up on our feet and wondering what might come next. To our happy surprise, the foul man produced a large, iron key and proceeded to free us from the last remnants of our shackles—the heavy neck rings. It was obvious that with nowhere to run, the hardware was unnecessary. The sense of physical and even emotional release was profound.

"Now, make fair use o' yerselves! Cap'n says the lad 'ere's fer the galley, so, be off wiv ye!" Snitch rasped, giving William a sound shove toward the fore hatch. "Look for a man wiv two fingers on 'is right hand. That'll be Wombwell, as fine a keep as ever roasted an oxhead. Mind ye don't steal so much as a crumb, my fine cuttl'fish or Master Wombwell'll have ye in 'is next pot o' Poor Jack Puddin'!"

A wide-eyed William gave us a fleeting look of apprehension and then made his way down the ladder and out of sight. Snitch flashed a sneering grin, then turned abruptly to Burrage and me.

"An' ye fine gentl'men shall 'ave the pleasure o' *my* comp'ny! It falls ta me ta make *seamen* o' ye, although," he mused, looking us over with the disapproving gaze of a farmer who had just purchased a three-legged cow, "ye can't draw rum from a piss-pot, I fear. Truth be told, after watchin' ye haul timber, I doubt ye could hold yer own weight in the riggin'. Ye ain't got the tooth for't. So we'll 'ave ye start from the bottom, so ta speak."

He motioned us to follow as he, too, disappeared below decks. As we made our way into the shadowy world below, I was struck by how similar it felt to the tunnels. Low ceilings, unexpected openings twisting this way and that and, always, the ever-darkening gloom as we descended each deck in turn. After the second ladder, a small candle was lit and the stoat-like pirate beckoned us walk forward toward the bow of the ship. Timbers glistened with black pitch and condensation in the flickering glow. Surrounding us was a complex landscape of close-set holds and compartments that contained all the stores essential for a voyage at sea— cables and line, galley wood, blocks and tackle tucked away in every conceivable nook and cranny.

At the forwardmost part of this lowermost deck lay a small hatchway, as yet unopened. Snitch placed the candle inside a small lantern and hung it on a peg. Reaching down, he gave a tug on the iron ring and swung the hatch open.

"This, lads," he said, pointing below, "is ta be yer new quarters!"

With a sinking feeling in my stomach, I stepped toward the opening and peered down into the dark hole. As my eyes adjusted to the light, I could barely make out what appeared to be hundreds of large iron eggs that were piled to within six inches of the ceiling.

"Aye! 'Tis the shot locker fer ye, an' a more snugger nest ye could ne'er find!" Snitch gaped, delighted with our shocked expressions. "Nay, nay, fear not, lads. It may indeed appear that ye'll have no room, but that's the *beauty* of't, ye see! The Cap'n feels our dear *Annie* is ridin' a mite too headstrong and wishes ta shift some o' her ballast to 'er hindquarters! That's the task at hand then, lads. Take a couple hundred or so balls 'tween decks ta the aft locker an' stow 'em tight an' even. Then you'll 'ave enough room for ten men in this locker 'ere!"

Snitch simply couldn't contain his own delight with the spontaneous wit he felt he had just displayed. With barely dry eyes, he staggered over to us and hooked a bandy arm 'round both our backs, drawing us close enough to sample his fetid breath.

"But first, shipmates," he chortled. "First, it's topside for a bit o' rum and dry beef ta toast our fine victory over Sir Robert! Plenty o' time for the hard work, eh, then?"

With that settled, he thankfully released us, and bade us follow him back above. Once on deck, I thought the fresh salt air never smelled so sweet.

Even the watered-down rum and leather-dry beef were eagerly received. It was just past midday and most of the crew lounged on deck awaiting a tour in the rigging or tending to small personal business such as the sharpening of weapons or mending of their tattered garb. As we finished our meal, a tall man with fair complexion made himself a place near the mizzen and proceeded to regard us with more than casual interest. In appearance, he reminded me of someone who might be found sprawled out on a piece of cardboard near a heating grate by the Boston Public Library. A virulent raggedness began at his clothing and infected his hair, his skin, and his very demeanor. His eyes darted about as if they had decided that he was always facing the wrong way. In the rare moments that they did settle on a thing, the eyes seemed to grow wide with a strange inner light indicating some profound sense of discovery. So it was when they settled on Burrage and me.

"Tom *seen* 'im!" the man announced, the words tumbling from a trembling lower lip. "There, in the dark!"

He paused to let the meaning sink in. Burrage and I glanced at one another.

"Are you talking to us?" I asked the darting eyes.

"Tom, 'e told old Worms, 'e did, an' Worms told me! Seen 'im behind the Door waitin' in the dark! Waitin' there in the dark like a spider, 'e was! Wiv those tiny lit'le eyes!'

With each word, the poor fellow shrank in on himself, as though he expected to be gobbled up by some unseen predator at any moment. My professional instincts kicked in.

"Why don't we start with your name," I offered, hoping to get his mind on a less threatening track. "Then we can hear what you have to say."

The man stared for a moment as if he didn't understand, then replied, tugging at his forelock.

"*Daggett*. Thelonius Daggett. Please ta make yer acquaintance," he said, although his gaze seemed to drift right through us and fix itself somewhere out on the horizon.

"Mr. Daggett," I continued, immensely unsure of my direction. "Pleased to make your acquaintance, as well. I'm not sure I understand what you were trying to tell me."

"*Good* lad, I am," he went on distractedly. "Keeps me eyes open, I does, jus' like Worms says. Keeps 'em on *ye*. Like a spider, 'e is. Like a spider!"

"A spider?" I asked. "Who is like a spider?"

Daggett drew back, his voice barely above a whisper and his eyes like saucers.

"Behind the Door! In the dark! Tom seen 'im! Told old Worms, 'e did! Ye'll tell old Worms I got me eyes on ye? I'm a good lad, I am!"

With that, Thelonious Daggett slowly backed away toward the rail and disappeared down the main hatch.

"What was *that* all about," Burrage snorted, and went back to chewing his last morsel of dried beef.

Odd, I thought. The Burrage I knew would have ordinarily been thrown into a frenzy by the bizarre encounter we had just experienced. And yet, here he was, sloughing it off as if nothing had happened. When had Burrage suddenly developed this calm, detached attitude? He used to imagine evil lurking in every corner of his life and yet, now that he was trapped in a world seemingly overrun with darkling entities, he acted as though he was watching some campy flick on late night TV.

"What's *with* you?" I asked.

"What?" he replied, with genuine surprise.

"Jesus, Burr! Wasn't it you who nearly went into seizures because some tree roots got in your face back in that tunnel? And wasn't it you who went brain dead in that little dungeon they had us in back there? Now we're being stalked by some borderline psychotic on a pirate ship in the 17th century and you act like it doesn't faze you? Is it me? Am I crazy or are we not in the deepest *SHIT* of our lives?"

Burrage seemed truly stunned by my outburst. He took a few seconds to reflect and then shook his head slowly back and forth.

"I don't know, Max," he began. "I just don't feel like it's all that bad somehow. I mean, the fact that we're still alive, it's already beyond belief, you know? And yet, here I am sitting on this unbelievable ship, drinking rum and eating this beef stuff. It really tastes pretty good, doesn't it? We're alive! Christ! Who'd have thought it! We're on a goddam pirate ship and we're alive and eating beef and we just kicked British ass! I mean, God, Max, I feel *good*."

I stared in disbelief as Burrage sprang to his feet and lifted his nose into the wind, taking deep draughts of salt air. I could almost see him flexing his arm muscles under his filthy tunic as he turned slowly about taking in the whole incredible scene around him. I couldn't believe it.

A few hours later, I found myself deep in the hold, alone. Snitch had brought me down shortly after the midday meal and set me to work hauling twelve-pound cannonballs from the bow locker to the aft. Having made untold dozens of trips, I now sat myself upon a water cask just above the powder room. As I sought to catch my breath, I struggled to understand my place in this terrible dream.

Burrage was not with me, as it turned out. It seemed that Ditty Gunn had overheard his remarks on deck and, sensing an opportunity, offered my friend the option of hauling shot below or trying his hand with a cutlass up on deck. There was no mystery as to which Burrage would

choose. My last glimpse found him under the tutelage of a certain
Spaniard—the only one tolerated on board ship as it turned out—named
Don Pedro Manual Ramirez de Santiago.

Don Pedro was a slender, dark-skinned fellow with poetic brown eyes
and a precisely sculpted beard upon his chin. His clothing was somewhat
more flamboyant than that of his peers and it was clear that he fancied
himself something of a dandy. He and his Anglo mates viewed one
another with mutual disrespect. He was prideful, self-absorbed, and an
unapologetic braggart and, while his boasts about his amorous conquests
were rightfully dismissed, his skills as a swordsman were unquestioned.
Although his weapon of choice was an evil-looking dueling sabre, he was
a master of any blade.

Don Pedro was the sole survivor of an encounter between the *Anne
Boleyn* and a Spanish vessel carrying sick and wounded soldiers back to
their homeland. Thinking he had somehow happened upon a wayward
treasure galleon, de L'Hiver had given chase and brought her to heel a
hundred nautical miles northeast of Old Providence Island. Though
pathetically short of able-bodied men, the larger Spanish ship had stood
toe-to-toe with the pirate for the better part of a day. She fought so well
in fact, that de L'Hiver had begun to feel that continuing the battle might
prove too costly and was about to order his gunners to stand down and
prepare to retreat.

Before he could give the command to disengage, however, an
enormous explosion had nearly torn the Spaniard apart. At first, de
L'Hiver believed one of his shots had found the powder magazine, but
then a man was observed leaping from the bow rail of the burning galleon
and frantically making his way toward the *Anne Boleyn*. As he swam
through the waves, several figures on the Spanish ship were seen shouting
in his direction although their intent was never clear.

Once dragged aboard the *Anne Boleyn*, the fugitive would come to
explain that he had been held prisoner on the galleon en route to trial
and certain execution in Spain. Don Pedro claimed that the governor of

Panama had falsely accused him of treason as a pretext to ridding himself of his wife's lover. The governor, he scoffed, was too much a coward to demand satisfaction and so had chosen to disgrace his rival instead. During the sea battle, Don Pedro said that he had been released from his shackles to fight for the undermanned ship, but, fearing the galleon was winning the duel, he had purposely thrown a lighted torch upon a cradle of powder kegs on the gun deck. Or so he claimed.

De l'Hiver, unmoved by the man's story, ordered him to be thrown back into the sea to join his hapless countrymen. But before the order could be carried out, Don Pedro, whilst suspended in the air above the rail, suggested rather aggressively that he had certain information about the routes and sailing dates of several New World treasure fleets. As he was lowered slowly back to the deck, he went on to add that he also could lead de L'Hiver to the undefended back gates of certain Central American strongholds in which the aforementioned treasure was being stored.

The French captain had decided that Don Pedro's tale might be of some value to him. If the story was true, they would all be rich. If it proved false, well, the fact was that the *Anne Boleyn* had not been very lucky over the past several months and a considerable grumbling had developed amongst the company. The Spaniard's story would excite the crew and purchase de L'Hiver several more months of sailing time during which their luck might change. Thus, Don Pedro became a fixture on board the *Anne Boleyn* and, in fact, proved a skilled, if somewhat reluctant warrior in times of conflict. Besides, the Frenchman reasoned, he could feed the fellow to the fishes at any time he became too tiresome.

Unfortunately, there had been no immediate opportunity to pursue the Spaniard's claims, as a combination of storms and several sightings of heavily armed vessels had driven the *Anne Boleyn* north to the Carolinas. Once there, the company was content to victimize a steady stream of lightly armed merchant vessels that seemed intent on crossing paths with the all-too-willing buccaneers. In terms of reward, the results were mixed and the pirates decided to take their hard goods north to the New

England colonies where they could trade them for stores and munitions and to recruit enough willing hearties to man a second ship for an attack on Don Pedro's treasure cities. Hence their ill-fated sojourn to Marblehead, a well-renowned haven for the sort of salty, amoral, hard-bitten scalawags de L'Hiver favored.

At any rate, when I had last seen him, Burrage was sporting a short, broad-bladed cutlass with a stout basket hilt. Don Pedro, a man not known for patience, stood before him spewing a rich, uninterrupted stream of Latin profanity inspired by his pupil's total lack of martial bearing. Burrage, for his part, was undeterred. Striking an aggressive stance, he raised his weapon to the ready and prepared to receive instruction from his new master. The Spaniard sighed and, with a thick accent, tried to communicate the basic skills involved in mutilating one's opponent before he mutilated you.

I was aghast. I felt as if I was witnessing a scene from *Lord of the Flies*. It was one thing to be titillated by romanticized visions of seafaring adventure, but it was quite another thing to throw aside centuries of social evolution and dive head-first into a vat of testosterone. And this, it seemed, was exactly what Burrage had done.

CHAPTER 13

As I sat on my keg alone in the dark, I shut my eyes and tried to evoke images of what had become my former life. The faint smell of wood smoke that never quite left my office; the fireman leaning back on an old kitchen chair in front of the engine house down the street; the color of Hannah Welkie's sweater as she clutched it to her throat in the swirling autumn wind. Like dying embers, each sensory snapshot glimmered ever more faintly in my memory. It was becoming so hard to even imagine that world, because this world—one which should have existed only in imagination—was all too real.

I lowered my head and the air around me suddenly felt damp and icy cold. The thin halo of light that had clung to the edges of barrels and crates in the storage bay evaporated, leaving a darkness blacker than any I had ever known. It entered through my eyes and filled my mind with an inky void. Every muscle in my body went dead as surely as if a switch had been thrown and I remained frozen to the top of the cask like a pile of rusted anchor chain. The sounds of the ship, which had surrounded me just moments ago, became lost in the cotton silence.

My senses, now completely bereft of stimulation, became a blank canvas. At that moment, a dim, red light entered from the hatchway amidships, then hovered just above my head. It flitted about behind me as though it was exploring every small corner of the hold. Still unable to budge, I contented myself to watch the furtive shadows it cast until it finally came to rest in the air just behind my right shoulder.

Within moments, a second light, this one cool blue, entered somewhere from the cable tier below. It, too, poked its way about the orlop beams and hatch coamings, eventually positioning itself just behind my left shoulder.

For several long moments the ghostly lights hung suspended in place, pulsing faintly. I wondered if this eerie display might have some natural explanation, but then the soft rustle of whispering voices began to rise behind me. At first the tone was calm, but as I strained to listen, the voices grew louder and more frenetic. Still, I could neither make out the words nor see the source.

As the cacophony increased, so too, did the intensity of the glowing lights. The voices began to rush like the sound of a mounting wind and the lights flashed like silent thunderbolts. Still, I could not move or turn to face them. The sharp flashes increased and the rushing wind began to roar in my ears and I felt as if the entire ship might come apart at any moment! But then. as quickly as it began, the roaring ceased and the ghost-lights raced briefly 'round the ceiling and shot away through a small crevice in the deck above.

Plunged again into utter darkness, I strained against my own inertia, yet I simply could not move. My eyes frantically searched the darkness when suddenly an image began to flicker in a distant corner of the hold. A pale but potent concentration of energy materialized before me. Whether my eyes were open or shut, I could see it pulsing ever more brightly.

At first I saw the spectral mass as nebulous and undefined, but as I watched it intensify, I realized that it not only had substance but an identity as well—that of Boden Welkie. A searing terror overwhelmed me, yet I could do nothing but sit motionless and silent. It struck me that my paralysis was no accident, but rather a prerequisite for our meeting. A pair of leaden eyes bored through me and for several seconds there was profound and utter silence. Then, a voice began to speak in a hissing, ragged squall.

"What's sworn by one is sworn by all!" it ranted with controlled fury. "And what's done by one shall all undo!"

At this point my sense of boundaries was all but obliterated. The words, so fraught with power and portent, meant nothing to me and yet, I had no doubt that in the end they would mean everything.

"The Door to Hell stands near to thee and those upon the deck! The key is turning in the lock unless the oath is kept!"

With that, the disembodied face shimmered brilliantly and the features began to dissolve in upon themselves and I watched Boden Welkie melt away. The eyes became deep-set, the forehead broadened and the bridge of the nose grew more pronounced. Sharp cheekbones emerged and a long, coarse beard crept round the chin and up along the jowls. Within a matter of seconds, I was looking at an entirely new and unfamiliar countenance.

"The Storm is nigh!" the entity bellowed, "Between both worlds it gathers now, like none that came before! Look not to bodies but to souls of those about to die!"

The eyes peered straight into mine and then exploded in a gigantic flash of red and blue light that left me sprawled on the deck, drenched in my own sweat and shivering with exhaustion.

It was twilight on the *Anne Boleyn* when I finally staggered back onto the main deck. The crew was clustered in little groups as the last light of evening fell peacefully across the rail. Clay pipes were lit and the sound of a fiddle drifted in the cooling breeze. Men lazed about playing games of chance or telling tales that evoked a gasp or a hearty laugh. Down near the foremast, a slender lad with angular features softly sung a tune to shipmates gathered about his feet. The words were of lost love and journeys home and the great ship rose and fell upon the shining sea with the gentle grace of a cradle rocked by a loving hand.

Then, without warning, the evening sky grew thick and black and the waves began to heave as if churned by a giant oar. A violent wind tore through the shrouds and hands leapt to the rigging to close-reef the sails, but as the first men ascended, they were tossed and shaken by the tempest until they lost their grips and plummeted into the cauldron below! The clouds themselves rose upward into the darkness and, as we watched, took on the shape of an immense figure looming thousands of feet above the ship! The men recoiled in horror and threw themselves face down upon the deck as a great, boiling chasm opened up in the surface of the sea. The doomed ship, now dwarfed by the cataclysm, clung momentarily to the precipice like a small twig above the falls, then plunged downward and disappeared into the thundering torrent! The screams echoed high and long until the black water closed in over us once more.

I felt a tug on my sleeve and as I regained consciousness, I leapt to my feet in a blind panic. Turning this way and that, I soon realized that I was once again in the hold of the *Anne Boleyn* and that the terrible storm was gone. It had never happened. Looking down, I saw the startled face of poor William staring back at me as if he feared what I might do next. I let out a low groan and sat back down on the water cask to get my bearings. The line separating dreams from reality had by now grown so blurred that I was on the verge of becoming immobilized. It was getting difficult to feel that anything I might do would have any real bearing on my fate.

I sensed how dangerous my state of mind was to my survival. I reasoned that if any part of my present experience *was* real, it would take all my emotional and intellectual strength to survive it. And I knew intuitively that if it all turned out to be some incredibly virulent psychosis, it would take acting as if it were real to pull myself out of it. Either way, inaction would spell my doom. I centered myself back in the moment and placed my hand on William's shoulder.

"I'm all right," I sighed. "It's good to see you, William. Are you okay?"

William nodded and I was struck by the unexpected calm that he seemed to exude. Whereas I could only imagine feeling complete terror had I been in his shoes, William actually seemed to be quietly thriving. I felt a momentary flash of anger as I realized that both William and Burrage were having an entirely different experience than I. Here I was, accosted by apocalyptic messengers and suffering horrific visions of destruction. And yet, there was William looking like a well-fed farm boy enjoying the benefits of fresh air, clean living, and hard work! And God knows what Burrage was feeling, yet somehow I sensed it was of no more concern than a day on a movie set. I spat on the deck.

"Where's Burrage?" I grumbled.

"With that man, Mr. Quill, and the Captain," William answered. "Mr. Quill sent me to get you."

A brief shudder ran through me and I shook it off.

"All right," I replied. "Lead the way."

William led me between decks to the ladder, then up two flights to the great cabin. There, seated on a cushioned bench was Bartholomew de L'Hiver. Standing to his left was Mr. Quill and seated on a small chair was Burrage, a dark cutlass resting across his lap. I gave him a sharp glare as I entered the room. The Frenchman motioned me to be seated and pointed to a small stool beside his writing desk. William took a seat on the floor and leaned back against the paneling.

The cabin was not what one would call overly ornate, but the woodworking was intricate and beautifully done. The paneling was a dark mahogany and a row of small-paned, leaded windows stretched across the stern just above a bank of low, built-in cabinets. A faded Oriental rug covered most of the forecabin and a number of fine silver chalices stood in a line behind a cup rail near the writing desk. Several rolled charts and four small sea chests were piled in one corner and a brace of flintlock pistols hung above the narrow berth. The cabin was illuminated by three brass lanterns, which swung gently with the roll of the ship. The captain did not allow me the luxury of a more detailed examination of his quarters.

"Forgive me," he said, bowing his head ever so slightly in my direction. "I cannot recall your name."

Not being sure I had ever given it, I introduced myself.

"Maxwell Blessing," I replied quietly.

He nodded and tilted his head forward, contemplating the rings on his right hand. His enormous hat hung on a hook by the door and his long tresses fell forward along the borders of his face giving him the appearance of a great cat peering out from its lair. I tried in vain to read his mood.

"Monsieur Blessing," he continued, not taking his eyes from his jewelry. "I am to understand that you may know the whereabouts of a certain document... a map. Is this true?"

His voice was calm and unhurried, yet I could feel the enormous tension that lay just below the surface. I glanced for a moment at Tobias Quill and he stared back at me unwaveringly.

"Well, *mon ami?*" the captain asked. "Your companions have already graced us with their knowledge in the matter, so do not feel an obligation to be discreet."

Both William and Burrage looked at me in silent agreement, although I had no idea what they might have said. I felt myself begin to panic. I realized that I didn't even know what Burrage was capable of at this point, or William either, for that matter. Both seemed swept up in some perverse fascination with the Baroque world in which we found ourselves. Did I even know them anymore? How much had they changed?

I reasoned that my best chance was to be truthful, but to go as slowly as possible in sharing any details of the matter. Perhaps in the process, I would get an idea of what the captain might believe and adjust my story accordingly.

"I assume you are referring to the small map that Mr. Quill asked me about earlier, the one that was taken from my wall apparently."

"*Oui, monsieur!* The very one! Perhaps you could share the circumstances of your acquisition and where you think the map might now reside," de L'Hiver purred, still not looking in my direction.

I shifted in my seat and glared again at Burrage.

"A friend gave it to me."

"Monsieur Burrage, I understand," the Frenchman interrupted. "And he acquired it from the keeper of a public house, did he not?"

"Correct, but that's all I know about where it came from. I have no idea how the fellow came by it and he's—" I hesitated nervously. "Dead, I'm afraid."

"Indeed!" exclaimed the captain. "And your friend, he brought the poor man to his end?"

"Burrage?" I stammered. "God no! The fellow froze to death. It was an accident."

I realized how tricky this was going to be. Everything I said sounded suspect even to me!

"Ahh. *C'est la vie*," de L'Hiver went on. "And so you put this map on your wall, *n'est pas?* Why did the map appeal to you so? After all, 'twas but a mean little rag, barely the scratchings of a chicken. And yet, you placed it there for all the world to see. Why would you do this?"

"I just liked it, I guess. It was quaint... curious looking. Anyway, it's gone. I have no idea where it is anymore. That's all I know."

The captain looked up for the first time. His eyes were hard, his voice cold and deadly.

"You know more, *mon ami*, much, much more! You saw the man that took it, did you not? A large man. And you followed him!"

My heart sank. Burrage must have told him everything. *Why?*

The Frenchman continued.

"Now, describe this man, this thief!"

My back began to stiffen and my left foot started to shake with tension. Again I shifted on my stool. I was cornered and I knew it. Any hesitation, any lie, and this man would not hesitate to slit my throat the way Snitch had done Ned Buckett! I had no choice.

"All right, it's true I saw the man, but not clearly. It was dark—

nighttime. I had been asleep and I was hiding in the shadows. I was afraid he would—"

"Kill you, *mon ami?* Describe this man. Leave nothing out!"

"He was large, huge it seemed. He wore a long, black coat. He was very ragged, I think. But that's about all. The room was so dark—"

"His face, *monsieur,* his eyes. Did you see his *eyes?*" the captain asked, leaning forward toward me, his hand caressing the hilt of the dagger in his velvet sash.

I pulled back, startled that I had not mentioned this most distinctive feature. I looked around the room and everyone was frozen, waiting for my reply.

"His eye—" I mumbled. "It was completely gone... this one," I indicated, pointing to my right eye.

✳ ✳ ✳

The black figure sat propped against the wall atop one of the disintegrating pine coffins in the catacomb known as The Works. And there, bathed in candlelight three fathoms below Burial Hill, he put the question to Evil Tom.

"What now, Tom?" he asked, cocking his disheveled head to one side. "Ol' Worms wiv Buckett's Bible. What should 'e do? Them's as sailed off, who knows what's ta become of 'em, eh Tom? A storm might drown 'em— aye—or ol' Robert might see 'em dance a pretty jig on Execution Dock!"

He let out a gleeful snort then, reaching casually into the dank recesses of the pine box, he pulled out the decaying head of its long-departed occupant. Holding the skull up to the candlelight, he brushed back such thin strands of hair as still clung to the flaking crown. The soft tissues were gone he noted, though a dark, walnut-colored mildew gave the facial bones a particularly melancholy aspect. Resting the grinning skull on his palm, Worms considered it carefully as Hamlet might have done Yorick.

"My, my, Tom!" he cackled. "She 'as yer very smile, does she not?

What's that ye say, Tom? An' quiet, too? The perfec' bride! I wonder if she's brung a dowry?"

Tossing the head aside, Worms quickly dropped to one knee beside the coffin and ripped the few remaining boards from the top. A cloud of fine, gray dust rose in the dim light like the spores of a toadstool as he rummaged about amongst the folds of the disintegrating funereal gown. He located one hand and then the other, the bones still intact. No rings adorned them. And neither could he find any trace of brooch or pendant, though it was not for a want of thoroughness. By the time he was finished, the poor departed lady had seen more excitement than she probably had experienced in all her years among the living!

"The grave digger done 'is best, it seems!" he growled with indignation. "An' shame upon 'im, too, what wiv 'er scarce gone cold! A Godless folk, Tom! Godless!"

As Worms slowly got himself up, his ears perked and the flame of the candle began to dance excitedly. With one motion, he suddenly whirled himself about and, drawing his dagger, fell upon the silent intruder, knocking him to the ground. With the dagger pressed firmly against the man's throat, Worms grabbed him by a shock of hair and roughly yanked his face into the light.

"No, no, dear God! It's I, Myles Castler!" came the desperate cry.

"Why, so 'tis," remarked the pirate as he dragged the poor fellow to his feet. "No harm done, then, save that nick upon yer gizzard, least ways."

Myles quickly brought his hand to his throat and examined the tips of his fingers. A small smear of blood made him grow momentarily pale, but then he regained his composure. Leaning back against the wall, he took a deep breath.

"An error in judgment on my part," he quickly offered. "Next time I shall make my presence known before it can be misconstrued. But on to more important things. Have you got it?"

Myles Castler seemed to have aged threefold in the time since he had entered the tunnels in search of his accomplice. His thinning hair hung lank and damp, plastered chaotically against his furrowed brow. A dark, stubbly beard gave his skin a sickly pallor in contrast and the formerly clear, steady eyes now scurried about like nervous beetles beneath his brows. His countenance, once the clean, confident study of a modern Englishman, had taken on a certain Uriah Heepish quality, that of someone who shunned the daylight.

Worms fixed him with a stare, then slowly reached under his coat and drew out the mysterious parchment. Myles Castlers' eyes widened expectantly and he reached out his hand to receive it, but Worms pulled back.

"Is there a problem?" the antiquarian asked nervously.

Worms turned aside, deep in thought.

"They've gone," the pirate said, suddenly bringing his loathsome face within a few inches of his companion. Myles found himself recoiling involuntarily, then caught himself. The odor of rot filled his nostrils, but he willed himself to remain steady.

"I know," Myles replied, stepping deftly to one side as if needing more room to fully express himself. "But really, that just makes things easier. After all, we've got the tunnels to ourselves!"

Again Worms moved in, this time nearly pinning the poor Englishman against the wall. The hideous eye was but inches from the smaller man's face and the pirate twisted his gristled mouth into a crooked sneer.

"They got that lad o' yer's as well!" Worms hissed.

"That's of no concern to me," Myles stammered, trying to affect an air of nonchalance. "He's not mine, you realize. I have no feelings for him one way or the other. He was merely part of—"

Worms bore in, his filthy skin almost touching that of his helpless companion.

"Aye?"

"It's a long story," said Myles, his mouth now gone dry. "It has to do with my time in prison. I—I needed a family, a normal life, to prove I had turned a new leaf, so to speak. Barrows & Wight are very conservative, you see. I needed to gain their trust. There was no other way! But my personal feelings never entered in."

Much to Myles' relief, Worms pulled back several inches as he continued the interrogation.

"Aye, yer masters, then... they paid a fine penny fer the things I brung ye, I'll wager!" Worms smirked, stroking his chin with blackened fingers.

Myles, now dripping with perspiration, could feel the buccaneer's hot breath on his face.

"They are fair to me as I have tried to be with you. The charts and books have been well received, yes. Your share of the profits have been placed in the small chest you provided me, just as you have instructed. It is there in my study whenever you wish to have it and none will be the wiser."

For a moment, Worms stared suspiciously into Myles Castlers' blinking eyes, then he stepped back and allowed the shaken man to gather himself. Sensing the pirate was considering his line of thinking, Myles sought to press the issue.

"This map, it was an extraordinary stroke of good fortune that it came to us. With this map, sir, we should have all we need for the rest of our lives! We have but to take it. But you must trust me!"

The buccaneer flashed with anger at the Englishman's pretense and again clutched the hilt of his dagger.

"I must trust ye? Not likely! Ask yer lad ta trust ye! This 'ere is Buckett's Bible, by thunder! An' it shan't leave me 'and until our work is done!"

Satisfied he had made his point, Worms backed off several steps and knelt down. Spreading the old map upon the floor, he brought the candle close to the yellowed surface and traced a line with what was left of his fingernail.

"There!" he whispered. "There's the key! You make sense o' them marks an' me an' ol' Tom'll do the rest!"

✳ ✳ ✳

"Worms!" the captain stormed, as he shot to his feet and began clumping furiously about the small cabin. "Curse me for the day I allowed that pestilent maggot on board this ship!"

"He has it then," Quill spat. "Or soon shall! Are we ta watch 'im have off wiv nine casks whilst we acts the fox fer Sir Robert Vole, by thunder?"

Realizing that he had forgotten himself, Quill immediately shot a lethal glance at Burrage and me and, though we had no idea what was being discussed, we understood that we already had heard too much.

De L'Hiver ceased his seething march about the cabin while the steady, acidic drip of inevitability seeped into his brain and slowly dissolved his former plans. After a moment of inner torment, the Frenchman suddenly reached for his great hat and his velvet coat and strode toward the door.

"*Alors,* we shall come about then back again to tunnels! And when I next see Melchior Wormsley," de L'Hiver announced, barely above a whisper. "We shall see how he fares with *no* eyes!"

With that, the Frenchman exited the cabin as a plume of molten lava might exit the cone of a volcano.

For several long moments, those of us left in the cabin sat riveted where we were. For Burrage, William, and myself, it was the result of stark bewilderment. But for Tobias Quill, it was the opportunity to refocus his agile mind on the crisis at hand. With a deliberateness that belied his considerable agitation, the gray man crossed over to the brandy cabinet and availed himself of a squat bottle containing an unidentified liquor. He poured what was left of the contents into a silver goblet, then turned and sat himself down in the spot lately vacated by the captain himself. Closing his eyes, Quill took a long, slow swallow of the fiery liquid, then wiped the back of his hand across his wet, stubbly chin. He sat for a moment longer, then spoke.

"The milk is on the ground, by thunder, on the *ground!*" he bellowed.

"But now that's done an' there's no denyin'. 'Tis time ye knowed somethin' of't, seein' ye've a part ta play."

I was taken aback.

"*We* have a part to play, did you say?" I asked, feeling even more suspicion than when I was being grilled by the captain.

"Aye, ye an' yer mates 'ere—all o' ye. So I best get on wiv't," he answered resignedly, resting the goblet upon his knee.

We could feel the jerk and luff of the sails as the *Anne Boleyn* swung her great body to larboard and looked to fetch a breeze. As she struck a bold, new tack to the northeast, I knew de L'Hiver was commencing an extremely desperate maneuver, what with Sir Robert presumably riding a favorable wind directly in our path. Should we be sighted, his frigates would have ample time to cut the angle without losing the wind and easily overcome any advantage in speed that the *Anne Boleyn* might ordinarily enjoy.

Quill, too, was aware of the risk but clearly was preoccupied with something far more ominous.

"Ta be sure," he began, shaking his head, "there's a tale ta tell, black as pitch! But there's times I doubts there'll be any left ta tell it."

Quill took another gulp of his drink, then commenced.

"We was all drove up from the Cays. First, 'twas gales what chased us nor'east for more'n a fortnight till there weren't a man could stand the deck wi'out he were tied about the waist! Waves as big as mountains—an' us awash wi' each man haulin' till he's like ta split in two! An' when 'twas done, there we lay like a whipped dog on a rainy night. But ol' *Annie*—aye—*Annie* kept 'er head jus' like she always done!

"But no sooner was we fit-out again than that devil Sir Robert come boomin' up from sou'west an' ne'er stops, damn 'is eyes! Keeps flyin' at us till we both o' us lose the wind! An' so there we sits two whole days, not three leagues apart, by thunder! Ya could nigh see 'im shakin' 'is fist at us!

"An' that's how it went, by the bones o' the prophets! Us wiv half our sail in shreds an' lookin' fer the wind, an' him the same! Two weeks later,

becalmed again! This time right 'ere off Salem Town an' driftin' east wi'
Catamount only two miles ta stern! We could see 'em wet the guns an' we
knows we're as good as stove if the air don't come soon!"

I noticed Quill's head take a slight bow and his eyes narrow as if he
was facing into a bitter wind. His mouth hardened and the chalky pallor
of his cheeks seemed to grow even more pale, if that was possible. But the
greatest change was in his voice. Where he had been telling a bold and
robust tale, his cadence now grew slow and hypnotic, almost as if he was
envisioning what he described in front of his own unblinking eyes.

"We was all on deck, every man-jack mendin' sheets and settin' lines,
tryin' ta coax a breeze an' deliver us from them terrible guns. The air were
heavy, dead almost, even the telltales hung down like they was made o'
wood. No man spoke a word fer there was naught ta be said.

"Then the Cap'n, 'e ordered down th' long boat ta haul us broadside
so leastways we might make a run afore we was blowed apart. Ol' Sir
Robert, 'e already swore there'd be no trial. 'Twould be ball or rope fer us
an' we all knowed it.

"But then," Quill's mouth grew dry and his lip trembled. "Afore a man
could make a move, we seen the blue light take out o'er the horizon then
beat back toward us, down o'er the *Catamount,* so close to 'er topgallants
that ye could see blue fire dancin' along 'er spars and down 'er riggin'!
Dark clouds, monstrous huge, was stackin' up in the sky an' the sun were
hid like night, but *still* no hint o' wind! We was all struck dumb, we was,
dumb an' froze ta the pin rail! The sea begun ta move like the wind were
strong out o' the nor'east, but nary a breeze touched cheek nor sail!

"The light come hard ta starboard, an' then a second one, red this
time, come up from the south an' crossed our 'T'! I never seen the like!

"Well, by now I'm thinkin' the Angel o' Death were come ta say the
Last Words, an' us such great sinners, ta be sure! Many a lad went knees
ta deck an' raised 'is 'ands in prayer askin' forgiveness an' beggin' mercy
in cries so piteous as ta make a stone weep! But them lights, they just
keeps movin' at us, an' the closer they gets, the louder the sound o' a great

storm-wind! Howlin' and churnin' the waves, it was, yet not a puff o' air!

"By now, I knows it ain't no angel but must be the Devil 'imself, come direc' ta carry our poor souls ta Perdition! The men, they jus' throwed themselves on their faces cryin' an' screamin' most profound! An' that was when we all heard the voice—there, high up in the wind!

"One lad, Able Peach, it were, 'e jumps ta 'is feet and yells 'Ol' Dimond! Ol' Dimond, ya come!' An' wiv that, every Marbleheader on board leaps up ta join 'im all laughin' an' dancin' like they jus' spooned gold in their slum-gullion!"

Quill paused again as if still entranced by the very memory of the encounter.

Old Dimond, I thought! And the *lights*! I could barely contain myself! *What should I do?!* Should I spill the truth about everything I had seen and heard? Was our fate now so woven with that of the *Anne Boleyn* that I should now throw caution to the wind? I glanced over at the quartermaster as he drained the last contents of the goblet. There was no logic and there was no clarity. I only knew that the burden of my encounters with Boden Welkie seemed to be shaking the very foundation of my emotional stability. Before I could pause to reconsider, I blurted it out.

"I've seen him—Old Dimond! Not an hour ago down in the hold."

Quill looked up abruptly and drew back as though someone had discharged a pistol. Burrage and William stared at me dumfounded, but there was no holding back now.

"Down in the hold. I was sitting on a barrel and I saw the lights! Red and blue. They flew about the room, then shot away. Boden Welkie, he just appeared there in the darkness. But then he changed... changed into someone else!"

Quill's eyes widened.

"It was just like a face floating there in the darkness. At first, I recognized him as someone I knew, but then it transformed into an old man I'd never seen before. He had a high, arched nose and whiskers all around the edge of his face. Like this..." I said, drawing my finger along the full arc of my jawbone.

"Dimond!" Quill gasped, as though struck by a boom. "'Tis the very one! Eyes like frozen fire, 'e 'as. An' he spoke ta us just so, 'is face jus' floatin' there like a gull on the wind. We all seen it! Gave me the fantods, it did!"

Quill had once again been transported back to the moment of that ethereal visit.

"He bade us all listen, but ta be sure, we 'ad no choice. It were Ol' Dimond what come ta save the 'Headers jus' like 'e done so many a time, an' us wi' 'em, by our good fortune! A miracle, by thunder! A miracle, indeed!"

Quill then leaned out toward me and dropped his voice so low that I could barely hear him.

"But how 'e done it—aye—there's the heart of't. There's the tale!"

Quill was now so immersed in the telling that twice he tried to coax another drink from the goblet, forgetting that he had already drunk it dry.

"Aye, indeed, that's 'ow we come ta be down in the tunnels."

"Yes, the tunnels," I prodded. "You dug them then?"

"Us? Dug them tunnels? Not likely! Why 'twould take a hundred men a hundred years ta dig the likes o' them. Most of 'em's struck through solid rock."

"Well, how did they get there?" I persisted.

"Some says they was always there or 'twas red savages dug 'em a thousand years ago. Ol' Dimond, even 'e don't know fer certain, but 'e warned us about the Door! Aye, 'Door ta Perdition' he called it. Solid oak but no handle, nor latch, nor lock neither. An' no one ever seen it so much as ajar nor wished ta. 'Tis said Old Scratch 'imself lurks behind there on a throne o' human heads, waitin' fer us ta break our oath. Me, I thinks maybe 'twere the spirits what dug them tunnels, cursed souls below Burial Hill tryin' ta carve a way up ta heaven, God forgive em!"

We were thoroughly enthralled as Quill's story unfolded.

"What was this 'oath' you keep talking about? And how did the tunnels protect you? Why couldn't the English still hunt you down, burn you out or something?" Burrage asked.

"Ahh, that were the beauty, ya see! All Sir Robert found is the *Anne Boleyn* empty an' rollin' in the swells at harbor mouth. He searched the town—kept 'is men on all the roads, but Ol' Dimond, 'e kept us hid. Eight score an' three we was, disappeared wi'out so much as a boot heel in the sand! Livin' 'neath the town for nigh on a year now an' Sir Robert swearin' not ta leave till we was all at the end o' a rope!" Quill cackled at the thought.

"But, how ever did you survive?" I asked.

"The nine gates," Quill whispered. "More like hatch-ways, truth be told."

"And these 'gates'... they have to do with time, don't they? The closet in my office is one of them, isn't it!" I challenged, as the startling reality started to take shape in my mind. "You took what you needed from the town all right, but you did it three hundred years later! Is that it? But how can that be? It would take truckloads of food to keep so many alive for so long and I know that never came through my closet."

"And the map, what does that show, then?" I went on, feeling I might never get so much in the way of information again. "Those nine crosses... those are the gates!"

Quill, realizing that more was being discerned than he had intended, grew immensely uneasy and began to pace the cabin deck. "Aye, gates indeed, each to a different time."

Burrage and I looked at one another unable to believe our ears. "You mean you have actually gone to other times as well? What years? What did you find?"

"Belay there!" Quill bellowed, clearly feeling pressed beyond his limits. "Enough o' that, then! 'Tis enough ta say we done it, though we paid dear. Every journey through a gate would age a man afore 'is time."

For the first time, he seemed to grow genuinely pensive. "Per'aps it were the pure wonder of't. Imagine, the colony at war wiv England, by thunder! Other queer an' terrible things as well, so terrible as ta make a man afeared ta see it! Nay, the food ne'er passed through the Key. Some salt cod come from the flakes in the year 1671. The rest from the docks in 1863. I confess, at times it took a stroke o' the cat fer the hands ta make the journey. 'Tain't natural,' the men would say. Weren't none o' us took any joy in it."

I was speechless. I took a moment to focus my mind and understand exactly what I was hearing. These ragged, desperate men, creatures of the 18th century, had basically been living off of supplies stolen from the docks of Civil War-era Marblehead and dried cod from 17th century fish-drying racks! *Who would believe it?* I asked myself, and yet, in light of my experiences during recent days, it was really no surprise.

"But the oath," Burrage persisted, getting us back to the main point.

"Aye, the oath," Quill sighed. "Ol' Dimond, 'e cast the terms, 'e did. As long as we stays in the tunnels, Sir Robert can't get at us, but there was the oath an' we daren't go against it! First, we must ne'er bring harm ta man nor woman beyond our time—the 'time folk' as we come ta call 'em—nor bring 'em back wiv us.

"Next, every hour a man lives beyond a gate, sees 'im age a whole day! That way, no man shall be tempted ta slip off, ya see—stay in a time where 'e don't belong! He'd die an ol' man in a year or two, 'e would!"

My God! I thought. *Did that mean WE were aging as well?* I did some quick math. It had probably been two or three days since we had first come down the ladder. That would be worth about two months if the rule held true. I looked at Burrage. He sported a normal, scruffy beard for the time we had been in the tunnels. With great relief, I concluded that we must not be subject to those same laws. I could tell that Burrage had come to a like conclusion and that Quill looked at me with the same subtle spark of realization, although he said nothing.

"So, you can't harm us and you can't go outside your time without shriveling up in a year or two and I assume that since we came of our own accord, you won't be held responsible for our presence here. Is that right? Is there more?" I asked.

Quill narrowed his eyes and turned his back to me as he returned to his seat.

"There may be," he replied, again choosing discretion over candor. "But no need ta preach a sermon when a prayer'll do."

I was suddenly confused. Why had Quill bothered to relate any of this to us now? The information had no bearing on our situation that I could see. Indeed, the whole crisis had been precipitated by something that Quill had not even addressed!

"All right then, what about the map? You clearly know where these gates are located already, so the crosses are of no importance," I said, thinking out loud.

I studied Quill's expression. He seemed nonplussed by my comments and yet, it had to be the map! Something was hidden on that old rag that was so important that de L'Hiver would turn his ship straight back into the path of his pursuers! And now this creature Worms possessed it, which seemed to be the true source of panic.

"There's something else! Something this Worms character can use," I mused.

"Those little *dots!*" Burrage chimed in. "The red ones near the drawing of the lady!"

The gray man's eyes flashed even though his head never moved. So that was it!

"It's a code," I whispered.

C H A P T E R   1 4

*S*tanding up slowly and arching his back, Myles Castler attempted to work the stiffness out of his aching shoulder. The manhandling he had just received from the brutish Wormsley had exacted a toll mentally as well as physically. As a co-conspirator, Myles was in the worst possible position. His well-being, indeed, his very survival, depended on correctly reading the moods of a man who was basically a vicious, 18th century psychopath. There was now no doubt in his mind that the moment he ceased to be of value, the buccaneer would likely put a blade to him.

Myles Castler also suffered from the knowledge that he deserved nothing better. He distinctly remembered the moment when he knew who he was and what he was. An Episcopal acolyte at the age of ten, he had once stolen several pounds from the collection box of his local church. When another boy was accused, he felt not only relief but a curious rush of joy. Even when the local bishop offered to withdraw the accusation in exchange for the anonymous return of the sums, Myles had opted to do nothing. The other boy, harshly rejected by a disgraced family, eventually hanged himself from the headstock of the tenor bell in the church tower.

At the time, even Myles was surprised by his lack of remorse and the perverse sense of power that the entire episode had instilled in him. After that, his life became a shadow-world of deceit, betrayal, and conscienceless acts. An insatiable need to procure money was secondary only to his desire to do so in the most deliciously illicit manner possible. And yet, in some parallel realm of his psyche, there remained a troubling sense that some day the ledger would be reconciled and that he would inevitably pay the price. By now, the sheer volume of his calumnies had outstripped his ability to imagine exactly what that price might be. He assumed that whatever line separated the forgivable from the unforgivable had long since been crossed and that the likely outcome was an untimely death, presumably quite painful.

"I need a break I'm afraid," he said, rubbing his eyes.

A small magnifier rested on the yellowed map and distorted the rows of pale red dots causing them to curve up behind the convex glass like a flight of elliptical geese. "I can hardly make out the details anymore. This candlelight is far too dim for this kind of work. Even with my glass, the marks are simply blurring together."

"Quit yer brayin'," came the harsh retort. "An' haul yerself back down again! The map were done by Quill's hand. I seen that right off. But 'twere Ned Buckett made them marks, I tell ye! An' a more clever piece o' meat ye n'er seen than Ned's brain. It's all there, damn ye. Ye jus' hafta see it proper. Now back at 'er. The sooner we're quit o' this place, the better!"

Worms pulled several more candle stubs from his coat and placed them in a small ring around the top of the parchment, lighting each in turn. With a weary sigh, Myles Castler knelt down and studied the patterns once more.

As the minutes passed, he could hear the thick, impatient rasp of Wormsley's breathing immediately behind his right shoulder. Beads of perspiration began to merge into slow-moving droplets that crept down Myles' cheeks and the bridge of his nose. Finally, one such drop gathered on his chin then fell like a small water balloon bursting upon the lens of the magnifier. He sat up to wipe it clean with his handkerchief.

"Here now!" Worms gruffed, poking the map with the point of his dagger. "What do ye make of 't?"

As Myles peered desperately at the rows of neatly placed dots, a vague sense of familiarity began to seep into his exhausted mind. Something about the patterns of the tiny dots, some on the horizontal, others on the vertical, and a few nestled on a diagonal plane amongst the rest, reminded him of prison. At first he could not place them whatsoever, but then, in the back of his mind, he imagined the sound of shouts and cheers, followed by groans and curses. The sounds grew louder and an image began to present itself: a hand thrusting quickly out, then jerking back again. The shouts. The groans. The hand once more.

And then it came clear to him. He recalled the games of chance played there in the shadows of the prison yard at HMP Dartmoor, the ancient stone keep in the Devonshire countryside. In his mind's eye, he could still see the hands flashing out and the small, tumbling cubes of ivory-colored plastic shooting through the air toward the granite wall. *Dice!*

"These look like rows of gaming dice!" he exclaimed. "See here... the little groupings of pips. If you use your imagination, they appear to stand in pairs! I'm sure of it!"

Worms pressed forward and squinted his only remaining eyeball at the mysterious symbols. As he stroked his ragged chin, a glimmer of recognition brought a small, grudging nod.

"Aye, Ol' Ned, 'e took ta gamin' the way another might ta rum. An' 'e won more'n 'is fair share, damn 'is eyes!"

By this time, Myles was hunkered down on his elbows counting the spots and scribing numbers in the moldering dust of the catacombs.

"See here? Simply add up the pairs! Two plus two is four, four plus two is six, then seven then another six and so on! Could it really be that simple?" he asked aloud.

By the time he was done with his audit, he had written five pairs of numbers in the dirt. In addition, the map offered the already discernable number of "1863" which, for some reason, had not been encoded like the rest.

"Now the question is, what do they mean? They're certainly not navigational coordinates. Dates, I wonder? Addresses?"

Worms, who had been studying the rows of dots and the numbers scribbled in the dust, licked his lower lip and squinted his eye. In a quick motion, he brought Evil Tom up to his ear and listened intently. With a loud shout he jumped to his feet and began to dance a lively jig, cackling and snorting as he spun about in the candlelight. He suddenly stopped, then stuck out his foot and smudged the numbers under the toe of his shoe.

"Ol' Tom, yer a trump, I tell ye, a trump!" he cried, turning to Myles. "Damn yer dates an' all the rest!"

Myles struggled to his feet, at once both startled and confused.

"Them's the game!" Worms crowed, pointing once more to the rows of dots. "Aye, the game. Called 'Duke o' Zed.' Damn ye, Ned Buckett for a clever stoat!"

"Duke of Zed?" Myles urged. "What is it? What kind of game?"

"A fine game an' one what Ned n'er tired of. Why, 'e carried the bones about in a goat skin 'e did, so's 'e could chance any man out o' his rum ration when e'er he pleased. The skin, ye see, it had letters writ on't, writ in squid ink they was. An' the bones—'fivers' we calls 'em—pips on five sides, one through five, then the last side bare, the 'Duke's Arse' we calls it!"

"So how is it played? And what's it got to do with the map?" Myles continued, starting to chafe at Worms' scattergun recollections.

"This is the way o' it," Worms explained. "The skin got five rows an' five letters each, one o'er t'other."

"Can you draw them?" Myles asked excitedly. "Here in the dirt."

He watched as Worms carefully scribed an 'A,' then a 'B.' The buccaneer hesitated, as if unsure how to proceed.

"Ain't got me letters," he growled.

Myles took over and quickly plotted out the standard alphabet— 'A' to 'E' on the first row, 'F' to 'J' on the second and so forth, until he came to the last.

"There, is that the way it was done?" he asked.

Worms considered for a moment, then nodded his head. "Aye, that's the way—jus' so!"

"And the 'Z,'" Myles inquired. "Where does it go?"

"Why, that's the Duke o' Zed!" Worms exclaimed. "The Duke don't consort wiv' the common folk. Nay, the Duke sits on the bones, ye see, as any high-born comes ta take yer money!"

"I see," Myles continued. "What next?"

"She goes like this: Once ye toss 'em, the larb'rd counts the row an' starb'rd counts the letter. If ye rolls a 'two' an' a 'four,' well, that makes..."

"Here!" Myles said, pointing to the letters. "Second row, fourth letter—the letter 'I'! Is that how it goes?"

"Aye, the bones decides," Worms answered, straying off into a flight of prurient fantasies. "Ye must love the bones... caress 'em like the innkeeper's daughter, tickle their pips till the sweat runs through yer fingers. If ye can make 'em wriggle afore the toss, why they'll fall on their backs like a two-penny frisker!"

"What are you saying exactly?" Myles forced himself to ask, although further details of Wormsley's sordid gaming fetishes threatened to numb his mind completely.

"Why, yer *wager*, damn ye!" Worms growled impatiently. "Each man, he lays a shillin' down, like this..."

The buccaneer tossed a coin on the letter "W" scrawled in the dust.

"Now, each man lays 'is wager," he continued, indicating other letters that might be covered. "Ye toss the bones an' reads the pips. If I toss 'five' ta starb'rd or 'three' ta larb'rd, I steers course straight ta the mark. If I toss 'em both on the same throw, why then I takes every coin on the skin. But when the Duke shows his bare bottom, well, ye lose yer wager an' that's an end to it!"

"I see," Myles said, anxious to test the concept on the map.

He carefully inspected the first pairing. The "larb'rd" pips, as Worms had referred to the left-hand grouping, numbered two. The right hand count was the same.

"All right then, that would be second row, second letter... 'G.'"

Worms drew closer as though he were monitoring the fair division of booty. Myles dutifully scribed the letter "G" in the dirt.

"Next, four and two, that would give us the letter 'Q.'"

This was drawn to the right of the "G." Myles leaned back for a moment to quickly check his work.

"There's our first pair!" he announced, feeling the same rush of excitement that he might digging through the last few inches of dirt above a treasure chest. "Now for the next pairing. We have a four and a three, that's 'R'. Five and one gives us 'U'. Splendid!"

He continued without a pause until the pairs of letters were stacked in five short rows before them. "G Q," then "R U," followed by "A I," "V L," and "E L". For several long minutes, they stared at the letters waiting for a sense of recognition to awaken in their brains.

Suddenly, Myles felt the hot glow of Wormsley's poisonous breath on the back of his neck. The razor sharp blade of the dagger sprang hard against the naked skin of his throat. With the finality of one who took deep pleasure in relieving a man of his windpipe, the buccaneer whispered in his ear, "Tom says 'e's done waitin'."

Snitch dug into his shirt and after a short search, emerged with a small chunk of biscuit. In one quick motion, he flicked off the twisting maggot that had taken up residence in the chalky crust and popped the morsel in his mouth. The biscuit being hard as a rock, he stashed it below his tongue and waited patiently for time and spit to soften it to palatability. With only thirteen remaining teeth, he was loath to bite down too soon.

Straddling the topgallant yard high upon the main, the sturdy yeoman leaned back against the mast and hooked his arm about the jeers. The once bright blue sky had tarnished to a dark smudge and the gusting chill caused the *Anne Boleyn* to stagger through the waves like a wounded animal. The horizon soared and plunged below the trestle tree, framed by the topgallant and main sheets. Snitch, and the dozen others who had been sent aloft, had been told by Ditty Gunn to sing out any sail the moment it appeared, but the constant pounding had made it difficult to stay focused on so much empty sea. That was why Snitch nearly lost his perch when the two large ships appeared.

"Sails ho!" he screamed. "Dead ahead!"

The deck exploded in a frenzy. Captain Bartholomew, already at the bow rail, sited his large brass scope out beyond the bowsprit and waited for a glimpse of the uppermost sails to come into view. The moment they did, he knew Sir Robert was upon them armed with a favoring wind. For all the action of her hull, the *Anne Boleyn* was making fewer than four knots as she bent to the wind on a larboard tack to the northeast. *Catamount* and *Dartmoor,* on the other hand, were in full bloom and running free, wind on the starboard quarter making eleven knots and closing fast.

Now was the moment by which these captains would be measured. The supreme chess match was about to begin with each master straining to anticipate what the other might do to ensure or avoid engagement. The great ships were pitifully ill-suited for deft maneuvering, square rigged, prisoners of the wind, and victims of their own momentum. As a consequence, courses set one minute might not show the result until many minutes later and those results could be disastrous. Even a minor miscalculation could easily mean the difference between escape and annihilation.

In this game of cat and mouse, assets could become liabilities in the blink of an eye. The ship with the favoring wind, while making greater speed, might also overshoot the mark. A vessel with the beamy dimensions to serve as a stable platform for the largest guns was invariably slower and less nimble.

As the Frenchman surveyed the scene unfolding before him, he quickly sorted through the more obvious possibilities. He made the assumption that Sir Robert, a pit bull and a braggart, would hold nothing back. With two powerful ships-of-the-line, the English outnumbered him two to one and out-gunned him at least ten-fold. The British guns were larger, reached farther and with greater effect. Some could throw a 48-pound ball well over a thousand yards. The gunners, having survived life in the Royal Navy, were tough as bar-shot and knew their business far better than the half-trained crews that de L'Hiver could bring to the touch-hole.

There seemed little doubt that short of the pirates' surrender, Sir Robert expected nothing less than to see every man-jack floating face down in the swells. With an obsession that bordered on sociopathic, Sir Robert had waited for nearly a year to see these rats exit their burrow and come out into the open. And each day he had spent rotting on the deck of his ship or holed up in some dank colonial hovel had added another cup of bile to his blood. No, this time there would be no denying him the cruel pleasure he felt was his just reward.

For his part, de L'Hiver knew that he could simply turn south once more and race the English all the way to Bermuda. He had no doubt that he could put leagues between them in a day or so, the wiser choice by far. But the Frenchman had not risen to his current office without taking a serious risk or two along the way. In reality, however, he had never been put to a test the likes of this one. He did not have a good feeling about what he was about to do. But the unbearable image of Melchior Wormsley sorting through the mysteries of Buckett's map drove de L'Hiver half-mad with fury.

As the vessels were poised to converge, it seemed clear that once the *Anne Boleyn* came within range, the English ships could easily swing to the broadside and deliver a thundering welcome. And yet, the Frenchman noted, *Catamount* and *Dartmoor* now stood a mere 150 yards apart, a tactical error which most likely reflected Sir Robert's arrogant belief that he would destroy the *Anne Boleyn* long before she ever reached the tiny corridor that ran between his warships. The danger to Sir Robert, of course, was that if the de L'Hiver's ship somehow survived the initial barrage and boldly sailed between her larger attackers, the English guns would be forced to stand down, lest they wound one another in the attack.

A second consequence, which might prove favorable to the smaller ship, was the fact that her assailants must slow themselves to a crawl in order to have any chance of hitting the moving target. If she was able to make it through the initial gauntlet of fire, the English ships would be stalled and facing in the wrong direction for pursuit, while the *Anne Boleyn* would be under full sail.

These thoughts and more raced in quick succession through the Frenchman's brain. As he now saw it, the best move was the boldest, lash the wheel and sail directly into the approaching storm. And so he did.

The first crash we heard was the sound of the crossjack yard letting go and one end coming to rest on the poop deck above our heads. Quill leapt to his feet and bolted from the cabin just as a second iron missile came flying through the upper rigging. Before a word could be spoken, William and Burrage were through the door as well and I was left standing alone, wide-eyed and shaken to the core. With every ounce of resolve that I could muster, I made my way to the deck in time to witness the mayhem that ensued.

Men were in motion everywhere, in the rigging, above deck, and below. Several gun crews surrounded their weapons. They scurried about with the agitated precision of worker ants ministering to a great, brass queen, washing her, feeding her, preparing her to give birth.

Above our heads, a half-dozen topmen armed with boarding axes slashed frantically at the damaged lines beneath the mizzen top. They had already begun to haul the crippled yard back into place and were trying to ready the tie to receive it. Realizing the tie chain could not be repaired in time, they quickly threaded stout lines through the undamaged links to secure the heavy timber and within minutes, the crossjack was back in action and doing its best to harvest wind for the gauntlet run.

Other than some lines and tackle, the initial damage was slight and Gunn soon had the crew immersed in its duties. On every face I saw the stark mask of fear, skin drawn tight across clenched jaws and mouths yearning to cry out. Yet none did. Every man seemed to sense that the die was cast and any fearful act would only diminish what could be his last moments on earth. For now, the only comfort any of them might find lay in the eyes of his shipmates. In this moment of truth, each man looked to the other for that fragile, unspoken pledge that he would hold his fear in check and do his duty. And if they all could somehow manage to do so, they just might survive the inferno they were about to enter.

And an inferno it was. With the three vessels now just a quarter mile apart, the sky burst forth in a hellish deluge of fire and shot. As darkness descended, a vast, mythic scene began to unfold. The forty starboard cannons of the *Dartmoor* spewed forth a boiling wall of smoke. As successive rounds were fired, the continuous thunder rolled across the water and struck the small ship like a shock wave. The mounting clouds of smoke, now illuminated from within, writhed above the waves like some amorphous, volcanic beast about to spew a pool of lava from its belly. The guns, relentless and cruel, hurled thousands of pounds of iron into the air and into the sea around the hapless *Anne Boleyn*.

And yet, throughout it all, the English ships had behaved just as de L'Hiver had anticipated with one critical exception. *Dartmoor*, the starboard-most ship, had turned to larboard in order to train her guns full-force on the approaching *Anne Boleyn* as was expected. But *Catamount*, rather than swinging to the starboard side, had also taken a larboard tack. So, rather than holding her position and joining in the bombardment, she was slowly narrowing the gap that lay between her and her sister vessel. This was extremely bad.

De L'Hiver had built his entire strategy on taking fire only from a distance. He had counted on silencing the British guns at the very moment when he would be closest and most vulnerable to them. In addition, he had counted on the relative immobility of the warships to give him a critical advantage on the first leg of his escape. But without access to the corridor between the vessels, the plan simply could not work. Sir Robert would maintain the deadly barrage even as the *Anne Boleyn* closed to within a hundred yards of his guns. And worse yet, *Catamount* was already positioning herself for an effective pursuit should the pirate manage to escape the first assault by *Dartmoor*. Even retreat was now impossible, for any attempt by the *Anne Boleyn* to come about and head to the south would parade her directly in front of the starboard guns of Sir Robert's flagship.

The Frenchman simmered with the realization that it was his own rash judgment, not Sir Robert's over-confidence, that would decide the fate of the *Anne Boleyn*. He turned to Ditty Gunn and in a voice as cold as ice, commanded him to take charge of the deck.

By the time de L'Hiver had pulled himself up the steps of the poop deck and clamped his angry fists on the wheel, the English gunners had found the range. Shot after shot tore through the shrouds and the air was filled with bits of rope dangling from the spars like vines in a burning jungle.

All this I witnessed in the span of twenty minutes. Burrage had made for the capstan, that being the closest thing to a battle station that he could identify until now. William crouched behind him and gazed with anxious wonder at the violent panorama unfolding before his eyes. Within minutes, Gunn hurried across the quarterdeck and beckoned them to follow. Motioning for me to join him as well, the first mate yelled down an open hatchway and the head of Thelonius Daggett popped up from below like a prairie dog. Daggett, for some inconceivable reason, had been put in charge of getting black powder from the magazine to the gunners on deck. And to my abject horror, I realized that we were expected to help him.

As we scrambled down the ladders to the magazine, I strained to see how Burrage and William were holding up. In keeping with the many contradictions of the past 24 hours, both behaved as if they were having the time of their lives. They could barely contain themselves now that they had become full, functioning participants in the surreal nightmare that had enveloped us. Was I the only one with the civility to remain terrified? My indignation was suddenly interrupted by the precarious piping of Thelonius Daggett's voice.

"Not my fault!" he huffed to no one in particular. "Tom knows who done it! Aye, now ol' Scabs got to bring the powder up afore the spiders comes out o' the dark. Afore the fire drives 'em out."

Daggett, an incoherent monologue still festering under his breath, turned abruptly and handed us each a worn, leather shoulder sling that could be used to support the small kegs of black powder. Having no idea how to reason with this marginal human being, I found myself dutifully taking hold of a keg of the highly explosive mixture that I would theoretically then transport up to the deck of the burning ship.

"Powder monkeys!" William exclaimed proudly. "That's what we are! Powder monkeys!"

With that he took his heavy keg and clambered out of the dark hold toward the roar of the battle above. I clutched Burrage's sleeve.

"Burr!" I choked. "You're not going up there..."

"Christ, Max," he answered, primarily with irritation, yet not without a touch of sympathy. "What else can we do?" Then he jerked his arm away and disappeared up the ladder.

I turned to Daggett, who stood staring at me with wide, luminous eyes made moist by some fleeting emotion that the sane world could only guess at. For a brief instant, he seemed to break free of his chronic disorientation and acknowledge the enormous moment that engulfed us all, but then turned his back and went muttering off into the nether regions of the hold. As I listened to the storm raging above, I turned and went back up the ladder.

The scene was even more horrific than the one I had left only minutes before. The *Anne Boleyn* had closed to within three hundred yards of *Dartmoor* and now found herself in the center of a maelstrom. Chain and bar shot hissed through the air ripping canvas and line from the masts like a flail. For every yard of sail that the topmen could replace or repair, a half dozen others hung in tatters. To make matters worse, the storm of red hot metal had started more than a dozen fires in the rigging. Splintered yards swung wildly about like stickbugs struggling in a spider's web. It had become so dangerous aloft that survival itself was now the only goal for those unlucky enough to find themselves there.

And yet, conditions on deck were even more terrible. The fiery rain of debris from above made every gun a potential bomb. The six surviving crews of the larboard guns bent into the withering fire as though they were braced against the wind in a snowstorm. Several mangled bodies lay about a seventh gun that had blown apart at the butt-end and now lay shattered like a trick cigar. One poor wretch sat propped against the gun carriage staring with surprise at the separated arm that lay cradled across his lap like a newborn baby. Within a minute, he was dead. The idea that six twelve-pounders could do battle with forty guns three to four times their size was so ludicrous that I almost laughed out loud. Ditty Gunn soon brought me back to my task.

"Powder! Ta the bow gun!" he screamed at me above the roar. "Lively!"

As I began a crouched scurry across the littered deck, I spotted Burrage out of the corner of my eye. He was down on one knee near a gun amidships pouring black powder into the bowl of a gun ladle. Holding the ladle's long wooden handle was the diminutive Irishman we had met when we first set sail. When the scoop was filled with the proper measure, the buccaneer leapt to the muzzle and slid the ladle down the barrel. With a half turn of the shaft, he dumped the load into the bowels of the gun and quickly withdrew the scoop. Within seconds, a twelve-pound ball was rolled down the barrel and rammed home.

The master gunner stood with his thumb covering the touchhole to prevent any lingering spark from being sucked down to the powder before the crew was ready. As the ship rolled on the swell, he sighted the gun and brought fire to the hole just as the *Anne Boleyn* reached the apex of her roll. A thick tongue of flame shot thirty feet out into the night illuminating the belch of smoke that soon followed. The gun jumped from the deck in a thunderous recoil and the four hands manning the train tackles stood ready to roll the gun forward again with a stout pull on the lines. The concussion knocked the unprepared Burrage to the deck where he flopped about like a gutted cod. Within seconds, however, he regained his composure and gamely made his way over to the next gun in line.

The bow gun, being nearest to the *Dartmoor*, seemed clearly in the most likely position to suffer complete annihilation. The closer I got, the more hesitant I became to journey the last dozen feet to the gun crew. The spray from the pounding hull seemed to pluck the sweat, grime, and blood out of the air and send it across the deck in an atomized cloud. I wiped the noxious mixture from my eyes and lips, but not before experiencing the taste of death as it seeped into my mouth.

Just as I was about to take the last few steps, a monstrous ball shattered the topsail yard on the foremast above me and a three-foot splinter plunged downward, lodging in the chest of the startled gunner. He pitched backward and fell writhing in my arms, his blood transforming the deck into a warm, red puddle below my feet. I lost my footing entirely and we both fell to the planks and commenced to slide about the gore with each roll of the ship. At that moment, a second ball cut through the remaining gun crew about a foot above the topgallant rail, taking three of them down—one headless. It seemed that everywhere I looked, another man was falling wounded or dead.

In what felt like the final death throes of the *Anne Boleyn*, the ravaged ship suddenly lurched upward atop a massive swell and then plummeted down the backside spewing bits of human flotsam from her deck across the surface of the sea. I knew we were all dead men.

❋ ❋ ❋

All that happened next comes hard in the telling, as when one attempts to put a dream into words and feels its essence evaporate before the story's done.

I can clearly recall the silent, slow-motion slide of the hull as it continued on its downward track along the nape of the great wave. I can see the figures on the deck, some tossed like bleeding marionettes against the bulwarks, arms and legs in a lifeless tangle of confusion; others still living, frozen to whatever bit of ship that was found in arm's reach. They waited quietly, long hair blowing in a noiseless wind, eyes fixed firmly toward the bow, as if poised to discover what face Death would be wearing when he came at last to claim them. Had we been Vikings, I would have said we were on our final voyage to Valhalla.

As the *Anne Boleyn* reached the nadir of her descent, there seemed no doubt that she would simply burrow beneath the waves and end her journey in the lightless belly of the cold Atlantic. As the bowsprit sliced deep into the black water and the first rush of ocean raced across the deck like an incoming tide, our world miraculously transformed.

Instead of plunging further beneath the waves, the *Anne Boelyn* righted herself with a smooth, graceful *swoop!* that left her gliding silently through the battle smoke as a swan might through the pale mist. The sea, which only moments before had been boiling like a witch's cauldron, became as still as an early morning pond, shimmering in the orange glow of the English guns. And though the battle still raged, there was no sound.

Next, I realized that the barrage of chain and ball, while still flying through the upper rigging as before, seemed for the moment to have entirely lost its effect. Shell-shocked and battered, we who had survived found ourselves spontaneously rising to our feet and migrating toward the rail. *Catamount,* which had been making way inexorably toward her sister, suddenly stood motionless, every breath of wind sucked from her shrouds. There still existed a narrow corridor between the two ships, though now it was fewer than one hundred yards wide.

As I gazed with wonder at the scene before me, my ears were pricked by the faint sound of an oar breaking the surface of the sea. Following the sound as best I could, I scanned the sea out beyond the bowsprit. What I saw left me dumfounded.

Out there in the water, in a small phalanx before the bow, three dark shapes slowly revealed themselves. At first, they appeared to be mere shadows, amorphous, liquid things like the water itself, a mesmerizing dapple of light and dark just below the surface. The shapes then seemed to emerge and yet, there was no outward sign—no ripple, no reflection of any kind. I recall a soft gasp arising from the several of us standing nearest on the deck, yet we struggled to understand what we were seeing.

In a later conversation, one of the gunners described them as shallops, small, open boats, each with a full complement of hands sitting silently at the oars. Others spoke of wraith-like figures, which never moved, their features nearly invisible in the changing light. I hold a picture in my mind of only the barest details, matted hair; a bony jaw; archaic clothing that clung dripping to their phantom bodies.

The boats themselves, if one could call them that, appeared rotted and filled to the gunnels with seawater, causing them to appear half-submerged on surface of the ocean. We distinctly felt the sensation of being towed steadily through the water, as though stout lines had been tied to the catheads and stretched outward toward the mysterious visitors. With no command that we could hear, the ghostly oarsmen seemed to bend their backs and lean into their oars.

"It must be them. On me mother's soul!" an old seaman had whispered at the time.

I later came to learn what the 'Headers on board believed about those kinsmen lost at sea during the late decades of the 17th century. They spoke of how long-departed shipmates would watch over Marblehead seaman and aid them in time of need. It was further rumored that Old Dimond himself had the power to call upon them at will and direct them as he saw fit. This, they claimed, was just such a time.

As the *Anne Boleyn* silently approached the corridor between the two English ships, we saw the guns go silent one by one. Just as de L'Hiver had predicted, neither vessel dared fire for fear of destroying the other.

We were now so close to the hull of the *Dartmoor* that we could literally see the hundreds of eyes that peered down at us from her main deck and from her gun ports. And yet, not a pistol was raised in our direction. The ghostly procession had struck every man dumb with a supernatural dread and none dared make a move to prevent it.

To starboard, the souls on *Catamount* paid similar homage, however, there at the rail of the quarterdeck, I observed a small, gaunt figure dressed in the finery of a gentleman. Even in the dark, I could see his face contort in a perfect rage at the prospect of our escape. Within an hour, without a breath of wind, we had left Sir Robert far in our wake. The last picture in my mind is that of a faint red light and a pale blue one darting here and there amongst the shrouds of the British ships like spirits cavorting among the dead.

CHAPTER 1 5

*H*annah Welkie sat looking out of the window of her sitting room. The sun had just disappeared behind Old Burial Hill and a cold, autumn wind sent small flocks of brown leaves circling about the frozen stones in the fading light.

In summertime, the old cemetery had always seemed so peaceful and green, a countenance suggesting that each occupant must have passed away softly, gently amongst family and friends. She imagined centuries of slow processions walking up the narrow, grassy paths and sweet hymns sung as loved ones found eternal rest upon this small, colonial Olympus. And here they slept beneath the jumbled stones, warmed by the sun and serenaded by white gulls wheeling in the clear, blue heavens overhead. In summertime, it was easy to imagine that the graves were merely hilltop retreats from which the dead could prop themselves up on an elbow and gaze serenely out upon the timeless town and always feel a part of the living.

But in autumn, with the grass grown pale and dry and the sky like a dark cellar wall etched with the last, dim light of day, Hannah saw each grave as a chill, lonely place in which the dead lay lost and forgotten. On late autumn afternoons life moved indoors and the townsfolk shrank from the rising wind. Deepening shadows spread over the village like a shovel-full of cold, black dirt spilling over the lid of a coffin. In this bare and brittle time of year, the living and the dead seemed as far removed from one another as distant spring does from autumn, with heartless winter in between.

She replaced the phone on the cradle, the doctor's voice now part of a past to which she could never return. Boden Welkie was dead.

＊ ＊ ＊

I cannot imagine a darker secret than the workings of Melchior Wormsley's brain. It was as if the endless, twisting tunnels below Marblehead were an extension of his mind and we were merely random thoughts trapped within. No consciousness seemed to more completely permeate this subterranean maze than that of Worms.

The map still lay before him and the letters Myles Castler had scrawled in the dust seemed almost animated in the flickering glow of the candles. Shadows danced in the shallow trenches and along the tiny ridges that outlined each character. Worms sat motionless, studying the mysterious markings as a cat might study a mouse. But the meaning carefully remained just out of reach, taunting him.

The body of his co-conspirator lay stretched out in the dim light at the base of the wall. Worms now began to regret his recent intemperance. It seemed the key was not yet in the lock after all.

"So, Tom," he whispered. "Ol' Ned don't wish ta spill 'is guts so easy, 'twould seem. Per'aps ye can trade wiv some o' them dark spirits ye thinks so high of, then. Aye! An' me, what just sent 'em a fresh soul fer their pleasure, ye might remind 'em!"

Worms rose up and gave Myles' body a sharp toe to the ribs.

"I s'pose we did act in haste, Tom," he went on, a touch of remorse in his voice. "He weren't a evil man, after all. An' he did know 'is letters most adm'rable, I should say. Ye shouldn't o' lost yer temper wiv 'im, Tom! Now who's ta make sense of't, I asks ye?"

Taking the map in hand, Worms sat down on the poor man's chest and considered his options.

"Now them letters in the dirt... I can't trust ye ta remember each one just so, Tom. You've not the head fer it, an' well ye knows it! An' we can't anchor here no more, that's certain! We must take 'em wiv us!"

He stood up and rummaged about in one of his great pockets, pulling out a bedraggled quill pen. Bereft of suitable ink, he was momentarily stymied, but then, looking upon the motionless body of Myles Castler, the buccaneer suddenly brightened and resumed his seat on the fellow's torso. Carefully studying the first pair of letters, he then looked to his victim's up-turned face and dabbed the pen point gingerly in the scarlet trickle that still flowed from the slit across his throat. One by one, he copied the letters on the map beside the small dots. It was delicate work but he accomplished it quite well for a big man with so little practice. When the task was completed, he dragged the sole of his shoe through the scribbling in the dust and set off toward the sea cave.

When Myles Castler had learned that the map had miraculously reappeared after three centuries, he knew he must keep it out of the Frenchman's hands at all costs. With it hanging there on the office wall, a mere dozen feet from a tunnel entrance, he realized that any of de L'Hiver's men could stumble upon it during one of their forays into the 20th century. The rediscovery of the map marked the culmination of a strange and complicated series of events that went to the very core of the dark relationship between Myles and Melchior Wormsley.

For quite some time, Myles Castler had been obsessed with solving the riddle of the mysterious sounds in the parlor closet. It was true that William had made the discovery and that Enid had never missed an opportunity to prattle on about it to visitors. Myles had feigned indifference and made every effort to discourage the curiosity of others. But whenever he had found himself alone in the house, he began a systematic search for the source.

For months he tapped the walls and shined lights into every crevice. He had even measured the entire building and created detailed drawings in hopes of discovering hidden spaces, but to no avail. As with William, it was Lady Jane who had eventually showed him the way. Once he had discovered the portal in the cellar, it was inevitable that he would explore the subterranean world. Even he was amazed at how comfortable he felt in the dark passages and he came to relish the Gothic dimension that the experience had awakened in him.

Soon, however, less exotic motives had taken over and he realized that he had stumbled onto a potential treasure trove of antiquities. On his first, brief trip below, he returned with several interesting artifacts—a pewter mug, an old shoe, and a sword hilt. Thinking he had discovered the old smugglers' tunnels alluded to in local lore, he set out to comb every inch of the ancient realm in search of profit.

On his return trip, however, it was *he* who had been discovered. In the most harrowing experience of his none-too-ordinary life, Myles had come face to face with Melchior Wormsley. For some reason that can never be explained, the violent reprobate had chosen not to murder him on the spot, but instead permitted Myles to frantically make a case as to why he should be spared. The result was an unholy alliance between the 20th-century swindler and the 18th-century psychopath.

For nearly a year, Myles harvested hundreds of priceless historical artifacts—old books, documents, and maps that were procured by the time-traveling agents, Wormsley and his inscrutable lackey, Ned Buckett. These prizes he would deliver to his enthusiastic patrons at Barrows & Wight at no small profit to himself. In return for their efforts, Wormsley and Buckett received payment in the form of diamonds (they thought). In actuality, the "diamonds" were an inferior grade of cubic zirconia that Myles had purchased in bulk at an East Boston pawnshop.

The partnership had proven satisfactory to all parties, until Quartermaster Quill had enlisted the services of Mr. Buckett. As I was later to find out, Buckett had been specially chosen to perform a crucial and most secretive task, one that led, among other things, to the creation of the troublesome map.

Fearful that Sir Robert might somehow breach the divide and gain access to the tunnels, Bartholomew de L'Hiver had ordered Quill to hide the spoils of their most recent voyage, a fortune in precious stones bound for Cadiz and hidden amidst an unassuming cargo of vegetable dyes. The small Spanish merchantman had hoped to avoid the interest of freebooters by appearing to be of too little value for an escort. But for the desperate crew of the *Anne Boleyn,* no ship was too modest to overlook. When they realized what they had stumbled upon, the company was euphoric and celebrated their good luck by getting drunk, marooning the Spanish crew, and burning the merchantman to the waterline.

The treasure was contained in nine small caskets, simple wooden chests no bigger than a large Christmas pudding. The boxes each bore a stout iron lock, the keys for which were found dangling on a chain round the neck of a Papal envoy accompanying the fortune to Spain. When the loop of chain was found to be too tight to fit over the envoy's head, the impediment had been calmly removed with the help of Wormsley's cutlass.

Each chest contained a fortune in diamonds, topaz, amethyst and opals. According to the hapless envoy, the caskets were en route from Africa and the New World to Cadiz, from which each would begin a separate journey to unrevealed destinations in Spain and Italy. It was whispered that the incredible fortune had been gathered secretly at the behest of a wealthy Spanish nobleman, a discrete solution to an unhappy marriage. In matters of this kind, however, the truth was rarely revealed.

In any case, Myles Castler had now joined a long list of those who would never set eyes on the mysterious treasure. With Ned Buckett now gone, the cryptic parchment offered all the guidance that Wormsley was likely to receive in finding the hidden gems. The small village of Marblehead, abandoned by pirates and pursuers alike, lay but a fathom or two above his head. Worms determined that he must risk a foray into the open and, if luck was with him, spy some symbol or character on a sign or building that matched the ones he had copied so meticulously on the map. Knowing Ned Buckett, the nine casks had been hidden right under their noses all along. Finding them was just a matter of time

It had been two days now since the phantom oarsmen had begun their tireless voyage to the north and west. The sea had been calm the entire time, though the sky was dark and brooding. Although the wind blew steadily against us, the pace never slackened and the *Anne Boleyn* slipped smoothly through the water on her invisible tether. Every now and then, we would catch a brief glimpse of red or blue lights dancing out over the wave tops in the distance. It was the strangest journey I had ever taken.

Little was said. The shock of Sir Robert's horrific assault had left us in a daze and by the time all our casualties had been counted, it became clear that we had lost more than half the company. Many had succumbed to their wounds since the battle and others were too ruined to hope for recovery. The devastation was so complete that there were barely 40 of us standing and most of those were so demoralized as to be of little use.

Once the last of the English ships had disappeared in the bank of smoke behind us, it had taken me nearly an hour to locate Burrage. I finally found him beneath a heap of toppled canvas, barely conscious. Even at the moment of discovery, I wasn't positive I had the right man. His hair had been nearly burned from his head and his skin was black with powder and dried blood. With tears running down my cheeks, I dragged him free and tried to clean his face with a rag soaked in seawater.

Where was the neurotic, quirky, asthmatic Burrage whose biggest fears had been bottle caps, aphids, and the six o'clock news? Once afraid of his own shadow, Burrage had last been seen hauling black powder to pirate gunners while the world exploded around him! And he had done so as full of life and purpose as I had ever seen him. Now, here he lay, battered and burned. I couldn't believe what we had come to.

William, who had found safe haven below decks during the worst of the firestorm, soon tracked me down and together we were able to get

Burrage cleaned up enough to more accurately assess his wounds. Fortunately, most were abrasions and minor cuts, bloody but superficial. The most significant injury turned out to be the loss of the last two fingers on his left hand, removed apparently by a shard of hot iron just before it had imbedded itself in the deck. The wound had appeared neat and clean, at least until the ship's carpenter had dipped the hand into a crock of brown paste, a poultice that he claimed would numb the pain and prevent the meat from putrefying. We were too weary to argue.

Over the next two days, Burrage improved at a remarkable rate and despite his lack of hair and the two missing digits, he seemed almost familiar again. Once he accepted the recent alterations to his physiognomy, he made the decision to simply shave the remaining stubble from his head. Resigning myself to Burrage's newly emerging identity, I accomplished his request with a razor-sharp dagger and a slippery coating of fish oil. The cosmetic transformation from neurotic nebbish to seafaring rogue was all but complete.

Having few other diversions, we spent the hours huddled below decks with the rest of the crew, thoroughly drained of energy. Bartholomew de L'Hiver and Tobias Quill had retreated to the great cabin leaving Ditty Gunn in charge of the dispirited company. In fairness, given our supernatural mode of travel, there was little essential work left to do. Gunn would periodically report back to the Captain and as the cabin door opened, sharp words could often be heard from within.

In truth, we had no idea what was happening to us and yet, none of the crew seemed anxious to find out. By rights we believed we should all be dead and it occurred to me that we might, in fact, be so already! Perhaps the ghostly boatmen were simply our escort to the nether world, silent witnesses on our journey to oblivion. And yet, I think, we all sensed that we still must be alive, though barely. It was hard to imagine that death would leave us so much in the flesh with aches and pains and weevily food.

✻ ✻ ✻

At dusk on that second day, a strangely energized Snitch clambered down the ladder and called us all on deck. As we made our way up, a chill wind sifted through my clothes and brought a shiver to my spine. Lanterns blazed in the tattered rigging and the yellow glow fell across piles of uncleared wreckage that still littered the deck. Captain Bartholomew, Quill, Gunn, and several others stood above us at the stern. It was clear that decisions had been made.

"Belay there!" barked the quartermaster, as the bedraggled crew gathered on the main deck. "Cap'n to address the Comp'ny! Stand for'ard an' hold yer tongues!"

The Frenchman, who had been standing with his arms folded across the pommel of his crutch, peered out darkly from beneath knit brows and then, with a heavy thump, came forward to the rail. His face was etched with fierce resentment as though he had been wrestling with some enormous conflict that remained still unresolved. He seemed bent on using the sheer force of his will to prevail, Job on his dung heap, cursing God.

"*Mes amis!*" he bellowed out into the growing darkness. "For two days we have been carried across the sea by a power that confounds our eyes and addles our brains. And though we have been delivered from the hands of our enemy, we are filled with dread, are we not? Some say it is the rebuke of God Himself, offended by our great cargo of sin. Others claim it is the angel Lucifer come to take us for his crew. But I say we have sailed this course before, my friends, and we all know who it is, do we not? It is Old Dimond, by thunder! And, though it yet may be found that he is the Devil, there is no doubt that his hand is on us now just as it was in the tunnels and just as it shall be until the debt is paid!

"One year ago we signed the Articles that spared us from Sir Robert's gibbet! But since then, we have lived like the dead beneath the ground and I say *NO MORE!*"

I watched in amazement as the crew around me, broken and weary beyond belief, let the exhaustion and the pain fall away. Their eyes burned with the warriors' fire and once more they became men.

"Who is this wizard if not another master to serve? Shall we come back to live like vermin below the earth? If so, then why not return to the plantations as slaves or in chains to the galleys? I am a free man of the sea, by thunder! So shall I live and so shall I die!"

An immense and unrelenting roar exploded from the deck. Cutlasses swung through the air and pistol shots lit the night as every man 'round me let his spirit soar into the darkening sky. I turned to find Burrage and gasped as I watched him mount the rigging and hurl a boarding ax out into the darkness toward the phantom longboats. William, only a boy minutes before, turned and fixed me with a gaze so confident, so strangely wise, that I felt I had become stunted while he had come of age. Once again, it seemed that I was the one seeking to substitute logic for inspiration, restraint for freedom, and maturity for mystery. At what point had my virtues become such vices?

Before I could bring forth any more of my useless, civilized instincts, the completely *un*civilized world around me was awash in a river of adrenaline. Broken spars, shredded canvas, and tangled lines were cut loose and hurled into the sea. Gun carriages were drawn back into place and the decks cleared of debris. Buckets of sea water washed the dried blood from the planks and—to the sound of a deep, rolling cheer—de L'Hiver ordered the black flag sent high aloft! Black velvet it was, with a white death angel, cutlass in hand, flying over a large, red "M" for the French word "mort." It was the captain's own design, inspired by a childhood spent amongst the gravestones of Bout.

The *Anne Boleyn* was soon a serviceable facsimile of herself and the carefully salvaged sails puffed out to feel the air on a larboard tack. But before she gained the wind, an unearthly blue light flashed in from the sea, circled the topgallants, then dove through the rigging, finally coming to rest but a few feet from the main mast. Every man on deck stood frozen

as the glowing entity hovered above the planks immediately in front of...
me!

Like a miniature cosmos, it pulsed its blue-white energy, a soundless,
mesmerizing sphere of translucent stardust. The light, seemingly refining
its effect on me, proceeded to construct an image directly inside my own
brain. I quickly recognized the glowering visage of Edward Dimond. His
face was the face of the tempest itself, a barely controlled fury in which
every detail of his countenance was in motion. His eyes flashed and his
hair danced in the gale. His voice rolled like thunder.

*"Each drop of blood that stains your hand, lets fall a grain of sand! The time
is gone, the storm is born, the Door awaits the DAMNED!"*

At the instant of his final words, an enormous flash of light exploded
in my brain and I fell back, collapsing upon the deck. When I regained
my senses a few moments later, it was clear that everything had changed.

The ghostly oarsmen and the mysterious lights were gone. The
northwest wind that had blown so steadily ever since we had left the
harbor of Marblehead had ceased and the telltales hung limp in the
lantern light. The air, so chilled with autumn, suddenly grew tropical and
a breeze began to rise from the southeast. A hearty shout arose from the
crew as they prepared the canvas to run before the wind. It soon
approached a scudding gale and the spanker was furled, the headsails
blanketed, and the black flag was snapping against the sky like a coach
whip. The seas grew larger and the once black sky took on an eerie,
greenish hue not unlike the phosphorescent glow along the tunnel walls.

The crew, just moments ago so jubilant when the wind had changed,
began to grow uneasy. Soon, pale flashes of lightening began to illuminate
the southern horizon and the clouds overhead started to boil against the
sky. William and Burrage had migrated to my side and we cast tenuous
glances at one another.

"I don't like the feel of this," Burrage warned. "Where did all this
weather come from?"

I felt a sharp tug on the back of my collar and whirled around. There stood Tobias Quill, his face pale and tense.

"He spoke ta ye, didn't he? Just before, when the light come!"

I nodded.

"'Tis the oath! 'Tis broke then, that's certain! I feels it 'round me throat like a hangman's noose," Quill whispered, fingering the front of his neck then mumbling as he turned to walk away "I'll tell the Cap'n."

"Sail ho!" came the cry from atop the mizzen. "Sails to the stern!"

We all stopped dead in our tracks and spun around to the southeast. First one, then two great ships were pounding toward us. Sir Robert had returned for the kill. Once more, the deck burst into frantic activity as all hands worked the *Anne Boleyn* for her final sprint. The wizard was gone for good. We were on our own.

I had never been at sea in a full-blown gale. The closest I had ever come was that night on Gerry Island, a night I had barely survived.

The *Anne Boleyn* was not at her best. The battle had taken a toll and even though she was now storm-reefed with little canvas exposed to the wind, the pounding of the gale brought a shudder to every plank and beam in her hull. And the conditions only highlighted my inability to contribute anything of use. In fact, de L'Hiver, fearing matters could only be made worse by the untimely demise of Burrage, William, or me, had relegated us to the lowest deck in the ship. We were now, in essence, little more than ballast.

Huddled there in the dim light, water dripping 'round about us on the cold stones, we did our best to hold ourselves together. Burrage knew that something extraordinary had just happened and wanted details.

"I'm not sure I can make sense of it," I replied in answer to his prodding. "Obviously, the worst has happened and our friend Quill seems totally demoralized. That voice, Old Dimond's—he said they are all 'damned.' I heard him, Burr, in my head. I have a bad feeling that someone may have died. That's why it all fell apart."

"Well, what does *that* mean?!" Burrage asked. "Lots of people just died. Ned Buckett, the British watch—hell, half the crew is gone! If dying is such a problem, we haven't exactly gone out of our way to avoid it!"

I looked at Burrage with more than a little impatience.

"*We?* 'We' haven't gone out of 'our' way? What's with you? What decisions have 'we' made? This is about *them*, not us! We're not part of this, Burr! We're not *pirates*, damn it!"

Burrage flashed me an angry look. It was almost as if he didn't want to be reminded. I knew things were changing with him, William, too, and it had gotten to the point where I had no idea where they stood anymore. It was time to find out.

"So what are you saying, Burr? You've joined the crew? You're a pirate now?"

Burrage was momentarily taken aback. It was clear he hadn't asked himself that question.

"I don't know. Jesus, I don't know what I am! I only know that for the first time in my life I feel free! I can't explain it, Max. I want to live! Christ, I'm just done with it—my half-assed job, worrying if I'll ever find the 'right' girl, worrying about my asthma, worrying about losing control. Hell, Max, we've lost control! You can't lose any more control than we have! And guess what? We're still alive! Can you believe it?"

I was truly stunned. He had described what was happening to him exactly right, it seemed to me, and, to my even greater surprise, I wasn't sure I felt the need to talk him out of it.

"Burr, are you telling me that you want to stay here? Stay in the 18th century?"

Burr hesitated.

"I don't *know*. I just know I don't want to go back to the way things were. I *won't*, Max! Anyway, it's not like we even have a choice, do we? Jesus, we may not even get back to land, for God's sake! All I know is that if I'm going to be here, then I'm really going to *be* here. There's a whole part of me that I didn't even know existed till now. That's all I have to say."

So now I knew.

William had been silent through all of it, but now he, too, had something to say and it was even more shocking than Burrage's revelation.

"I know who died," he stated quietly.

Burrage and I turned abruptly.

"I think it was—my father."

"What?" I asked. "What are you talking about?"

"The Articles," he continued. "They say you can't kill a person from another time. That's how you get damned. Isn't that what they said?"

Burrage nodded.

"So, if someone got killed, it must be someone from *our* time, then," William said, looking down at his hands. "I mean, it *has* to be, right?"

"We don't *know* that, William. We don't really know what's going on yet," I cautioned. "But even if something did happen, what's that got to do with your father?"

"Because he's here," William answered, looking me straight in the eye.

"You *saw* him?" I shouted. "When?"

"Just before we got on the boats—back there in the tunnels when that man, Ned Buckett, had me trapped. He *knew* Ned Buckett."

I was almost speechless. "Why didn't you say something? My God, William! He may be our way out of here!"

William turned away entirely and I resisted the urge to turn him back around. Within a few seconds, he was crying softly in the darkness.

"William, I'm sorry. I didn't mean to shout. It's just that we need every bit of help to get out of here—every bit! If your father is in the tunnels, he may know of a way out. Or, he may have already gone for help. Did he see you? Were you able to speak to him?"

William lowered his head. I could barely hear the reply as it came in a thick, choking sob.

"I *hate* him! I hope he *is* dead!"

"What are you saying?" I asked incredulously. "Why—"

"Because," William interrupted, with more bitterness than I could ever imagine. "Because, he's with *them!* Ned Buckett and Worms. He left me here—he was never coming back! He said so!"

With that, William completely fell apart. Great heaving sobs bent him low in the shadows as the *Anne Boleyn* rose and fell in a dark, stormy sea.

✳ ✳ ✳

It's hard to say exactly how long the storm lasted and, even after the worst was over, it showed no inclination to move on. Instead, it lingered, glaring angrily down from the heavens, threatening to roar in at full throttle if provoked. We had been blown all the way back to Cat Island and, even though the seas had calmed a bit, a brisk wind continued to blow up from the southeast and the sky stayed as dark as pitch. As near as I could tell, it was about six o'clock in the morning when we finally sighted Marblehead.

A quick summons from Ditty Gunn brought us back on deck again and we marveled at the gigantic storm clouds that still frowned ominously from the heavens. And though he had supposedly abandoned us to our fate, I sensed Edward Dimond's sulphurous presence looming high up in the thunderheads.

Although nearly fatal to the battered *Anne Boleyn*, the violent gale had served us well on one score, for while the ocean raged, Sir Robert had been held at bay. But as the storm waned, a new danger came to the fore. We could see the English ships no more than three or four miles astern, two great, angry bees silhouetted against intermittent flashes of lightning. Until now the tempest had prevented them from closing the gap or bringing their gunners into a position where they could renew the attack. But with the lull in the storm, *Catamount* and *Dartmoor* were poised to drive us hard against the coast. The extraordinary danger only underscored the fact that de L'Hiver was willing to risk everything for his mysterious ends.

With the winds at a more manageable level, Gunn soon dressed the yards in as much canvas as the conditions would allow. *Anne Boleyn's* shallower draft gave her the advantage of a short cut or two and she slipped over several submerged rocks and beat her way toward the mouth of the harbor. But the sharks were circling for the kill. I could imagine the gun crews, grim-faced and already furious at our earlier escape, preparing to blow our crippled ship out of the water.

Within minutes we were at the mouth of the inner harbor. The small ship came about just off the promontory that would someday become Fort Sewell. On this day however, it was merely a wind-blown bluff of earthworks, brambles and scrub pines. In the dim light, I could barely make out the shadowy entrance to the sea cave and I dreaded the thought that we might again be forced to leave the open world behind.

The fact that he was so close to something that he wanted so badly made Wormsley's head throb. By this stage in his life, he had become an emotional windsock. The smallest stimulation could evoke climactic changes in his brain chemistry. As he strode toward the sea cave en route to the sleepy village of Marblehead, the juices churned in his belly, not merely with the excitement of locating nine chests of jewels. He was driven as much by the desire to deprive others of that pleasure as he was to reward himself.

He lived for such moments. Nerves twitched. Muscles pulsed with random bolts of chemical energy. His clothes became soaked in an oily effluvium as sweat mixed with the foul compost that perpetually coated his skin. Even his breath, fetid in the best of circumstances, grew positively poisonous in his heightened state.

As the hulking buccaneer hurried along the passages, his breathing became labored and a frothing trickle of foam began to build up in the corners of his mouth. Navigating in the dim light with only a single eyeball was a strain indeed and the exertion caused a pale discharge to seep from beneath the lid.

As repulsive as Worms' physical state had become, his mental condition was by far the more noxious. Any basic human sensibilities had long since been distorted to the point where they were now unrecognizable. And while his intellect still operated with cunning precision, it was no longer attached to what might be called a conscience. To sustain a conscience, one must have access to such feelings as empathy, guilt and regret, feelings he hadn't experienced since early childhood. And yet, conscience is the cord that binds our essential humanity together. Without it, the mind is simply a soulless engine driving something that can no longer be called human—a monster.

And so the monster that was Worms stumbled the last few yards through the ankle deep brine that slopped about the floor of the sea cave. Emerging into the early morning air, he immediately turned his back to the harbor and clambered up the cold, wet face of the shallow cliff that wrapped itself around the point. Had he not been in such a distracted frame of mind, he might have noticed the silhouette of a small, dark ship bearing down on the entrance to Marblehead Harbor.

An elderly woman leading a pair of cows along a muddy slough barely looked up as the ragged seaman made his way down the harbor road. The brief glimpse was enough however, and she quickly raked the animals' ribs with a willow switch to hurry them on their way. In a place like Marblehead in the early 1700s, the residents had honed their survival instincts early on. Like a fly giving wide berth to a spider, she knew what response a stranger with the look of Melchior Wormsley should elicit.

As he passed, the buccaneer doffed his moldering tricorn, swept it low along the ground with an exaggerated bow and bared his teeth in an obsequious grin. The incongruous gallantry discomfited the old woman to such an extent that she let out a startled chirp, kissed the small, wooden talisman that hung about her neck, and trundled off down the muddy path leaving her livestock to find their own way to the grazing yard.

Worms watched her disappear between two clapboard buildings and placed his hat back upon his head. Before doing so, however, he slid the stubbed, clay pipe from the tacking ribbons along the brim and filled the bowl with a stout pinch of Virginia weed. Finally realizing he had no fire with which to light it, he growled and gripped the stem in his mouth as if determined to ignore the physics of the situation.

"Well, Tom, a fine welcome, I should say! What comes o' low breedin' I 'spect. It's clear this place'll never amount ta more'n a bucket o' fish guts! An' me wiv'out a tinderbox, too!"

Resigned to the situation, he continued his westward journey along the harbor road and as he passed the small cottages and harbor front buildings, his working eye revolved in its socket trying to identify any potential matches for the cryptic symbols on the old map. There being the barest examples of signage in the crudely built village, the possibilities were few, but he eventually came upon a weathered plank with the words "Publik House" carved into it with a shallow stroke. Flecks of marine tar clung to the channels where the sign maker had attempted to highlight the letters in a darker hue, but most of the pigment had peeled away. Though Worms couldn't honestly read the words, he knew their meaning well enough.

The sign was chained to a stout beam that protruded from the corner post of a squat two-story building. The exterior was sheathed in random scraps of wood that clearly had been scavenged from the various docks and dumping grounds about the village. It appeared that whenever the wind blew too easily through the wall or a trickle of water grew too steady, the owner had searched out the nearest bit of refuse and tacked it over the offending crevice. It was just the sort of derelict establishment in which Worms felt most comfortable.

Ducking beneath the low-slung door, he found himself blinking in the gloom of a cramped chamber that wound its way through a thicket of stout posts and below a plank ceiling barely six feet overhead. A small blaze burned in the back corner of a stone fireplace and provided the only source of light, the shutters having been latched fast across the two small windows at the front of the room.

A dozen wooden chairs and several stools had been placed along the perimeter of the room and two simple rectangular tables stood near the center. There was little else about other than a large iron pot on the hearth and several handfuls of herbs hung upside down to dry along a beam above the fireplace. Even without his hat, the lumbering seaman was forced to stoop forward with his neck hunched uncomfortably to one side as he took stock of his surroundings.

Dawn had broken barely an hour before, though with the heavy clouds one could hardly tell. Still, in a fishing town such as this, the day was well under way. Within moments, a lone figure buried beneath rough-woven skirts and a dingy shawl shuffled down the narrow stairs and made her way to the fire. Prodding the sticks with an iron, she fell into a spasm of coughing as a plume of smoke snaked up her arm and curled about her head.

"Beggin' yer fergiveness, goodwife," Worms purred. "But would ye have a small cup o' rum near ta hand, now?"

The ragged woman grunted an assent and gestured toward the wall.

"Take a stool ta thyself and mind how ye foul the floor. The bowl is there beside ye."

Worms glanced down at the small spittoon tucked against one of the table legs. He chose the largest of the chairs and drew it up to the table, content to hold his head erect once more. The woman disappeared around the corner and returned shortly with a pewter tankard with two fingers of clear rum swirling across the bottom. Worms held the brim to his nostrils and took a long sniff of the sweet, sharp odor, then drained the contents in three quick gulps.

"Well, then, ain't that a stiff breeze in the mains'l! Pray blow another afore ye stop the bottle!"

The woman was neither old nor young, comely enough considering the times and the burden of life in a place such as this. Her hair was dark and her skin a ruddy pink. The mouth looked unnaturally pinched, probably the result of missing teeth, but her eyes were shining black, clear and strong. She knew her business and the ways of the men who frequented her establishment and it was obvious that she would brook no mischief. Most importantly, she knew a man like Worms was bound to make landfall every so often and that, with a little care and clear thinking, it was possible to survive him.

Most of the local fellows were not much different than any of the other seamen who found themselves here in the course of a voyage. Some were brash and others brawlers; some barely spoke a word but preferred to sit with a quiet pipe and a hard eye for any who might intrude upon them. All were men who could haul till their backs broke and who knew that each storm, each freezing night at sea brought them a day closer to a sailor's death. Mostly, they were survivors who managed to be as decent as was required to avoid hastening their day of departure from this earth. The same might be said of any fisherman, trader, or pirate for they were all seamen and, taken one by one, there was scant difference among them.

But occasionally, a man appeared who lived outside the boundaries of common understanding, who was dark and inscrutable and made everyone around him speak softly and stare into their tankards. The man might be quiet or loud, subtle or loquacious. He could be of any rank. The one trait that marked him, however, was that unmistakable air of evil that lurked beneath every expression and behind every word, no matter how innocent it might seem on the surface. One could sense it as surely as the sparrow senses the hawk the moment before it drops out of the sky.

The woman realized that she was in the company of just such a man and that she could never guess exactly where or when his evil hand might fall. She knew that she could not show a modicum of fear, but must instead behave as though he was like any normal human being. Then, if luck was with her, he would eventually be gone from her life and she could go back to serving common sailors once more.

"Come, trollop—lively then! I'll not drink ye dry, by thunder!" Worms roared, brandishing his empty cup.

"Hold thy tongue, sir, or the dogs shall see thee out the door! I'll have no man say me wrong in my house. Thy money, sir, afore another drop I'll pour."

Worms' eye became a slit and twitched with uncertainty. So bold an answer left him wondering from whence it sprang. He was not used to it, not from a tavern wench alone in a tiny fishing village, anyway. Because his mind worked best when survival was at stake, his response was restrained.

"Now, Tom," he whispered to himself. "No call ta insult the lady. We've other business ta tend."

Worms returned to his former manner.

"Pay Tom no mind, goodwife. His bile's up on account o' past wrongs too ghastly ta recount," Worms declared, reaching into his purse for tuppence. "Here's good English coin for yer trouble. Truth be told, I 'ave ta be takin' my leave."

Rising from his chair, the buccaneer leaned forward with his palms on the table and fixed the woman with a cold stare. She could feel the skin on the back of her neck tingle with apprehension.

"Afore I slips me cable, Missus, can ye answer me a small question?"

"I may," she replied as calmly as her nerves would allow.

"Have ye seen a stranger here about o' late, a seafarin' man o' middle years what wore a scarlet sash about 'is throat?"

The woman answered straight away with a steady voice.

"There are many sailor men who cross the threshold as thee may well believe. I serve them their rum and victuals and pay them no more heed than I would a stray cat."

She watched as the face of her visitor hardened. He moved from behind the table and closed in on her until he was barely an arm's reach away. Her jaw clenched and she did her best to stand her ground and conceal the fear that was working its way up her back.

"He were a p'culiar sort," Worms pressed, his looming frame blotting out all the light in the room. "He couldn't speak, ye see. An' him a man wiv' so much ta say. No tongue, poor lad. He just made a sort o' watery sound in the back o' his throat. Sad ta see, it were. Are ye clear ye don't recall such a man?"

He had no sooner asked the question than he flashed his dagger with a flick of his wrist and held the point so close to her left eye, that her lashes brushed against the razor edge like the panicked wings of a butterfly caught in a web. She gasped and brought her fingertips up to her cheek.

"P'raps if ye had but one eye ye could narrow the view and separate one man from t'other," the buccaneer hissed.

His lips were now so close to her ear that the spittle ran down her neck. She could feel the blood begin leaving her brain as a prelude to losing consciousness. With her last ounce of gumption, she reached deep down her throat and brought her voice back within range of her tongue.

"As I have told thee, sir, I know him not."

He stared at her as if trying to pick a lock. Then, in an instant, he drew back the knife and plunged it deep and twisting into the smooth skin of the oaken post next to her head. A noiseless gasp escaped her lips and she slid down to the floor as the muscles in her legs turned to quivering jelly. Sitting there at the base of the post in the disheveled nest of her own skirts, she was simply overwhelmed by sheer horror. Her eyes glazed over and her arms fell limply at her sides as she awaited her fate.

"So, Tom!" Worms chided. "Now ye've gone too far wiv' yer harsh ways an' brought the creature ta this sorry state. We're left to puzzle it out on our own, damn ye!"

He withdrew his blade from the splintered post and turned to the door, picking up the tuppence on the table as he left and slipping it into his purse. As he cracked the door, a low, rolling rumble met his ears.

"Tain't thunder, Tom," he mused, sniffing the air. "Them's guns—"

C H A P T E R   1 6

*H*aving come so far, we watched in disbelief as the first 24-
pounder arced out over the water and came hurtling toward us. Running
on grit and gristle, the tattered *Anne Boleyn* had somehow staggered from
Cat Island to the mouth of the harbor and now, a mere three hundred
yards from the sanctuary of the cliffs, luck and the wind had run out. Our
spirits plummeted.

Skillfully using the last of the wind, *Catamount* had come 'round the
northernmost side of the island and stood off the point not a quarter of a
mile away. Meanwhile, *Dartmoor* had swung to the southeast and stared
down on us from that direction. Realizing that we were becalmed and
completely helpless, Sir Robert had maneuvered his flagship with cold
deliberation, withholding fire until every larboard gun was perfectly
aligned, a firing squad awaiting the final order. That first shot sailed
overhead and plunged into the sea to the southwest. We knew it would
likely be one of the last to do so.

When the firestorm began to tear through our rigging, we
immediately flattened ourselves on the deck and tried to become
somehow invisible, but the outcome was brutally obvious. We simply had
nowhere to hide. In desperation, several of the crew chose to take their
chances in the water and swim for shore, though they must have known
that exhaustion and the cold would claim them long before they reached
the rocks. One by one they leapt from the starboard rail but within

minutes disappeared from sight with flailing arms and pathetic cries.

Snitch was one of those for whom water seemed preferable to fire. But as he scrambled to the bow rail amidst raining debris and prepared to launch himself into the cold harbor, he made a startling discovery. A small fishing shallop lay anchored a mere twenty yards to the larboard side of the bowsprit. In addition to her mast, useless without canvas or the breeze, he saw that she had been fitted out with several pairs of oars. She was a beautiful sight. Within minutes of informing the captain of his find, Snitch and six shipmates were dragging themselves out of the sea and over her side. A short time later, the shallop hugged the hull of the *Anne Boleyn* and the remaining crew climbed, jumped, or fell into her broad belly. Oars were set and she began a frantic pull for the sea cave—34 grateful souls clinging to one last miracle.

As the shallop pulled away from the beleaguered *Anne Boleyn*, a lone figure watched intently from atop the bluff.

"So, Tom," the dark man croaked. "'Twould appear our ol' shipmates 'ave fell inta the fire now, eh? Look at 'em pull, Tom! Now, there's a sight ta be sure. Like Ol' Scratch hisself set 'is horn in their hinder parts. Not done wiv ol' Worms yet, I reckons. Nay, not nearly."

With that, Worms slipped down the amongst the shadows and quickly made his way into the entrance of the cave before any on the shallop could take notice.

Burrage, William and I did our best to remain inconspicuous as more practiced hands manned the oars. Given this unforeseen chance at escape, the men of the *Anne Boleyn* pulled as though reborn and in their fevered brains they could almost see themselves gathered on the near shore. With each stroke, the effort grew more frenzied, but the closer we drew to safety the more vulnerable we felt and, in fact, our luck abandoned us once more.

A mere ten yards from water's edge, a ball of angry iron shattered the hull barely an oar's length from where Burrage, William, and I sat huddled against the mast. Splintered wood exploded through the air mixing with the flesh and screams of the wounded. I heard a sudden cheer roll faintly across the water from the decks of *Catamount* as our tiny vessel broke apart and men were dumped into the sea like so much chum.

In all honesty, I can't recall by what miracle we made landfall. I imagine that only the relative calm of the harbor prevented our tired bodies from being battered like rag dolls on the barnacle-encrusted rocks that lurked just below the surface at the foot of the cliff. By the time the last man had dragged himself into the black shadows of the sea cave, there were but 25 or so left alive.

We lay blinking and exhausted along the walls of the cave, bodies half immersed in the debris and seaweed that slopped about the floor in the shallow tide. The cannonade had ceased within minutes of our reaching the rocks. I later reasoned that Sir Robert Vole, now with full knowledge of at least one entrance to our heretofore hidden sanctuary, was not about to see a small mountain of blasted rubble keep his men from us.

In the eerie silence that followed, the smoldering ember that was Bartholomew de L'Hiver slowly worked itself into an angry flame once more. Separating himself from the flotsam at his feet, the Frenchman steadied his bad leg against a large boulder and surveyed the bedraggled remnants of his once fearsome crew.

I, too, took stock of the shivering survivors. Burrage and William were barely visible as they propped themselves up in the darkness against the back wall. Ditty Gunn, as always, had found himself near the captain, as had Don Pedro, Scabs Daggett and the man they called Jack Wager. I saw Tobias Quill, the quartermaster, head in hands with his gray braids hung like limp tell-tails against his wet face. And there, too, was the indestructible Snitch who, like a cockroach, seemed always to scuttle away just before the squashing. A full score more were scattered about in various states of disrepair although the severely wounded never made it out of the sea.

I also recognized the diminutive Irishman, though I had never learned his name. He lay bent and bruised against the pile of timbers that Burrage and I had gathered so recently. As I watched him gather himself up and rearrange his tattered clothing, his waistcoat momentarily fell open, revealing a pale white female breast! Never would I have imagined that this rugged shipmate, a skilled sailor and uncomplaining member of the crew, had been a *woman* all along.

With a quick tug of her linen blouse, the lady quickly regained a modest and concealing state. I could not tell from her manner whether her gender was a secret to others as well, but I resolved to treat it as such for the time being. I had read of female pirates, Ann Bonney and Mary Read among the most infamous, and I wondered if she might be one of them. I doubted she was, but this was no time to inquire.

Stunned at the result of his count, the French captain wiped a strand of seaweed from the side of his cheek, his dark face trembling with rage.

"Know this!" he bellowed, his accent thickening with every word. "Robert Vole may be the sword that cuts us down, but it is one of our own who wields it! *Wormsley!*"

As he spoke, he slowly turned his head, inviting every man to drink in the full meaning of his words.

"Wormsley, *mes amis*, has Buckett's Bible. *Oui*. Buckett's Bible. And each of you knows what that means."

Though barely a muscle moved, I could see that this revelation had a profound effect on the men. What color was left ran out of their cheeks at the thought of the pernicious Worms in control of the priceless map. And with Ned Buckett now resting at the bottom of Salem Harbor, the crude parchment was the only hope of ever seeing their treasure again. The thought that everything they had suffered might be for naught was the final straw. The blood returned to their faces and without uttering a word, they rose to their feet and found their resolve once more.

"Worms *must* be found!" de L'Hiver went on.

Even as the Frenchman spoke, the British were deploying a small armada of longboats bristling with musketmen who would be upon us directly, hungry to finish the bloody business that their gun crews had begun so well. De L'Hiver addressed the situation.

"Look into your hearts, *mes amis!* We are so few now, *c'est vrai.* But think on this—we have the tunnels! With stout hearts and a quick brain, we can make these pig-dogs squeal yet, I think."

A cheer went up once more. And it was true; even I could see it. The narrow passages, so familiar to their defenders, would become a disorienting chamber of horrors to Sir Robert's infantry, no matter what their number. Her Majesty's troops, so well-drilled in warfare on open ground, would be reduced to fighting single file, a style perfectly suited to de L'Hiver's battle-hardened mariners, adept at small arms and used to tight quarters. And then there was the matter of motivation. What reason did an underpaid foot soldier have to battle crazed hellions in an underground maze? The crew of the *Anne Boleyn*, on the other hand, was fighting for a fortune for which they had already risked all.

Buoyed by the response of the crew, de L'Hiver quickly laid out his plan. The company would split into two groups. The larger, under the command of Ditty Gunn, would be charged with holding Sir Robert's shock troops at bay, causing as much pain and suffering as possible. The other, led by de L'Hiver himself, would attempt to find the elusive Wormsley and the precious map. Still concerned about the ramifications of our well being, it was determined that Burrage, William and I would join the latter party, which also included Tobias Quill and Snitch.

Personally, I was unsure which assignment held the least appeal, a confrontation with the British army, or one with a man who seemed to inspire fear and revulsion in all who knew him. Burrage had another response.

"Excuse me, sir, Captain," he stumbled.

De L'Hiver, clearly chafing to get on with things, growled for Burrage to be quick about it.

"Sir, could I please join Mister Gunn's party and help with the defense?"

The only jaw that dropped lower than my own was that of the incredulous captain. But as amazed as he was by the offer, he decided that even a piece of cannon-fodder like Burrage might be of some use in a fight, if only to give the British another target to occupy their time. When Quill raised the expected objections, de L'Hiver reminded him that the Oath had already been broken; Old Dimond had been clear about that. Whether Burrage lived or died was no longer of any consequence, as far as the Frenchman was concerned. In fact, he reasoned, dividing our trio might discourage any thoughts of escape on our part, implying that such an attempt would mean death to those left behind, each held hostage for the survival of the others. The Quartermaster had to agree.

I, of course, was totally beside myself. And yet, there was nothing I could do or say. It was obvious that the transformation of Peter Burrage was complete. The extraordinary events that had torn us from our 21st century moorings had meant far more to my friend than I ever could have imagined. Something deep within him had lain dormant his entire life. Now it had been awakened and had captured his soul. I was in awe.

Ditty Gunn stepped forward and placed a cutlass in Burrage's hand.

"Until we reach dry powder in the stores," the Scotsman said, "we've no but our blades ta fight wi'. Stay close ta me an' ya might live yet!"

I couldn't help but notice the glint of new found respect that had shone in the first mate's eye. I felt myself grow momentarily jealous. My determination to hang on to my modern values had left me completely isolated and at cross-purposes with everyone else around me. One look at William confirmed it. Although he dared not ask, I knew that William longed to fall in with his companion and brave the coming storm. I squeezed his shoulder to let him know he was to stay with me.

"So be it," the captain announced.

"*Lively then!*" shouted Ditty Gunn to the company, now bristling with resolve and in full lather.

And with that, de L'Hiver motioned for his party to follow and disappeared into the blackness.

* * *

Only minutes after they had set off into the tunnels, the larger party began to execute a defensive scheme that could only be described as brilliant in concept. The plan was to entice the English troops into the cliffs, project an illusion of weakness, and then retreat deeper into the labyrinth. When the pursuit began, Gunn would attempt to lure small groups away from the main force and then destroy them piece-meal with a series of small, furious assaults.

And so it went. Gunn positioned Jack Wager and a half-dozen hands in the rocks around the cave entrance to stage an ambuscade when the longboats drew close to shore. As the first boat approached to within thirty yards, the pirates leapt from cover brandishing their pistols and preparing to open fire. When their wet powder appeared to fail, they feigned panic and staged a headlong retreat back into the cave. This fine bit of theatrics only made their pursuers more bold, convinced that what was left of de L'Hiver's crew had been reduced to a disorganized rabble. They couldn't land their boats soon enough!

By the time, the troops had disembarked, no easy task on the rocky promontory, Wager and his men were long gone and hidden in the darkness deep within the tunnel. Sure enough, the British found the going nearly impossible. One by one they were ordered into the passageway and immediately struggled with their headgear and long muskets, these made even more unwieldy by 24-inch bayonets. To avoid stabbing one another in the back, they opened up their line until they were a good ten feet apart.

When at last the lead man, a young ensign, rounded the bend, he found himself alone in an eerie phosphorescent glow facing Jack Wager and his band of cutthroats. I have no doubt the unlucky fellow must have considered himself doomed, but Wager was not yet done with his trickery. Instead of overwhelming the man, as could easily have been done, the buccaneers turned and fled screaming into the darkness. The officer was so rattled by the startling turn of events that he immediately lost a grip on his sword and counted himself very fortunate not to have soiled himself.

Once the initial shock had passed and the ensign had decided the pirates were nothing but a pack of cowardly scoundrels, he retrieved his weapon, raised his voice in a bold rallying cry and went hurtling off in pursuit. It wasn't until the butt of a flintlock pistol crashed down upon his skull that he realized things were not as they had seemed. Scabs Daggett and another hearty hoisted him by the armpits and stuffed his unconscious body in a pickle barrel just inside the storeroom.

As for the rest of Sir Robert's men, they entered the Hub on the run and were left wondering what had become of the dashing young officer. It was decided they should split up and head down the various passages, killing every buccaneer in sight until they had found their leader and, who knows, a chest or two of pirate gold perhaps. The trap had been sprung.

What followed could only be described as mayhem. Gunn and his men knew their business and carried it out with deadly precision. One by one, small groups of British soldiers found themselves led down ever-narrowing passageways, lost, trapped and virtually blind in the darkness. Confused and panicky with no room to maneuver, they were easy prey. Gunn's assassins fell upon them from above, rushed out at them from side passages and dragged stragglers screaming into the blackness before their companions knew what had happened. The British, once they realized that firing their muskets in the tunnels was more of a threat to themselves than their enemies, were virtually disarmed. The labyrinth had become a house of horrors. Cutlass, ax, and dagger flashed in the shadows until so much blood had been spilled that the dust had turned to a dark red paste in areas of the fiercest fighting.

When it was all over, only one man in Gunn's command, a surly brute named Droan, had been injured. He died of bayonet wounds within hours. Of the eighty-odd British soldiers who entered the cliffs, not one returned.

The subterranean battle claimed one other victim, however, and, to my profound regret, I was there to witness it. Once de L'Hiver had left the cave, William and I fell in behind him with Quill and Snitch to the rear. We moved as swiftly as conditions would allow and I was amazed at how familiar the tunnels had become since I had first stumbled into them a lifetime ago. The glowing algae was enough to light our way, although I was sure that I didn't wish to find what the Frenchman was looking for.

Our path took us to the Hub and then on to the storeroom. De L'Hiver motioned for Snitch to light the candles and conduct an inventory of potential weapons. The three buccaneers were soon heavily armed, each with a cutlass and dagger, as well as several flintlock pistols apiece. It was clear that they believed Worms would prove difficult to bring down.

To the surprise of no one, I was provided with nothing, a decision which, under ordinary circumstances, would have been fine with me. But this was different. I truly felt as though we were tracking a monster and even a peasant's pitchfork would have brought some sense of security. Instead, I felt naked.

Before we left, the Frenchman walked over to William and presented him with a short, thin dagger. He fixed the boy with a look that said this was not done lightly. Bending his head, he spoke in a low voice and in a tone that was not without a touch of genuine concern.

"Keep this, *mon petit poisson*. If the shark tries to bite, aim for his eye!"

Despite the fact that I was seen as having no more value than an leaky bucket, I was somewhat moved by the Frenchman's gesture to my young companion. At any rate, we were now prepared to move. For a reason known only to him, de L'Hiver chose to search in a passage that I had never seen before. It forked off of the one in which Burrage and I had become lost that first night we entered this world. As soon as we made the turn, Quill brought us all to a sudden halt as he placed a finger to his lips.

"*Whisssht!*" he cautioned in a hoarse whisper, his eyes darting this way and that. *"Someone comin'!"*

We all flattened ourselves against the wall. Sure enough, I could hear the heavy tread of boots coming down the tunnel behind us. A single man.

My God, I thought, realizing that William and I had somehow ended up at the back of the file without any defense between us and the intruder. The terrifying image of Melchior Wormsley had been etched in my brain ever since the encounter in my office. The thought that within moments I might be face to face with the creature again left me weak with dread. I watched William slowly drawing the dagger from his belt. Without thinking, I reached for the knife.

William, startled by my actions, instinctively stepped away from me and fell against the opposite wall of the passage. At the same instant, an enormous, dark figure emerged from the shadows and stopped dead in his tracks before us, a look of near madness splayed across his face.

"Hold!" he shouted, pointing his weapon directly at William's head.

As he did so, both Quill and the Frenchman darted from hiding. As if in slow motion, with the gun still aimed directly at William's temple, the intruder squeezed the trigger! A blue cloud of smoke poured from the muzzle and when the thunderous crash had finished echoing from the rock walls, all that remained was a deafening silence. I can still see the flame knifing out of the barrel like an vaporous sword thrust into the blackness. Reeling backward, I smashed the crown of my head against the wall and felt my mind begin to mist over. I tried to scream out for William to move but my voice was frozen with terror.

As I fought to regain my equilibrium, I felt someone clutch my shoulder and drag me upwards to my feet. It was Snitch.

Half shielding my eyes with a cupped hand, I forced myself to look at the body heaped in the dust. To my amazement, there were two, one fallen full across the other. The uppermost was a complete surprise. The intruder, it turned out, had not been the creature Worms after all, but an English soldier who must have become separated from his fellows. Driven mad with fear, he had the further misfortune of stumbling upon us, causing him to panic and fire at poor William. Now the redcoat lay dead, de L'Hiver's cutlass embedded in his chest.

As Snitch rolled the soldier's body away and his victim was revealed, I received the second shock. One of my companions was dead, it was true, but it was not William. It was the enigmatic Mr. Quill. The unfortunate quartermaster had apparently leapt into the line of fire at the last second and prevented the musket ball from ever reaching the still-trembling William. Whether he had been attempting to dispatch the English soldier or whether he had purposely sacrificed himself for the boy, we can never truly be certain. I only know that there was no weapon in his hand when he fell and for this last noble act, I will honor him forever.

The moments following Quill's tragic demise were hard ones. William was practically catatonic with shock and I could not stop shaking. Snitch was impossible to read, but at least he had the decency to remain silent. It was the captain that I most wondered about. They had been together for many years now, Quill and de L'Hiver. And it was clear that they had developed a certain trust in one another.

It seemed to me that men in their profession might need at least one shipmate on whom they could depend and if that was true, then Quill was that man for de L'Hiver. After all, Quill was responsible for all the business aspects of the crews' welfare. Just a hint of betrayal or poor judgment could have meant unrest or even mutiny. In many ways, Quill had been the glue that kept this band of desperate, suspicious cutthroats together, a testament to his ability to cultivate that curious brand of "honor" that was so essential to a company of thieves. I had a feeling that the Frenchman knew his loyal quartermaster could never be replaced.

Whatever he felt, de L'Hiver chose not to reveal even a hint. The task at hand was to find that for which Quill and most of the company had given their lives to retrieve—Buckett's Bible. With Quill gone, our firepower had been reduced by a third and I wondered if de L'Hiver might rethink his decision to flush Worms from hiding until he had more in the way of help. One look at his face and I knew he had no such concern. It was as though Quill's death had infused him with a strength and purpose that even Worms could not shake. We moved on.

As we picked our way along the twisting passage, I could hear the sporadic battles between the English and Gunn's men as they echoed from every direction. Shouts, screams, and the occasional roar of muskets surrounded us, sometimes faint and far away, other times seemingly just around the next bend. As the acrid smell of black powder permeated the tunnels, there was a real fear that, at any moment, we could be overrun by a party of soldiers who were as panicked and trigger-happy as the poor fellow we had just left lying on the tunnel floor. Snitch and the captain both inched their way forward with pistols drawn and cocked.

Our path took us perilously close to the sound of one particularly fierce struggle that seemed to rage both in front and behind us. Sure enough, the clash of steel and the cries of men began to close in on us with startling speed. De L'Hiver raised a hand to halt, when dead ahead, in the momentary light of a muzzle flash, we could see a clutch of British troops being driven our way amidst a cloud of dust and smoke. The captain signaled a quick retreat, but that too proved impossible as a second skirmish pressed us from behind. Before we could even move, one fleeing soldier hurtled towards us and fell dead at our feet.

We knew that we would momentarily find ourselves trapped in a frenzied hornets' nest of British soldiers. I could only imagine how they would deal with us, as desperate and enraged as they were sure to be. With the lurid vision of our last encounter fresh in my mind, my breathing grew shallow and my hands turned cold as ice. Unconsciously, I began to back against the wall pulling William alongside me. This section of the tunnel featured several deep alcoves and I could only hope that we might somehow remain concealed in the shadows and avoid notice, but I knew that the odds were pathetically low.

To our left, a retreating soldier turned to reload his musket. As he rammed the wadding down the muzzle, he chanced to look up and, for a brief instant, his eyes grew wide as saucers. He raised his hand, pointing squarely in our direction, and turned his head to alert his companions. At that moment, from the opposite direction, an errant pistol ball ripped across the front of my shoulder and passed but an inch above William's head. As I turned in horror to see if he was hurt, he blinked, then flew backwards and disappeared in the shadows behind us.

Before I had a moment to react, I, too, found myself dragged into the blackness. A heavy weight had come down upon my shoulder and yanked me inward, throwing me to the ground like a sack of wheat. A second later I turned to see Captain Bartholomew and Snitch hard on our heels, convinced, no doubt, that we were in the midst of an escape!

"Hold, damn you!" the Frenchman bellowed. "Stand fast or I'll slit your bellies, manhood to maw!"

I saw de L'Hiver framed against the pulsing glow of the battle beyond. Within seconds, he and Snitch were upon me, prepared to make me pay for my apparent betrayal. Just as Snitch was about to bring the butt of his pistol down upon my head, there was a muffled "thump," and the passageway went dark as night.

For a moment, there was no sound, no movement as we all strove to get our bearings. Then, the tunnel was suddenly bathed in light as a lantern appeared from behind the folds of a long, black coat. Standing above me was the hulking figure of Melchior Wormsley.

De L'Hiver and Snitch, also sprawled in the dust, immediately struggled to their feet, but as the Frenchman made a grab for his cutlass, he found a pistol leveled straight at his head.

"Belay, Cap'n, belay!" came the taunting response. "An' tell my ol' shipmate ta drop 'is pistol there, by thunder, or won't a soul leave this chamber wiv' his skull unstove!"

With a look as black as I have ever seen, the Frenchman hesitated then motioned Snitch to drop his flintlock. Worms gestured for us to sit back against the rock while he surveyed his catch in the lantern light. I finally saw William on the ground behind our captor and called him over to us. As Worms stepped aside to let him pass, the buccaneer laughed softly to himself.

De L'Hiver seethed.

"I swear to you, Wormsley, on my father's soul—"

Worms immediately glowered and spat.

"Tom don't take ta threats, Cap'n, if ye please!" Worms retorted venomously, the foul skin in his empty eye socket twitching with malevolence. "'Specially when them what's spewin' 'em 'as a ball aimed square at 'is brain."

Worms watched coldly as the full meaning of our predicament sank in. And yet, as terrified as I felt, I couldn't escape the nagging feeling that there was something truly odd about this whole situation, something that didn't make sense. Worms knew what the Frenchman was after, certainly. So, why reveal himself? After all, Worms *had* the map. All he had to do was stay hidden until the rest of us were killed, captured or gave up the search for him. Why would he reach out of the shadows and literally pluck us from the jaws of death as he had done? I was sure that de L'Hiver must be puzzling over the very same question.

Just at that moment, Snitch recoiled in a display of profound distress.

"Cap'n! Cap'n, it's the Door!" he cried, pointing to the thick oaken planks that had swung shut behind us when the tunnel had gone dark. "The Devil's Door, by all the Saints! An' we come straight through 'er!"

I immediately stared at de L'Hiver. A look of primal fear flashed across his dark face and I could see him struggle to regain the mantle of control that he wore so easily as a buccaneer captain. His reaction unnerved me. The "Door" from what little Quill had said was an object of immense mystery. Like any mystery it had become a magnet for fear and superstition. It would be difficult to find anyone with a greater reservoir of fear and superstition than a band of 18th century mariners with all their talk of the Devil and a throne of skulls. As a modern day psychologist, I would be the first to look beyond the supernatural and search for the real roots of such poppycock. But I now inhabited a world where even the most outlandish nightmare had substance. I now had first-hand experience with disembodied wizards, spirit lights, ghostly oarsmen, not to mention the flesh and blood creatures that now surrounded me. Why not the Devil, too?

As I tried to make sense of it all, I saw that Snitch had been struck by the same horrifying thought. Worms certainly *looked* the part—foul, evil, and demonic. Who knew what shape the dark angel might take when walking amongst thieves, murderers, and cutthroats? What guise more appropriate than the most depraved among them! That one instant of illumination sent a wave of terror through me unlike any I had ever felt. When it had passed, I realized that under no circumstances must I ever allow myself to believe such a thing, not even for a moment. Our only hope for survival was to believe that Worms, as horrific as he might appear, was simply the warped product of an often barbaric time in human history, no more than that.

"Aye, Master Snitch," Worms purred. "The Devil's Door as ever was! An' it's a blessin' indeed that brave hearties such as yerself think it so. 'Tis a peaceful place, is it not? A fine place ta be alone wiv' yer thoughts when others might deign ta interrupt. Now, Tom, what do ye guess they'd be thinkin', all brung together wiv' Ol' Worms, as they be? Well, says I, they might be grateful, bein' as it's me what done 'em such a service."

De L'Hiver was in no mood for such banter.

"And what service might *that* be, *monsieur?* That you spared us your company at table and so kept our food in our bellies?" he scoffed.

It was probably best that Worms never latched onto the full meaning of de L'Hiver's sarcasm, but he still suspected the captain had not shown him proper respect, considering the trump card he held.

"*Food*, Cap'n? Nay, not a feast for yer *tongue!*" he chuckled. "For yer *eyes* more like, an' I knows where it's hid. Aye, Cap'n, Buckett's Bible! Ye knows of't, do ye not? An' here ye're prob'ly thinkin' it were lost or stole by some n'er-do-well, eh? Well, says I, there's a service indeed! Ye can't deny it. So what say ye? A cause ta give Ol' Worms 'is due, I reckons. An' 'im so misused of late."

Worms was clearly enjoying his triumph. What was more of a surprise was the change that came over the Frenchman. Far from growing more angry, a look of serenity began to settle over his countenance. I could only assume he believed that control of the situation, the map, the treasure, and the renegade Worms, would be his soon enough.

"I think you play me false, *monsieur*," de L'Hiver reasoned. "If you *had* this map, you would have the chests and if you had the chests you would not be here. Is it not true?"

Worms was momentarily taken off stride and I saw his remaining eyelid narrow as he considered his next move.

"I might say the same, Cap'n," Worms countered. "Ol' Ned, why, he's better'n any map, says I. Ol' Ned knows every hole them jewels is in. But Ned ain't 'ere, *is* he! I 'spec Ol' Ned ain't nowhere. What's that, Tom? A bargain, says you? Why, there's a thought!"

I couldn't help but wonder how Worms seemed so sure that Ned Buckett must be dead. I tried to recall the night of the mute's demise but the mystery was never explained. I had assumed he had died at the hands of the English watch, but the ease with which Worms drew his conclusions made me question what really had happened. I watched the Frenchman handle the response and plot his next move. Still unsure of the options, he invited his adversary to continue.

"Think on *this*," Worms replied with steely certainty. "Wiv'out poor Ned, ye needs the map, an' Lord knows, I has it! Now, Ol' Tom, here, 'e don't have 'is letters an' n'er do I, but that Mr. Quill can read a word or two, God bless 'im. I 'spec ye takes my meanin'."

The Frenchman considered a moment, then responded.

"Suppose we have a man who could read this map. What then?"

"Why, *halves*, says I! Half fer Tom an' me on account o' Buckett's Bible. Half fer the man what can read it, divide it as ye please!"

A tremor of rage rippled across the Frenchman's face. It was clear that both men knew that neither could realize his goal without the help of the other. But it was equally clear that, once that goal had been achieved, the real contest would begin. I certainly couldn't imagine that Bartholomew de L'Hiver would ever allow Wormsley to walk away with anything.

"*Done*," the Frenchman hissed. "But I regret that Mr. Quill is not available to perform such a service."

With that, de L'Hiver pointed his finger directly at me.

"*You* shall take his place!"

CHAPTER 17

*E*ventually, the mayhem in the tunnels had been reduced to the occasional scream as a soldier was dragged from hiding and dispatched with cold efficiency. In due course, even these melancholy sounds had ceased entirely. The survivors, all members of Mr. Gunn's ragged band, were found lying exhausted in the large storeroom. By the time we joined them, they were already nursing their wounds and pouring large quantities of rum down their parched throats. I was greatly relieved to see Burrage alive and unharmed and he returned my silent salutation.

When Wormsley made his entrance, Ditty Gunn cursed and spat while the rest simply stared anxiously, unsure of exactly what had transpired. The news that Tobias Quill was dead came hard to the entire company and as a first order of business, de L'Hiver chose a burial party to retrieve the fallen quartermaster and to inter his remains on Burial Hill. To avoid any chance that they might be seen by one of Sir Robert's roving patrols, it was decided that the party should use one of the time gates. And so it came to pass that Tobias Quill was buried in the year 1777, by that measure, more than one hundred years after his birth.

Once the burial crew had been dispatched, the Captain stationed most of the remaining hands at posts throughout the tunnels, there to keep an eye out for any British stragglers who might somehow have been missed. Once the others had been set about their duties, we were joined by Ditty Gunn, Jack Wager, and Burrage. With barely a word spoken, we were soon on our way with Melchior Wormsley to recover the infamous Bible of Ned Buckett.

As we followed the one-eyed buccaneer toward his undisclosed hiding place, my apprehension grew with every step. From what I understood, de L'Hiver had offered me up to Worms as the one who would now decipher the mysterious map. This was a puzzle that I had *already* taken to an expert antiquarian and one that I was no closer to solving than I had been the first night I saw it hanging on the wall of Eddie McCool's pub. What chance did I have of discerning anything of use, particularly amidst the murderous atmosphere that had permeated the entire proceedings? I decided that my only hope was to feign some understanding and stall for time.

We marched for approximately a quarter of an hour, then found ourselves standing in the web of burial catacombs known as the Works. Several lanterns were lit and the Frenchman stepped forward.

"Very well, *monsieur*," he said to Wormsley. "You have led us here! Now the map!"

"Not so hasty, says Tom," Worms replied, bringing a filthy finger to the side of his nose. "This bears thinkin'! This map, what were bought so dear by so many, why, she's got the smell o' death all about 'er! What's one more, says I! What's ta stop ye from puttin' a ball in me throat once I shows ye where she lies?"

De L'Hiver knew that his word, whatever it was worth, would not appease the ever-vigilant Wormsley. As much as it sickened him to think about it, there was only one option that would keep things moving ahead. He dropped his baldric, dagger, and pistols to the ground and motioned for his companions to do the same. The weapons were gathered and placed in an alcove just across the tunnel.

"There, then," the Frenchman countered. "You have nothing to fear, eh? But hear me, *cochon!* You have weapons enough to kill no more than *two* of us before we reach you. When the map is found, we shall all stay together and learn her secrets. Understood?"

Worms agreed, delighted to see that he alone was heavily armed, although he suspected there might be more than one blade yet hidden in a pocket or boot. Grabbing my sleeve, he yanked me from the group and shoved me toward a small archway that was partially hidden amongst the rotting coffins against the far wall.

"Through there ye'll find 'er!" he cackled. "Through that hole ye'll find a box wiv' a stone upon the lid. Remove the stone and ye'll find 'er wiv'in!"

I could see the fire burn in his eye—a manic, obsessive light that made me shudder. I took a few halting steps, then felt a small stone catch me in the back of my ribs.

"Lively, now!" Worms bellowed.

"I need light," I said. Gunn stepped forward and handed me his lantern.

"Ta' this, laddie," he whispered. "Stout heart now. I'll stand your watch."

Only marginally reassured, I knelt down before the low archway and held the lantern out ahead. A fat, moldering spider, so large and so ugly that it resembled a troll more than a bug, lumped its way up a scrap of silk and hung looming over the entrance, daring me to proceed. The interior of the tiny cave was lined with webs and the light seemed to bring their residents to life. By now, my skin was crawling.

Sure enough, in the center of the low chamber was a single, aged coffin. I ducked down as low as I could and crawled through the archway, dragging myself into the cave, desperately trying to avoid putting my hand on anything that moved. Setting the lantern beside me, I struggled with the large stone that I pushed toward the far edge of the pine lid until it fell to the ground with a soft thump. *Jesus*, I thought. I could only imagine what kind of place a creature like Worms would choose to hide something. It would have to be somewhere that even *he* believed gruesome enough to discourage intruders. I dreaded my next task.

"Here, now!" I heard him bark from the outer chamber. "Lively there!

The dead moves more sprightly than the likes o' you!"

Knowing that the sooner I retrieved the map, the sooner I would be quit of this place, I flung open the lid of the coffin causing a plume of dust to rise up around me. With the lantern on the floor, the coffin interior was cast in murky shadows, a black hole. I slowly raised the light to where the first rays could catch the features of the unfortunate occupant. The pale, contorted face of Myles Castler stared up at me with an expression of such profound surprise that it appeared as though being dead was something illicit that he had been caught doing. His eyes were clouded over with a thin layer of dust giving them a wooden look, as if he were a piece of faded folk art. The fact that he had once been a living human being seemed strangely remote, though I knew he had been so only a short time ago.

My throat was so dry and constricted that I could hardly breathe. I longed to cry out but I immediately thought of poor William. If I was shocked and confused, I could only imagine what would go through William's mind. Something terrible had transpired between William and his stepfather, a betrayal so deep and painful that I knew the scars would last a lifetime. Were he to see Myles Castler in this condition, or even know of it, I was sure the horror, guilt, and anger would simply congeal into a viscous mass of psychological trauma.

My concern for William was the only thing that gave me the strength that I needed to finish what I had begun. I reached into the coffin and rolled the body on its left side. The dark black groove across his neck said all that needed to be said about how he had died. I put my hand down into the bottom of the coffin and pulled aside a dirty piece of cloth, clearly a memento left by the previous occupant. Holding the lantern above my head I could see the old parchment spread neatly across the pine boards. Within moments I had rolled it up, tucked it under my arm and was backing out of the tiny crypt.

Soon the map had been spread upon the ground and surrounded with lanterns. With a stern glance, de L'Hiver beckoned me to sit before it. I took a deep breath and leaned forward, praying that something would

present itself that would begin to satisfy them. The first thing that caught
my eye were the newly added rows of letters. Worms explained that he
had already done the hard work by deciphering the cryptic dots and that
I had but to make good use of them. For many minutes I watched the
letters dance mockingly in the flickering candlelight. Burrage, intrigued
by the puzzle and wishing to help me, squatted down by my side. There
they lay, five pairs—GQ, RU, AI, VL, and EL. As we studied the
mysterious pairs of letters, it dawned on me that I had no clue to their
meaning.

"I can't do it," I said softly. "There's nothing to *read*, you see? I have
no idea what these letters refer to. They're not words, that's plain. And I
have no idea what they are."

At that moment, a fuming Wormsley brought his great hoary head
down level with mine. His eye scanned my face as though he was looking
for the chink in my armor, a place where he could thrust in his hand and
yank out proof of my treachery for all to see. All of a sudden, his right
hand shot out and grabbed the hair on the top of my head, holding me
immobilized. He then reached forward with his other hand and slowly
brought his greasy, black fingers down toward my neck. In a flash of
motion, the fingers darted past my ear and then withdrew again, clutching
the abdomen of the great spider that had apparently dropped down upon
me when I exited the burial chamber. With one motion, he brought the
wriggling creature to his mouth and bit down, spitting the remains against
the tunnel wall.

"I 'spec ye can do better," he glowered, then stood up and folded his
arms across his chest.

Burrage and I wrestled with the puzzle for more than an hour until we
were drained. The patience of our antagonists, never in abundance to
begin with, had run out entirely. De L'Hiver and Worms took turns
berating us for our ineffective work and at one point we suffered several

hearty kicks and blows at the hands of the one-eyed buccaneer. In the end, it was William who made the great discovery.

It was he who stood pointing at the ornate compass rose that had been drawn in the upper corner of the map. The complexity of the rendering had nearly hidden the clue that William's father had discovered when he first examined it.

"Of course," Burrage exclaimed, kneeling forward. "The compass—it's pointing in the wrong direction entirely. It's pointing *east* instead of *north!*"

For a moment, we had forgotten that we were prisoners of murderous cutthroats and we were transformed into three boys with a treasure map. A thrill of excitement shot through me and I grasped the edges of the old parchment and began to rotate the map a full ninety degrees in a counter-clockwise direction.

With the north arrow in its proper vertical position, the columns of letters now lay on their sides though, at first glance, they seemed no more decipherable than before. This time it was Burrage who broke through.

"Max, *look!* We've rotated the map so the north arrow actually points north, right? What if we rotate the letters back in the other direction so they read as they would have if the compass had been drawn correctly in the first place?"

I tried to see them in my head, but by that time Burrage had scribbled them in the dust on the floor of the passage.

"*See,*" he shouted.

Sure enough, what had been nonsense became clear. The two rows of letters now lay one above the other and when read in order, they spelled: "QUILL GRAVE".

By this time, Worms was beside himself with de L'Hiver in a similar state.

"Come on then, ye cow guts! Hold out on me an' I'll have yer bollocks fer breakfast! Mind the truth now! Out wiv' it!" he howled, grasping Burrage by the throat.

"QUI—QUILL!" Burrage stammered, the words barely audible as they fought their way through his constricted windpipe.

In an instant, de L'Hiver produced a small dagger from the sleeve of his coat and held it but a foot from the side of Worms' neck. Worms, not to be out done, brought his pistol toward the captain in what became a classic standoff.

"Let him *speak*, damn you!" the Frenchman cursed. "Let him speak."

Worms gained control of himself and slowly let Burrage go free. The Frenchman stepped forward and bade him continue.

"It says, 'QUILL GRAVE,'" Burrage croaked. "That's all. That's all there is."

"Quill, 'e ain't in no grave, Cap'n!" Snitch chimed in. "Not yet, 'e ain't!"

"He will be, *mon ami*—in the year 1863," de L'Hiver answered, pointing to the date on the map.

Of course! I thought. What a poetic game the brilliant Ned Buckett had concocted! Not only had he hidden the treasure in another time, he had apparently hidden it with the very man who had sent him on his mission. Since 1777, the enigmatic quartermaster would have lain peacefully at rest in a tomb on Old Burial Hill. It would seem that in his quest for an undisturbed hiding place, and what better place than a cemetery, Ned Buckett had stumbled upon his old shipmate's grave. And while he may never have known the time or cause of the quartermaster's demise, I can only imagine that he delighted in the discovery. Little did he realize that he himself would meet his maker but a few short days later on the *Anne Boleyn*.

And that fact begged the question—*who* killed Ned Buckett? Having seen him nearly done to death at the hand of the venomous Snitch, it might appear that the captain ordered the job completed during the skirmish with the British watch. But I thought that unlikely. Clearly, until an hour or so ago, the precious map had been missing and Ned Buckett was the only living link to the treasure's whereabouts. It was unthinkable that anyone not in possession of the map would permanently silence the only man who might be able to recover the nine caskets. Which left but the one obvious suspect.

No, Snitch's previous attack had clearly been a message to the sly mute—produce the map that Mr. Quill had directed him to create or suffer the wrath of the company. I knew, of course, how the parchment ended up in the avaricious hands of Melchior Wormsley. The question was—how had it found its way to the wall of Eddie McCool's pub?

While I was trying to fill in the gap, Bartholomew de L'Hiver prepared us for the next step in this increasingly captivating process. His demeanor told me that everything that happened from this point on would be unpredictable and desperately dangerous. I knew that both de L'Hiver and Wormsley had decided a long time ago that the other would never see one farthing's worth of treasure. It was simply a question of how and when the outcome would be played out, and who else might end up a casualty along the way. In their minds, I could tell that they were circling one another like a cobra and a mongoose in a death match.

"Worms," the Frenchman announced. "I shall recover my pistols, but the others will leave their weapons where they lie."

I could immediately tell that the others were not real keen on this arrangement, but were wise enough to bide their time. A cutthroat without the wherewithal to "cut a throat" was at a distinct disadvantage.

Worms nodded his agreement and the party set out down a tunnel marked with a carving of a grain sack. With a feeling of surreal anticipation, I had no doubt that in a matter of minutes we would be emerging somewhere in the vicinity of a dockside warehouse in 1863, the third dark year of the War Between the States. When we arrived at the gate, de L'Hiver had us wait until after midnight before we could exit. Our work had to be done in the utmost secrecy.

By 1:00 AM, we finally emerged from beneath a stone cistern near an old wooden pier at the harbor's edge. A thin, crescent moon had just risen over the now larger village of Marblehead. Once again, I thrilled at the realization that I had slipped time's cable and was gazing on a scene that had vanished from the earth nearly a century and a half ago!

Kegs of mini-balls, manufactured for the war effort, sat stacked along the pier awaiting shipment to Union troops in the south. Though the narrow streets were nearly deserted, I spied a citizen or two afoot dressed in the fashion of the mid-19th century. Watching from the shadows beside the Eldridge Gerry House, I marveled at the sight of two Federal soldiers passing in an open carriage as it made its way down Washington Street. What I wouldn't have given for a conversation with them! Not on this night certainly—de L'Hiver kept us well hid and moving along the meandering alleys and dark steps that climbed up between the hillside homes to the top of the town.

We soon found ourselves huddled amongst the tumbling old gravestones of Burial Hill. A chill wind had risen from the sea as though the spirits were letting us know that our presence on this sacred ground caused them great offense. I shouldn't wonder. With a cloaked lantern de L'Hiver led us quickly from stone to stone, glancing each time to see if I could read Tobias Quill's name carved upon one of them. It was no easy task, as there were many stones to examine.

When we were about halfway across the cemetery, de L'Hiver, struggling with his crutch on the uneven ground, placed the lantern on the horizontal slab of a small brick tomb as he rested for a moment. Almost immediately, William let out a small cry.

As I rushed over to see what he had discovered, I found, carved in antiquated text, the names of several generations of Quills. Nervously scanning the entire surface of the stone, I could see no "Tobias" listed among them. I immediately realized that while the 1777 burial party must have chosen this resting-place for their quartermaster they certainly could not have taken the time to add *his* name to the list.

"This *must* be it!" Burrage exclaimed. "The map said 'QUILL GRAVE,' not 'QUILL'S GRAVE.' And this *is* an existing tomb, one of the only ones on the hill! They wouldn't have taken the time to dig a grave. I'm sure of it!"

If anticipation had been electricity, our party would have lit the night sky. As he stood at the head of the grave holding the lantern, de L'Hiver motioned us all to grab hold of the heavy tablet and, upon his signal, we slid it aside and let it fall to the ground where it cracked into two large pieces.

There, atop a large stone vault, lay a skeleton in the distinctive clothes of an old-time mariner. His long, gray hair hung about in the several crude braids that Quill favored and his great black hat had fallen to one side. Even in the heat of our purpose, the sight of the noble quartermaster, now suddenly centuries removed from his existence, gave each man pause and a moment of genuine homage was paid by all of us, with the exception of the remorseless Worms, of course. The sinister pirate hung back, fingering the stock of his belted pistol, an act that did not go unnoticed by the canny French captain.

"*Monsieur,*" he growled, placing his own hand on the corresponding weapon, "there is more than enough room for another in this melancholy house. Perhaps you should step over into the lantern light and help us see what we have found."

A few minutes work revealed that the grave was void of even a ha'penny. The effect on the party was immediate and devastating.

"Why, it's been stole certain!" Jack Wager spat. "Grave robbers, no doubt. An' us what done all the work so's they could live like kings!"

Snitch and Ditty Gunn simply sat on the ground and stared at the crypt with blank expressions. Burrage, William and I found ourselves in the strange circumstance of having no real stake in the outcome, other than survival, and yet, we felt as deflated as those who would have claimed the prize. *Is there any mystery as captivating as a hunt for lost treasure*, I thought? At that moment, I couldn't imagine one and I hung my head as low as the rest of them.

We were all too numbed to notice that de L'Hiver had not given in to the wave of despondence that had so profoundly infected the rest of the party. He continued to hold the lantern above the small crypt and peer down at the disheveled contents within.

"One moment, *mes amis*," he intoned with striking calm. "Let us not forget that the treasure would not have been placed here at the time *Monsieur Quill* was brought to this place, God rest his soul. *Monsieur Quill* has slept in this house for nearly one hundred years, *c'est vrai!* But Ned Buckett made his visit here not seven days ago, *ne c'est pas?* Little time for robbers to discover a treasure, I think..."

Every face turned toward him. He was absolutely correct. Unless someone had actually witnessed Ned Buckett placing the caskets in the tomb, there was little likelihood that someone would have happened upon the jewels by chance in such a brief period. There had been no recent interment, that was clear.

"We are looking for something else, *mes amis!*" the captain announced.

Within seconds, several pairs of hands had reached anew into the shallow vault and began a search for some other sort of clue. We had no idea what. Ditty Gunn proved the winner.

Secreted in an inner pocket of the quartermaster's frayed black coat, was an oblong pewter box and inside that box was a parchment scroll. The scroll was handed to me. We were dumfounded by what we found. Written on a piece of fresh parchment in the clear, cursive hand that de L'Hiver immediately recognized as Quill's own, was the following message:

> It werr Here. No More.
> Nine Cask. the full Measur.
> Each a Gate. Each a Home.
> Ask Me Where they Live.

De L'Hiver's face clouded over like a lunar eclipse.

"Back to the tunnels," he said in a halting voice. And while his features held firm, his eyes seemed to age three hundred years.

CHAPTER 18

*O*n the ensuing days, shards of truth were found glinting in the dark debris. The Company, reduced to a mere twenty-six souls, ourselves included, set about the business of coming to terms with its fate. And bitter terms they were.

After long hours spent examining pieces of the puzzle, I constructed a fragile theory about what had transpired. Whether it would prove the correct one, I didn't know for certain. But at that point, it was the best I had to offer.

I came to believe that Bartholomew de L'Hiver, trusting no one to hide the treasure, yet prevented by the Articles from doing so himself, had selected Ned Buckett for the task. The decision was based on the belief that, if captured, Buckett could not be forced to talk, regardless of what torture Sir Robert might bring to bear. The fact that Buckett could read and write, skills that the British would not likely ascribe to one so humble in appearance, enabled him to create a record of his deposits, cryptic as it might be. The infamous map immediately became known among the company as Buckett's Bible. That much was agreed upon by all.

Burrage considered my next bit of conjecture a bit fantastic, but while I was sorely tempted to agree with him, I could not come up with any other plausible explanation. I think Tobias Quill, aware of Ned Buckett's long and unsavory association with Wormsley, suspected that it was only a matter of time before the mute would be coerced into betraying his shipmates. Quill, therefore, followed the unsuspecting Buckett on his journey into the nineteenth century and, hidden from view, watched him deposit the chests into the very same crypt that bore the quartermaster's family name. The inscrutable Buckett undoubtedly found the irony delicious. Once the task had been completed, the clever fellow contrived the code that Worms, with the help of Myles Castler, I suspected, ultimately managed to crack.

But long before the map ever found its way into the greedy hands of Melchior Wormsley, Quill removed the fortune chest by chest and, as explained by the note in the tomb, spirited it away. He then apparently hid a single casket somewhere beyond each and every one of the nine gates, a bow to symmetry that would be consistent with the methodical quartermaster. It was my theory that, throughout what we now call the Old Town, there was hidden a fortune so vast as to defy the imagination.

I was encouraged in this belief by the fact that for many years Marbleheaders recognized a kind of "treasure day" during which the good citizens packed picnic lunches and searched the town for olden pirate riches long rumored to lay buried within there. And though this practice continued for quite some number of years, as far as I know, not a single precious stone of the great fortune has ever been recovered in this manner. Now, it seems, memories of this bygone ritual have long ago faded, as have those of so many other wonderful, eccentric bits of the town's past.

The most extraordinary part of the tale was an irony that only Quill could have appreciated. I could not imagine what the quartermaster must have felt when he slid aside the stone tablet, only to discover his own noble bones resting peacefully within. I can only conclude that he mistakenly assumed the interment had occurred much later in his life and that he, too, must have smiled at the mystery of his own transcendence.

I have no doubt that, as a final jest, he placed the small scroll in his own pocket believing that any who made their way to it using Buckett's map would then be compelled to do everything in their power to ensure both his longevity and good will. For without Quill, the treasure was truly lost. Little did he dream that, like himself, his great secret would be gone so soon. It was this final truth that now rested so heavily on those of us who had survived him.

Within a week, Sir Robert's ships had vanished from the horizon. It was rumored that, after their year of oppressive boredom and an assessment of their losses, his crews were on the verge of mutiny, so the decision was made to declare victory and sail back to England. Three years later, Sir Robert Vole himself would be hanged on Execution Dock, having defrauded a duchess of her lands in Cornwall.

In the greatest of all ironies, Melchior Wormsley was held harmless by his fellows once it was determined that, when all was said and done, his only real crimes were the recovery of Buckett's map, the rescue of de L'Hiver from the British, and his desire to be a wealthy man, a quality admired among those in his profession. These findings of innocence, while built upon facts that no one could refute, went hard with Bartholomew de L'Hiver. I took from his seething silence that his business with the one-eyed rascal was not at an end, but had merely sunk below the surface in the manner of a crocodile awaiting its prey.

With regard to the influences of the mysterious wizard, Edward Dimond, nature had taken its course. Once his supernatural protections had been rescinded, most of *Anne Boleyn's* crew had perished. Those who had momentarily escaped their fate had done so as the result of their own wits and gumption and it was apparently of no immediate concern to Dimond. However, his brooding presence still seemed to lurk amongst the shadows and I could not help but feel that I had not seen the last of him.

As for Buckett's Bible, the map itself mysteriously disappeared shortly after our journey to Old Burial Hill, about the time that the diminutive "Irishman" also vanished. I was later to find out that the buccaneer with the feminine charms was named Brighid Doolin. She had left the tunnels and Marblehead in 1705, eventually making her way to Charlestown, where it was said that she married a cordwainer named Fergus McCool, who lived with his twin brother, Edward.

Within a short time, the Company held a council and it was decided that the shortest road to wealth led right here to Marblehead. And so the crew came to an understanding, each man swearing to search time and town until the caskets were unearthed. It was agreed that when any box was found, the contents would be divided according to shares. Those who wished to do so could take their leave foregoing all claim to any riches uncovered at a later date.

That left only the fate of myself and my two companions to be decided. De L'Hiver wasted no sympathies and put it to the Company that we were dangerous still. As long as we remained, he warned, luck would give them a wide berth. Therefore, the best solution would be to commandeer a vessel at the earliest opportunity and deposit us upon some uncharted island there to let Destiny take its course. The crew saw some logic in this, but the idea lost momentum when it was realized that such a journey would take time and draw some of them away from the more rewarding task of locating the treasure. At that point, Ditty Gunn got up to speak.

"I know each man a' ya hath paid dear ta be sittin' here t'day. But I ask ya ta consider this—where we were once o'er a hundred, now we're barely a score! God knows it'll take all our wit an' wiles ta find tha' which we seek. I say three more pairs a' eyes, an' the only among us tha' can read a word, well, I'm nay so keen ta give 'em up so soon!"

De L'Hiver rose to his feet and glared, first at us and then at the mate.

"And I say they are more trouble than they are worth! If it were not for the Articles, I would as soon see them tied to a chain and dumped into the harbor. We have no need of them. The map is gone and its work is done. Monsieur Quill's last words are known to one and all, bitter as they may be. At the best, they are three more mouths to feed and, forget not, shares to be given! At worst, they bide their time waiting for the moment when they can make an escape back to their world. And what then? What foul mischief might they make if given *that* chance?

"They are coiled snakes, *mes amis!* Who among you would dare to keep them close?" the Frenchman thundered.

"—I," said Gunn, as all eyes turned in his direction. "They stood wi' us on the foredeck when Sir Robert's guns slaughtered us like rats. I'll stand for 'em now."

Again, de L'Hiver glowered at the sturdy Scotsman.

"And will you take their place on the gibbet when they betray you?" the Frenchman asked quietly.

Gunn stared at Burrage and me for a long moment. I returned his gaze with as much reassurance as I could extract from my raging ambivalence.

"If I do this thing, ya will nay run, ya will do no act ta bring harm ta your brothers here assembled. Will ya swear upon your mortal souls an' those a' your very mothers?"

"Aye," came Burrage's answer in a firm, clear voice that surprised even him.

And so Peter Burrage's journey was complete. He had resolved that he was willing, eager even, to be reborn in the 17th century. The danger, the deprivation, the physical demands of his new life were a small price to pay for the profound awakening he seemed to have experienced. There is something of the pirate in every boy, I suppose, and there is something of the boy in every man. And for Burrage, at least, the 20th century offered no honorable counterpart. William let it be known that he felt the same, albeit for reasons of his own.

"And *you?*"

Gunn's question cut through me like a knife. Up until now, I had managed to keep my feelings, my intentions below the radar of those around me. I had cooperated as the circumstances dictated and I had managed, with great difficulty, to control my impulse to scream in the faces of all those around me that *I* should not be here! I had been a model sort of prisoner, I thought. I had harmed no one and clung to the belief that should the situation present itself I would be free to make an escape. I assumed this was expected and that no reasonable captor would question my right to *try*. I had not counted on an appeal to my honor, for God sake. What was this man asking me to do? To forego my freedom in exchange for my life?

Gunn's willingness to risk his own welfare on our behalf was not lost on me. And yet, I could not help but wonder what I was really gaining in return. By allowing me to remain with the Company, he was offering me my best chance not only to survive, but to escape. On the other hand, in order to receive that precious gift, I was being asked to renounce the essential use of it! Was I bound to honor such a promise? Bartholomew de L'Hiver wasted no words.

"As before, if even *one* shall escape, the lives of those who remain are forfeit and in a manner more cruel than imagination can conjure, *comprendez-vous? And yours* with them, *Monsieur*," he snarled, whirling on his first mate. "Agreed?"

"Agreed," Gunn answered, without even looking in my direction.

And so my promise was exacted and my fate sealed without a single word from me.

Once our status had been established, I was surprised at how attitudes toward Burrage and me changed. I must say that we were treated as any other crewman. No keepers. No physical restraints of any kind. The key was William. As ship's boy, he reported to Mister Gunn and Gunn made sure he was always accounted for.

In the several days that followed, de L'Hiver began to execute a ferocious, yet carefully controlled campaign to ferret out the nine lost chests. It would not be easy; it was like finding a "biscuit in the ballast" as Snitch had groused. And then there was the ever-present prospect of betrayal. For the most part, the two dozen surviving hands knew the whereabouts of the time gates. All it would take was the odd theory or chance clue to lead some lucky seaman to a fortune. But what of the others? Would he share his find? Or would he choose instead to bide his time and slither off to recover the stones, then disappear forever?

Such fears gnawed at de L'Hiver like a nest of termites burrowing beneath the bark of his brain. He could not sleep. He could barely eat. And the very sight of Melchior Wormsley made him feverish with rage. Therefore, the captain resolved to manage the process to the minutest detail.

No man could pass through a time gate without at least three shipmates in tow. Each search party was carefully composed to avoid close friends or companions being grouped together. And each had to report in detail every observation and every act. The crew was amenable, for each man was aware of what he had to lose in the event of some foul deception. The shares of even one recovered chest would make every man wealthy beyond belief.

One disconcerting factor was the accelerated aging that afflicted members of the company who journeyed beyond the gates. This phenomenon kept the forays to the point and guaranteed that each party would return in short order. They were not unlike pearl divers battling to search a moment more, as precious bubbles of time drifted away one by one.

Ultimately, it was our immunity to this time assault that made Burrage and me at once desirable and dangerous as foragers. Because we suffered no ill affects, there was no deterrent to our escaping to another time, treasure or no. On the other hand, we offered staying power that no other searcher could match. We were so valuable in that regard, that we were both included on virtually every expedition. I could tell that de L'Hiver felt great resentment at his dependence on us, yet even he had to believe that, because of our loyalty to William, we were a safer bet to return than his arch-tormentor, Melchior Wormsley.

True to his irrational nature, the one-eyed miscreant seemed oblivious to the risks involved and he tried to attach himself to any party involved in the search. His eagerness infuriated the Frenchman, but de L'Hiver had to yield to the vote of the crew and no man was eager to replace him at the cost of his own longevity. Consequently, we often found ourselves in the close company of this foul bully and dreaded the time spent with him as one might dread sharing the sidewalk with an ill-tempered Doberman. In spite of these circumstances, Burrage and I had become infected with the same obsessive desire to find the treasure as our companions and we threw ourselves into the challenge.

And so it happened that, on our 23rd day in the tunnels, Burrage and I found ourselves lingering over a bit of stew in the large storeroom that served as the galley. We had just returned from a fruitless excursion into the year 1777. While scouring Burial Hill for recently dug graves, we were flushed by a constable and a small contingent of militia from the rebel garrison at the Gale's Head earthworks. Being as we were strangers, our small party must have been taken for Tories or spies as we skulked about on the high ground overlooking the fort. Fortunately, it was dark and we disappeared into the night shadows just as several lead balls whistled past our heads. We took off at a run, and several minutes later, we had wriggled through the stones at the base of the Old Powderhouse and beyond the time gate.

Burrage was exhilarated.

"*Jesus*, Max!" he gushed. "That last shot almost took off a piece of my ear!"

He held up his hand and examined the spot that his missing fingers once occupied.

"Oh, please!" I huffed, not sharing the same sense of accomplishment in his various encounters with mayhem.

"What the hell, Max, even *you* have to admit that got your heart goin'! No one ever chased me through a graveyard when I was living in Cambridge."

"Let's not get started on the joys of life in a war zone for God sake," I sighed. "We're here for two reasons. There's a fortune in jewels somewhere under our noses. And they won't let us leave. Let's just stick with those, okay?"

Burrage stood up and stretched. He was newly outfitted in a decent pair of slops and a crimson tunic that he had taken off of a dead British officer. His shaved head was wrapped in a piece of black silk that hung down his left shoulder and brushed the worn leather of his baldric. A German dueling sabre dangled from the hanger and a short boarding ax was tucked in his waist sash. I had to admit, he cut a swashbuckling figure standing there in the candlelight.

If I hadn't known the old Burrage, I would have found the new one pretty impressive. And while he had taken on this new, mythic persona, I, in contrast, had seemed to shrink. Where he had become Brom Bones, I was now Ichabod Crane. It irked me. I resolved that if I was going to be a prisoner and a tool of those around me, I was going to get more respect for it.

"Burr," I said, consciously making my voice an octave lower and as loud as I dared. "I'm sick of this stupid 'plan.' All we do is race around the decades hoping some sign will pop up saying, 'This Way to Treasure!' No one's thinking! I mean, it could be hidden anywhere. Marblehead may be small, but it ain't *that* small! We need to sit down and figure this out."

Burrage hesitated, then took a seat on a keg across the small table that separated us.

Leaning toward me, he whispered, "What are you saying? You want to have your own private search going?"

I paused. I hadn't really thought about it that way and hadn't mean to suggest it.

"I don't know, I mean, let's look at it from another angle. We have a lot of advantages, you and I. We can go to any time without any ill affects.

I have to think we're a lot brighter than most of these guys. Why can't we do this on our own, then grab William somehow and take off? We don't owe these guys anything. It isn't *their* treasure, for heaven's sake!"

I could see a troubled look come into Burrage's eyes. I knew he was struggling. On one hand, I still saw Burrage, my old friend. But looking deeper, I saw a man who had found a part of himself that he never knew existed, a part that he now cherished. The question was, how much did he associate his new identity with the company of shipmates that I was now suggesting we betray? How far would Burrage the Friend go in risking the welfare of Burrage the Buccaneer?

For a second, a cloud seemed to pass over his face. Was it the falling of the candle flame or something more ominous? Burrage rested his chin on a fist and stared ahead.

"And where would you look?" he asked quietly.

"I don't know," I replied. "That's the question, isn't it? We've been searching only a few of the nine gates. There's the one under the wharf during the Civil War; the one that comes out near the fish flakes on Little Harbor in 1692; and the one we just tried."

We knew of a fourth gate, The Key, but for obvious reasons, we hadn't been permitted to return through it to search.

That was four. *Where were the others*, I wondered? The majority of the Company had been focused on 1704 at the end of the tunnel to the harbor below the fort. That made sense, of course. It was the one year that didn't punish them. It was *their* time and they could search it at their leisure without suffering the mysterious ravages of the other portals.

"Well, I'd stay away from the 'Boat,'" I mused, referring to the carving that led to the sea cave. "The crew is out there pretty much all the time. It would be too much of a risk. Wait a minute. The carvings! They aren't just guides to the tunnels, they're guides to the gates!"

"They are?" Burrage asked.

"Yeah, sure. Think about it! The 'Boat' takes you to the harbor— 1704. Those three cannonballs? They take you to the Powderhouse in

1777. The 'Key'—that's obvious Now—1692—that's the 'Cod' and the 'Grain Sack' is 1863. What's left?"

Burrage scratched his stubble with a dirty finger.

"There's that tombstone thing. That takes you to the Works. You think there's a gate in the catacomb? Then, there's the 'Well.' I thought that just led you to the water. The top of that shaft's all closed over. That's all I remember except for that skull by the Door. Jeez, you think the Door is a time gate?"

"I don't know—that's seven carvings, though. I bet you anything there's a couple more. I'd bet my *life* on it!" I answered.

Again, a cloud passed over Burrage's face.

"So, what now?" he asked.

"Pick one," I answered, looking directly into his eyes.

I wanted to see the familiar spark. I almost didn't care what he said. The old Burrage would have told me I was crazy and tried to talk me out of it. I wanted to know what the "new" Burrage was about—where he began and ended. He shifted on his keg and turned his eyes away.

"I don't know."

What was he thinking? Was he *with* me? Damn! I didn't care! I was going to have to risk it. I figured, even if he had left my world behind, well, hell, he could pick any time he wanted to and spend his share! Stay in 1692 or 1704, what's the difference? It's not like the FBI could track him down! I'd make him see that. Burrage wouldn't fail me.

"The 'Skull,' " I said.

He jerked his face up with a look of amazement.

"You're kidding! Why *that* one?! Christ almighty, why not the 'Well' or even the 'Tombstone?' Why pick the one that everybody thinks takes you straight to Hell?"

"*That's* why," I replied. "Think about it. Everyone's scared to death of that door. Who's gonna bother us if we go *that* way? They're not even guarding it! Sure, Worms used to hang out near the entrance there, when he was hiding from the captain, but that's done. He stays with the others now."

Burrage wasn't convinced.

"Look," I pressed. "Did you ever stop to think that maybe the Skull carving is just meant to scare people to keep them away? What better place to hide something? We can take it slow. If it starts to get bad, we'll turn around. We've already been in there anyway, when Worms first caught us. There was no 'devil' or throne of heads. We can do this!"

The next morning, Burrage went out with a small party to the fish flakes, but he was back within twenty minutes.

"I don't know why de L'Hiver keeps pushing them out there like that," I grumbled. "No one will stay long enough to find anything. And it's getting worse. They all feel like they're using themselves up. "

"I guess," Burrage answered, as he took a long drink of well water from a goat skin.

"You ready?" I asked.

Burrage didn't answer.

"Burr?"

"Yeah...yeah, let's go."

It took us about twenty minutes of steady walking to reach the great oaken door with the skull carved above it. I had a lantern, some hard crackers, and the goat skin of water. Burrage had his sabre and boarding ax.

William had been assigned to Snitch's care that morning and he was learning how to use a knife in close quarters. What was happening to William was troubling. He had become almost a recluse, rarely speaking and, when he did, he used as few words as possible. I was certain the shock of his father's betrayal still weighed on him. It seemed as though he had thrown all his energy into learning the pirate's trade. I shuddered to imagine what the outcome might be—repressed rage combined with such lethal training. William, like Burrage, was changing. As we pushed open the ominous door, I was glad he was not with us.

The last time we had been in this place, I was too panicked to take in many details. The tunnel was cut through solid rock, like so many of the others. But there was something different about this one. There was none of the iridescent algae that lit our path through other passageways. The walls here were black as pitch. On the floor, I saw numerous small fish bones and the hooves of pigs, a layer of filth created during Worms' occupancy, no doubt. A torn goat skin lay against the base of a wall. I felt as though I had stumbled upon the subterranean lair of some foul demon. For a brief moment, the idea that Worms might indeed be the Devil crossed my mind once more. I quickly shook the thought out of my head. Not since peering down the gloomy shaft in my closet wall had I experienced such a feeling of dread combined with an irresistible urge to continue. The sense of déja vu caught me off guard and I staggered for a moment. I felt Burrage's hand in the small of my back, but he said nothing.

Unlike most of the passages we encountered, this tunnel moved distinctly downhill. The path convulsed with many twists and turns, a great, stone intestine. There were no side tunnels, only a relentless, single-minded, downward track that seemed to grow ever more steep. I began to fear for our safety.

"What do you think, Burr?" I asked, marching steadily forward, the lantern held out ahead.

There was no reply.

Before I even turned, I knew he would not be there. I froze. What to do—call out? I didn't dare. If I went back, what would I find? And forward? A penetrating sense of fear began to overwhelm me. The candle flickered in the lantern and the flame slowly, steadily shrank to a pinpoint of glowing wick. Within seconds, I was engulfed by total darkness. With no means of relighting the lantern, I immediately turned and began to inch my way back in the direction from which I had come. My breathing grew shallow. The tips of my fingers scuffed along the harsh grain of the wall and a caustic, burning sensation began to assault my flesh.

I had no sense of how far I had come. I felt as though the air itself was disappearing. To avoid fainting, I slowed my pace even more, then came to a complete halt. Fighting for breath, I sank to one knee and clawed at my throat, leaning against the jagged tunnel wall. *Jesus*, I thought, *I'm going to die!*

At that moment, I felt a slight pressure on the back of my neck. Unable to stand and barely conscious, I waited for the inevitable.

"You don't belong here," came a soft voice from the darkness.

I strained to turn my head and sank down with my back against the coarse stone. A frail, spectral light shimmered just beyond my left shoulder. I struggled to identify the voice. It spoke again.

"I was afraid it would come to this."

Welkie! I was sure of it. The pale, lavender vapor grew brighter and vague features presented themselves. Boden Welkie's eyes peered at me with sad familiarity.

"My God, is it really *you?*" I stammered.

"You don't belong here at all, Mr. Blessing. Do you know where you are?" he asked, a slight tremor in his tone.

"No, not really. I was looking for a gate. One of the time gates," I replied. "Was I moving in the right direction? What kind of place *is* this?!"

Without saying a word, he motioned that I should sit back and look out into the darkness. At first, there was nothing, just an infinite, black void. And then, as the moments crept on, I saw a long procession of pale figures moving slowly toward me. I was completely mesmerized by the soft aura that surrounded their forms. As they came closer, images sharpened and I began to make out individual features.

One by one they passed, my old, departed shipmates from the *Anne Boleyn* and her battles with Sir Robert. They came like a phantom army, rags fluttering slowly from broken bodies and faces like death masks. Some left the odor of brine in their wake; others the smell of burnt flesh. As they moved by me, I thought I saw an occasional glimmer of recognition.

The figures were translucent, brightening then fading like plumes of foxfire in a darkling wood. Each face bore the pain and anguish of that tiny moment when life had slipped away and the heart was gripped by the cold fingers of eternity.

"Where are they going?" I asked in a voice compressed by the weight of the question.

"To a place that each has shaped with the passions of his life," Boden Welkie answered.

"What do you mean?"

My wraith-like companion hesitated, as if to consider my readiness for the answer.

"Think of those gates through which you have passed," he said. "Each one transported you to a different realm, a realm defined by time. For the dead, there are gates, as well, defined not by time, but by experiences that penetrated most deeply into his or her being. Those moments carved out 'realms' in the afterlife, which they will now inhabit. The ninth gate is a passageway, a path for the dead to reach that place where each will spend eternity. That is why you do not belong here. It's not your time."

I was dumfounded. If it was not my time (thank goodness!), how was it that I was here at all? I sensed that Boden Welkie had anticipated my question.

"Ever since you and your companions entered the tunnels," he went on, "you have been 'backstage', so to speak."

"Backstage?" I prodded. "What do you mean?"

"It's a physical realm, to be sure," he replied. "A theater is a good analogy. Most people experience life as performers acting out the scenes of their existence. They are out front 'on stage', if you will. But you, you have been 'backstage'. It is a physical dimension that allows you to move behind the scenes through time. You're not supposed to be able to do that, unless you are invited, of course. But you were not."

I was totally bewildered.

"I, however, *was* invited," he continued.

"By whom?" I asked.

"By Edward Dimond."

"The wizard?"

"Precisely. You experienced the discomfiture of his attempts to call me here. I didn't understand what was happening at the time, all those troublesome feelings, which is why I sought your help. I thought I was losing my mind. But even as you tried to help me, you sensed the calling yourself, I *know* you did. But it was not meant for you."

"Well, then," I asked, "If I was not invited, why am I here?"

At that moment, the line of specters reached an end and the last figure drifted past me on its downward journey. It was Myles Castler.

"*Jesus,*" I gasped, in a barely audible whisper.

"Ah, yes, Myles. He was not invited either, but he met his fate here nonetheless, thanks to the one you know as 'Worms.'"

"Do you know him—Worms, I mean?" I asked.

"Only as an observer," he answered. "That was why I was invited."

"I don't understand."

"My being brought here was a gift," he replied. "My time on earth was coming to an end and because of my love of Marblehead history, my fascination with 'time,' Old Dimond reached forward and drew me into the tunnels. He gave me a vehicle for exploring the centuries, and so I have."

Boden Welkie went on to relate an anthology of fantastic stories, some of which you have read elsewhere in my writings. Welkie had become intrigued with various members of the Company and had journeyed back through their lives on a enthralling tour of the 17th century. Quill, de L'Hiver, Worms, he had traced them all to their origins.

When he finished the account, he turned his attention back to my circumstances.

"Now and again, someone such as yourself stumbles upon the tunnels. Myles Castler has been visiting them for some time. But now you must understand You are in grave danger!"

That I was in peril was not exactly news to me. It seemed like I had been on the verge of disaster ever since my attempt to rescue Welkie himself on Gerry Island.

"Do you mean Worms?" I asked. "De L'Hiver?"

"Oh," he replied, "there is immense danger where *they* are concerned, no doubt. Both are capable of terrible violence. But I am referring to something far more insidious. I am talking about the seduction of time."

"I don't know what you mean—"

"Ah, but you do!" he countered. "Your friend intends to stay, does he not? And the boy as well?"

I nodded.

"That is a very bad idea," Welkie exclaimed. "It is one thing to visit another era. It is quite another to remain there for any extended period of time. Old Dimond was so concerned about such disruptions that he accelerated the ages of the *Anne Boleyn's* crewmen as a way to keep them where they belonged."

"What *is* it? Will something happen to Burrage and William if they decide to remain?" I asked.

"Indeed," he said. "But worse, the longer they remain, they more they will contaminate the era they inhabit. The physics of time are very volatile, apparently. There are aspects of your makeup that are in balance with the events, the influences, the sensibilities of the 20th century. Here, they are out of balance. There is a subtle, corrosive effect that derives from the inherent incompatibility of your energy with that of this time. The longer you remain, the greater the risk that certain disruptions could damage you and this place."

"Disruptions?" I exclaimed. "What kind of disruptions?"

"That I cannot tell you because I do not know. As I said, I have been a guest here only briefly. It is time for me to move on to my destiny. With my death, I fell into harmony with all realms. I have none of the corrupting baggage that accompanies the living. You, your friend, the boy, you are all threatening the equilibrium of the times you occupy. You must find a way to leave. You simply must!"

Leave? I thought. Was Welkie even aware of the obstacles that had been put in front of me? Before I could protest, the ghostly visage began to dim. In his remaining moments, he made one, final plea.

"Mr. Blessing," he asked. "When you return, could you visit Hannah? Tell her... tell her that I'm fine. Tell her that I love her. Would you do that for me?"

With that, Boden Welkie's spirit slowly drifted down the passageway, then disappeared.

When I finally stumbled out of the oaken door again, I felt completely energized by the clarity of Boden Welkie's message. As I ran along the passage toward the Hub, I had no doubt what I must do. My stubborn, nagging belief that I did not belong here had been validated. It no longer mattered that Burrage felt "fulfilled" by his bizarre infatuation with this place. There was no question that William needed to return to his home; to his mother; to a place where he could be given the care and support he must have if he was to become whole again.

My mind, my emotions, and my spirit were at long last moving in one clear, unambiguous direction. I wasn't sure how I was going to do it, but I had no doubt that my job was to find a way to bring us back and leave this strange, awful world far, far behind.

I burst into the Hub and whirled around. *When had Burrage disappeared?* Had he followed me down the tunnel at all, or had he simply slipped away early on, filled with doubt and conflicted loyalties? Or worse, had he embraced his dark side altogether? Was he, even now, leading Gunn, de L'Hiver and the others in an effort to hunt me down and make me pay for my treachery?

I knew I could not afford to think such thoughts. I had to pray that Burrage and William still had enough 20th century humanity left in them to provide me with a doorway back into their lives. Besides, I had no choice! Boden Welkie had made it clear that our presence in this world was a ticking bomb. I had to find Burrage!

The Hub was deserted, as was the storeroom. I cocked an ear, desperate to pick up any trace of my friends. In an instant, I heard the familiar rushing of water upon the rocks, the sound that had taunted me for so long. Without a moment's hesitation, I hurtled toward the sea cave. My mind was filled with a thousand and one images: *Had Sir Robert returned and wreaked a terrible vengeance upon one and all? Had the simmering hatred of de L'Hiver and Worms finally burst forth in some volcanic eruption and engulfed all those around them?* A growing sense of disaster began to gnaw at my gut.

Stumbling the last few yards, I lurched into the sea cave and sprawled on a blackened heap of seaweed and shells. I struggled to catch my breath and, with a final heave, pulled myself up from the stinking compost and fell back against a large out-cropping of stone. For several long moments I stood blinking into the shaft of sunlight that knifed through the shadows and illuminated the far wall. At last my eyes adjusted and I gazed across the small, domed room.

I saw Lady Jane crouching on a small boulder across the floor. The sunlight caught the small beads of sea water that clung to her matted coat and flew through the air as she let go a sharp, convulsive shake. When she composed herself once more, she resumed the delicate washing of her fur. Her curled paw rose and fell, scrubbing the scarlet blotches that encircled her nose and mouth. I watched in horror as she slowly turned her head, then licked contentedly at the broad smear of blood that ran down the face of the dead man.

A great gash cleaved his left temple and a cutlass was embedded in his chest. I recognized him as Wombwell, the sea cook. From his prostrate body, I followed the light across the floor counting no fewer than six other corpses before my eyes found the entrance to the cave. Staggering to the opening, I gulped in the cold, fresh breeze and tried to purge my nostrils of the death-smell that hung in the air like thick, fermented syrup.

As I caught my breath and stared wide-eyed in every direction, I was struck by the profound silence around me. Where was Burrage? Was he still alive? Was William? I sensed that the tunnels were empty, that whatever deadly storm had blown through had left nothing alive in its wake. I inched my way down to the water's edge and splashed a handful of cold sea water across my face. Resting back on my haunches, I closed my eyes and drank in more of the chill air that blew in across the mouth of the harbor. When I opened them again, I noticed the small, stout, wooden chest half-submerged in the waves. It appeared to be empty and the ornate, hinged lid flung open. As it bobbed low in the water, four lifeless fingers curled over one edge as if trying to prevent it from drifting further out to sea. Bowing my head in disbelief, I caught sight of a single, glowing sapphire staring out at me from the shallow water like a pale blue eye. From deep within a submerged crevice it blinked several times and then disappeared from view in a rush of sea water and kelp.

CHAPTER 19

Across the harbor, the last light of day began its slow climb up the shallow hill on the Neck, the shadows chasing it around boulders and across the tall grass until it climbed a lone pine tree and clung briefly to the topmost branches, finally melting softly upward amidst indigo clouds on the eastern horizon. It was the rising tide that finally awakened me from my stupor and I dragged my cold, water-logged shoes up the steep rock face to a small granite shelf above the sea cave. By now the sea had obscured the cave entrance and the coming night had turned the shallow cliffs into a formless black void. Rolling surf had long since carried the small chest out into deeper water and the grasping hand of the submerged buccaneer had been swallowed by the forest of kelp nodding in the swells. I could imagine the bodies bobbing like fleshy corks against the domed ceiling of the cave, battered by the rocks as the cold water washed the blood from ragged wounds.

I sat back against the embankment and gave in to my exhaustion. Everything around me, the chill wind shuffling the dead leaves on the great oaks overhead and the deepening blackness of the night sky, only underscored my feelings of abject misery. I couldn't help but dwell on the enormity of what had been lost.

Burrage was gone. I didn't know if he was dead, dying, or simply stolen by the rogue spirit that had been awakened by me, for *I* was the reason he had come. I had been so full of my own need that I had ignored his pleas to hold back, to be sensible, to stay safe. With supreme hubris I had assumed that only *I* was in danger, that only *I* had demons to fight. I had believed that I could manage Burrage's quirky compulsions and drag him behind me like a human security blanket while I trembled forth to confront my own personal bogeymen.

What an arrogant, pathetic fool I had been! And when we finally found ourselves in the belly of the beast, it was *I* who had blinked. It was *I* who had played the victim and clung to the helpless, civilized sensibilities of another time. After all, I was a representative of a "superior" world, where powerless-feeling inhabitants had learned to manage their daily angst by sitting in front of a psychologist, a pulpit, or a TV screen. I came from a time where fear was a commodity, used and abused by advertisers, preachers, and politicians. Make us anxious enough and we'll buy what we're taught to buy, hate who we're taught to hate, and kill who we're told to kill. I think Burrage just got tired of all the fear. As for me, it seemed I had learned to eat, sleep and breathe it.

And then there was William. In a way, I think his story was so enormously painful that I had barely been able to consider his emotional state since the horrendous betrayal of his father. I had been content just to see him calm and fed and warm at night. In truth, I realized that William's stoicism had been a great relief to me and allowed me to concentrate on my own survival and a plan for our escape.

But here, staring out across the dark water, I let myself think of the young boy whose life had become a waking dream. The terrible moments had clearly seared him, and yet William had managed to find his way through a crippling sadness that might have overwhelmed him. He, like Burrage, had looked outward instead of inward and dared to fit himself into our strange, new world. Instead of cringing like a civilized person might, he had embraced what was offered and found the part of himself that could survive, indeed, thrive. I shook my head. It all seemed so wrong. And what if Boden Welkie had been correct? What if our presence in this place threatened our health or our sanity, perhaps the fabric of time itself?

For the rest of the night, I lay trance-like upon the naked rocks chasing my thoughts through the gloom. Even the wind rifling through my loose rags couldn't blow away the mists of my confusion. Burr, William—where *were* they? Dragged to the bottom of the harbor or lying in a pool of blood in some forgotten passageway?

As the first, cold light of dawn began to feather the far horizon, I propped myself up on an elbow and rotated my neck to release the stiffness. Suddenly, my bleary eye caught a gentle movement out near the far shore of the harbor. Squinting into the shadows, I homed in on two small shapes rising and falling with the swells. Long boats!

I was too far away to make out who the figures were or how many pulled so relentlessly at the oars, but their deliberate course led my gaze down the harbor toward a merchantman resting peacefully at anchor. I was hypnotized. With all the innocence of a baby rocking in her cradle, the anonymous vessel lay asleep. A lantern blinked below the yard, although the watch was likely below warming their bones with a cup of rum or stealing a bit of sleep before the start of a new day.

I looked back again at the slender black hulls gliding noiselessly down the harbor. Were the boats simply carrying mates back to their ship? If so, why were they circling around from the barren headlands of the Neck? The docks and taverns were on the other side of the harbor, the only destination of interest to any honest seaman.

It was a struggle for me to follow the tiny craft against the dark shore and, as they approached the anchored hull, I lost sight of them altogether. For what seemed an eternity, I screwed my eyes into the shadows, but the only thing I could see was the watch light winking furtively in the distance. The wind had disappeared entirely and the water grew so still that I could barely hear the ripples lapping against the rocks below. It was as if all of nature was straining to hear what might come next.

The answer soon came. The watch light blinked out and for a brief moment there was nothing. Then, a short, jagged flash of fire ripped through the darkness where the ship lay tethered. An instant later, another and then another! A barely discernable "*pop*" blew in across the water followed by two more in sequence to the flashes.

"Jesus Christ!" I said out loud as I sprang to my feet.

There was no doubt in my mind what was happening. Whomever remained of the *Anne Boleyn's* crew had set sights on a new vessel. The hapless sailors aboard the unknown ship had no doubt been overrun and their bodies were likely settling to the bottom of harbor that very moment. As troubling as the scene was, the fact that Burrage and William might have been with the boarding party gave me hope.

I immediately turned to make for the village. Despite the low odds, my only chance was to alert the townsfolk and convince them to row for the victims. I would worry about my next move once we had gotten to the ship. I only knew I had to keep Burrage and William within reach!

I clambered wildly along the crest of the cliffs, several times losing my balance and nearly falling to the rocks below. At the far side of the promontory, the ground sloped downward toward the shallow cove that ran along the harbor and the sleeping village. As I struck the beach, I saw a small skiff tethered to a stump just above the tide line. To my surprise, a pair of crude oars lay within, the blades peeking up beyond the bow. She was no more than ten feet long and I knew that I could handle her myself.

I dropped to my knees in the damp sand and my cold fingers tore at a knot in the line. The tiny vessel swung expectantly to starboard as though anxious to be on our way. With the rope finally free, I splashed through the gentle waves and fell into the boat. I notched the oars within the pegs, swung her bow out toward a space between the rocks and began to pull like a man possessed.

Once beyond the headland, the harbor came to life and the small craft rose and fell with the growing waves. Sweat soon soaked my back as I settled into a rhythm, though my pace felt excruciatingly slow. I stole a glance over my left shoulder and saw the sheets begin to fall from the yards on the merchantman. The ship was preparing to sail. I knew I couldn't hope to catch her before she got under way, so I adjusted my course to the harbor mouth giving myself a chance to intercept her before she reached open water.

My God, I thought, *suppose I <u>do</u> get to her in time?* The wind was picking up again and she could be flying by the time she reached our rendezvous. *What then?*

But what choice did I have?

The minutes seemed to race, though my progress felt like a crawl. Again, I shot a look down harbor and saw that the merchantman was now fully under way. Her sails rippled and caught the breeze, peach-colored in the morning light. She rose and fell and small bursts of white foam began to shoot forward from below her nose. As best I could, I tried to anticipate her course and saw that I was not yet on her line. I bent my back and pulled till the skin on my palms began to crimp and burn against the rough oars, sweat now pouring down my forehead and my heart pounding in my chest. Despite it all, I had no idea if I could come close to reaching her.

As the minutes passed, I checked my bearings more often and wondered what those on board must be thinking of this tiny, bobbing spec ahead of them. Would they steer a wide course and leave me floating helplessly in their wake? Most likely. In any case, I would soon have my answer, for the ship was now growing rapidly larger and less than 200 hundred yards to starboard. No matter where I set myself, the next few minutes were in her hands. I had orchestrated my own moment of truth. A great ship would soon be upon me and she would either fly by or run me down. There was nothing I could do about it either way.

I don't know what had made me think that a ship under full sail was going to somehow stop and politely wait while I made my case. And what case was it to be? The only thing I controlled was how I would comport myself over the next few minutes. Would I cower and dive for cover?

Would I scream and rage against the unfairness of it all? Or would I stand and look this moment in the eye?

As my small boat rocked in the swells, I shipped oars and dropped them across my seat. The merchantman still bore down upon me, showing no signs of slowing or changing course. For the first time, I saw the black figures poised in the rigging and dotting the rail. No one seemed to move. And still she came.

When she was 60 yards away, I stood up in my boat, which now lay with her tiny broadside to the oncoming vessel. The bowsprit of the approaching ship moved to and fro like a giant rapier angling for the kill. Faces began to take shape, each one expressionless as though carved from the same oak as the timbers and masts. Forty yards now and still she came, the rising sun suddenly bursting upon her sails like fire.

Then, without warning and without will, my pounding heart grew quiet. The icy hand along my spine loosened its grip and fell away. Even the small boat beneath my feet seemed to pause in its rocking and lie still in the waves. An enormous peace flooded my mind and my field of view began to fill with the great ship running towards me. I closed my eyes and heard the rush of the wind and the crash of the hull against the waves. When my eyes finally opened again, the huge ship towered over head. I felt a strange smile spread along the corner of my mouth.

So, this is what it's like.

"*Max!*" the tiny voice screamed.

I looked up. Clinging to the nets below the bowsprit was Burrage. He hung over the edge, extending an arm as the hull rose and fell before me.

"*Max!*" he implored. "*Now! Do it now!!*"

In the next instant the ship was all around me. Spray stung my eyes and a chaotic blur of timbers and lines was everywhere I looked. Her bow made one last downward lunge and I saw Burrage's hand clawing the air a few feet from my face. I felt the skiff crack and then disintegrate below my feet just as I leapt outward, both arms stretching further than I imagined I could ever reach. And when the tips of my fingers curled 'round Burrage's hand and I clung to the cuff of his coat, I felt the bow rise like a great fish from the sea and lift me up into the boundless blue sky.

The end

A F T E R W O R D

So, there you have it.

If nothing else, one may choose to see it simply as a tale told in the ancient tradition of the New England coast. Needless to say, Max Blessing's incredible account defies the laws of natural science. In fact, my first instinct was to dismiss it as a rousing bit of fiction worthy of a dark night and a warm fire to read it by. However, since concluding that a publisher might find it appealing, I have happened upon several facts that are worth sharing with you, the deserving reader. I believe they cast the story in an entirely different hue.

First, I discovered that there really was a Wizard of Orne Hill—an Edward Dimond—and that reports of his mysterious life have been part of Marblehead lore for more than 300 years. In fact, his home at the foot of Old Burial Hill still stands.

My research also revealed that Marblehead's history is fraught with innumerable accounts of piracy, smuggling, and other dark activities. Many of these stories still lay hidden deep beneath the dust waiting to be uncovered. So before I leave you, I will relate two curiosities that may shed some light on the narrative just concluded.

Some number of years ago, I have been told, this house—*my* house— was abruptly sold by foreign interests and passed into local hands. For some unexplained reason, however, all records of those transactions have disappeared entirely. Nothing can be found that suggests the Castlers,

Max Blessing, or Peter Burrage ever set foot in Marblehead.

I also learned that an elderly widow living somewhere in the Barnegat district left town a decade ago amidst rumors that she had unexpectedly come into a considerable fortune. What struck me about this story was an off-handed comment concerning a strange, blue light that had supposedly been observed dancing about her chimney one night several weeks before she put her house up for sale. Her name was Hannah Welkie.

—Kenelm Winslow Harris